W9-CCN-703

TALON OF GOD

TALON OF GOD

WESLEY SNIPES AND RAY NORMAN

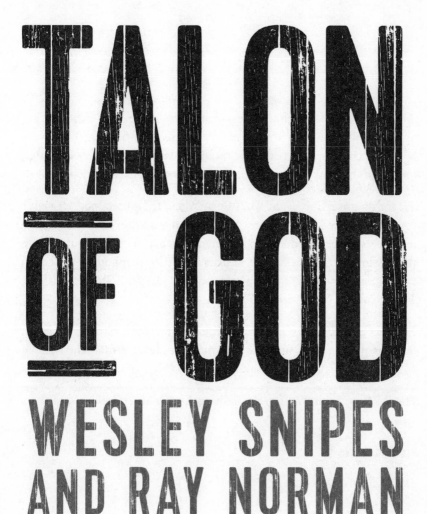

HARPER Voyager
An Imprint of HarperCollinsPublishers

TALON OF GOD. Copyright © 2016 by Maandi House, Inc. All rights reserved. Printed in the United States of America. No part of this book may be used or reproduced in any manner whatsoever without written permission except in the case of brief quotations embodied in critical articles and reviews. For information address HarperCollins Publishers, 195 Broadway, New York, NY 10007.

HarperCollins books may be purchased for educational, business, or sales promotional use. For information please e-mail the Special Markets Department at SPsales@harpercollins.com.

Harper Voyager and design are trademarks of HarperCollins Publishers LLC.

FIRST EDITION

Designed by Suet Yee Chong

Map by Globe Turner / Shutterstock, Inc.

Library of Congress Cataloging-in-Publication Data has been applied for.

ISBN 978-0-06-266816-5

17 18 19 20 21   RRD   10 9 8 7 6 5 4 3 2 1

TO THE MOST HIGH,
TO OUR LOVED ONES,
AND TO THOSE WHO FANNED THE FLAMES AND KEPT THE FAITH.

CONTENTS

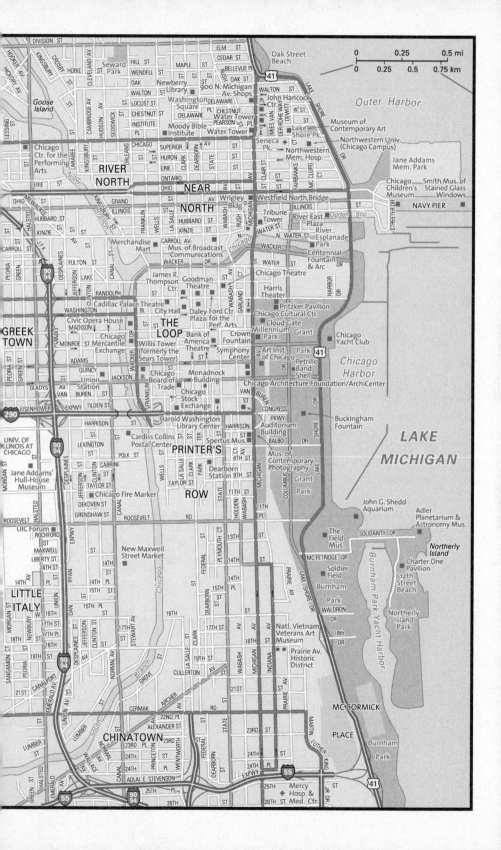

TALON OF GOD

PROLOGUE

MY TEARS HAVE BEEN MY FOOD
DAY AND NIGHT,
WHILE PEOPLE SAY TO ME ALL DAY LONG,
"WHERE IS YOUR GOD?"
—PSALM 42

S pare some change for a veteran?"

His words were empty, barely loud enough to be heard over the trains thundering on the elevated rail overhead. Some days, Lenny didn't know why he bothered. No one listened. Most of them didn't even look. They just walked by at top speed with their eyes locked on their phones, the sidewalk, the sky—*anywhere* but the homeless man huddled in his nest of newspapers, rattling his paper cup.

Lenny didn't blame them. He couldn't stand the sight of himself, either. Or, at least, he couldn't when he was *there*. Present. Sometimes he drifted away, lost into memories that felt more real than the late November cold. When that happened, he didn't care about anything. This afternoon, though, he was most definitely here. Here and hungry, so he kept at it, repeating the words and rattling his cup at every person who passed.

"Spare some change for a veteran?" *Rattle rattle.*

More shoes walking by. No one stopping. No one *caring*.

Sure, they were cold, too. But theirs was a temporary inconvenience. For him, this was as real as it got, and it was about to get worse. The sun was getting low. He needed to head for a shelter—November nights in Chicago were no joke—but he couldn't go in with nothing, so he decided to push, raising his raspy voice over the roar of the trains in the growing evening cold.

"Spare some change for a veteran!" *Rattle rattle.* "Spare some change for . . ."

His voice faded. Someone had stopped, a young black man in a heavy, black coat with the shiniest shoes Lenny had ever seen. That was a good sign. Stopping at *all* was a good sign, but shiny shoes meant money, so Lenny rattled his cup again, giving the smart-looking stranger a snaggletoothed smile. "Spare some change for a veteran, sir?"

"I can do better than that," the man said, reaching into his pocket to draw out a crisp, folded bill. "What's your name?"

"Lenny," the homeless man replied promptly, reaching eagerly for the bill. He so rarely got paper money, but when he did, it was usually good. A five, maybe even a ten. Enough for a hot dinner, and maybe coffee tomorrow, too. But when his fingers closed around the money, the man with the shiny shoes didn't let go.

"Tell me, Lenny," he said, crouching down so they were at eye level. "Are you a God-fearing man?"

Lenny knew how this went, and he nodded rapidly. "Go to church every week."

The man arched a skeptical eyebrow, but Lenny wasn't lying. He hadn't believed in God since the war, but when you were homeless you spent a lot of time in churches because they were open, they were warm, and that's where the food was. Unfortunately, technical truth didn't look like it was going to earn him dinner tonight.

"Is that so?" the young man said, gripping the offered money tighter than ever. "Show me. Quote me some scripture, and the money's yours."

Lenny didn't know a word of scripture, but he tried anyway, reciting some phrases he'd seen typed on the church bulletins he took for fire kindling. It must not have been good enough, because the man snatched the bill right back out of his hands, making Lenny cry out. "Come on, man," he begged, watching the man pocket the money again with loss in his eyes. "Have a heart. I'm just trying to survive."

"Really?" the man said. "Just survive?"

Lenny nodded. "Ain't we all?"

For some reason, this made the man smile. "And what if I were to offer you something better?" he asked, reaching his gloved hand inside his heavy winter coat to pull out a small glass bottle filled with a liquid so bright green, it almost seemed to glow in the dim light. "Something new?"

Lenny recoiled at once, swearing to himself. Just his luck. The one bite he got tonight, and it was a pusher. Unlike a lot of people he'd met on the street, though, Lenny didn't truck with drugs. He'd had enough chemicals sprayed on him in 'Nam to last five lifetimes.

"Nah, man," he said, scooting backwards farther into the shelter of the bridge. "I don't touch that stuff."

"It's free," the man said, tossing the green vial casually in his hand. "Try it."

The first hit was always free. "Nah," Lenny said again, backing away. "I'm clean, man. I don't do that."

Even if he had been a druggie, he wouldn't have touched the stuff in the man's hand. Lenny had never seen anything like the green liquid in the bottle, but it reeked of rotten eggs. Yet another reason to get out of here quick, before things got weirder. But as Lenny pushed himself off the pavement to walk away, the man in black grabbed his arm.

"I think there's been a misunderstanding," the stranger said softly. "That wasn't a request."

Lenny swore and yanked, trying in vain to escape. It should have been easy. He'd been a soldier once, and still made a point to keep himself in decent shape, despite his life on the street. But the man in black was freakishly strong. No matter what Lenny did, the stranger moved him as easily as he'd move a child, letting go of his arm to grab Lenny by the jaw. He started to squeeze then, forcing Lenny's mouth open with one hand as he popped the lid off the vial with the other. Eyes wide, Lenny lashed out with his feet and fists, but the man just seemed to absorb the blows as if they were nothing as he poured the green substance down Lenny's throat.

It tasted as vile as it smelled, and Lenny tried to spit it up, but it was as if the liquid was *climbing* down his throat. Worse, it *hurt*. The burn was so bad that Lenny couldn't even scream. His body had clamped up the moment the green crap touched his tongue. He didn't even feel the sidewalk when he fell backwards, his body convulsing in the alley as the burning liquid rolled down his cheeks and sank into his skin. He was still fighting to take a breath when he heard the man whisper in his ear.

"Thank you for your service."

Lenny's eyes bugged open, but he couldn't say a word. He couldn't breathe, couldn't move, couldn't do anything but lie there and watch the stranger's shiny shoes as they walked away, vanishing into the crowd of oblivious evening commuters pouring down the stairs from the elevated train station across the street.

No one caring at all.

1

FIRST THINGS

auryn didn't know it was possible for a cell phone ring to sound furious until hers went off, screaming like a banshee through the heavy fabric of her winter coat. She grabbed it as fast as she could, smiling apologetically at her clearly annoyed fellow commuters cramming the Chicago L car before turning to the window and whispering into the receiver, "Not now."

"Yes, now!" Naree yelled on the other end, her normally faint Korean accent thick with righteous anger. "Are you out of your mind?"

Lauryn winced and hunched farther into the cold train window, meeting the annoyed gaze of her own exhausted, brown-eyed reflection as she adopted her calmest roommate-soothing voice. "I wasn't trying to—"

"Do you know how many asses I had to kiss to get you that interview? I sold you to the head of HR like you were the second coming! That job was as good as yours. All you had to do was show up and say yes. So why didn't you?"

"Because I didn't want to work there!" Lauryn snapped, all attempts at calm abandoned. "I'm grateful you did this for me, Naree, I really am. But as I told you last week, yesterday, and *this morning*: I don't want to work at a private hospital in the suburbs!"

"Why not?" Naree demanded. "The money—"

"It's not about the money," Lauryn said, pinching the bridge of her nose to head off the stress headache she could already feel building. "I could get a better-paying job anywhere, but I *like* working at Mercy."

"Don't feed me that martyr crap," her friend growled. "No one likes working at a chronically underfunded inner-city hospital."

"Well, I do," Lauryn said stiffly. "They need me there. I became a doctor to help people, not treat rich ladies' tennis elbows."

"Rich ladies need help, too," Naree reminded her. "And unlike Medicaid patients, they *pay*. You want to do charity work, join the Peace Corps."

"Why should I go all the way to another country when there are people who need help right here in Chicago?" Lauryn argued. "I don't fault you for using your new med degree to get a sweet job in a cushy private practice, but that's not what I want for my life. Why can't you understand that??"

"Because it makes no sense!" Naree said. "You need this job, Lauryn. I get your mail, remember? I know you're drowning in student debt even with all your scholarships. It's all well and good living on instant noodles when you're a poor student, but we're done with that. The only reason I graduated number two in med school is because *you* were number one. Number one from the *University of Chicago*—you know, one of the best schools in the world? You could get any job you wanted, so why the hell are you still hanging on at Mercy? Do you *like* being poor?"

"No," Lauryn said. "But I like Mercy. And I'm *not* poor." Mercy couldn't pay its attending physicians what other hospitals did, but it was still doctor money, which might as well be millions compared to what many of her patients lived on. "I make enough to pay my bills, make my rent, and feed myself. That's more than a lot of people have."

Her friend snorted. "Maybe you can be happy just making ends meet, but what about your family? They scrimped and saved to put you through college and med school. You owe them payback. Isn't your dad poor?"

"And we're done," she said, her voice flat. There were few topics that Lauryn liked talking about *less* than her father.

"You need to face facts," Naree said. "Your dad could totally use—"

"Just leave my dad out of this," Lauryn said. "He has nothing to do with my life now, and he wouldn't take my money anyway. He's a preacher. He works for a 'higher reward.'"

"Like you're any different, Miss I-Don't-Like-Money-I-Just-Want-to-Help-People."

"It is *totally* different," she said, raising her voice as the commuter train's breaks began to squeal. "I have to go. This is my stop."

"This isn't over," Naree warned. "You're too smart to be this stupid, Lauryn!"

"Yeah, yeah," Lauryn said as she pushed her way to the doors. "'Bye, Naree."

She hung up right after, cutting off her friend's inevitable attempt to have the last word. It was a childish move, not to mention a temporary fix—it was hard to escape your roommate, especially one as in-your-face as Naree—but after a twelve-hour shift, Lauryn just didn't have the patience to deal with her inability to let things go. The fact that she meant well only made the situation worse. Naree was as good a friend as she was a doctor. So long as she thought Lauryn was hurting herself with this job, she'd never give up trying to save her. And that was the problem, because Lauryn didn't *need* saving. She was already doing exactly what she'd gone to med school to do: helping the people who needed her the most. At Mercy, she routinely saw patients who'd never been to a doctor before her because they couldn't afford to. And while it was frustrating and stressful and draining to work in a place that was always overcrowded and underfunded, it was also incredibly fulfilling. The way Lauryn saw it, working at Mercy meant making a difference, and that was more satisfying than any paycheck.

She just wished she knew how to put that deep satisfaction into a form her friend could understand.

Well, at least Lauryn wouldn't have to deal with the fallout immediately. Even with her fancy new job, Naree would still be stuck at the clinic until midnight. Since it was only seven, that meant Lauryn had at least five hours before she had to have this argument again, and she was determined to spend as many of them as possible asleep in her own bed. That lovely thought was enough to send her racing down the stairs from the elevated train platform, but as she walked through the turnstiles and out into the icy street, something caught her eye.

Directly across from the train station, at the end of the narrow alley between the support beams for the L's elevated track, a man was lying facedown on top of a pile of newspapers. He was clearly homeless, which sadly wasn't uncommon in this area. What *was* uncommon was the fact that he was still outside this late on a November evening in Chicago. The sun hadn't even set yet, and it was already below freezing. If he stayed exposed like that all night, he'd die.

Cursing under her breath, Lauryn hurried across the street, dodging cars and hopping over the frozen puddles. When she reached the alley's mouth, she stopped to assess the situation. Working with the homeless was a delicate business. No one chose to live on the street in winter, which meant there were always complicating factors in a situation like this, generally drug use or mental illness. Or both. Either of those could make accepting help very difficult, but as Lauryn peered down the alley for clues to the homeless man's situation, she spotted a familiar navy-blue veteran's baseball cap lying beside an empty paper cup, and she relaxed—she knew that hat. She'd seen it in her ER just a few days ago, which meant the dirty man lying at the end of the alley wasn't some unknown. It was Lenny.

Lenny was one of Mercy Hospital's "frequent fliers," people who used the emergency room as their one-stop shop. Most frequent fliers were pill poppers, opiate addicts looking to get more pain meds. That wasn't Lenny, though. For all his other problems, he had never been a druggie. He was just confused, a Vietnam vet who'd never been able to leave the war behind. Years of poorly treated PTSD had left him unable to hold down a job and chronically homeless, but he'd always been a gentleman to Lauryn. But even if he'd been an ogre, she wouldn't have left him outside in this cold.

"Lenny?" she called down the alley. "It's Dr. Jefferson."

She paused hopefully, but the man didn't stir.

"Lenny!" she said again, louder this time. "It's Lauryn from Mercy. The sun's going down, buddy. We need to get you somewhere warm."

Again, there was no reply, and a cold dread began to curl in

Lauryn's stomach. Pulling out her phone to use as a flashlight—and in case she had to call for an ambulance—Lauryn stepped into the dark alley beneath the tracks.

The cold hit her like a slap. It was like a meat locker down here. The gap between the elevated subway's support beams and the stone retaining wall, which kept back the hill that had been cut in half to build the track originally, was sheltered from the famous Chicago wind—but the shadow from the track above meant that no sunlight could get down to warm it up. Even here at the front, the alley leading back into the underpass was a good ten degrees colder than the street beside it. If Lenny stayed down here, death from exposure became a "when," not an "if," and that knowledge gave Lauryn the push she needed to keep going, walking farther into the dark below the bridge toward he sheltered nook at the back where her patient was lying motionless.

"Come on, Lenny," she said, squatting down to grab his shoulder. "Time to wake—"

She let go with a gasp, snatching her hand back. She hadn't seen anything in the dark, but the moment she'd touched his faded jacket, something slimy and cold had coated her bare fingers. It was still there, a thick, viscous liquid that shone sickly green when she held her hand under the light of her phone's screen, and Lauryn shot back to her feet with a curse. How could she have been so stupid? Touching an unassessed, unconscious patient without gloves was a newbie mistake, and now her bare fingers were coated in an unidentified slime that smelled like a mix of rotten-egg sulfur and the sickly sweet reek of decaying wounds.

"Stupid, stupid, stupid," she muttered, wiping her hand on the cement wall beside her while frantically dialing 911 with the other.

It took three rings for Dispatch to pick up. When the girl finally answered, Lauryn didn't give her the chance to finish asking "what is the nature of your emergency?" before launching into doctor mode.

"This is Dr. Jefferson from Mercy Hospital," she said, crouching down beside Lenny. "I've got an unconscious male down across the street from the Indiana CTA station. Early sixties, known mental illness, currently unresponsive to voice and touch. I'm going to need—"

A horrible, inhuman shriek cut her off as Lenny's whole body seized, jerking up off the pavement like his belt was attached to a string someone had just pulled tight. The sudden movement made Lauryn jump as well, and she nearly dropped her phone in the process. Luckily she held on, but just as she was sucking in a breath to yell at the dispatcher that he was seizing and she needed that ambulance STAT, Lenny started to . . .

Change.

Despite only getting her actual degree six months ago, Lauryn had already seen plenty of seizures in her career. She'd seen drug addicts spaz off their beds in the heights of violent overdose and patients arch bad enough to throw out their backs during cardiac arrest. But she'd never seen anything like this.

Lenny was bouncing off the pavement like water on a hot griddle. With every violent jerk, the blood was visibly draining from his pain-twisted face, leaving his normally dark skin a morbid shade of gray. His eyes, previously closed, were now wide open and bulging, the blood vessels bursting as Lauryn watched, leaving his corneas a solid wall of red.

After that, Lauryn didn't care about the green crap. She dropped her phone and grabbed Lenny's shoulders, forcing him back down to the ground with all her weight. "I need that ambulance!" she yelled at her phone on the pavement. "How long until—"

Lenny lashed out with both arms, throwing her off him and knocking her phone clear across the alley. Lauryn scrambled to stay on her feet, but he continued to flail his limbs, slamming his elbow into her chest. As soon as she felt the blow connect, Lauryn knew it was going to hurt, but what she didn't expect was for the hit to send her *flying*, launching her backwards across the alley and into the chain-link fence that separated Lenny's hiding spot from the rest of the bridge's support structure.

The metal mesh caught her like a net, bouncing her face-first onto the asphalt below. She caught herself with her hands at the last second, nearly breaking her wrist as she went down hard, but the pain barely registered through Lauryn's adrenaline rush. So the moment she landed, she shoved herself back up, hands raised and ready to defend herself as she looked around for Lenny.

He wasn't hard to find. In the time it had taken Lauryn to get back to her feet, Lenny's jerking body had pulled itself upright. Considering he'd been unconscious when she'd found him, Lauryn wasn't even sure how that was possible, but he was most definitely standing . . . and his bloody eyes glinted in the low light as they locked on hers.

The look was enough to send the frantic breaths whooshing right out of her lungs. Until this point, everything Lenny had done had been bizarre and terrifying, but still inside the realm of medically possible. Looking at him now, though, all Lauryn could think was that the person standing in front of her didn't look anything like the homeless man she'd come here to help.

And that made no sense to her trained, rational mind.

The Lenny she knew was a wiry old veteran with slumped shoulders and hooded eyes that had seen too much. This *thing*— the man-shaped shadow looming over her in the dark—was a good half foot taller, with shoulders that barely fit inside Lenny's ratty old clothes. His limbs looked too long for his body, and his raised hands were veiny and gnarled, the lengthened nails looking almost like claws. As awful as all that was, though, his face was the worst, because when he looked at

Lauryn with his bloody eyes, his lips curled up to reveal a wall of yellowed teeth below his horrifying grayish-blue-tinged gums. This wasn't Lenny anymore.

She wasn't sure it was even still *human*.

Lauryn was a first-response emergency room doctor. It took a lot to spook her, and even more to make her panic. But the sight of Lenny's horrible, inhuman face lifting into a snarl did the job. She screamed at the top of her lungs, her body moving faster than ever before as she launched herself back toward the lit street and, hopefully, safety. She was halfway through the squeeze between the wall and the support beam when Lenny's gnarled hand grabbed her arm, closing down on it like a bear trap.

This time, Lauryn didn't even get a chance to scream. He yanked her back into the alley, nearly snapping her neck as he threw her hard down on the bed of newspapers where he'd been lying when she'd found him. The padding softened the blow a little, but the impact was still enough to knock the air out of her lungs. Gasping, Lauryn scrambled through the greasy sheets of newsprint toward the cement wall. But when she put her back against the stone and whipped around to face her attacker, the violent monster who had been Lenny froze.

The change was so sudden, so complete, Lauryn's first thought was that she'd imagined it. But while his body was still facing her, Lenny's head was turned over his now massive shoulder, his bloody eyes fixed on the alley's entrance, where a new figure—a tall shape in a long winter coat—stood framed against the glare of the floodlights from the train station across the street.

Crouched down against the wall at the back of the tiny alley, Lauryn couldn't see the newcomer's face. With the lights behind them, she couldn't even tell for sure if it was a man or a woman.

Whatever it was, Lauryn didn't care. She'd never been so

happy to see another human being in her life, and the moment she got over her shock, she screamed at the top of her lungs once more.

It wasn't the most articulate cry for help, but it must have been enough. The moment she yelled, the newcomer charged Lenny like a linebacker, knocking him to the ground. Lauryn barely managed to move out of the way before the man—for it was obvious now that her savior was a middle-aged dark-skinned man under that bulky, well-worn winter coat—grabbed her arm and pulled, lifting her back to her feet like she weighed nothing at all.

"Thank you," Lauryn gasped.

"Don't thank me yet," the man replied, his deep voice unnaturally calm as he turned back toward Lenny, who'd already rolled back to his feet, snorting like a bull as he turned to stare them down with his blood-filled eyes.

It was at this point that the absurdity of the situation finally began to beat its way through Lauryn's panic. She was in an alley under the elevated train track less than a hundred feet from a busy train station during the evening rush, facing off against her patient, who'd apparently turned into a monster—a *legit* monster with red eyes, incredible strength, clawed hands, the works—with an unknown savior who didn't look like he found any of this out of the ordinary.

Quite the opposite. The man who'd just pulled Lauryn to her feet looked so calm, he might as well have been waiting for the train. Lauryn was still trying to work her brain around that when Lenny's bloody eyes locked onto the two of them, and his ashen face contorted into a mask of pure, insane rage.

"Um," she said, voice cracking as she took a step back. "I don't know who you are, but I think we should run. I already called EMS. They'll be here in just—"

"I know," the man said, his voice calm and still as a deep winter night. "That's why we can't run. Look around." He nodded at the sheltered square at the end of the alley, formed by the retaining wall, the support beams, and the chain fence that separated this alley from the rest of the underpass. "Right now, he's in here with us. If we leave, he'll follow, and then the whole street will be in danger." He reached into his bulky coat, keeping his eyes locked on Lenny, who was now stomping the dirty pavement like a rhinoceros about to charge. "We have to fight him here."

"Are you *crazy*?" Lauryn hissed. "We can't fight him! He's sick. He needs medical attention, not to be hurt more."

Even as she said it, though, Lauryn wasn't sure. She liked to think she had a high threshold for weird situations—a necessity in her profession—but *nothing* about this made any kind of sense. She could probably come up with some kind of explanation for the red eyes, discolored skin, and obvious violent psychosis, but that didn't change the fact that this thing in front of her was over nine feet tall. On his best day, Lenny just barely topped six feet. He was so tall now, his head was actually scraping the bottom of the train bridge overhead, and that simply wasn't possible. Just thinking about it made Lauryn feel like the whole world was sliding sideways. A feeling that only got worse when the man in front of her reached into his coat to pull out—not a stun gun or a pepper-spray canister or anything that might actually be useful—but a *sword*. A huge two-handed, cross-hilted sword with a wide blade so finely polished it glowed like molten silver in the dark alley.

"Unclean spirit!" he said, his deep voice ringing as he raised the sword in front of him. "I command you to leave this servant of the Lord and torment him no longer."

The loud words bounced through the dark like shots, and the thing that had been Lenny recoiled with a hiss. Lauryn hissed, too, but for completely different reasons. *What the hell are you doing?*

"I'm attempting an exorcism," the man replied, never taking his eyes off Lenny.

That's what Lauryn had been afraid of—this guy was clearly mad, too. She looked down at her hand, wondering if whatever she had touched had psychotropic properties. At the same time, she still found herself saying, "An exorcism? Like, for demonic possession?"

The man answered her blatant skepticism with a patient look and a nod toward Lenny. "Do you know of anything else that could do that?"

Lauryn did not, but just because she didn't have a rational explanation didn't mean she had to buy a crazy one. Unfortunately, she was literally not in a position to argue. The lunatic with the sword was the only thing standing between her and Lenny. But while she wasn't sure how she was going to handle *two* crazy men, Lauryn was still a doctor and Lenny was still her patient. It was her duty to help him survive . . . whatever was going on. Before she could think of how to actually *do* that, though, Lenny's discolored lips peeled back in a snarl.

"Your words mean nothing, soldier," he said, his voice grinding in a way that should never come from a human throat. *"He is already ours, as you all will be."*

"Nothing is yours but death," the man with the sword said, his booming voice making Lauryn jump. "I command you to be silent and come out of him!"

Again, the force of his words bounded through the narrow alley like gunshots, and again the thing that had been Lenny snarled like a beast, running its hand possessively over the veteran's discolored face. For a moment, Lauryn worried it was going to try to speak again in that awful voice, but thankfully it didn't. It did something even worse. It jumped.

The thing that had been Lenny flew at them like a tiger, its clawlike hands going straight for the stranger's throat. Fast as it was, though, the man with the sword was even quicker, spinning away like a leaf on the wind. He dragged Lauryn with him, snatching her out of the way a fraction of a second before Lenny slammed into the cement support beam they'd been standing against. The moment the monster's back was to them, the stranger brought his silver sword down, slamming the flat of the wide, heavy blade across Lenny's shoulders.

The blow landed like a hammer, propelling the transformed veteran to the ground. His scream of pain as he landed was the most human sound he'd made since this whole thing started, and it stabbed Lauryn like a knife.

"*Stop!*"

She didn't even realize she'd yelled until the word left her throat. The sudden sound made the man with the sword jerk in surprise, and then he jerked again when Lauryn's hand shot out to grab the cross hilt of his sword. "Don't," she ordered. "He's my patient. I won't let you hurt him."

"I don't want to hurt him," the man said, his patience, which until this moment had been flawless, slipping slightly. "But he is a threat to everything. If the demon won't listen—"

"There is no demon!" she cried. "Look, I don't know what's happening to him, but he needs help. Not *this*." She pushed down on the sword and let go, turning back to the transformed man, who was already pushing himself up from the pavement. "Lenny!" she yelled. "Snap out of it! This guy's going to hurt you!"

"*I'll hurt* him," Lenny snarled. "*I'll*—"

"No one's hurting anyone," Lauryn said in her doctor's voice, the one she used when patients needed to be shocked back to their senses. "Help is on the way. We're going to get through this, Lenny, I promise, but you need to stop this *right now*. Come back to us."

The command echoed through the alley, making Lenny

shake. Lauryn stepped back, ready to run, but this time, Lenny didn't attack. He just shook his head, blinking his bloody eyes in confusion, and then he whispered, "Doc?"

The word was tiny and broken, but it was the sweetest thing Lauryn had heard all night, because it was Lenny's real voice. "Yes," she said with a gasp of relief. "It's me. It's Dr. Jefferson. Hang in there, Lenny. Help is on the—"

She cut off as Lenny grabbed his head. "You gotta make it stop! The voices, the *voices*—"

His voice started to change back as he spoke, the words rasping and flexing like a rusty saw. But when Lauryn tried to go to him, the man with the sword beat her to it, stepping in front of Lenny as he reached into his coat yet again to pull out—not a sword this time, but a plastic bottle of water, which he proceeded to upend over Lenny's bowed head.

"What are you—"

"You are cleansed," he said, his voice taking on a chanting tone. "'He will wipe away every tear from their eyes; and there will no longer be any death; there will no longer be any mourning, or crying, or pain.' With this, you are washed clean, Lenny. Be at peace all the days of your life."

The words lingered like fading lights in the dark, and then Lenny toppled to the ground. He changed as he went, his transformed body crumbling like ash that scattered when he hit the pavement. When it was over, Lenny was all that remained, lying still as a corpse on the pavement.

Lauryn was at his side a heartbeat later, shoving her fingers under his torn shirt collar to check his pulse. Her own heart leaped for joy when she felt it fluttering, faint but clear. She was rolling him onto his back to take the pressure off his airways when the stranger sheathed his sword and knelt down beside her.

"Are you hurt?"

"No," Lauryn said, but only out of habit. Between her bruised ribs and the scrapes on her hands from the struggle on the pavement, she was actually pretty roughed up, but it was nothing life-threatening. Lenny was in a far more precarious situation. Though the most extreme changes seemed to have faded, his eyes were still blind with blood, and his face remained the color of old ash. She still had no idea what was going on, but an injured man she could handle, and after all the chaos, Lauryn was determined to make this one thing right at least.

"I can save him," she said firmly. "I'm a doctor."

"So I gathered," the stranger replied, looking at her like he was seeing Lauryn for the first time. "He listened to you."

"Of course he did," she said smugly, turning her attention back to Lenny. "He's my patient."

"That's not what I meant," the man said as he slid the water bottle back into his coat. Which reminded her.

"What did you do back there?" Lauryn asked, glancing pointedly at the water bottle. "What is that stuff?" When he didn't answer immediately, she added, "You were quoting Revelations, right?"

The man nodded, looking impressed she'd recognized the passage, but didn't explain. He was too busy staring at her hands, which she'd just moved to Lenny's abdomen. "What's that?"

"I'm palpating his organs to check for internal bleeding," she explained as she began to press her fingers into the soft flesh below the old man's ribcage. "His pallor's anemic, but there's no visible blood loss, so I'm feeling around to see if I can—*hey!*"

The man had grabbed her wrists, turning her hands palms up. "What's *that*?" he asked again, nodding at a long discolored mark across the fingers of her right hand that stood out clearly from the rest of her minor scrapes and bruises.

Lauryn frowned, unsure. Then she remembered. "Oh, that's from when I first arrived. I touched Lenny to try and wake him up, but he had this glop on him that burned my . . ."

She trailed off, frustrated. Halfway through her story, the man had stopped listening. He grabbed his bottle of water again and yanked off the cap, upending what was left over Lauryn's fingers.

"Hey!" she cried. "What are you—*OW!*"

She tried to jerk away, but he held her fast, which was a problem because whatever he was pouring over her hands, it *wasn't* water. The clear liquid had no scent, but it burned like fire everywhere it fell, making her gasp in pain.

"*Stop!*"

"No," the man replied calmly, gripping her squirming fingers. "That burn is dangerous. You need to be cleansed. Remember what was written—'I will sprinkle clean water on you, and you will be clean.'"

Lauryn bared her teeth at him. "You're using Ezekiel as an excuse for burning my damn hands?"

"Language," the man chided, though once again, he looked impressed. "You know your scripture," he said as he released her.

Hazard of being a preacher's daughter, Lauryn thought bitterly, clutching her fingers, which were now burned and blistered. "And you don't know what 'stop' means—that was assault!"

"No, it was necessary," the man replied in that infuriatingly calm way of his, placing the now empty bottle back inside his coat once more. "If my hunch is correct, the stuff you touched is the same substance that caused Lenny's troubles. Not the sort of thing you want on your skin."

Lauryn went silent, her anger forgotten. In hindsight, it was obvious, but in the panic and chaos of the fight, she hadn't had much chance to consider that the strange green slime on Lenny's coat might have caused whatever had just happened to him. Now that the stranger had pointed it out, though, Lauryn couldn't dismiss the worry that the stuff might also have gotten to *her*. After all, she *had* been the one who'd seen Lenny double in size and grow *claws*. Two observations she would have dismissed as hallucinations if she'd heard them from one of her patients.

That was a thought that could bring you down fast, and Lauryn closed her eyes with a shaky breath. But terrifying as it was to realize she might have come in contact with some kind of mind-altering psychotropic, now was not the time to panic. She still had a patient to take care of, and it wasn't like she was alone in her delusion. The man with the sword had seen it, too. He could help her figure out what was real and what wasn't.

And then we can all *panic.*

The thought was ridiculous enough to help her focus. But the idea of the man helping her wasn't. He was her proof that this craziness wasn't just, well, craziness. But when Lauryn opened her eyes again to tell the stranger that she'd need him to stick around for a statement, she discovered she was alone by Lenny's side.

Lauryn shot to her feet, turning in a confused circle, but the dark alley was empty.

There'd been no footsteps, no noise at all, and now there was no strange man with a sword, either. Her dropped cell phone, however, was sitting right in front of her, the screen displaying a text from emergency services saying they'd be right there. Sure enough, sirens were already blaring in the distance. Half a minute later, an ambulance screeched to a halt in front of the alley entrance, the flashing red lights filling the alley with chaotic motion as Lenny woke up screaming.

2
PHYSICIAN, HEAL THYSELF

By the time they got Lenny loaded into the ambulance, Lauryn was more worried than ever.

He had woken up screaming when the ambulance arrived, having clearly slipped further into his delusions, yelling about flying castles and demons and armies of monsters pouring out of the sky. This would have been creepy under any circumstances, but everything was made infinitely worse by the wounds to his corneas, which caused him to weep blood. Given the extent of the damage, Lauryn wasn't sure his eyes would recover, and there was still the matter of the strange necrotic discoloration that covered his skin, particularly his face, neck, and hands. At this point, the best she could say was that at least Lenny wasn't violent anymore, though she didn't have much hope as the paramedics lashed him to the gurney in the back of the ambulance.

"Doc?"

Lauryn tore her eyes off her patient to see Manny Ortega, one of her favorite paramedics, walking over with a first aid kit. "Your turn," he said, holding up the kit.

"No need," she said, shaking her head. "I'm fine, really. But can I catch a ride back to Mercy with you guys?"

Manny gave her a funny look. "You want to go *back*? But I thought you just got off shift."

She had, in fact, just gotten off a twelve-hour shift. *And* she was less than a block from the apartment she shared with Naree. But sleep was impossible given everything that had just happened, and she'd be damned if she let Lenny go into the cattle call that was the general emergency room after all that.

"Just give me a lift. I'm already acting as attending physician. Might as well see it through. I can sleep when I'm done."

"Why is it doctors make the worst patients?" Manny said, shaking his head. "Fine. You can ride along, but only if you let me patch you up. For the love of God, Lauryn, I can see the burns on your hand from here. What did you do, grab the crack pipe out of his mouth?"

"It wasn't like that," Lauryn said irritably, shoving her burned hands into her pockets. "Lenny doesn't do drugs. I can't even get him to take his prescriptions."

"No drugs," Manny repeated, turning to look at Lenny, who was still shouting at the top of his lungs about the end of days. "You sure about that?"

Lauryn wanted to say yes, that the Lenny she knew wouldn't have touched a street drug if his life depended on it. But she couldn't, because this—not the monster who'd attacked her earlier, but the raving madman being tied down now—*wasn't* the Lenny she knew. Now that she was back in the familiar medical world, the strangeness of everything that had gone down under the bridge was finally starting to hit, and as much as Lauryn hated to admit it, Manny was right. Drugs were the most likely explanation.

"Come on," Manny said, hopping up into the back of his truck. "You can tell me the rest while I deal with your hand."

With a defeated sigh, Lauryn climbed into the ambulance beside Lenny. When she was safely strapped into the little fold-down seat, Manny banged on the door to signal his partner, and the ambulance pulled out, the sirens kicking up as they started down the street toward the hospital.

"So," he said, gently taking her injured hand. "What happened? Really."

"To be honest, I'm not sure," Lauryn admitted, wincing as he started smearing the freezing cold burn salve all over her fingers. "I was on my way home when I saw Lenny down at the end of the alley, so I came over to help. When I touched him, he had some kind of slime all over his face and shoulders."

"Is that what got your hands?"

Lauryn nodded. "I wiped it off as best I could, but not well enough apparently. He didn't respond to his name, so I called you guys. He attacked me immediately after."

Manny shook his head in disbelief, which was exactly how Lauryn felt. Manny'd worked this route for years, and he'd picked up Lenny before. She wasn't sure how well they knew each other, but anyone who'd spent time with Lenny knew the old man was terrified of violence since the war. "It's *gotta* be drugs, then. Poor bastard wouldn't hurt a fly otherwise." He shook his head again and turned back to her. "What about you? You look a little freaked, and I'm not talking upset. Do you think you could have been exposed, too?"

Lauryn dropped her eyes. She'd been trying very hard not to think about it, but given how all the weird stuff she'd seen tonight—Lenny's transformation, the fight, the Bible-obsessed stranger with his sword and burning water—had happened *after* she'd gotten the green goop on her skin, Manny's theory made way more sense than she liked. She'd never heard of a hallucinogenic drug that took effect instantly and could be absorbed through the skin, but toxicology wasn't her area of expertise. Plus, however much she hated it, the idea that she'd been accidentally tripping made a lot more sense than Lenny *actually* turning into a monster.

She must have looked horrified, because Manny patted her arm reassuringly. "Don't worry, Doc," he said. "We'll get you taken care of. To be honest, though, I knew it was drugs the moment you told me about the slime."

Lauryn's head shot up. "What do you mean? I've never even heard of a drug like this, and you know we get the full spectrum in the ER."

"You wouldn't have heard of this one 'cause it's brand-new," Manny said as he finished wrapping the bandage around her fingers. "I don't even know what they're calling it yet, but Lenny's the second druggie gone loco we've picked up tonight. First guy had green slime all down his front, too. He also attacked someone who tried to help, but his rescuer wasn't as lucky as you. By the time we got on site, he'd torn her into confetti."

That description was enough to make even Lauryn's iron stomach turn. "That can't be a coincidence, can it? The green slime?"

"Don't know," Manny said with a shrug as he tied off her bandage. "Cops wouldn't tell us nothing, but my buddy in Dispatch says everyone's going nuts about some new drug on the streets. A bad one. Don't know what it does, but the police are freaked real good." He gave her a worried look. "I really hope you didn't stick your hand in a hornet's nest, but just in case, I'm going to have to ask you to put this on for the rest of the ride."

He reached up to grab the restraint straps hanging from the wall of the ambulance, and Lauryn's heart began to sink. "I'm not hallucinating."

"I know," he said. "But better safe than sorry, no?"

Lauryn couldn't argue with that. Cover Your Ass was the mantra of modern medical work, and that was all Manny was doing. It was what *she* should have done in the alley, and so, with a sigh, Lauryn dutifully put her wrists behind her back, letting him bind her to the steel wall of the vehicle as the ambulance careened down the snowy street toward the bright glowing tower of Mercy Hospital.

And this was how, twenty minutes later, Lauryn ended up a patient in her own hospital.

She felt like the main show at the circus. Even though she was technically only there for observation, her room was a nonstop stream of visitors. Everyone she'd met over her two-year internship at Mercy, from nurses to tech staff to desk workers, seemed to have found a reason to drop in and ask how she was doing.

All the attention would have been touching if Lauryn hadn't been well acquainted with how hospital gossip worked. She was the interesting case of the evening, *and* she was the new doctor. Combine the two, and everyone on staff was itching to get all the gory details firsthand so they could tell the others later. Even her boss stopped by, though he was only there to bitch her out for saddling them with Lenny, a known write-off patient who could never be expected to pay for his treatment. He also wanted to make sure she was going to show up on time for her shift tomorrow, something Lauryn was also wondering about, because despite all the uproar, she felt fine. Sure, her hand hurt, and she was bruised all along the side where Lenny had thrown her on the pavement, but none of that required her to be in a bed hooked up to the full diagnostic suite. Constant monitoring was part of standard drug-reaction observational procedure, and until her blood work came back from the lab to prove exposure one way or the other, there was nothing Lauryn could do but wait.

Lauryn *hated* waiting. She was well aware of the irony, since waiting for test results and transport and rooms to open up was a core part of working at a hospital, but at least when she was on duty, there always some kind of task to keep her busy. As a patient, though, Lauryn was stuck. All she could do was sit in her bed and wait for the labs she'd ordered to finish processing. In an effort to speed things up, she'd asked for all the results to be sent straight to her, but she couldn't do anything about the number of tests in line before her or how long each one actually took to run. Given how late it was getting, she supposed she could have slept, but even that was impossible thanks to the parade of nosy coworkers—not to mention the thoughts flying through her mind at a thousand miles per hour.

Finally, around midnight, Lauryn gave up all pretense of politeness and closed her door, the universal hospital sign for GO AWAY. She starting to think she might actually be able to get some sleep at last when someone knocked.

"Unless you're my blood work, bug off," Lauryn grumbled, pressing the pillow over her head. "I have work in six hours."

The door opened before she could finish. But when Lauryn yanked the pillow down to chew out whatever nosy secretary, nurse, or junior med tech had stopped by "just to see how she was doing," she saw it wasn't a hospital employee at all. It wasn't even her roommate, though she was sure Naree would come storming in the moment she got Lauryn's email about what had happened. The man standing in the doorway was someone she hadn't seen in a long time, and he was the very last person Lauryn expected—or wanted—to visit tonight.

In hindsight, she didn't know why she was surprised. Tonight had already gone to utter crap, and if there was anything that could put the crap bow on top of the crap cake, it was a nighttime hospital visit from her ex-boyfriend Will Tannenbaum.

"Hi," he said awkwardly, looking around at the darkened room. "Is this a bad time?"

Lauryn's answer was a long, silent stare. Will looked exactly the same as he had when she'd last seen him. Like, *exactly* exactly, right down to the scruffy, curling dark hair, five-o'clock shadow, and tired eyes he'd stared at her with the night they'd broken up. He was even wearing the same jacket, the leather one she'd bought him back before things had fallen apart, and for a stupid moment, Lauryn's heart sped up. When she saw him standing in the doorway looking just like he used to, she could *almost* believe he was here because he wanted to be. That he'd heard she'd been attacked and had rushed to the hospital to make sure she was okay . . .

And then she remembered Will was a cop. Worse, a detective. A *vice* detective . . . and she was currently under observation for possible narcotics exposure.

With that, all her stupid hopes fell right back into the gutter. Will wasn't here to see Lauryn, Girlfriend Who Got Away. He was here to see Dr. Jefferson, Witness. His work brought him to the hospital like this all the time. It was how they'd met in the first place, when she was a student doing her clinical rotations. Back then, it'd seemed like a perfect match. Since in addition to being a very attractive man, Will was also a vice detective, he was one of the only people in the world who'd understood Lauryn's crazy schedule, because his was just as bad.

Unfortunately, this common ground was what had ultimately ended their relationship. Not because they hadn't gotten along—when they actually managed to spend time together, things were great—but because those moments were just that:

moments, little teases of what could have been if only they were less busy. And that was the trouble, because neither of them was willing or able to *be* less busy. Lauryn had tried for a while, re-organizing her classes and even taking one less shift at the hospital, but despite promises to the contrary, Will hadn't made the effort to match her. There was always something else he had to take care of—a case, an emergency, a bust—and after a month of constantly being stood up for his work, Lauryn had decided she was better off cutting her losses and ended it.

That was half a year ago, ancient history, and Lauryn had every intention of keeping it as such. But it had also been a long, scary night, and she was only human. That was a combination tailor-made for bad decisions, and seeing Will like this after so long, Lauryn was teetering on the verge of a horrible one. She *almost* told him she was happy to see him, that she missed him . . . but thankfully he opened his mouth then and saved her from herself.

"Don't worry," he said, pulling out his badge. "I'm here on business."

For the second time in as many minutes, Lauryn's newborn hopes flatlined. "Of course you are," she said, slumping back down into the scratchy hospital pillows. "Never thought otherwise."

"I won't be long," he assured her, grabbing the battered plastic visitor's chair and moving it closer to her bed. "I just need to take your statement about the attack tonight."

She looked away. "I didn't realize detectives did that kind of grunt work."

Angry or not, that still came out snippier than Lauryn had intended. Thankfully, Will seemed to be as oblivious to her feelings as ever.

"I don't, normally," he admitted, pulling a hand-sized spiral notebook out of the back pocket of the department-provided brand-name jeans that were part of his street-clothes uniform. "But we're shorthanded, so I'm taking this one on myself. I actually came here to interview the homeless man. I didn't even know you were involved until I arrived."

Lauryn didn't believe that for a second. Will had been a lousy boyfriend, but he was an excellent cop. He might look like the nice Jewish boy next door, but he was a smooth operator with a network of informants reporters would kill for. He'd probably known she'd been hospitalized before the ink was dry on her admission form. Lauryn supposed the lie was proof that he really had sought her out, which meant he must still care at least a little, but after the crash and burn of a few seconds ago, she wasn't going down that road again. If he wanted to pretend everything was normal, that was fine with her, so she pushed herself up, folding her hands in her lap as she gave him her best "nothing you say can possibly surprise me" doctor stare.

"Ask away."

Will cleared his throat as he glanced down at the questions he'd written in his notebook. "Why don't we start when you left work?"

For what felt like the millionth time that night, Lauryn told the story of how she'd gotten off the train, seen Lenny, gone to investigate, and been attacked. She'd also explained how she'd known the victim, a detail Will seemed particularly hooked on.

"So, again, you claim Lenny had never shown signs of violence or drug use before tonight?"

"Never," Lauryn said firmly. "He's a vet who suffers from severe PTSD and a whole host of other unmanaged mental issues, but he's terrified of violence and has a pathological mistrust of chemicals, including medicines. The guy won't drink artificial sweeteners, for God's sake. I can't believe he'd take a street drug knowingly."

Will shrugged. "Life on the streets makes people do a lot of things they'd never consider otherwise."

"Maybe," Lauryn admitted. "But Lenny's been on the streets for at least a decade without incident. Why would he change now?" She gave him a sharp look. "One of my EMT buddies told me there's a new drug on the streets. Something you guys don't understand. Do you think that's what's going on here?"

"You know I can't answer that," Will said, shaking his head. "You're a witness. If I tell you what I'm looking for, it'll change your answers." He looked back down at his notebook. "Just describe what happened after you got the stuff on your hand."

Lauryn shifted uncomfortably in the bed. Lots of people had asked about that, but Lauryn had yet to actually tell anyone what she'd actually seen—or thought she saw. But dodging nosy coworkers was very different from an official police interrogation. If they were ever going to get to the bottom of what had been done to Lenny, she needed to tell Will the truth. The *whole* truth. But while that made sense in her head, getting up the nerve to say it out loud was another matter entirely.

"It's going to sound kind of crazy."

"I work Vice in Chicago," Will reminded her with a wry smile. "Whatever you saw in that alley, it won't even ping my Strange-o-Meter. Just tell me what you think happened, and we'll go from there."

Lauryn still wasn't convinced, but there was no turning back now. So, with a deep breath, she told him everything she remembered, which was actually a surprising amount. In her experience, trauma victims and people suffering hallucinations both had trouble recalling specifics, and yet Lauryn could remember every stumble and fall and blow of the fight with Lenny so clearly, it made her lingering bruises ache.

But while the physical stuff was easy, describing Lenny's

transformation was a lot harder. Even with a doctor's vocabulary for describing bodies and how they broke, she just didn't have the words for the way Lenny's shape had shifted and changed into something that didn't even look human. By the time she got to him throwing her around, Lauryn was sure Will thought she was out of her gourd, but the conversation really broke down when they got to her unlikely rescuer.

"Let me make sure I've got this straight," Will said, his voice locked in that calm "I don't want you to know how much bull I think this is" voice Lauryn herself used with truly delusional patients. "While you were being attacked, a third party—a man carrying a *sword*—came out of nowhere and saved you from Lenny using Bible verses and holy water?"

"Yes," she said, cheeks burning. "He was going to fight Lenny, but I didn't want him to hurt my patient, so I stopped him. He used the water after that, and then again on my hand once Lenny was down. That's how I got burned."

She held out her bandaged hand for him to examine, but Will didn't give it more than a cursory glance. "I think it's safe to say you were hallucinating," he said, leaning back in his chair. "And honestly, given what you touched, we should be damn happy that's all it was."

Lauryn sat bolt upright in her chair. "It *was* the new drug, wasn't it?"

He shrugged. "Officially, we don't know anything until we see your blood work. Off the record?" Will sighed and leaned forward in the creaking chair, resting his elbows on his knees. "This is bad, Lauryn. I don't know if you've been following the news, but a new group's been muscling into the Chicago narcotics business."

"I don't need to follow the news," she said. "I've seen the results in the ER. So is it a new gang or something?"

"Not sure yet," Will admitted. "Whoever they are, though,

they're thorough. You wouldn't believe how many dead gangsters and cartel members we've fished out of the river in the last two months. At this point, these new guys have to control most of the drug business in the city, if not all of it, simply because there's no one else left. But that's not even the weird part. Where things *really* get strange are the drugs themselves. Over the last few months, we've had product flooding into Chicago. Meth, heroin, coke: the whole pharmacopoeia. I've busted enough stockpiles to make the whole city high twice over in the last three weeks, and I don't think we're even making a dent. And that's still not the worst part."

"What's the worst part?"

"The quality."

"Is it tainted?" Lauryn asked, biting her lip. Laced drugs were even worse to deal with than normal ones. With common drugs, you knew what to expect and how to treat it, but when junkies started shooting bargain drugs cut with who-knew-what into their arms, all bets were off. But while she was already making a mental checklist of complications from compromised drugs to look for, Will was shaking his head.

"The opposite," he said. "Every cache we've seized has been some of the purest stuff I've ever seen. I'm talking expensive, pharma-grade dope, and they're selling it for dirt cheap."

Lauryn frowned. "Why would they do that?"

"That's what we don't get, either," Will said, frustrated. "Generally cartels take over the drug trade in a city to eliminate competition so they can *raise* prices, not drop them. But these guys have been pushing cheap pharma-quality drugs on the city like they're on a mission to get the whole city hooked."

"That *would* explain the rise in overdose cases we've seen lately," Lauryn said. "But what does this have to do with Lenny? I mean, he didn't OD, and certainly not on heroin or coke."

"He didn't," Will agreed. "But I've been working this case

for a month now, and over the last twenty-four hours, all hell has broken loose." He stood up and started pacing around the room, his face distant. "It started this morning. One of our informants—a homeless man we were paying to keep an eye out for new dealers in the area—went beserk. Ripped the door right off a patrol car before officers took him down. Not three hours later, another guy we've been following did the same. Before he bled out, one of the witnesses claimed he saw the junkie tear two bystanders to pieces like they were made of paper. He also said that his eyes glowed red the whole time, and that his mouth was dripping with green slime."

"Green slime?" Lauryn repeated, her blood running cold.

"Now do you see why I got here so fast?" Will said grimly. "We've had six incidents so far today, all homeless and, except for Lenny, all known addicts connected with the new cartel investigation. As of right now, Lenny's the only perp who's survived. All the others were either shot by cops or died from heart attacks at the scene. When we searched the bodies, the one connection we've made is finding traces of green slime you just mentioned in your report."

"And you think that's what's making them go nuts?" Lauryn said, leaning forward. "Is the slime a new kind of drug or something?"

"I don't know," Will admitted. "But if my hunch is right, you're damn lucky a wandering swordsman street preacher with magic water's all you saw after you got it on your fingers."

Lauryn was starting to get that impression, too. "Well, whatever it is, the drug has to still be in their blood," she said authoritatively. "Nothing that causes such huge changes can be flushed that fast. Your morgue must have done autopsies on the other cases by now. What was their toxicology?"

Will glanced back down at his notebook. "As I mentioned, all the perps were habitual junkies, so their blood was a cesspool.

Since they all seemed to die of the same thing, Forensics' plan was to look for a common denominator, some chemical they all had in common that we could use as a key. So far, though, they haven't found jack. The only condition they all had in common was . . ." He trailed off, squinting at the paper in front of him before turning it around so Lauryn could see. "I can't pronounce this."

"Sulfhemoglobinemia," she read, eyebrows furrowing. "Weird. Sulfhemoglobinemia happens when there's too much sulfur in the blood, and only in really rare cases. Sulfur's pretty common, and nontoxic to most people, but an excess in sulf-hemoglobin *would* explain the cyanosis."

Will blinked. "Could I get that in English, please?"

"Extra sulfur in his blood would explain why Lenny's skin was discolored," Lauryn said, getting excited as the pieces fell into place. "I thought I was hallucinating when I saw Lenny turning that ugly blue gray, but that part might have actually been real. Unlike normal red blood cells, sulfhemoglobin can't carry oxygen."

"And that makes you dead," Will finished with a grim smile. "See? I'm learning."

"I don't know how useful that is, though," Lauryn admitted. "You said the victims died of heart attacks, not hypoxia." At his blank stare, she translated. "Lack of oxygen in the blood. Also, too much sulfur wouldn't explain the hallucinations or psychosis."

"Good to know you're just as stumped as we are," Will said with a self-deprecating laugh. "Personally, I don't care what the chemical compound is. I just want to find whoever's pushing this crap and bag 'em. Street drugs are poison, but something that turns normally docile addicts into monsters? That's a nuke, and we need to stop it yesterday."

"No argument here," Lauryn said. "But I still don't get the sulfur thing. It just doesn't make sense." It might explain how the green stuff had burned her fingers, since sulfur was mildly corrosive, but no amount of sulfur exposure could possibly cause the other symptoms. Even if it was just being used as a chemical base for something nastier, any dangerous compounds would have shown up in the lab report way ahead of sulfur. She was still thinking it over when yet another knock sounded on her door. This time, though, it was the one she wanted.

Lauryn's face lit up like Christmas when the girl from the lab stuck her head in. "Dr. Jefferson? I have your reports." She stopped there, casting a wary look at Will, who was obviously a police officer despite his street clothes. Even if he hadn't left his badge lying on the bed, everything about his posture and bearing screamed "cop"—and anyone who'd been in a hospital long enough could play "cop or fireman" with 90 percent accuracy. "Is this a bad time?"

"For blood work?" Lauryn flashed her a grin. "Never."

She reached out with both hands for the thin manila envelope. But rumors about Lauryn's drug exposure must have been reaching critical mass, because the tech handed it over with only her fingertips, keeping maximum distance like she was giving food to a leper. That was going to be annoying to deal with later, but for now, Lauryn was too busy ripping open her results to care.

As the priority case, Lenny's report was on top. At first glance, it looked like every other set of tests Lauryn had ever ordered run on him. He had all basic vitamin deficiencies you'd expect from someone who didn't have access to regular meals or shelter, though no hepatitis or HIV, which was a miracle considering how long he'd been on the streets. But despite the thorough report she'd ordered, the section Lauryn was *really* interested in, the toxicology report, was infuriatingly blank save for a one-word note at the very bottom.

Sulfhemoglobinemia.

"That's the same thing the others had," Will said, reading over her shoulder. "Anything else?"

"Nothing," Lauryn said, flipping the printout over just to be sure she hadn't missed a page. "I told you, he's clean." And while she was very happy to be right about that, it made *no* sense. It was like the more information she got, the more infuriating the puzzle became. For example, the last report she'd had from Lenny's nurse said that he was still hallucinating, claiming to see all kinds of horrors. For a patient with zero history of hallucinatory psychosis, drugs were the most likely culprit. Even if it wasn't a street drug, the toxicology report should still have found *something*.

Frustrated, she moved on to the second report in the folder, the one with her name printed at the top. Here again, however, there were no surprises. She was slightly anemic with terrible vitamin D from never getting outside in the sunshine, but no trace of anything that could possibly account for what she was almost positive was her hallucinatory episode under the bridge. Frustration levels moving up a notch, Lauryn skipped to the end to check her sulfur levels. She already knew what it would say, but still she wanted to confirm the proof with her own eyes, which only made the whole thing even more frustrating when she opened the second page only to find it was blank.

Staring at the empty sheet, Lauryn's first thought was that someone must have fucked up. When she checked again, though, all the toxicology tests she'd ordered were there. They'd just managed to fit the results on one page because there was nothing to report. Everything, including Lauryn's sulfur, was perfectly normal.

And she had no idea what to make of that.

D o you need a ride home?"

Lauryn looked up from her paperwork to see Will standing over her. "I need to get back to the station, but I can drop you off at your apartment on the way." He smiled. "It'll be like old times."

Him driving her home from the hospital before heading back to work would, in fact, be *exactly* like old times, and that was precisely why Lauryn didn't want to go.

After her clean report, there'd been no more need to keep her under observation, so Lauryn had abused her status as a doctor and written her own discharge. She'd already changed back into her normal clothes and checked out of her room. The paperwork was the last step, but the whole process was still taking longer than she liked. It was now nearly one in the morning, and even though she'd just have to come right back in five hours for her 6 AM shift, all Lauryn wanted to do was go home and go to sleep. She was trying to decide if she wanted that badly enough to risk being alone in a car with her ex when her phone began to ring with a jangling tone she hadn't heard in a long, long time.

"What the—"

Lauryn dropped her pen and dug out her cell phone, eyes going wide when she saw her father's name on the screen. She hadn't talked to her dad since Easter, when he'd called to guilt her for skipping church. Unless there was a holy day in November she'd forgotten about, there was only one reason he'd be calling now. But while her dad was the absolute last person Lauryn wanted to talk to after the night she'd had, ignoring him wasn't an option. On the rare occasions Pastor Maxwell Jefferson remembered he had actual, physical children in addition to the spiritual sons and daughters in his congregation, he tended to go overboard. If Lauryn didn't answer, he'd just keep calling until he got fed up enough to come find her in person.

That would lose her even more sleep, so Lauryn gave in, hitting the button to accept the call. Before she could say anything—or even get the speaker to her ear—her father's voice boomed out loudly enough to make everyone in the hallway turn and look.

"*Why didn't you call?*"

Lauryn sighed bitterly. That was her dad. No "hello" or "how are you doing?" or "oh my God, I heard you got attacked, are you okay?" Just accusations for not living up to how he thought she should have acted. Like always.

"Lauryn!" Maxwell barked.

"Sorry," she muttered, rubbing a hand over her face. "I'm fine. It was nothing serious."

"Then why were you in the hospital?" His voice grew suspicious. "I heard you were on drugs."

"Who told you that?"

"Solange Peterson from the prayer circle works at the front desk," he reminded her. "She called to let me know the moment she heard."

Lauryn rolled her eyes to the ceiling. She'd forgotten all about Miss Solange, which was very stupid of her. When hospital gossip collided with church gossip, nothing was safe. "Well, she was mistaken," she said stiffly. "I was attacked and put at risk, but I didn't actually get exposed to anything." At least, not according to her toxicology. "I'm fine. I just want to go home and get some sleep."

"Good," her father said. "I've got your room all ready. I'm already on my way to pick you up."

That threw Lauryn for a loop. "Wait, what? You're coming *here?*"

"My daughter was attacked," Maxwell said angrily. "Of *course* I'm coming to get her. At times like this, you need to be at home with your family."

"But I've got my *own* place," she said. "All my stuff is there. I don't even have clothes—"

But it was too late. Maxwell had clearly already made up his mind, and nothing short of Jesus himself was going to make him change it. "Home is where your family is," he said, his preacher's voice booming through the phone's tinny speaker. "I've already left a note for your brother. I'll be there in five minutes. Be waiting out front."

He hung up immediately after that, cutting off the call before Lauryn could get a word in, and she jerked her phone down with a frustrated groan. "'*Be waiting out front*,'" she mimicked, seething. "I'm a doctor, dammit! Not a high schooler who needs to be picked up from band practice."

Will flashed her a sympathetic smile. "So I take it you won't need me to give you a ride?"

"Not unless we can leave right now and you're willing to put the sirens on," Lauryn said, only half-jokingly. If she'd thought a cop car or sirens would have actually stopped her father, she would have jumped right in and told Will to floor it. "Looks like I'm spending what's left of the night at my dad's house," she said bitterly. "Oh well, at least I'll get to see my brother. I haven't seen Robbie since he was in high school."

For some reason, that made Will's smile turn sour. "Don't get your hopes up," he muttered, which struck Lauryn as a weird thing to say. When she tried to ask him about it, though, Will had already turned away. "Thanks for your help tonight, Lauryn," he said without looking back. "Take care."

"You, too," she said, trying not to feel like she'd just been stood up again. Thankfully, the insurance section of her remaining discharge paperwork was complicated enough to take her mind off it.

Fifteen minutes later, officially discharged, Lauryn walked out of the administration office, through the darkened main lobby, and out into the covered hospital pull-through where her father's pristinely maintained 1982 Buick LeSabre was waiting to pick her up, exactly as promised.

"You're late," Maxwell said when she opened the door.

Exhausted, emotionally drained, and royally pissed off, Lauryn didn't even dignify that with a reply. "Let's just go," she muttered, collapsing into the couch-soft seat. "It's been a hell of a day."

Maxwell scowled at her language, but must not have been in the mood for a fight, either, because he just pulled out, coasting under the hospital's glaring lights toward the empty street.

And behind them, unseen, a solitary man on a motorcycle with what appeared to be a sword strapped to the side pulled out and began to follow.

3

SOMEONE TO DEVOUR

The roads were empty tonight. A mercy, because Will was already late.

He made it to the Chicago PD's main office in record time, parking his unmarked car in the vice department's section of the icy, sprawling lot. He slammed his door as he got out, stomping through the freezing night as he cursed himself for a damn fool.

He shouldn't have gone to the hospital.

It had made sense at the time. The new group taking over the Chicago drug scene was his case, and since the green stuff had been popping up on his informants, that made Lauryn his witness. His territory. And like most detectives, Will was possessive of his territory. This time, though, he wished like hell that he'd let someone else take the job, because seeing Lauryn again had hurt a lot more than he'd expected.

"Idiot," he muttered as he tapped his ID against the electronic pad that opened the bulletproof door. "Stupid—"

His self-recriminations were cut off when one of the guys from Homicide came sprinting through the door, nearly bowling Will over in the process. That was pretty normal for this time of night—the wee hours of the morning were prime time for police work—and the fact that he hadn't even seen it coming through the glass door was yet more proof of what a distracted moron he'd become, mooning over his ex like a lovesick high schooler.

The only thing he could say in his defense was that she'd looked exactly like he remembered—a tall, lovely woman with a knowing smile, warm brown eyes, and a steel backbone. Even lying in a hospital bed listening to him describe the terrifying drug she might have been exposed to, she hadn't looked scared or beaten. Exactly the opposite. She'd been radiant with the same alluring mix of energy, intelligence, and competence that had drawn him in from the very beginning. *Still* drew him in like a moth to flame . . . which was exactly the problem, because he'd burned that bridge right down to the ground. There was no going back for a man who'd already wasted his second and third chances. Not with a girl as smart as Lauryn. He knew that perfectly well, and yet he'd still rushed straight in like an idiot the moment he had an excuse to talk to her.

Moron.

The only good thing he could say about this mess was that at least Lauryn had given him a lead. That was more than he could say about the rest of his witnesses, so Will gave his regrets the boot and got back to business, jogging up the stairs to his desk in the vice department to type up his report.

Personal issues aside, it had been a good interview. Before her, he'd had five dead druggies, three murdered witnesses, a dead cop, some unidentifiable green glop . . . and nothing to show for any of it. This Lenny stuff, though, this was useful. The old vet might not be talking sense yet, but at least he was *alive*. Even better, the green stuff seemed to be the only drug in his system. If he snapped out of it, he might be able to tell Will who'd sold it to him, which would be a huge breakthrough. Until then, Lauryn was the closest thing he had to a reliable witness, and her comments on the sulfur angle were invaluable. There was also her report of a second witness, the man with the sword . . .

That might not be as valuable.

He knew Lauryn wasn't a liar, but even though her blood work had come back clean, the second half of story was just too weird to convince Will she hadn't hallucinated her savior. But a good detective records everything, no matter how ridiculous, and so he dutifully added the swordsman to his report, typing it up exactly as Lauryn had told it to him, along with his own observations about her seemingly clear state of mind.

When he'd recorded absolutely everything he could think of, including the not-admissible-in-court glimpse he'd stolen of Lauryn's lab report over her shoulder, Will saved the document to the department's case file and grabbed his phone to call the lab.

"This is Tannenbaum from Vice," he said the moment the line picked up. "I need a list of street drugs that contain or could be mixed with sulfur."

"Sulfur?" the man asked, clearly puzzled.

"That's right," Will said firmly. "It's for the new drug case."

That should have been all he needed to say. With eight casualties and a dead cop in less than twenty-four hours, Will's case was at the top of the department's list. But instead of jumping to get Will the information he'd asked for like he should have, the man on the phone just sighed.

"Sorry, Detective, no can do. We're backed up till Monday,

and the chief made it clear that no one gets to reorder the schedule until we're back on track."

Will ground his teeth. "I'm not asking you to *test* anything. I just need someone to make me a list."

"Which takes time," the tech replied. "And time's exactly what we don't have."

"Are you guys smoking the evidence down there?" Will yelled. "I didn't just pull a twenty-four-hour shift 'cause I felt like it. People are dying! I can't wait till Monday. I need this *now*."

"Sorry, man," the tech said, not sounding sorry at all. "I'd help you if I could, but my hands are tied. Chief Korigan was very clear: no more messing with the schedule. You'll just have to wait. Other departments have priority cases, too."

Not like this one. But ticked off as Will was, badgering the tech was pointless. If he wanted to actually push anything through, then he was going to have to take this to the man who actually had the power to make things happen.

He hung up without even wasting the breath to say goodbye, ignoring the worried looks from his fellow plainclothes detectives as he stormed out of the vice office and down the hall to the elevator that would take him straight up to the chief's floor.

Even as he slammed his thumb down on the button, Will knew this was a bad idea. Technically, this was a problem he should have taken to his superior, but the idiot paper pusher Chief Korigan had put in charge of the vice department didn't work nights—*God knows vice doesn't happen at* night—and Will wasn't about to let this sit until morning. Besides, this confrontation had been a long time coming.

In the ten years he'd worked for the department, Will had outlasted seven police chiefs, all of whom had either been drummed out on corruption charges or sleazed their way further up the political chain. It was all business as usual for Chicago, but even in the cesspool that was Illinois politics, Victor Korigan was in a class by himself.

A former military contractor, Korigan was different from the usual brand of incompetent hack or crooked city government crony who traditionally passed through the revolving door of Police Chief. Both he and the mayor—who'd practically handed Korigan the job on a silver platter—had expertly dodged all questions about his past, but Will (being Will) had done some digging, and hadn't liked what he'd found.

In the very few comments he'd made about his past work experience, the mayor had called Korigan a "hardworking immigrant and veteran of the Bosnian War who understood what it took to keep a city safe." But while that made a good soundbite and was technically true, Will's research had uncovered that Korigan's military career during the conflict had been firmly on the Serbian side, often as an officer commanding suspiciously undocumented "civilian detainment" units.

There was no direct evidence linking him to ethnic cleansing or any of the other war crimes that had shadowed that horrible conflict, but the connection was still too close for Will's liking, and the picture only got worse when you added in the unpleasantness Korigan's private military company had been involved with since. The man seemed to be playing war-zone-tragedy bingo with jobs in South Sudan, Somalia, Yemen, and Afghanistan. Now he was heading up the police here, and while Chicago was the most dangerous major city in the US, Will didn't think bringing in a man with hands as bloody as Korigan's was going to make things any better.

But, of course, no one else had seen it that way. According to the mayor, Korigan had been brought in to bring "private sector efficiency" to the eternally overbudget Chicago PD, and for all his other sketchiness, Korigan had done just that—mostly by slashing the budgets on every part of police work that actually mattered. This crap with the lab was a perfect example. Rather than hiring more techs or expanding the lab to deal with the overflow in casework, he'd just ordered everyone to wait their turn. Screw priority, screw the victims, screw actually solving cases. No, even knowing that there was often a tiny window after a crime was committed to solve the case, cops were expected to take a number, like the forensics lab was a deli counter. But it had put them back in the black, which meant the mayor was now holding Korigan up as the genius who'd saved the Chicago PD from themselves. Meanwhile, the people of Chicago were paying the price in backlogged cases and cops too hamstrung by budget cuts to actually do their damn jobs.

It was directly because of Korigan's cut-and-burn policy that this new drug cartel had been able to grow as fast and big as it had. Will had been warning the department about it for weeks now, but no one had listened. Now, things were going even crazier than he'd predicted, and it was only fitting that the chief bear the brunt of the mess he'd created when he'd decided to put money before people.

He just hoped he didn't get canned for saying so.

Will quashed the nagging doubt with a sneer. He'd always prioritized the case over his job, and he'd yet to be fired, because he got the job done. Even for a golden boy like Korigan, it was hard to sack a detective with a case-resolution rate as solid as Will's, and that knowledge gave him strength. By the time the elevator reached the top floor, he was almost looking forward to the fight, and he got off with a spring in his step, half jogging down the carpeted hall.

Unlike the rest of the bustling station, the top floor of police headquarters was dark and empty. This was where the bureaucrats nested, the army of lawyers and experts and overpaid managers who got to do their police work in tidy nine-to-five chunks. The only people up here at this time of night were Will and the janitors, but he knew from months' worth of department emails that Chief Korigan was a night owl. Sure enough, there was light shining through the expensive frosted-glass door when Will reached it.

At least he hadn't walked all this way for nothing. With only a cursory knock, Will grabbed the door and shoved it open, exploding into the office only to stop in his tracks when he saw Police Chief Korigan sitting at his desk in a tux and white tie like he was on his way to the opera. It was so unexpected, Will was actually struck speechless, but if Chief Korigan was surprised or angry to see a detective storming into his private office at one in the morning, he didn't let it show. He simply folded his hands on his brand-new custom glass desk, smiling through the frame of his perfectly groomed goatee as he said, "May I help you?"

The genteel question snapped Will out of his shock, and he met his boss's smile with a feral one of his own. "You sure can," he said. "I need you to put the new drug case back on priority right now."

"Is that so," Korigan said slowly. "Why?"

"Because we've got addicts going nutso and killing people all over downtown," Will snapped. "Sounds like a priority to me."

Korigan shook his head, leaning back in his leather chair to study Will's face. "You're Detective Tannenbaum from Vice, correct?" When Will nodded, the police chief glanced at his computer monitor. "I presume you're talking about the new overdose cases?"

"They're *not* overdoses," Will growled. "I keep telling you, this isn't a standard drug case. Whatever's causing this, it's something new, and it's killed nine people, including one of our officers."

"I am well aware of the situation," Korigan said. "But while I agree it is very tragic, that's no reason to disrupt the order and efficiency of this office. We have procedures in place already that—"

"Screw your procedures!" Will shouted. "We're talking about what could be the beginning of an epidemic here!"

"First off—watch yourself. I respect your passion, but I have no problem docking your pay until you remember your place in this department. Am I clear?"

"Yes."

The chief arched an eyebrow. "Excuse me?"

"Yes . . . *sir.*"

Korigan smiled. "Good. Now, on to the second matter. I can't help but think you're overreacting. There are 2.7 million people in Chicago. Seven cases is *hardly* an epidemic."

Will opened his mouth again, but the chief cut him off. "You want to do your job. So do I. But this is a public office, not a crusade. I was brought in precisely to keep hotheads like yourself inside the lines. We have rules, we have a budget, and we have a duty to the taxpayers of Chicago to respect both."

"With all due respect, *sir,*" Will said through clenched teeth. "How are the taxpayers of Chicago going to react when they find out there's a drug on the streets turning people into monsters and their police chief is too concerned with keeping accounts in the black to do anything about it?"

By the time he finished, the polite smile had fallen off Korigan's face, leaving something much colder that Will didn't like at all. "We *are* doing something about it," he said flatly. "Whatever you might think, I have, in fact, read all of your admirably detailed reports, and despite your dramatic conclusions, I stand by my decision. This case will be processed like any other: in accordance with the documented procedure."

Will's hands clenched into fists. "But—"

"The resources will be allocated when they're available," Korigan went on like he hadn't spoken. "That's how procedure

works. That how *I* work. That's what it means to have a *system*."
His eyes narrowed. "I've let you skate by for a long time now,
Tannenbaum. You've got a fantastic record, and I've let you handle things your way so far out of respect for that, but I can't look
the other way forever. You've put almost two hundred hours of
overtime into this new cartel investigation alone, and for what?
You're no closer to cracking the case now than you were last
month."

"Because I didn't have the resources," Will snapped. "If you'd
given me more people—"

"You'd have worked them to death, too," Korigan snapped
back. "Police work is work just like everything else. You can
throw man hours at it all you like, but sometimes you just have
to accept your limits."

"By which you mean *your* budget."

"Partially," Korigan said with a pitying look. "But has it ever
occurred you that my policies are about more than just the
budget? Think about it. We're cops. We see the worst of this city
every damn day. When we start panicking, people notice. The
press notices, and that's a problem for everyone."

"Who cares about the press? We—"

"You *should* care about the press," Korigan said. "You think
seven junkies going nuts is bad? Try dealing with a terrified
population whipped into a media-induced panic once the papers
announce that Chicago's in the grips of a new, unknown, violent
drug epidemic. I don't care how many people are OD'ing, it'll
be nothing compared to violence we'll have when people start
thinking every bum they see on the street is one bad hit away
from going berserk. *That's* an emergency, Tannenbaum. That's
what's going to get people killed—panic, chaos—and that, not
the budget, is why your case is officially on the back burner from
now on."

He finished with a low glare that dared the detective to try him, but for once, Will was speechless. That was a much better explanation than he'd expected when he'd stormed up here. Clearly, he'd underestimated the new chief, but that didn't mean he was done just yet.

"I get that this is the sort of case that would freak people out," he said calmly, changing tactics. "But I don't think you understand how bad things are getting. This isn't your normal vice case of drugs and sleaze. People are getting literally torn to pieces for reasons we can't explain, and worse, the first two victims were both criminal informants. Our *only* informants on this new cartel, I might point out."

"And the other five had nothing to do with us," the chief reminded him. "Two points don't make a trend."

"That's not how the rest of my guys will see it," Will said, leaning over the desk. "If word gets out we can't protect our informants, no one will tell us anything ever again."

"They're not telling us anything *now*," Korigan said. "We don't have so much as a parking ticket on this new cartel. We certainly don't have anything linking them to this new drug."

"We don't need a link," Will argued. "They're the only pushers left in town. Who else could be selling it?"

That bit of undeniable logic finally seemed to get through, and the chief looked down with a sigh. "You're *sure* it's a new drug?"

Will nodded. "As sure as I can be. I just got back from interviewing a witness, and—"

"Witness?" Korigan's head jerked up to look at his computer screen. "I thought all the witnesses were dead?"

"Not this one," Will said proudly. "Both the witness and the perp from the last case tonight pulled through. Better still, the victim is a doctor at Mercy who knows the perp and can testify that he had no previous history of drug use."

The police chief looked deeply skeptical. "If the perp wasn't a junkie, what was he doing taking a drug?"

"I don't know," Will said. "Like I keep saying, *nothing* about this case is normal. I don't know how he got hold of that green slime or why he used it tonight, but you don't have to be psychic to know there's something bad coming. I'll bet you anything you want that the mess we saw tonight is just a warm-up. That's why you have to make this a priority, before anyone else gets killed."

That was as good a case as he was ever going to make, but the chief just shook his head again. "I know you want a big case," he said tiredly, "but let's be reasonable. Say you're right, and the new cartel that's taken over the Chicago drug market is actually pushing some kind of new drug that makes people go nuts. *Why* would they do that? What kind of business kills off their customers?"

"What kind of business sells pharma-grade street drugs at ditch-weed prices?" Will countered. "These guys haven't made sense since they came here. Why should they start now?" He put his hands down on the glass desk, leaning forward until he was inches from Korigan's face. "You want to keep this out of the papers? You want to look good for the mayor who got you this cushy gig? Back off and let us do our damn job. Give this case priority. Give me what I need and I swear I'll put a stop to this before it gets anyone else killed."

He was breathing down the chief's neck by the time he finished, but the man in front of him hadn't even flinched. He just sat there, staring right back up at Will with the hard eyes of a man who'd seen it all. It was a sharp reminder that despite his fancy office and expensive tux, Victor Korigan was a veteran of some of the world's worst hellholes, and he was not intimidated now.

"This is not open for debate, Detective," he said coldly. "While I appreciate the spirit behind your theatrics, my decision is made. The case stays off the priority list. We'll continue normal investigations as required, but I don't want to hear a peep out of you about your unfounded conspiracy rumors. From here on out, our official statement is that this whole tragedy was caused by a big drug cartel pushing a bad batch of meth. End of story."

"You don't know what you're doing," Will warned. "If we don't act fast, we—"

"End. Of. Story." Korigan growled. The sound was almost guttural, making Will take an involuntary step back. When he looked up again, though, Korigan was back to normal, smiling and slick as ever as he stood up from his desk. "Go home, Detective," he said, turning to grab his heavy felt overcoat from the hook on the wall. "You've been working too much, and it's starting to affect your judgment. Don't make me put you on medical leave."

The tone was friendly, but Will knew a threat when he heard one. He was starting to see how Korigan had wormed his way into the top law enforcement office in the city. The man was a smooth operator who knew how to control those below him. He certainly had Will by the balls. With those two terrifying words—"medical leave"—the chief had all the ammunition he needed to take Will off the case entirely. At this point, Will's only choice was stand his ground and possibly lose everything, or back down and play along. Neither appealed to him, but Will was used to hard choices, and just because he was being forced down didn't mean he was out of the game entirely.

"If you say so, sir," he said quietly, looping his thumbs through his belt. "But where are *you* going? Little late for an opera, isn't it?"

"My affairs are none of your business," Korigan replied. "But for the record, I'm off to a party." He flashed Will a sharp smile. "An active social life is important for maintaining mental health. You should try it sometime."

Will scowled, but before he could think of a comeback, Korigan walked around his desk to open the door. "Thank you for telling me your concerns, Detective. My door is always open to my officers—although next time I'm going to insist you actually knock. But I'm afraid I have to get going. *Good night*, Mr. Tannenbaum."

The obvious dismissal made Will bristle. It was not in his nature to back down from a fight. He'd learned long ago that the only way to get what you wanted in life was to bite down and never let go. Tonight, though, the practical cynicism from a decade of police work told him that pushing back now would only make things worse, so he forced himself to let it go, stepping back out into the dark hallway seconds before the police chief closed the glass door in his face.

The cold silence of the empty hall was insult to injury. But while Chief Korigan could threaten his job, he couldn't tell him what to do during his free time, and all of a sudden, Will was in the mood to do a little driving. That thought brought a smile to his face, and as fast as he'd been kicked out, Will changed course, hurrying out of the building with only a brief stop at his desk to print out a copy of the case file that was no longer marked priority to anyone but him.

The moment Tannenbaum was gone, Victor Korigan locked his office and walked down the hall to the private elevator that went down to the underground lot reserved for high-ranking government officials. After checking his bow tie one last time, he climbed into the armored Hummer the city provided for his safety and told the driver to take him to the address on the invitation he'd been waiting for all day.

The one he'd received mere moments before Tannenbaum had charged into his office.

That had been unfortunate. Men like Tannenbaum were ticking time bombs—overinvested, convinced of their own righteousness, and, worst of all, highly resistant to bribes. Even so, he'd hoped to put off dealing with him for a little while longer. Obnoxious as he was in other ways, Tannenbaum was a good detective. He did his job, kept his nose clean, and was popular on the force, all of which made him difficult to remove. But removed he would have to be. Korigan had been given control of the Chicago PD precisely to keep chaos elements like Tannenbaum from disturbing carefully laid plans. It was a position he'd fought long and hard for, and if Tannenbaum insisted on threatening his cultivated equilibrium, then the detective would have to go. Simple as that.

But that was tomorrow's problem. Tonight, he had far bigger, far better fish to fry, as the engraved summons in his hands proved. Technically, it was an invitation to a party, but the name at the top told Korigan that it was so much more than that, and he could hardly keep himself still as his driver followed the GPS through the slushy, frozen streets of late-night Chicago until he reached the giant brick-faced four-story mansion sprawling at the center of a mile-long stretch of Lake Michigan–bank property on the edge of the city limits.

Despite the fact that it was now nearly 2 AM, the party inside was still in full swing, the energy coming from the house almost tangible. The moment Korigan's Hummer pulled up to the front entrance, a uniformed valet rushed out to get his door, welcoming him without once glancing at his face. Returning the favor, Korigan ignored the man and dismissed his driver with a wave as he walked toward the entrance, climbing the carefully swept and salted stone steps to the Gilded Age mansion's elegant double doors.

Stepping inside was like walking into Hollywood's ideal of debased opulence. Everywhere Korigan's eyes fell, beautiful people—male and female—were lounging on antique furniture, gazing up at the fat, graying bodies of Chicago's elite with the sort of overt sexual excitement only lots of money could buy. White-coated waiters circled through the rooms offering guests silver trays laden with flutes of champagne, delicate French pastries, and mountains of coke. In one parlor, two huge men were trying to kill each other on the billiard table while a circle of gentlemen in tuxes cheered them on, yelling out bets and trading huge rolls of cash every time a punch landed. In another, a pair of identical girls lay naked on the dining table, their slender bodies covered in a rainbow of beautifully cut sushi that guests removed with long silver chopsticks.

The excessive debauchery made Korigan's pulse quicken, but not for the usual reasons. He'd sold his military services to dictators and kings for decades now. Sins of the flesh were just part of doing business. Even to his jaded eyes, though, this was a party for the ages, but he'd expected nothing less from the home of Christopher St. Luke.

St. Luke was Chicago's most eccentric billionaire. Notorious, too. His weekly parties were the stuff of tabloid legend, as were the untold millions he'd donated to the campaigns of local politicians. But what the papers didn't know was that the lion's share of St. Luke's fortune wasn't due to his pharmaceutical empire or the massive Chinese corporations he partnered with, but from a ruthless, multi-decade effort to take over the illegal drug market in the Midwest. A highly successful effort, as poor Tannenbaum was only now finding out.

Thinking about the detective made him chuckle. Poor boy would have had a heart attack if he knew where his boss had been headed when he'd burst in. But even if Korigan had laid out his evening plans in full, Tannenbaum couldn't have grasped a tenth of what it really meant. His worldview was simply too small to comprehend the full scope of St. Luke's ambitions. Korigan, however, understood them all too well, which was why he was here tonight.

Because he wanted in.

He'd courted St. Luke's favor—protecting his opium farms in Afghanistan, punishing his enemies in Africa and South America, even bringing in a sub to sink his rival's drug-running shipments off the coast of Florida—Korigan had finally hit the big time last summer when St. Luke had personally invited him to be part of his main team in his home base at Chicago. The promotion had cost him more than he was wise to give, but Korigan had learned the hard way that power in this world— *real* power, the kind that outlasted death—was a matter of birth and privilege. After years of scrapping in the dirt, he'd turned his pack of war dogs into one of the world's most profitable mercenary companies. But even then, despite all his work, all his money, he'd been a fly to men like St. Luke. No matter how far he'd climbed, the glittering world of real power was always as far above him as the stars above the desert. Now, though, his work was finally paying off. After almost a decade of service, the dragon had finally looked down and taken notice, and Korigan was determined to do whatever it took to climb the last few rungs of the ladder and take his rightful place at the top of the world.

That was the plan, anyway. And it's why he was in Chicago. But for all his time here, this was his first invitation to actually meet his mysterious employer. Now, standing in the entry of his famous mansion, even the ever-steady Commander Korigan was shaking with excitement as he grabbed the nearest servant and spoke the words he'd been waiting ten years to say.

"Take me to St. Luke."

The name alone was enough to make the young man look nervous, but he clearly knew who Korigan was, and he didn't ask questions. He simply motioned for the police chief to follow him as he made his way through the wild drug-fueled escapades going on in the front of the house to the slightly quieter, but no less extravagant, party going on in the back.

The huge hall that ran along the side of the mansion facing the lake had clearly been intended as a ballroom. Now, though, it looked—and smelled and sounded—like the inside of a sultan's harem. Everywhere he looked, beautiful, naked bodies of both sexes lay in writhing piles on enormous silken pillows. Interspersed between them were giant hookahs and opium pipes, their trays of coals glowing like hellfire in the smoky dark as they filled the room with their heavy, intoxicating scent.

Just stepping into the place was enough to give Korigan a slight contact high, but he'd spent enough time in the worst scumholes in the third world to be virtually immune to narcotics at this point. Which meant that he was able to scan the room and see that, while this was clearly the party's inner sanctum, the man he'd come to meet wasn't here. Instead, the servant who'd led him here motioned for Korigan to wait and scuttled over to the nearest pile of pillows to speak to a man currently buried under multiple women. There was a brief exchange, and then the man stood up, his drugged lovers rolling off him like raindrops as he shrugged his muscular fighter's body into the dark jacket and leather pants the servant discreetly handed him. When he was presentable, the man reached down and picked up a sword off the floor. Not a replica or showpiece, either, but an actual long-handled slightly curving blade with clear wear marks notched into its edge. The man checked his weapon and slipped it into a sheath on his belt before sending the servant fleeing with a wave of his hand as he turned to greet Chicago's chief of police.

"Well, well, look who's wandered in out of the cold."

Korigan's jaw tightened. This was not the man he'd come to see, but it also wasn't someone he could ignore. He'd never personally met the tall, lanky, dark-skinned man, but he'd talked to him on the phone enough to recognize the voice. This was Lincoln Black, head of St. Luke's operations in Chicago for the last eight months and, if one gave credit to the rumors, St. Luke's own personal monster.

Personally, Korigan wasn't sure how much of that last part he believed. Every two-bit gang lord and drug kingpin cultivated a bloody reputation to keep the troops in line, but he'd played up his own reputation as a monster enough to have very high standards for the real thing. Still, watching Lincoln Black as he slipped on a pair of mirror-polished black leather shoes before turning to walk soundlessly toward him through the smoke, a killer's smile stretching his face, Korigan couldn't help but think that maybe this time, the rumors didn't go far enough.

"Nice monkey suit," Black said, stopping to look Korigan's best tux up and down. "Lemme guess, you're all dressed up to see the wizard."

"I'm here to see St. Luke," Korigan said coldly, lifting his chin to show Black just how unimpressed he was by the attack-dog routine. "He wants a report on operational security after the recent series of junkie freak-outs." He narrowed his eyes. "You wouldn't happen to know anything about that, would you?"

Black smiled. "We all have our roles to play, policeman," he said as he turned around, beckoning over his shoulder for Korigan to follow.

Grudgingly, Korigan did, moving behind Black and stepping out of the ballroom turned opium den, through a door into a side hallway lined with picture windows overlooking the mansion's snow-covered lawn. Unlike the rest of the house, though, there was no party here. Just a plain, empty hall running down the length of the house to what appeared to be a dead end. As they got closer, however, Korigan realized that the subtly striped paper covering the wall at the hall's end was actually an optical illusion. There *was* a door here, an opening lined up perfectly with the stripes so as to be invisible when viewed from the front. Even after he'd spotted it, it wasn't until Black actually stepped through where the wall should have been that Korigan's eyes finally realized the deception, leaving him a little dizzy as he walked through himself. Korigan stepped sideways past the hidden corner and through a small wooden door into a room completely cut off from the bacchanal just feet away.

It was not large, but unlike the hall leading up to it, the secret space was anything but plain. Everything inside—the walls, the floor, even the ceiling—was swarming with ornate decorations that, in keeping with the man who owned them, seemed to be competing to display the most outrageous examples of sin in all its myriad forms.

Elegant oil paintings depicted Catholic nightmares of satanic rituals and cloven-hoofed women tempting priests from their churches, while the long runner carpet was a nest of snakes and apples. But while Biblical themes were dominant, the decorations weren't limited to Western debauchery. Beautifully detailed Japanese watercolor depictions of unclean souls suffering appropriate punishments at the hands of demons in the eight Buddhist hells hung beside Hindi carvings depicting Yama, God of Death, overseeing the torture of a wide variety of sinners. It was the sort of collection you'd expect being protested at an edgy museum looking for press, but other than a quick assessment, Korigan didn't spare the art more than a glance. His eyes were locked on the man standing in the middle of it all.

Not surprisingly, Christopher St. Luke looked exactly like he did on television: a handsome, fit man in his late fifties with winking blue eyes, silver-fox hair, and a wry smile that made him appear like he was constantly appreciating a joke you weren't sophisticated enough to understand. Like the partygoers at the front of his mansion, he was dressed in a suit that cost more than the average American made in a decade, but unlike them, he wore it like it didn't matter. The ridiculously expensive tux—which Korigan could have traded for a year's worth of food for him and his men in the old days—was just clothing to him. Black-and-white fabric not worthy of special regard. It was like he lived in an entirely different reality, one Korigan would trade any life on the planet to be part of, and he could barely keep his fingers from shaking as he reached out to take the billionaire's offered hand.

"The infamous Victor Korigan," St. Luke said, shaking Korigan's hand not quite hard enough to hurt. "It's a pleasure to finally meet you in person. I've been very impressed with your work so far keeping the police so agreeably out of my hair."

"I do my best, as always, sir," Korigan said, keeping his voice carefully neutral. This was his big shot. He wouldn't ruin it with overconfidence. "Thank you for inviting me tonight."

"It was long past due," St. Luke said with a wide smile. "You've done good work for me for some time now, and today was no exception. I'm very pleased with how you handled the curveball we threw you today."

Korigan's jaw twitched. "You're talking about the ODs."

"I am," St. Luke said. "Bet your boys weren't expecting those."

"They weren't," Korigan agreed, suddenly angry. "And neither was I. It would have been simpler if you'd warned me you were trying something new beforehand. If I'd known you were looking to get rid of police informers, I could have come up with something far less disruptive."

"But if I'd warned you, I wouldn't have seen just how well you handled emergencies," St. Luke said. "And that was far more valuable to me than what kind of noise it created. In fact, the noise was a crucial element. It was a test, Korigan. One of many, and you passed your part with flying colors. Seven crazed junkies go flying off the handle over the last twenty-four hours. One even managed to kill a cop, and yet the only blip I've seen about it is a statement on the Chicago PD website warning about a bad batch of meth." He grinned. "That's some quality situation control, Korigan. *That's* why I brought you into my Chicago operation. And now that I know you can live up to expectations, I think it's time I brought you in on the rest."

Korigan's heart skipped a beat, the surprise neatly washing away his anger at being played like a fool. If he hadn't heard it himself, he never would have believed it. It just didn't seem possible that after so many years of fighting and crawling and killing his way up the ladder, he was finally being invited into the inner circle. He'd worked for St. Luke long enough to know he was much more than a drug kingpin with a respectable front. The man in front of him represented power on a global scale. Power untouchable to someone like Korigan.

He'd been born with less than nothing, an unwanted child of an unwed mother in the worst days of the failing Yugoslavia. Shunned by his family and branded an embarrassment, Korigan had scraped by after his mother abandoned him for a new husband and a second shot at life, not caring that her son was barely being given a chance at a first. So he'd begged and stolen, done whatever it took to survive until he was old enough to join the one group that didn't care about his background: the army.

He'd been a soldier ever since, serving first under Tito, and then joining the Serbs when the civil war broke out. He'd served the Croats, too, and the UN when they'd come in. His gun had belonged to whoever could pay, and it shot whatever target got him the most money. Women, children, his own men—it made no difference. He'd already learned that money was the only real power in the world—the force that made good men kill and bad men do far worse. It was literally the currency of life, more precious than blood.

Yet as his mercenary operations expanded and his wealth

grew, he began to realize that there was yet another tier. A place above what money could buy. A world inhabited by men like St. Luke, those *so* rich and *so* powerful, the price it took to buy them off didn't exist. From the moment Korigan glimpsed even a piece of it, he knew nothing else would do. It was the ultimate victory, the final goal for a man who'd dedicated his entire life to chasing and hoarding power, forever out of reach.

Until now.

"I see you like that idea," St. Luke said, his blue eyes flashing as he took in the hunger Korigan knew must be plain on his face. "You've always been an ambitious man, Commander Korigan. I've always liked that about you. Our ambition is all we truly own in this life . . . and I'm now going to let you in on a bit of mine."

"I'm honored," Korigan began, but St. Luke cut him off with a single raised finger.

"I didn't invite you for your honor," he said, shooting Lincoln Black a conspiratorial smile. "I'm sure you won't be surprised to hear that we're working on something . . . very special here in Chicago. Something beyond the usual narcotics trade. I brought you to Chicago because I needed to see if you could handle it, but I called you here tonight specifically because I want you by my side as we move to the next step. But what I want and what you can give are two very different things . . ." He trailed off, looking Korigan over like he was trying to find his weakness. "Tell me, Commander, how far are you willing to go?"

To join you at the top of the world? "As far as I have to."

St. Luke's smile widened to a grin. "I was hoping you'd say that," he said, turning to walk over to the corner of the room. He waved his hand as he went, and the painting-covered wall slid sideways to reveal a brushed steel elevator. St. Luke stepped inside as the doors slid open, motioning for his guest to follow. Heart pounding with anticipation, Korigan obeyed, stepping into the hidden elevator as fast as he could without running. Lincoln Black followed at a more relaxed pace, slinking into the elevator like this was all old news.

When they were all inside, St. Luke pushed the single button on the command console, and the doors snapped shut, sealing them inside seconds before the elevator dropped like a stone.

4
UNCLEAN SPIRITS

The elevator stopped as quickly as it had dropped, the doors sliding open to reveal a hallway very different from the one above. There were no paintings here, no debauched guests, no servants. Just a harshly lit cement-floored hallway stretching off into the distance, its walls lined with iron bars holding back the dark. It was so unlike everything else he'd seen so far, Korigan didn't actually realize what he was looking at until he saw something move in the dark.

"Is that—" He stopped, swallowing against the sudden dryness in his throat. "Is this the zoo?"

St. Luke chuckled beside him. "So you've heard about my collection?"

Of course he'd heard. Every human trafficker and warlord in the world knew about Christopher St. Luke and his preferences. The billionaire famously paid top dollar for the odd and inexplicable. Korigan himself had sold him a pair of albino conjoined twins he'd stumbled across in Africa just a few years ago. But knowing that St. Luke must be keeping a private human freak show somewhere in his empire and actually walking through it were two entirely different things, and even Korigan—who'd walked through the worst of what war could do without blinking—felt himself begin to shake as St. Luke strolled over to the closest set of iron bars.

"I've always had a passion for the odd and inexplicable," he said as he scraped his neatly trimmed nails over the metal. "Even in this dull modern age when all the unknown lands are already discovered, the world is still so much bigger, so much *stranger* than the human mind can imagine. There are so many mysteries, so many things we don't, can't, maybe even shouldn't understand." He dropped his arm and turned back to Korigan. "Some men find that frightening, but I choose to celebrate it and, when possible, learn from it."

He lifted his hand, beckoning Korigan closer. After a moment's hesitation, Korigan obeyed. As he got closer to the bars, though, he saw that the darkness behind them wasn't darkness at all. It was an illusion caused by the glass wall just inside the bars, which had been carefully tinted to *appear* dark, probably so that whatever was inside couldn't see when it was being observed. From the elevator, the glass looked like a flat black nothing. But when you were standing right in front of it, you could see straight through into the cell beyond, though that didn't mean Korigan knew what he was looking *at*.

"What the—"

He turned away and rubbed his eyes, telling himself to get a grip. But when he looked again, he saw exactly the same thing:

a ten-by-ten room with walls that appeared to be *crawling*. He was wondering if it was another optical illusion when he realized it wasn't the walls that were crawling. It was what was on them.

The entire cell was filled floor to ceiling with wasps. They crawled over every surface except, for some reason, the glass right in front of St. Luke and Korigan. But while they swarmed over every other inch of the cell, they especially seemed to favor the far right corner where a giant lump of insects were climbing into and over what looked like a rounded hive. On closer inspection, though, Korigan realized he was wrong again. The thing in the corner wasn't a hive at all. It was a person. A man.

And he was *moving*.

After that, it was a hard fight not to be sick. Korigan had seen a lot of horrors in his life, but he'd always had a special hatred for insects. The only thing that kept him from sprinting back to the elevator was the fact that St. Luke was still standing beside him, watching him intently like he was waiting for Korigan to crack. But while it had never been for such high stakes, Korigan had played this game before, and he knew better than to show any sign of weakness. In the end, the only trace of his inner panic was a slight waver in his voice as he calmly asked his host, "What is that?"

"An experiment in the limits of human endurance," St. Luke replied proudly, tapping the glass behind the bars. "Mankind is capable of so much more than we give ourselves credit for. But the only way to know *how* much more is to push. That's what I do here, Korigan. I push limits." He lifted his eyebrows with a smile that sent shivers down Korigan's spine. "Would you like to see the rest?"

Korigan would have been happy if he never saw anything like this again in his life. These were Dr. Mengele–level atrocities, and even Korigan had his limits. But he hadn't reached them yet.

"Tell me, Commander, how far are you willing to go?"

"As far as I have to."

He wasn't sure what game St. Luke was playing: if he was actually proud of the things in the cages, or if this whole zoo tour was just another test. Either way, Korigan was determined not to lose, so he buried his fear and nodded to his host, matching him grin to feral grin.

"What else you got?"

This answer seemed to delight St. Luke more than anything else Korigan had said. His host was practically bouncing as he started down the hall, showing off cage after cage of horrors. In one, a pair of twin teenage girls were methodically slaughtering and dismantling a goat, arranging the pieces in a disturbing mosaic across the bloody floor of their enclosure. In another, a seemingly normal young man sat crouched with his hands over his face, hiding from the walls of his cell, which was entirely covered in broken mirrors. Yet another held an old man who was naked save for a cloth around his waist and a chain around his neck where he'd been tied like a dog to a post in the cell's center. In his hands, he held a pot of something black and viscous that he was using like finger paint to write enormous, complex messages on the wall in a myriad of languages. Having studied several, Korigan recognized Greek, English, and Coptic. Before they passed out of view, he also spotted his own name scrawled amid the rest, which had to be the creepiest thing he'd seen all night. Or, at least, it was until they reached the double doors at the hall's end.

Up until this point, the path through the zoo had resembled a prison hallway. Once St. Luke pushed open the doors, though, Korigan could see that the room on the other side was much larger, a modern-looking underground lab complete with bright white walls and techs in full-body hazmat-style lab suits hovering around banks of computers. The sudden switch was enough to make Korigan jump, but while they were clearly at the more modern end of St. Luke's experiments, even this space was obviously no ordinary lab.

Half of the equipment—the computers, centrifuges, lab tables, chemical hoods, sample fridges, and so on—looked like it could have come from any hospital. But the rest of it, the strange objects interspersed between the normal ones, defied explanation. No two were the same. Some were tiny, some giant, some were made of metal, others of stacked brownish-white tiles that looked disturbingly like bones. But while Korigan didn't understand any of it, he recognized the rusty, reddish-brown stain that covered their moving parts.

Blood was everywhere, actually. Even the normal lab equipment was splashed with it, the white and steel surfaces splattered, old and new drips overlapping like the room had been repeatedly sprayed with blood and then haphazardly wiped down, but never actually cleaned. The smell certainly lingered. The rusty, musky scent of dried blood was so thick in the air down here, even Korigan found it hard to breathe. But unnerving as an underground lab soaked in blood and filled with strange artifacts was, the stained equipment was nothing compared to the six-foot-tall black cube sitting at the room's center.

From a distance, it looked like it was made of matte black glass. As he got closer, though, Korigan saw that the cube didn't actually have walls at all. It was just . . . dark. A box of deep shadows cast by nothing, and that didn't make sense at all. You couldn't just have a cube of *dark*. And yet, there it was, standing in front of him like an ink stain in the air. It had no physical borders, no walls, just a clear, invisible line that the light from the banks of fluorescents overhead simply could not—or would not—penetrate.

Given the other, more obvious, horrors they'd passed by to reach this place, a box of dark should have been the least of Korigan's worries. But hard as he'd learned to be, Victor Korigan was above all a practical man. He valued money and steel and leverage, things he could touch and hold and wield. Things that had *purpose*. He had walked over corpses and felt nothing, because corpses he understood. But the sheer physical impossibility of that thick, inky darkness, that shadow from nothing, scared him more than all the blood in the room combined.

"Beautiful, isn't it?"

The whisper made him jump, and he whirled around to see St. Luke standing right beside him. "It's awful," he said, the words tumbling from his lips.

He regretted the admission of weakness at once, but surprisingly St. Luke's smile grew bigger. "It is, isn't? That's what makes it so compelling to me."

"What is it?"

St. Luke's smile turned sly. "I can't tell you *all* our secrets," he said, walking over to a metal lab table where the masked techs had laid out a grid of shoebox-sized white specimen containers marked with blood-red biohazard symbols. "For now, let's just say that that black box is the alpha and omega of my operation here, and the reason for *this*."

He removed the lid from the closest box and reached inside, pulling out a two-inch-long glass vial filled with a sickly green, viscous liquid that glowed like emerald fire under the lab's bright lights. "You know what this is, of course?"

Korigan had never seen the green slime before, but he wasn't stupid. "That's the drug," he said, turning all the way around so he wouldn't have to look at the terrifying box of darkness anymore. "The one that's been making junkies go crazy."

"It does a lot more than that," St. Luke said, putting the vial back in its box. "But this was just our first attempt, and as you saw from today's experiments, far too strong. But we learn from our mistakes, and I think you'll find the next version is far more up your alley."

He opened the next biohazard box on the table, reaching inside to pull out not a vial, but a normal-looking plastic baggie filled with dull gray-black powder. "This is our finished product," St. Luke said, tossing the baggie at Korigan, who caught it just in time.

Korigan frowned at the bag of powder in his hands. "Is it a drug, too?"

"Not specifically," St. Luke said. "It's called Z3X, and it was developed to be an . . . additive of sorts. By itself, it does nothing, but when mixed with other drugs—amphetamines, opiates, hallucinogens, uppers, downers, even cannabis and alcohol—it acts like a booster, multiplying the effects of whatever drug it's taken with."

Korigan's face broke into a smile. For the first time since he had arrived down here, things were starting to make sense. *This* was business, and business he understood. "I always wondered how you were able to sell so cheap here in Chicago and still turn a profit, but now I see. This lets you give your customers the same high for less."

It was brilliant. With an additive like this, you could give a cokehead the same high while only having to fork over half as much actual cocaine. It was exactly the sort of ballsy, game-changing move he'd expect from a man like St. Luke, but the billionaire was shaking his head.

"No, no, no," he said angrily. "You're missing the point. This isn't about money. Look around. Does it look like *I* need more money?" He scoffed. "Money's so easy, even a third-world thug like you can get rich if he's willing to do things no one else will. But this is bigger than money." He held up the baggie of Z3X. "*This* is about control."

He finished with a grin, but Korigan was still bristling over the thug comment. He didn't need anyone, not even St. Luke, to remind him where he'd come from. But as much as he wanted to teach the rich man a lesson, that wasn't why he was here. Pride got you nowhere in life, and Korigan had learned long ago to swallow his if that's what it took. "What kind of control is there that you can't buy?" he asked, his voice perfectly cordial, like he hadn't even heard the insult. "Everyone has a price. Whether you buy it with that powder, blood, or money doesn't matter. The end's the same."

"That's where we're going to have to agree that you're wrong," St. Luke said, looking him in the eyes. "There are more ways to control a man than leverage, my friend. Debts can be paid, addictions can be broken, lives can be saved, but you can never escape what's in here." He tapped his fingers against his forehead. "Who we are inside, the person we become when our backs are to the wall, *that's* what Z3X unlocks."

Korigan was getting frustrated. He could deal with a certain amount of mockery from St. Luke, but he hated the feeling of being so far out of his element. "How? Is it a psychotropic?"

"You'll see," St. Luke promised, holding out his hand to take the baggie of Z3X back. "For now, though, all you need to know is that we're moving ahead with our final production push."

"Final push? I don't understand. You just said the green slime was the first experiment that led to Z3X. How can there already be so much out there if you just tested it today?"

"I already told you," St. Luke said dismissively. "The incidents today were a test for *you*. We've been working on this for months now. Today's experiments were just a way to use up old stock and test my tools at the same time, and I'm happy to say both were a success. You've proven you can handle what I throw at you, which is good, because I'm about to toss you one hell of a bomb."

He moved closer, grinning at Korigan with a smile that made the former merc step back. "I know you, Korigan," he said quietly. "You clawed your way up from nothing, became the rich and powerful man you are purely because you were willing to do what others weren't. There are many who call you a monster for that, but I've always thought if you weren't willing to be a monster, then you weren't really trying." He glanced over his shoulder at the table full of white boxes. "This Z3X isn't just a drug. It's a change. With it, I intend to turn this city into something greater, and I'm reaching the point where I can't do it alone."

Those were words he'd been waiting a long time to hear, and Korigan took a deep breath. "What do you need me to do?"

"Steer the ship," St. Luke said. "I've set everything up. Z3X is already coursing through Chicago's drug-addled underbelly, but there still has to be a push. A kick that can launch this city into my control."

Now they were talking. "You mean a military coup?" Korigan grinned wide. "No problem. My men—"

"No, no, nothing like that," St. Luke said quickly, shaking his head. "Quite the opposite. I had the mayor make you police chief because I need you to *keep* order, not break it."

Now Korigan was really confused, but before he could ask another question, St. Luke held up his hand.

"I brought you into this because you're famous for keeping your command no matter what happens," he said. "That's what I need from you now. The Z3X is already everywhere, but it's all for nothing if I can't activate it. The green slime was just the beginning. Soon, this whole city is going to be tearing itself apart to reinvent itself into the Chicago I want. *That's* what I mean by control: the ability to take an entire population and push it to the limit. All the groundwork is already laid, but it will still take time to build up to the critical mass I need. While that's happening, I need to know that when push comes to shove, you can keep the Z3X flowing. That means my factories in the city stay open, my pushers keep operating unharassed, my name and the name of the drug stay out of the papers, and the Feds don't get involved until it's far too late. And it all happens as if it's just another day in the office for you. I need your composure. I need you to control the city. Do that for me, Victor, and I'll give you what you've always wanted."

Korigan swallowed. "Which is?"

"Power," St. Luke whispered. "The power to be above those who would pull you down. Power no one can ever take away." St. Luke pointed at his chest. "*My* power."

He couldn't believe what he was hearing. "You'd give that to me?"

"Gladly," St. Luke said. "I've been me for almost sixty years now. Frankly, it's time for a change, and I've been looking for an heir for some time."

"An heir?" Korigan repeated, unbelieving.

"Yes," St. Luke said with a smile. "Someone with the experience and ruthlessness needed to take over my business concerns while I focus on more . . . spiritual matters."

That was a crock if Korigan had ever heard it. St. Luke didn't have a spiritual bone in his body. But while his explanation didn't fly, he did seem serious about the offer.

"To be clear," Korigan said slowly. "If I do what you want here in Chicago, you'll make me your heir, the person who inherits this." He swept his arms upward, indicating the mansion overhead. "All of it?"

"All of it," St. Luke agreed. "You won't even have to wait until I'm dead. I'm actually planning to retire soon. Consider this operation my going-away present."

It was too good to be true. Korigan knew that meant he shouldn't trust it. Hell, with that hovering darkness over his shoulder, no sane man would. But he was having trouble fighting against his desire for it to be true. After all, wasn't he *owed* a stroke of good fortune? He, who'd worked so hard to pull himself out of the gutter? Who'd thrown away pride countless times to court the same billionaire who was standing in front of him, offering the impossible? No. It was past time for Victor Korigan's ship to come in.

That said, he couldn't get aboard by being stupid.

You can't cash in wishful thinking.

"I want it in writing," he said, crossing his arms. "All of it."

"Of course," St. Luke replied. "We'll draw everything up nice and legal for my protection as well as yours. We both have to do our part in this agreement. And I want you to be clear: none of this is worth a dime if you can't keep my operations going until the end. If this fails, I fail. And if I fail, you *certainly* fail."

Lincoln let out a chilling laugh at that, which Korigan ignored. "And what end is that?"

"You'll know," St. Luke promised. "Believe me. When it comes, you'll *know*."

That was a warning bell if ever Korigan heard one, but he was in too deep to care. He had no idea what St. Luke was thinking, but he was now certain the billionaire had finally passed eccentric and gone straight to mad. But that was fine with him. If the old man wanted him to play along with this Z3X scam, Victor would play the best game he'd ever seen. It's not like he gave a damn about Chicago. This cold, windy place was just another job to him. He'd bring the whole damn city to its knees if that was what St. Luke wanted, because when the end did come, it wouldn't matter. With St. Luke's wealth at his disposal, Korigan could escape any hell the crazy old man brought down on their heads. St. Luke was one of the richest men in the world. Even if Korigan only managed to salvage a fraction of that, he'd still have enough money and power to finally stop worrying about finding that next job and keeping ahead of all the people who wanted him dead. With that much money, he could finally rest, finally relax.

Maybe even have enough time to wipe off all the blood he'd gotten on his hands throughout his life . . .

To hell with that—someone else can wash my hands for me.

And it was almost in his grasp. He just had to keep doing what he was so good at doing.

Winning.

"All of your wealth," he said again, voice shaking in eagerness. "Transferred to me. Legally. In writing. Notified and witnessed."

"Yes, yes," St. Luke said, waving his hand dismissively. "All the bells and whistles. Now do I have my man or not?"

Korigan thought it through one more time, searching madly for the catch. In the end, though, he couldn't find one big enough to risk losing the reward. "You have a deal," he said, holding out his hand. "I want the papers in my office first thing tomorrow, and I want full access to your illegal operations here in Chicago. As soon as I have guarantee of payment and control over all the necessary pieces, I will lock down this city so tight, there won't be so much as a kid shoplifting without my say-so. Come hell or high water, you will have no disruptions to your Z3X operation."

"Spoken like a true mercenary," St. Luke said proudly, gripping Korigan's offered hand and shaking it for far too long. "I'll have it to you by noon tomorrow. Lincoln will deliver it personally so he can fill you in on our Chicago narcotics operations."

Black did not look happy about that, but he nodded just the same, and Korigan's stomach began to flutter. He was close. He was *so* close. But he had to get out of here now, before St. Luke's apparent madness shifted and he changed his mind. "I should go, then," he said as he finally pried his hand out of St. Luke's. "It's late, and we've much to do."

"Of course, of course," St. Luke replied. "But do feel free

to enjoy the party upstairs before you go. I always encourage people to make the most of their baser urges."

Another time, Korigan gladly would have taken him up on that, but right now he wasn't even thinking about the pleasures upstairs. Nothing would satisfy him now other than the promise this apparent madman had just made him, and the only thing on his mind was what he was going to do to make sure he didn't lose it. He was already making contingency plans as he said goodbye to his host and strode away, barely even noticing the horrors this time as he half walked, half ran through the zoo, back to the elevator and the work that lay beyond.

Y ou're making a mistake."

St. Luke glanced away from Victor Korigan's retreating back to see Lincoln Black sitting cross-legged on top of one of the long lab tables with his sword in his lap. "How so?"

"The police chief," Black said. "He's a blind idiot."

"You underestimate him," St. Luke said, shaking his head. "He is blind, true, but no more than most men. Despite that, he's as scheming and ambitious as I could ever ask, and that makes him useful."

The swordsman snorted. "Only if you like dull knives. What kind of fool do you have to be not to accept that there's more going on than meets the eye after seeing *that*?"

He nodded toward the black box in the center of the room, and St. Luke chuckled. "Not everyone is as open-minded as you. But it's not that he didn't notice it. It's that he chose to ignore it in favor of his own goals." He grinned. "Like I said, ambitious. And very good at his job. He's certainly kept you out of trouble. Or did you think it just happened that no one noticed all those gang lords you decapitated and threw in the river during the takeover?"

Black shrugged. "I figured it counted as a public service."

"If you ever do a public service, it really will be the end times," St. Luke said with a laugh. "But don't worry. We won't have to put up with him for long." His lips curled into a cruel smile. "Wise generals make sure that soldiers like Korigan don't outlive their wars."

"I did notice you left out a few key bits of information while you were promising him all the kingdoms of the earth," Black said, reaching down to poke the baggies of Z3X. "But are you sure about trusting him with so much? It'd be some dramatic irony if the great St. Luke got taken down by the underling *he* underestimated."

"I'd never fall prey to such melodrama," St. Luke said in disgust. "Trust me. I know how to deal with men like Korigan. He's learned to play it smooth, but deep down he's still the same frightened little boy willing to do anything for the power to keep himself safe. Why do you think he jumped so fast and so high when I offered him my fortune? To a man like him, *I'm* the top." St. Luke laughed out loud. "He has no idea."

"We don't need him."

"Not technically," St. Luke agreed, rubbing a hand on his chest like it pained him. "But we can still *use* him, and, it's nice to have someone covering our backs. Federal investigations can be quite annoying when you're on a deadline."

"Feds die just like anyone else," Black pointed out. "But we're about to have bigger problems. Ones Korigan can't touch."

St. Luke's smile faded. "What do you mean? Was there a problem with the last catalyst?"

"Not at all," Black said, shaking his head. "For all his protests, the veteran bum went out nice and big. Full transformation, just as predicted. The problem came later when he tried to attack a woman, some doctor who'd treated him in the past. Things were about to get nice and ironic with him ripping the arms off the very person who'd come to help him, when who should appear but our favorite Bible-quoting, sword-wielding friend."

The billionaire's eyes went wide. "Are you kidding me?" When Black shook his head, St. Luke slammed his hand down on the table, denting the metal surface. "And you're only telling me this now *because*?"

"You're the one throwing wild parties upstairs. What was I supposed to do? Not get laid?" Black scoffed. "Anyway, our *friend* pulled one of his vanishing stunts at the end, and I've hunted his kind long enough now to know it's a waste of time to try and find him after that. But it doesn't matter. I know where he's going."

"Where?" St. Luke growled impatiently, his blue eyes so bright with anger they almost seemed to glow.

Black smiled at the light. "Remember I told you there was a doctor?" he said casually. "Well, she was a real piece of work. She stopped him from killing the bum *and* managed to reverse the transformation. But it gets even better."

St. Luke arched an eyebrow. "Actually better, or better in that it amuses you?"

"Both," Lincoln said. "The doctor got some of the green junk on her hands, and wouldn't you know, it *didn't work*. Strongest crap we had, and she just shrugged it off. All she got was some burned fingers."

"That's impossible," St. Luke said. "No one can take that much concentrated sin."

Black spread his arms wide. "Hey, man, I'm just reporting what I saw. But what you're missing here is that Mr. Holy Warrior saw it, too, and it got him *good*. He spoke more words to that girl than I've heard him say in decades. There's no way he'll let her go. Way I see it, we just got a chance to take down two birds with one stone."

St. Luke saw it, too, but he was already thinking bigger. "Can *you*?"

"That depends," Black said. "You're asking me to take out our oldest enemy and the doctor who impressed him, and move your plan ahead at the same time. That's a lot more than two birds for this one stone. I can still do it, but it's going to make a pretty big mess."

"So what?" St. Luke said dismissively, turning to gaze into the black cube at the center of his lab. "Now you see why I brought Korigan in. Your 'messes' are his problem from tonight forward, so do what you have to do. We've fought too long and too hard to tolerate risks this close to the end, and a SEE warrior in the city represents a catastrophic risk. I want him dead, and I want the doctor dealt with as well. I don't know what her story is, but anyone who can shrug off the effects of the Emerald Compound is too good for this world." He paused, before finally looking up at Black and saying, "I don't care how you do it, but I want both problems taken care of and all of this pushed into the next phase by tomorrow. Understood?"

Rather than answer, Black just tucked his sword into his belt and reached down, gathering up as many boxes of Z3X—both the concentrated green liquid form and the black powder—as he could fit in his arms. When he was loaded down, he gave St. Luke a final wink and walked off, whistling a cheery tune as he made his way back toward the elevator.

Satisfied that his predator was on the hunt, St. Luke put the matter out of his mind and returned his gaze to the black cube at the center of his lab, staring into its endless depths lovingly before yelling at his lab staff—who were still staring in horror at the massive chunk Black had taken out of their supplies—to get back to work.

They had a city's worth of orders to fill.

> THE COMING OF THE LAWLESS ONE IS BY THE ACTIVITY OF
> SATAN WITH ALL POWER AND FALSE SIGNS AND WONDERS.
> —2 THESSALONIANS 2:9

5

FALSE SIGNS

Technically, the drive south from Mercy Hospital to her father's home in Englewood took fifteen minutes. Thanks to the time dilation effect of awkward silences, though, Lauryn would have placed it closer to fifteen hours.

She sat awkwardly in the passenger seat of her father's car, staring out the window at the dark city. About halfway through, thick, wet snow started to fall, covering everything in a muffling blanket until all Lauryn could hear was the putter of the engine, the soft strains of the ever-present gospel music from the car radio, and the pointed huff of her father's angry breathing. Even so, it wasn't until they stopped at the light that marked the entrance to Lauryn's childhood neighborhood that he finally said what he'd clearly been thinking since they left.

"You should have called me."

The words were full of recrimination, but Lauryn was too tired to even roll her eyes. "There was no point," she said. "Everything was under control. By the time I had a chance to call, I was already fine. It wasn't a big deal, Dad."

"You were attacked," Maxwell said, his big preacher's voice filling the car until her ears rang. "How is that not a big deal?"

"It was scary when it was happening," she admitted. "But I couldn't have called you in the middle, could I?"

"So why didn't you call when you got to the hospital?" he argued back. "I had to find out from someone else!" His hands tightened on the leather-wrapped steering wheel. "I'm your father. Your family. You should have told me."

"Why?" Lauryn demanded. "So you could be worried, too? I'm twenty-seven, Dad. I'm also a *doctor*. I know when to call in families, and I can definitively say that a burned hand is not a medical emergency. The only reason I was even admitted was because there was a chance I'd been exposed to narcotics, but even that turned out to be nothing. There was absolutely no medical reason for me to call you and ruin your night as well."

That was the logical truth, but Maxwell's scowl just got deeper. "You still should have called," he growled, tapping the gas as the light turned green. "Grown or not, children should have more respect for their parents."

Lauryn gave up after that, slumping down as far as she could into the Buick's cushy seat. Seriously, her father could take offense at anything. The worst part was, she *had* actually considered calling while she'd been stuck in bed waiting for test results. The only reason she hadn't was because it was Wednesday. Wednesdays were potluck and choir practice at the church. If she'd done as he'd asked and called, her dad would have scolded her for interrupting his work. As always, there was just no winning with her father, so Lauryn decided to stop trying. Her goal tonight was to get Maxwell off her back, get some sleep, and get back to her normal life first thing tomorrow.

Thankfully, by the time they pulled up to the modest two-story house she'd grown up in, it was late enough to go straight to bed without the usual small talk. Lauryn popped out of the car like a cork the moment it rolled to a stop in front of her dad's postage-stamp yard. It was a sign of how upset she was that she made it all the way to the porch steps before noticing the *other* car that was taking up her father's tiny driveway: a brand-new souped-up electric-blue Dodge Charger.

"What is *that*?"

It didn't seem possible after their previous discussion, but her father's voice grew even more disapproving. "That's your brother's car."

Her jaw dropped. "That's *Robbie's*? But he's only nineteen! How the hell—"

"Language," Maxwell barked.

She gaped at him. "Your son is driving around in a car there's no way he could legally afford, and you're worried about *my* language?"

"Lauryn, that's enough."

The hell it was. Twenty minutes ago, going home had been the last thing Lauryn had wanted to do. Now she was kicking herself for not checking in sooner. Robert had always loved to party, and unlike Lauryn, who'd had exams and frantic studying to keep her out of trouble, he never missed a chance to have fun. Combine this with his pathological aversion to anything resembling honest work, and she was certain that shiny new car meant no good. Growing up, if someone in the neighborhood had something this nice, it almost certainly came from working a corner. She was about to march into the house and give her derelict brother a piece of her mind when the front door slammed open, and—as if summoned—a young man in a puffy jacket and spotless white sneakers shot out like a bullet.

"Dad!" he yelled. "Move your car! I gotta—" He stopped short, blinking in surprise as he finally registered that Maxwell wasn't alone. "Lauryn?"

Lauryn blinked back. The tall man in front of her looked nothing like the baby brother she remembered. Despite going to school only a few miles away, she'd been terrible about visiting her family since she'd left home . . . because she'd left home precisely so she *wouldn't* have to deal with her family. She couldn't avoid her dad—Maxwell knew where she lived, and he showed up at her door like clockwork every month no matter how much she changed her schedule—but she hadn't been back to the house or seen her brother since Robbie's first year of high school.

Back then, he'd looked like any other poor preacher's kid: cherub-faced, modestly dressed, and sporting a haircut that hadn't been in style since the seventies. But for all he'd looked like a choirboy, Robbie had been trouble from the moment he was born. For as long as she could remember, he'd been surly, in and out of suspension, always giving her and her dad a hard time— which only made sense when you considered how everyone was constantly comparing him to his sister, the valedictorian.

That was a huge part of why she'd stayed away, actually. When she'd left for college, Lauryn had hoped her being out of the house would help Robbie shed the stigma of being the eternally underachieving sibling and grow up a bit, or at least stop being such a delinquent.

Unfortunately, this seemed to be wishful thinking. The kid she remembered had at least looked wholesome and clean-cut, even if he hadn't acted the part. By contrast, the man on the porch looked like he'd just stepped out of a music video. Everything on his body—clothes, hat, shoes, watch—was name brand

and out-of-the-box pristine. If it wasn't for the fact that Robert's baby face still looked exactly the same as it had when he was twelve, she wouldn't have known him at all.

He seemed to be suffering the same problem. For a moment, he just stared at her like he wasn't sure what he was seeing, and his face fell into a sour sneer. "Look who's back," he said, crossing his arms over his chest. "What's wrong, Lauryn? Fancy med school kick you out?"

"That'd be kind of hard to do since I graduated six months ago," she replied, glaring back at him. "And it's Dr. Jefferson now."

Robbie rolled his eyes. "Whatever. Just tell Dad to move his car. I'm going out."

"Going out where?" she demanded. "And where did you get the money for that Charger?"

"From my job at None of Your Damn Business, Inc."

"Funny how you having a job is the least believable part of that," Lauryn said, climbing up the stairs to the porch where she could glare at him on equal footing. "Where'd you get the money, Robbie?"

"Uh-uh, Queen L," he said, using his new height to loom over her as he waggled his finger in her face. "You don't get to boss me around anymore. You left, remember? Believe it or not, my life goes on even when you're not here to tell me how to live it. Now get out of my way. I got business."

"And that's exactly why I'm not moving," she growled, putting her hands on her hips. "Any business that gives a nineteen-year-old kid a car like that isn't the kind of business you should be doing."

"For your information, no one gave me a damned thing," Robert snapped. "I bought that car with *my* money. You don't gotta go to med school to make bank, you know. I make damn good cash as a rapper. I do private parties and gigs all over this city. I'm probably going to get signed soon, and then I'm out of this Dumpster fire for good, so you can shove the attitude."

By the time he finished, Lauryn was rolling her eyes so hard it hurt. Forget the car. If Robbie had earned half what his jacket cost from freelance rap gigs, she'd eat it right off his back, puffy sleeves and all. Before she could tell him as much, though, her brother stepped around her, bumping their father, who'd just finished moving his car a half foot farther down the curb and onto the grass.

"Robbie!" Lauryn yelled, spinning around. "Get back here! I'm not done with—"

He got into his car before she finished, cutting her off with a slam of his door. A second later, the oversized engine gunned to life, brand-new tires squealing on the icy pavement as the car roared down the quiet street before disappearing around the corner.

"What was that?" Lauryn cried, turning on her father. "Are you just going to let him go?"

"What else can I do?" Maxwell said, shuffling into the house like an old, old man. "He's nineteen."

"So?" she said, running after him. "You still try to run *my* life, and I don't even live with you anymore."

"You're different," he said. "You still listen sometimes."

"So will he if you just try harder," Lauryn said. "But you have to do *something*. He's acting like an idiot."

"I'm doing all I can," Maxwell argued as he walked into the small kitchen and opened the fridge, taking out casserole dishes—the same ones the ladies from his church had been re-filling for him every week since Lauryn's mother had died—and placing them on the table. "I take him to church. I pray for him daily."

"He doesn't need church or prayer," Lauryn said, frustrated. "He needs an intervention. He needs *Scared Straight*! He needs you to be his *dad* and tell him he can't do this crap!"

Maxwell slammed the dish in his hands down on the table, and Lauryn braced for the storm . . . that never came. Fast as it had flared, all the anger in her father's face fell right back out of him, leaving him deflated.

"'Judge not lest ye be judged,'" he quoted softly, shaking his head. "I'm proud of all you've accomplished, but you left, Lauryn. You don't know what we've been fighting. I've done all I know how to do for Robert, but I can't force him to live how I want. It's like when you were living in sin with that policeman—"

"Detective," she corrected. "Will was a detective, and he has nothing to do with this. This isn't a matter of morality, Dad. Robert could be mixed up in something really bad." Because Lord knew nineteen-year-old boys didn't get brand-new cars from doing anything good.

"I know," Maxwell said sadly. "Jesus knows, I know. But if I push, he'll leave, and then there won't be any godly influences in his life at all." He shook his head. "It's better this way. God will guide him back to the right path."

That was the stupidest thing Lauryn had ever heard—and that was saying something, standing in this house. Her brother was out there driving recklessly to who knew where in the middle of the night, and their dad's solution was to cross his fingers and trust in some mystical man in the sky to make things right. But then, "Trust in God" was Maxwell's answer to everything. It was the same ridiculousness that had made Lauryn move out in the first place, despite the fact that living at home through med school would have been MUCH cheaper than splitting an apartment downtown with Naree. But even when money had been so tight she'd felt like she couldn't breathe, Lauryn had always considered the extra rent a small price to pay to avoid the daily spike in her blood pressure that came from living in the same house as her father.

Speaking of which, the old headache was already starting to

pound through her temples, and Lauryn decided it was time to end this. "I'm going to bed," she announced, walking out of the kitchen. "It's too late for this mess, and I've got to be back at the hospital in a few hours for my shift."

She paused there, bracing for the inevitable lecture, but Maxwell just sighed. "Go on, then. Your room's just like you left it."

Shaking her head, Lauryn stomped up the rickety stairs to her childhood bedroom. She barely took the time to strip off her coat before falling face-first into her old princess bed and closing her eyes in an effort to will herself to sleep as fast as possible, before anything else could happen.

Surprisingly enough, it worked. Lauryn had always been a terrible sleeper, and her old bed was just as lumpy as she remembered, but somewhere in the tossing and turning and general anger with the world she must have drifted off, because she woke up with a start when a loud, low sound rumbled through the house. To her sleepy brain, it sounded a bit like a growling lion, but as she sat up, the rumbling resolved itself into the sound of a very powerful, and thus very *loud*, engine.

"Dammit, Robbie," she moaned, peeking over the edge of her comforter at the dusty, sticker-covered alarm clock that was still on her nightstand to see it was 5 AM. On a good day, that was when Lauryn tried to wake up at home for her six o'clock shift. After a night like last night, it was the last straw.

She shot out of bed, taking the old flower-covered comforter with her like a cloak as she stomped over to the window to give her delinquent brother a piece of her mind. But when she pulled back the lace curtain, the vehicle making the racket outside wasn't Robbie's car. It wasn't a car at all. It was a motorcycle, and sitting on top of it, looking straight up at her window like he'd been sitting out there waiting for her to appear, was the man who'd saved her life in the alley.

Lauryn's breath left her body in a rush. Seeing him again was a bit like seeing a ghost. Even after getting a clean screen on her drug test, Lauryn had half convinced herself that she'd imagined the tall, stoic man with the sword, because that was the only explanation that made sense. But now, somehow, there he was, just sitting on his bike under the streetlight across from her old house. He even waved at her, causing Lauryn to jump back and yank the curtains closed. A silly reaction in hindsight since he obviously knew she was there, but how and why, Lauryn had no idea. All she knew was that she didn't like it. Sitting outside someone's window before dawn was stalker behavior. That said, jumping to conclusions was a bad habit for a doctor, and he *had* saved her life. Either way, she definitely wasn't getting back to sleep, so Lauryn threw on her shoes, grabbed her coat from where she'd tossed it on the floor, and crept downstairs to give her mysterious savior the benefit of the doubt.

He must have cut his motorcycle off after she vanished from the window, because by the time Lauryn made it downstairs, the predawn morning was unnervingly still. Even the normal sounds of the city seemed to be holding their breath as she unlocked her dad's triple-chain/deadbolt setup and crept out onto the porch, wincing when the subzero cold struck her in the face. The shock was almost enough to send her right back inside, but she was in the pipe now, so Lauryn kept going, clutching her coat tight around her shivering body as she walked down the frozen porch steps and across the tiny yard to the chain-link fence, stopping at the gate to stare across the empty street at the stranger who'd saved her life.

At least this time she could get a better look at him. In the dark alley where she'd found Lenny, she'd only gotten a vague impression of a dark-skinned man with broad shoulders and a deep voice who carried himself like a soldier. It was still dark now, but between the orange streetlights, the snowy road, and the city's glow reflected off the low clouds, Lauryn could see that the man wasn't as old as she'd originally thought. His age was actually very hard to place, but though life—or maybe his ever-present look of absolute seriousness—had left a few trace lines on his face, his body was that of a young man in his prime. His clothes were just as oddly timeless, and clearly custom-made. There was just no other way his long winter coat could fit him so perfectly. Odd as all that was, though, what really caught Lauryn's eye was the long, cloth-wrapped object strapped to the side of his bike. The one she knew was actually a large cross-hilted sword.

The whole situation was so bizarre and surreal, Lauryn didn't realize she hadn't actually said anything yet until the man stepped off his bike and dipped his head in greeting.

"Lauryn."

The sound of her name spoken in that calm voice made her stiffen in alarm. "How do you know my name?"

The man arched a dark eyebrow, amused. "You were yelling it at Lenny."

"Oh," she said, biting her lip. "Right. Well, that still doesn't explain what you're doing *here*. How did you find me?"

"I followed the ambulance to the hospital," he said, shrugging like ambulance stalking was no big deal. "After that, I followed your father's car. I would have let you sleep longer, but our enemy is moving quickly, and I wanted to introduce myself before they struck again."

By the time he finished, Lauryn was no longer sure giving him the benefit of the doubt was a good idea. "What do you mean, 'enemy'?"

"This might be easier to explain if I told you my name," the stranger said, walking across the street and holding out his hand. "I'm called Talon, and I work for a higher power."

Lauryn shoved her own hands deeper into her pockets. "Is that a euphemism or a really bad company name?"

"It's the truth," he said, lowering his offered hand but still keeping it where Lauryn could see. "I came to Chicago following a sign. At the time, I didn't understand why. Now, I'm sure I was sent here to find you."

This was getting crazier by the second. "Hold up," she said, cutting him off before he could push them any further down the rabbit hole. "Following a sign? What kind of sign?"

"A sign from above."

Lauryn sighed. Of course. After all that Bible quoting, what else had she expected? "Look," she said, reaching up to rub her suddenly aching head. "I swear I'm not trying to be as insulting as I know this is going to sound, but are you one of those religious crazy people?"

"I've been called such," Talon said, not seeming insulted in the least. "But what others think of me doesn't change the truth."

She was certain she was going to regret this, but . . . "Which is?"

It was a simple question, but Talon frowned, clearly thinking hard about how best to answer her. "There's something very bad going on in Chicago," he said at last. "I'm not sure yet how you're connected to it, but when I see a miracle, I can't just dismiss it. Things like what happened in the alley last night don't occur without reason, and I learned long ago to listen when God speaks."

"What miracle? We got lucky, and I already had an ambulance on the way."

"You and Lenny both survived when everyone else who touched that green stuff died," Talon reminded her, his thin lips curving into a knowing smile. "Sounds like a miracle to me."

Lauryn shrugged. "You say potato, I say biochemical good fortune. I had very limited exposure, and there's lots of reasons why Lenny survived and the others didn't, starting with the fact that he *wasn't* a junkie. That's a pretty big factor in his favor."

"But that doesn't explain why Lenny could hear your voice when he could hear nothing else," Talon said. "He was lost, but when you called him, he answered. That's a sign, Lauryn. Jesus said, 'Unless you see signs and wonders, you will not believe.' No one can deny you were shown both last night, but while you might still refuse to see, *I* can't ignore the writing on the wall. My eyes were opened long ago, but even if they hadn't been, I would've had to be truly blind not to see that something critical happened in that alley, and you were right in the middle of it. That's enough to make me believe you have been chosen to play an important role in what's to come."

Again, Lauryn knew better, but she still couldn't help herself. "Important role, huh? For what play?"

"I don't know," Talon confessed. "But it's going to be big."

"Riiiight," she said, shaking her head. "Listen, I don't believe in—"

"Doesn't matter," he said, staring her in the face. "You don't have to believe in good to know that there is evil in this world. You're a doctor who works with the poor. You see the evil men do to themselves and each other every day. But there is something even greater out there than the petty sins of mortal men, and its claws are digging into this city as we speak." He lifted his head, scanning the cloudy sky. "You can feel it if you try. All you need to do is pay attention."

Lauryn was already opening her mouth to say she felt nothing of the kind, but before she could get the words out, a wind picked up. It was nothing, just a breeze carrying a faint hint of rotten trash. But the timing was enough to make her pause, which Talon apparently took as his cue to continue.

"Just as you knew your brother was walking the wrong path when he left last night, I can feel the city tilting off its axis," he said solemnly, his dark eyes boring into hers. "I came to stop it, and on my first night here, I was led to you." He smiled. "I believe you have been chosen for a great task, Dr. Lauryn Jefferson. That makes it my duty to stay with you and guard you until that task is complete and his will has been done on earth as it is in heaven."

From anyone else, that would have sounded ridiculous, but Talon spoke the ridiculous words with such doubtless certainty that, for a crazy moment, Lauryn wanted to believe him. He just sounded so confident, so sure, so unlike how she felt most of the time. But tempting as it was to follow someone who so clearly felt no doubt, Lauryn was *not* crazy, and it was too early for this crap.

Just as she was about to go inside to call the cops to come place Talon under a psychiatric hold, however, it occurred to Lauryn that maybe she was looking at this situation the wrong way. Sure, the crazy dude with a sword from the alley showing up uninvited in front of her father's house before dawn was alarming, but it also proved that he was *real*, which meant Lauryn now had a witness who could corroborate her story from last night! Plus, despite his raving about evil afoot in Chicago, there was still the chance this Talon might actually know something useful about whoever it was that'd hurt Lenny, which made him *very* important in Lauryn's book. She might not believe in hell, but Lauryn liked to think that there was a special punishment waiting for people who hurt her patients. Even more important, though, was the fact that despite being weird as hell and armed with a *sword*, Talon didn't set off any of Lauryn's danger instincts, which years working in the ER had honed to a fine point.

For Lauryn, that was the deciding factor. She prided herself on being a rational woman of science, but anyone who worked the front lines with the public developed an almost supernatural sense for when someone was a threat, and Lauryn's was telling her that Talon wasn't. Crazy, maybe. Delusional, definitely. But dangerous? No—at least, not to her. She couldn't explain what made her so certain, but her gut was positive that Talon was one of the good guys.

Too bad he wasn't one of the sane ones.

Can't have everything with your stalkers, I suppose.

"Okay," Lauryn said, shoving her sleep-tousled hair out of her face. "I'm still not sure why you're here, but I appreciate that you want to help, so I'm going to go inside and call my friend. He's the detective who's working Lenny's case, and I'd really love it if you could give him a statement about what happened last night."

"I'd be happy to," Talon said, looking up at the dark sky again. "But I don't think we have time."

"Why not?"

His face grew grim. "The birds."

Still confused, Lauryn looked up as well, squinting at the dark sky. For a moment, nothing seemed out of the ordinary, and then, suddenly, she saw it. The predawn sky was full of birds. She wasn't sure what kind, but they were huge with black feathers and strange, oddly naked heads that made her skin crawl. "What are those?"

"Vultures," Talon replied, walking back to his bike.

Lauryn grimaced. For all her claims not to believe in the supernatural, that was creepy as hell. "And you think they're a sign?"

"Are you used to seeing vultures in Chicago? Especially in freezing weather? Yes," he said, climbing onto his seat, "it's a sign.

"But not one I follow."

He glowered at the circling birds. "'The coming of the lawless one is preceeded by the activity of Satan with all power and false signs and wonders.'"

That was a Bible quote for sure, but Lauryn was too distracted to figure out the book and verse this time. She was sure he was right about vultures in Chicago, but then again, she wasn't really much of a birdwatcher, so she wasn't as up on the migratory patterns of buzzards. Still . . .

"So you're saying, in all seriousness, that you believe those birds are a sign from Satan."

"Yes," he said simply, starting his bike. "Get on. We have to follow them."

"What?" Lauryn jumped back. "*No!* I'm not going to just get on your bike and go bird chasing! I don't even know you."

"So take a leap of faith," Talon said, flashing her a smile. "It'll happen whether you believe it will or not, Lauryn. You might as well get a head start while you still can."

That almost made a strange kind of sense, but Lauryn had reached the end of her patience. "That's it," she said, turning around and marching back toward the house. "I've officially reached my limit for crazy. I'll tell Will to get your statement later. You want to chase birds, knock yourself out. I'm going to get ready for work."

"You can't run from this, Lauryn," Talon called after her. "You're part of the plan now. You'll play your role one way or another, and it's generally a lot easier if you just have faith and go along from the start. Trust me on this."

"I'll keep that in mind," Lauryn said without looking, waving over her shoulder as she climbed the steps back to her front door. "Freaking crazy dude."

That last part was muttered under her breath. But as Lauryn was reaching for the knob to open her father's front door, her work pager began vibrating like crazy in the pocket of her winter coat. Her private phone went off a few seconds later, blaring with the impossible-to-ignore piercing ring she'd assigned to the emergency desk at work. Either sound was enough to put her instantly into doctor mode. Combined, she moved so fast she almost sprained a muscle, grabbing her phone and speaking before the call even connected.

"This is Jefferson."

"Lauryn!"

It took her several seconds before she recognized the voice as Sandy, one of the ER's head nurses and the most levelheaded person Lauryn had ever met. This was partially because the call was still connecting, but mostly because Lauryn had never heard Sandy in a panic before.

"We need you in here STAT," the nurse said breathlessly. "We've got three separate 2050s coming in as I speak."

That couldn't be right—2050 was their internal code for a massive incident like a bus crash or a big fire, basically any emergency situation where you were dealing with more than ten people in critical condition at one time. In her six months working in the Mercy ER, Lauryn had only seen two 2050s, one of which barely met the minimum. Three at once didn't even seem possible. "What happened? Was there a terrorist attack or something?"

"No one's sure yet," Sandy said. "But we're up to our noses in ambulances with more waiting to unload. The director's called all hands on deck. Get down here!"

"On my way," Lauryn replied, but Sandy had already hung up, leaving Lauryn scrambling to open the door and get inside when Talon's calm voice spoke behind her.

"Need a ride?"

She whirled around to find him perched on his bike, which was now idling directly in front of her house. "You don't have a car," he pointed out. "I'd be happy to take you to the hospital."

Lauryn didn't care how many 2050s were coming in—she was *not* getting on a motorcycle in subzero weather with a crazy stranger. "Thanks, but no thanks," she said. "I've got a ride."

Talon looked skeptical, but Lauryn didn't care. She was already running into the house, yelling up the stairs to her still-sleeping father that she was borrowing his car. By the time Maxwell's door opened, she'd already grabbed his keys from the hook in the kitchen and headed out the door. It took four tries to start the old Buick in the cold, but she got it going in the end, spinning the tires on the frozen pavement as she floored it down the street toward the hospital.

And behind her, she could see Talon in her rearview mirror, calmly following on his bike, his head constantly swiveling to the north.

Where the circle of vultures was getting bigger in the growing gray of dawn.

MATTHEW, MARK, LUKE AND JOHN, BLESS THE BED THAT I LIE ON.
FOUR CORNERS TO MY BED, FOUR ANGELS ROUND MY HEAD;
ONE TO WATCH AND ONE TO PRAY AND TWO TO BEAR MY SOUL AWAY.
—*THE BLACK PATERNOSTER, 1656*

6

ONE TO WATCH AND ONE TO PRAY AND TWO TO BEAR MY SOUL AWAY

Talon followed her all the way to work.

Another day, that would have been cause for concern, but right now Lauryn was too busy to care. An elephant could have been waiting for her in the emergency room and she wouldn't have seen it past the mass of patients being wheeled in from the ambulances like victims coming in from a war zone.

"Dr. Jefferson!"

Lauryn tore her eyes from the chaos to see one of the trainee nurses sprinting toward her. "Dr. Jefferson," she said again, panting. "Thank goodness you're here!" Her eyes flicked over Lauryn's shoulder at Talon, who'd somehow managed to park his bike and come right back to her side in thirty seconds flat. "Who's that?"

"Never mind him," Lauryn said quickly, determined not to waste any more brainpower on the Talon problem. If he was stupid enough to get in the way during an emergency, security would boot him. She had more important disasters to handle.

"What's the situation?" she asked, pumping a generous amount of sanitizing gel into her hand from one of the wall dispensers before donning a pair of latex gloves. "Those gurneys are headed for the burn ward in the basement. Was there a fire?"

"No," the nurse said quickly, hurrying to the computer to pull up the charts for Lauryn to review. "There's just too many patients for the normal ER to hold, so Sandy ordered us to move everyone downstairs to the burn ward."

Lauryn swore under her breath. At a hundred and fifty beds, Mercy's ER wing was made to handle anything Chicago threw at it. If the head nurse was already moving overflow patients into the burn ward, things were even worse than she'd thought.

"Let's see," she muttered, leaning down over the computer screen as she tabbed through the enormous list of ambulance reports. "Wait, these are *all* drug cases?" There had to be a hundred in the system already, and that wasn't counting all the patients still pending admission. But while their symptoms varied wildly, every single one was marked with the code for an overdose.

"This can't be right," she muttered, paging through the files. "Did admin get lazy with the coding?"

"No, the code's correct," the nurse said, wringing her hands. "They started coming in around 3 AM, all showing signs of different street drugs. What makes it weird, though, is that they all presented with the same secondary symptoms of disorientation, cyanosis, subconjunctival hemorrhaging, and hallucinations, even for those who tested negative for all known hallucinogenic drugs."

A lump formed in Lauryn's stomach. Cyanosis meant a bluish or gray tinge to the skin, and subconjunctival hemorrhaging was bursting of the blood vessels in the eyes. Add in the hallucinations and you had the same nightmarish combo she'd observed in Lenny last night. But tempting as it was to jump to conclusions, a good doctor knew better than to make a diagnosis without solid proof, so she went ahead and brought up the results of those patients who'd been here long enough to have lab work done.

Sure enough, just as the nurse had reported, every patient admitted under the 2050 emergency code so far had come up flagged for different substances, ranging from heroin and meth to plain old pot and party drugs. Other than the list of secondary symptoms the nurse had just rattled off, the only common thread linking all the cases together was a small note at the very end of each lab report.

Sulfhemoglobinemia.

"Too much sulfur."

Lauryn almost jumped out of her skin. She whirled, her anger spiking when she found Talon standing right behind her at the nurse's station, reading the patient lab result summaries over her shoulder.

"*Get out of here!*" she yelled, shoving his broad chest with both hands. "This area is for authorized personnel only!" She turned to the nurse, who was gaping at Talon with a confused mix of fear and wonder. "Call security to come kick him out."

"No need for that," Talon said, backing off immediately. "But you know, there's another name for sulfur. In the old days, they used to call it brimstone."

"Who *cares* what it's called," Lauryn said. "You're lucky I'm not calling the cops. Now *get*. Go be crazy somewhere else. I've got work to do."

She turned away after that, not even bothering to see if Talon obeyed as she jogged out from behind the nurse's station to join the stream of EMTs pushing gurneys toward the burn ward deep in the hospital's basement. She was so sick of this cryptic crap. She had no idea why Talon had fixated on her, but he could take his brimstone and vultures right back to hell. Meanwhile, she had *actual* work to do saving *real* people's lives. And speaking of . . .

Without slowing her pace, Lauryn pulled out her phone and tapped through her contacts until she reached the number she'd never thought she'd call again. She still wasn't sure dialing it now was a smart move, but she had to tell someone, and Will was the easiest. As usual, he picked up on the second ring, though she must have woken him up, because his voice was thick and muffled.

"Tannenbaum."

Even with the emergency going on all around her, the intimate sound of her ex-boyfriend's sleepy voice hit Lauryn harder than she'd expected. "It's me," she said when she'd pulled herself back together. "You need to get down to the hospital. We're having a massive influx of drug cases, and they've all got the same sulfur readings Lenny showed last night."

For a long moment, nothing happened, and Lauryn began to wonder if she'd gone too fast. But she needn't have worried. Though he was clearly still half-asleep, this was Will. If it involved a case he was working, he'd rise from the dead to investigate, and this morning was no different.

"I'll be right there," he said, sounding more awake with every word. "Thanks for the tip. Don't let anyone leave."

Lauryn looked around at the four gurneys the transport team was currently trying to wedge into the elevator. "I don't think that'll be a problem. See you when you get here."

Will grunted and hung up. Lauryn hung up as well, dropping her phone into the pocket of her white coat as she abandoned the glutted elevators and ran for the stairs, taking the heavy cement steps two at a time as she rushed down to the hospital's fluorescent basement.

The sun still wasn't up over the horizon when Will screeched his unmarked patrol car into the Mercy Hospital deck. He was out before the vehicle stopped moving, barely slowing down enough to lock the door behind him as he raced through the freezing predawn dark toward the hospital's side entrance . . . only to find it was locked until nine.

Frustrated and in too much of a hurry to go all the way around to the ER entrance, Will banged on the glass, flashing his badge at one of the orderlies inside. Even then, it took some serious convincing to get the man to open the door, not that Will blamed him. Unshaven, in street clothes, and running on less than two hours' sleep out of the last thirty-six, he wouldn't have believed he was a cop, either, badge or no.

After leaving Korigan's office, Will had spent the rest of the night working his street contacts for any hint of the sword-wielding man who had helped Lauryn, as she'd reported to the police. He'd also pressed hard to try to find out where this new drug was coming from—who was supplying it, who was selling it, that kind of thing. Unfortunately, he'd had zero success on both fronts. No one seemed to know anything about a guy with a sword, and the few pushers he could find who would admit to having heard about a weird green ooze that reeked of sulfur didn't seem to know anything beyond that. He knew they were lying, but the fear in their eyes was enough to convince him to back off and try again later. Spooking the few informants he had was the last thing he could afford right now. Still, that meant he had nothing, and after hours of dead ends, Will had given up and gone to bed. He'd just drifted off when Lauryn called, yanking him right back into the fray.

And it was quite the fray. He'd barely made it into the main lobby before it became obvious that the hospital was under siege. Everywhere he looked, patients with discolored, grayish skin and horrifying bloody eyes were lying on gurneys. Some were comatose, while others were strapped down to keep them from rolling off their beds, their bloody eyes wide and rolling as they babbled about voices that Will could only hope were hallucinations.

He grabbed a nurse, who said Lauryn was in the burn ward. Making his way downstairs, he almost gave up right there. The chaos of the upper floors was nothing compared to the madhouse that was the basement.

Down here, the otherwise modern Mercy Hospital took a decided turn for the 1950s . . . or maybe the 1850s. Rather than being divided up into several smaller rooms, all the patients had been lined up together field-hospital-style in a huge underground room that made Will think of a combination between a fallout shelter and a Civil War medical tent. But even this basketball court–sized space wasn't enough to handle the massive flood of EMTs constantly wheeling new patients through the propped-open fire doors.

Even in the scrum, though, Will had no trouble finding Lauryn. All he had to do was look where the trouble was thickest, and there she was, working with another doctor and a team of nurses to restrain a large man near the back who looked like he was having a fit.

It was hard to watch. Even with all the help, the man on the gurney was so much bigger than Lauryn, and his long arms were flailing violently as he tried to fight whatever hallucination was attacking him. As always, Lauryn was a medical machine, calmly dodging the man's violent outbursts as she and the other doctor worked together to push his arms down long enough to administer some kind of shot. Whatever it was, the junkie went quiet a few seconds later, and the team let go of him to move on to the next patient. Lauryn was moving with them when Will ran over.

"Hey," he said. "Got a moment?"

"Do I look like I have a moment?" she asked irritably, giving him an exhausted look.

"Anything will do," he said. "Just give me the basics."

"You're looking at them," she said, nodding at the rows of patients on gurneys. "You got here too fast. We haven't even finished the initial assessment, and we've *still* got more coming in."

So Will could see. "And these are *all* drug cases?"

Lauryn nodded. "Once I pointed out the sulfur to the director, we went ahead and separated all the ones with signs of sulfhemoglobinemia from the normal ER patients and wheeled them down here. We're still not sure what's going on, though, or what's causing the hallucinations. Right now we're in survival mode. But we should know more after we finish triage."

"When's that?"

"No idea," Lauryn said, and then her eyes lit up. "But I do have some good news for you. You remember the guy I told you about? The one who saved me from Lenny? I found him."

"You did?" Will was shocked. He'd looked all night and hadn't found a trace. "How?"

"Well—actually, it was more like he found me," she admitted, putting Will's guard up at once. "He's over there if you want to ask him some questions, and if you could do that somewhere else, I'd love it. I've tried everything I can think of to get him out of here, but he won't leave, and we don't have the resources to make him. We need all the staff we've got just to keep up with—"

A scream cut her off, and they both whirled around to see the big patient she'd just calmed down arch off his gurney like he'd been electrocuted, screaming at the top of his lungs that something was eating his legs. The patient started to convulse a second later, and the already loud room got even louder as a team of people in blue uniforms charged over.

"Crap, he's coding," Lauryn said, racing away from Will to join the team of techs as they hoisted the convulsing man onto a CPR board. "I gotta help with this. Take care of Talon for me."

"'Talon'? *That's* his name?" Will called after her, but Lauryn was already locked back into doctor mode, yelling for a nurse to get her fifty CCs of something Will couldn't begin to pronounce.

After that, he decided he'd best get out of the line of fire. He was wondering how he was going to find this "Talon," since Lauryn hadn't gotten a chance to tell him what the suspect looked like, when he spotted a tall, muscular, dark-skinned man wearing a long, plain, but very well-cut winter coat standing in the ward's far corner, his dark eyes watching Lauryn in a way Will didn't like one bit.

Bingo.

Target acquired, Will slipped into his own version of professional mode, checking his pistol and making sure the badge hanging from his neck was out and facing the right direction before strolling over to the stranger like he had all the time in the world. "Hey," he said when he got there, taking a long moment to look the man up and down. "You Talon?"

The man's dark eyes flicked to Will's face for only a moment before going right back to Lauryn. "I am."

"Great," Will said, tapping the badge on his chest. "I'm Detective Will Tannenbaum with Chicago Vice. I'd like to ask you a few questions."

"I'm sure you would," Talon said, his voice surprisingly deep and calm despite the chaos around them. "We all have questions, Detective, but now is not the time."

"Actually, I'd say it's the best time," Will replied flatly, stepping sideways to block the man's view of Lauryn. A move Talon didn't seem to like at all.

Too bad Will didn't give a damn.

"Lauryn says you were the one who helped her when she was attacked last night," he said, pulling out his notebook. "How did you come to be in that alley?"

"I was following a sign," Talon said, moving his head to get Lauryn back into view.

Will didn't bother writing that down. "Do you live in Chicago?"

"I go where I am sent and remain where I am needed. Right now, that's here."

Will arched an eyebrow, but that seemed to be all the man had to say on the subject, and he suppressed the urge to sigh. "Look, pal, I don't have a lot patience this morning, so we're going to cut the crap and make this real simple. I'm betting you know a lot more about *this*—" he tilted his head back over his shoulder at the sea of patients "—than your average guy wandering through Chicago should. I've also heard tell that you've been stalking my friend Dr. Jefferson, which is illegal in the great state of Illinois. That puts you in a bad spot."

"Which I can alleviate by telling you everything I know about this situation," Talon finished for him.

Will grinned. "Nice to see you've got a brain under that scowl." He tapped his pen against his open notebook. "What you got for me?"

"Nothing you can use," Talon said, finally turning to look at Will head-on. "I am sorry to disappoint you, Detective, but I'm not involved in this. At least, not in the way you hope. As I said, I arrived in Chicago yesterday following a call—"

"A call from who?"

"The one who calls us all."

Will sighed. This was going to be a long morning. "Look, buddy, I—"

"You don't believe," Talon said, giving him a pitying look. "But that's all right. You'll come around. They always do. All you need to understand at the moment, Detective Tannenbaum, is that you and I follow similar callings. We both enforce laws and protect the innocent. That makes us allies, and right now, you *need* an ally."

Will gave him a flat look. "Do I?"

Instead of answering, Talon just waved his hand at the rows of beds. "It must be clear to you by now that these people are suffering from no ordinary drug. It might have started that way, but what we are seeing now is the evidence of something far more sinister."

Will didn't know about that, but he wrote it down anyway. "And what is that?"

"A malady of the soul."

I had to ask. "Really?"

Talon took his blatant skepticism in stride. "Doubt does not change the truth, Detective. Just ask Thomas."

"Who's Thomas?"

"The disciple."

Will rolled his eyes to the ceiling. "Listen—"

"That is advice I should be giving you," Talon said, cutting him off. "Because if you would stop trying to be right for a moment and actually observe what's going on around you, you will see that this is no common sickness, which is why Dr. Jefferson's medicine isn't working."

As he said this, Will heard Lauryn's distinctive gasp. Seconds later, the code alarms went off again as several more victims went into cardiac arrest. He was still watching in shock when he felt Talon step in closer beside him.

"You can't repair a malady of the spirit by treating the flesh alone," the strange man said quietly. "You have to approach the problem as a whole."

"And how do we do that?" Will asked, just to see where this was going.

"I don't know yet," Talon admitted, showing a hint of frustration for the first time. "I don't know how they got to this state, but I *can* tell you there's no way they did it on their own. No matter how addicted or hopeless or fallen to sin a person becomes, you can never fall farther than God can catch. No soul is cursed beyond salvation. There is always a road back. But for some reason, these people all seem to be stuck in a dead end. Look."

He moved to the victim closest to them, a young woman with eyes so full of broken blood vessels, Will didn't know how she could see. Even so, her eyes were moving rapidly, while her face was contorted in fear, her hands pressing against the restraints in her efforts to fight off something only she could see.

"I can't reach her," Talon said sadly. "Even when I pray, she doesn't hear my voice."

"Of course not," Will said, nodding at the track marks on her arms. "She's high as a kite."

"Do drugs do this?" Talon asked, pointing at her neck where a strange bruise had begun to form on her blue-tinged skin, almost like a hand was choking her from the inside.

"Damn!" Will whispered, his eyes going wide. "What *is* that?"

"Something that should not be here," Talon said angrily. "Like I said, Detective, this may have started with a drug, but no one knowingly invites this kind of horror into their bodies. Something is pulling these people apart, and we need to work quickly to discover its source and stop it before it's too late."

He looked at Will like this was supposed to be some kind of huge revelation. Will, on the other hand, was starting to wish he'd taken Lauryn's warnings about Talon being nuts a bit more seriously. But while he didn't buy this "malady of the soul" mumbo jumbo for a second, he couldn't deny there was something seriously messed up going on here.

"Okay," he said slowly, placing a hand on Talon's arm and steering him back to the corner. "For the record, I don't believe you, but just for the sake of argument, let's say you're right. That would mean these people are . . . what? Possessed?"

"That's one way to describe it," Talon said. "But true possessions are extremely rare. They require either an enormously vulnerable victim or a person who's actively willing to invite a demon into their bodies. Even then, the demon in question still has to be able to make the long journey from hell to Creation."

"Demons?" Will repeated, hopes sinking. "You mean to tell me you think all this is the work of the *literal* devil? The serpent, the dragon, the Great Deceiver, all that crap?"

"He has many names," Talon said, giving the detective a weighing look. "I understand your skepticism, Detective, but if you can't see the devil's hand in a disaster where hundreds of otherwise normal sinners are struck down by an unknown malady whose primary symptom is an overabundance of *brimstone* in their blood, I wonder how you can see at all."

"Easy," Will growled, snapping his notebook shut. "Because I see *facts*, not religious hocus-pocus."

"So their cries mean nothing?" Talon countered. "It doesn't strike you as odd that an entire ward of hallucinating people—several of whom are on drugs that don't cause hallucinations—all happen to be having visions of the same demons?"

"No, I find that incredibly odd," Will snapped. "But that doesn't mean I'm going to take the hallucinating drug addict's

word for it. I deal with junkies every day. Lots of them see demons. I'll spot you that this is some strange behavior, but that
doesn't mean we're dealing with actual demonic possession."

"There, at least, we agree," Talon said as he turned back to
the victims in the gurneys. "I can't believe hell has come so close
as to allow this many possessions at once. This cannot be a true
mass possession. Something else has to be going on, but we still
have a problem. Whatever has dragged them down to this state,
so long as they stay like this, these people are lost sheep. Easy
prey. And where you have easy prey, you have predators."

"Predators, huh?" Will said, putting up his notebook. "Let
me guess, more demons?"

Talon's eyes narrowed. "Not every evil in this world comes
from hell. I've met men whose cruelty would put devils to shame.
But whatever guise the wolf comes in, the Good Shepherd will
protect the flock."

"Good Shepherd, huh?" Will said, shaking his head. "Let me
guess, that's you."

"I do my best to serve," Talon said proudly. "Just like you."

This was getting so crazy, Will could only laugh. "Me, huh?"
he said with a chuckle. "What's my role in your fantasy, then?"
He grinned wide. "Am I the wolf?"

"You give yourself both too much and too little credit, Detective," Talon said, shaking his head. "You are just a man. The
wolf is behind you."

Will's eyes shot open, and he spun around, scanning the
room, but all he saw was more of the same chaos. However, when
he turned around to tell Talon that was a nice try, his suspect
was gone.

Cursing himself for an idiot, Will whirled around, his eyes
going automatically to every exit. Unless he was sprinting, which
Will definitely would have noticed, there was no way Talon

could have gotten out of the ward in the split second Will's back was turned. But even knowing that, it took Will far too long to spot his target, because Talon hadn't made a break for the doors at all. Quite the opposite. When Will finally spotted him, he was cutting a straight swath into the middle of the room toward Lauryn, who was tending a patient while talking to a tall doctor Will didn't recognize but instantly disliked.

That set off a whole new round of warning bells. Will couldn't say what it was about the tall black man with the suave smile and pristine white doctor's coat standing beside her that unnerved him so much, but he'd learned to trust his gut in matters like this. If he didn't like someone, that usually meant his subconscious had spotted a warning sign that his brain simply hadn't caught up with. He wasn't alone, either. Now that he was looking, he could clearly see that Talon—who strangely *hadn't* set off those warning bells—was moving toward the new man, not Lauryn. He was positioning to corner them both when the strange tall man in the doctor's coat reached into his pocket and pulled out a small glass vial that glowed green as envy.

That was all Will managed to make out before everything went to hell.

Lauryn couldn't believe how badly this was going.

She'd been here for almost an hour, and they *still* weren't done with the initial triage. She'd already had four patients code on her, which was three more than she'd ever had to deal with in a single day. No one had died yet, thank God, but Lauryn had a sinking feeling this mess was going to get worse before it got better. The only good thing she could say about the situation was that at least they were finally getting enough hands in to help. Pretty much the entire staff of Mercy Hospital—doctors, nurses, nurse assistants, techs, volunteers, anyone who could tie a bandage—was now in the ward working at top speed. As a result, there were a lot of people running around that Lauryn didn't know, but even if she couldn't put names to their faces, they all knew their jobs, and they did them faster than ever before, racing to stabilize patients whose illness they still didn't understand.

Except one man.

"Dr. Jefferson?"

Lauryn looked up from the patient whose red eyes she'd been checking to see a handsome young doctor with dark skin smiling crookedly down at her from his impressive height. It was shocking to see—this was hardly a situation for smiling—but people had all kinds of ways of dealing with stress, and smiling was hardly a bad one. She just wished his looked less . . . predatory. "Yes?"

"I'm Dr. Lincoln Black, from Herpetology," he said, his smile never wavering. "I understand you're the one who pinned down the sulfur connection?"

"That's me," Lauryn said, confused. "I'm sorry, did you mean *Hep*atology?" Because unless her Greek was wrong, she was pretty sure herpetology was the study of snakes. But rather than dying of embarrassment like any normal doctor would if they got their own specialization wrong, the unnerving man just shrugged.

"Of course, of course, Hepatology," he said, stepping in a bit closer, which in turn made Lauryn step back. "But you *are* Dr. Lauryn Jefferson, right? The one who was attacked by the junkie last night?"

Lauryn nodded, glancing back at her patient, who was starting to writhe again. "I'm sorry, Doctor, we'll have to talk later. I need to get back to—"

"I'll only be a moment," Dr. Black said, reaching into his pocket. "I have something to show you. I think it could be the answer you're looking for."

That got Lauryn's full attention. "Really?" she said, head shooting back up. "What did you find? Did someone isolate the compound that's causing the hallucinations?"

"I wouldn't know about that," Black said. "But I can say for sure that you're about to get some firsthand experience."

With every word he spoke, Lauryn felt like the ground was crumbling under her feet. She couldn't say when it became obvious, but by the time he finished, Lauryn was certain this Lincoln Black was no doctor—of the liver, snakes, or otherwise—and he didn't mean anyone any good. She was already taking a breath to yell for security when his hand emerged from his lab coat clutching a glass vial that glowed like green fire.

Unfortunately, by the time her stumbling, panicked brain caught up with what her eyes were seeing, it was far too late. The tall man was already bringing the vial straight down into her face. It all happened so fast, she couldn't even close her eyes. All she could do was stand there watching her death come down. Oddly enough, her last thought was the prayer her dad used to make her say every night before bed.

Matthew, Mark, Luke and John, bless the bed that I lie on.
Four corners to my bed, four angels round my head;
One to watch and one to pray, and two to bear my soul away.

Lauryn had always thought that prayer was macabre what with angels watching over you just in case you died in the night. Now, though, in the terrifying time dilation of panic, it just kept running through her head over and over, getting shorter and shorter with each cycle until it was only one line spinning through her head wildly like a broken record.

Two to bear my soul away. Two to bear my—

And then, without warning, he was there, the avenging angel, standing over her with his sword flashing like lightning as he smashed the green vial inches from her nose, sending the emerald liquid flying as he positioned his body like a wall between Lauryn and the grinning doctor who wasn't a doctor at all.

"Well, hello, Talon."

FOR THERE ARE THREE THAT TESTIFY: THE SPIRIT AND THE WATER
AND THE BLOOD; AND THESE THREE AGREE.

—1 JOHN 5:7–8

7

THE SPIRIT AND THE WATER AND THE BLOOD

The emerald liquid flew out in an arc, splattering onto the linoleum floor with a violent hiss. But though the sulfurous stench of the vile concoction rose up like a physical presence, miraculously, not a drop hit Lauryn. It was the kind of luck that deserved a prayer of thanks, but Talon didn't dare lower his head or take his eyes off the grinning monster in front of him.

"Haven't seen you in a while, old man," Lincoln Black said, showing no concern at all for the three-foot-long mirror-bright sword Talon was holding between them. His eyes instead flicked over Talon's shoulder to Lauryn, who was still frozen in shock. "Still at it, I see?"

"Always," Talon said, turning his sword so that the edge was angled at his enemy's neck.

"Okay, that's enough!"

The shout was loud and close, but neither man moved. Then, at last, Talon glanced to the side just long enough to see Detective Tannenbaum standing beside them with his gun drawn . . . and pointed at *him*.

"You're aiming at the wrong target, Detective," Talon said quietly, turning back to Black, who was smirking.

"Yeah, well, he's not the one with a sword," Will growled, finger hovering over the trigger. "But don't worry—he's under arrest, too. Now drop the weapon and put your hands up."

Since Lauryn was still in Lincoln's reach, Talon didn't move. Black, however, raised his arms languidly over his head. Aside from that token gesture of compliance, though, he didn't even spare Will a glance.

"I see you found yourself a new girl to attach to," he said, flashing Lauryn a charming smile. "Word of advice, sweetheart: don't stick around. Ladies who hang out with Talon tend to end up with a bad case of dead. But then, maybe that's how he likes it?" He turned back to Talon with a cruel smile. "A little less temptation in your life, holy man?"

The taunt hit harder than Talon would have liked to admit. For a horrible second, he was back in that night, with Black standing over him, laughing as the blood dripped from his curved sword. And then, like a drowning man catching a lifeline, he remembered.

"Your words mean nothing," he said, glaring at his oldest enemy. "'You are of your father, the devil. Whenever he speaks a lie, he speaks from his own nature, for he is a liar and the father of lies.'"

Lincoln rolled his eyes. "Really? Gonna pull out this boxed Bible nonsense again? Can't you come up with your own lines?"

Talon had no intention of responding to that, but even if he'd wanted to, Will didn't give him the chance.

"What part of 'under arrest' do you crazy assholes not understand?" the detective yelled, physically forcing his way between them. "Sword down, hands up, *now*." He glanced over his shoulder at the two hospital security guards who were standing in shock by the doors. "Little help here?"

"They can't help you," Lincoln said, lowering his arms. "No one can. Not anymore."

"Dammit, I said hands *up!*" Will barked, moving his gun off Talon to point the barrel in Lincoln's face. As always, though, the threat fell flat. Talon knew from experience that Black feared nothing, least of all death. All that was human and fearful in him had withered and died years ago, leaving a grinning shell who lived only to tear others down. If there was a chance the detective would listen, Talon could have explained this and saved him the trouble, but there was no time. Black's smile was already growing, and Talon had the horrible creeping sensation that he'd missed something vital.

"You sure you want to be pointing that thing at me, hot shot?" Black asked, his voice mocking. "Not to spoil your fun, but you might want to save your bullets, because you're about to have a lot more to shoot at."

Will gritted his teeth, but before he could yell whatever he was clearly about to yell, Lauryn screamed.

"*Shit!*"

Talon whirled at once, turning just in time to see Lauryn grab the patient in front of her. The man was convulsing on the gurney, his mouth opening in a scream of pain as he clutched his hands to his face where three drops of the emerald liquid from the vial Talon had cut out of Black's hand had missed the floor and landed on his flesh.

"Oh, dear." Black tsked as the smell of burning flesh filled the room. "Should have been paying more attention."

Will shouted something back at him, but Talon couldn't hear it over the chaos exploding around them. Up to this point, everyone in the room—staff and the patients cognizant enough of their surroundings to understand something exciting was happening—had been watching the unfolding police drama with absolute attention. Now that Lauryn's shout had broken the spell, everyone started moving at once. Especially the code team, who practically knocked Will over in their rush to get to Lauryn's patient.

A mistake Talon didn't realize until too late.

"No!" he shouted, grabbing for the closest nurse. "Don't touch—"

A roar drowned out his voice as the man on the gurney sat bolt upright and wrapped his arms around the burly tech who'd been trying to slide the cardiac board under his back. The moment he had the man in his grips, he lurched up and bit down hard, sinking his teeth—his long, yellow, no longer human teeth—into the man's shoulder. He was still gnawing when the other techs yanked him off, ripping his teeth out of the screaming man with a sickening sound. It wasn't until the bitten man's skin started to change color, though, that Talon realized just how badly they'd been set up.

"*Black!*" he roared, whirling around, but his enemy was already gone. In the split second Talon had been distracted, Lincoln Black had made it all the way to the giant fire doors that separated the burn ward from the rest of the hospital. He was out of the ward entirely by the time Talon finally caught up, snatching him by the collar and slamming him into the hallway's cement wall. But when he put his sword to Black's neck, the wiry man went limp in his grasp, laughing like this was all a big joke.

"Shut up," Talon said, pressing harder as he jerked his head toward the chaos exploding through the ward behind them. "How do I stop this?"

"You can't," Lincoln giggled. "That's what's so funny."

"I don't believe you," Talon said. "You might not value your life, but your masters are too selfish to create a weapon with no counter. There has to be a way to shut this down, and you're going to tell me what that is, or I'll do what I should have done years ago."

"Like you could," Black taunted, grinning wider than ever. "I know you, Talon. You believe *everyone* can be saved. Even me. That's why you've never been able to kill me despite all the times we've done this. Because you know if you do, your God loses. But that's the joke, isn't it? 'Cause I ain't ever going to repent, and I'm never going to stop. So what's it going to be, holy man? Are you finally going to accept that your God has no power over me and cut off my head? Or are you going to let me live and keep our little dance going for one more round? Either way, I win. But you'd better decide fast, or your little doctor's going to end up just like that other girl you thought you could—"

Talon slammed him into the wall hard enough to crack the cement. Black was still wheezing when Talon dropped him and turned away, striding without a word back into the chaos in the ward behind them. He'd just made it to the doors when he heard Black's laughter chasing him down the hall.

"You're too late, you know!" he yelled. "The green stuff's just the catalyst. The match to the kindling. They're all already damned, and you know it."

"No one is damned who cannot also be saved," Talon replied quietly, taking a deep breath before he pushed through the crowd of increasingly panicked nurses and EMTs and made his way back to where he was most needed.

At Lauryn's side.

The moment Lauryn saw the green goo on her patient's face, she knew it was going to be bad. She might not have understood the rest of it—like why a man dressed as a doctor would try to punch her in the face with an unknown drug or how he knew Talon—but when it came to her patients, things got very simple: do what had to be done to save the life. It was the part of being a physician Lauryn had always understood, and it was what she clung to now, shutting the rest of the craziness out to focus on the emergency in front of her.

"Get him tied down," she ordered, dropping to the floor where the bitten tech was rolling around in a panic, getting blood everywhere. She put a stop to that by locking her hand on his shoulder, pushing him gently but firmly onto the floor. Above them, the nurses managed to get the patient lashed back down to the bed. Surprisingly, he went down without a fight, rolling and crying and rubbing his bloody mouth on the sheets. But when the nurses tried to approach him again, Lauryn stopped them.

"He'll be fine," she lied. "Just leave him be, and stay away from that green stuff." She pointed at the splatter of emerald-green goo that was lying on the floor between the beds a few feet away. "That's the hallucinogen that started this mess, and it's absorbed through the skin. I need everyone to stay away until the biohazard team can come handle it. I don't want anyone else going nuts on me."

After what they'd just seen, it didn't take much convincing to get the nurses to back down. She'd barely finished her warning before the whole team cleared out, putting five feet minimum between themselves and the spilled green liquid. When Lauryn was satisfied no one else was going to be accidentally exposed, she turned her attention back to the downed tech, who was looking worryingly ashen despite the pressure Lauryn was applying to his wound. A few seconds later, though, she realized the man's skin wasn't turning ashen from lack of blood. He was changing color, his face slowly shifting from flushed tan to a very familiar shade of sickly bluish gray.

"Damn," she muttered, prying open his clamped-tight eyes. Sure enough, they were already going, the blood vessels popping right in front of her.

"What's wrong?"

The question made her jump, and Lauryn looked up to see Will crouching beside her with his gun still in his hands.

"Put that away!"

"No," he snapped. "Not until I'm sure he's not going to Hulk out on us again." He shot a poisonous glare at the druggie who was still lashed down to the gurney before returning his attention to the ashen-faced tech Lauryn was holding down. "Please tell me that's not what it looks like."

"It can't be," Lauryn said, letting go just long enough to catch the roll of wound tape one of the nurses tossed at her. "I don't care what he's on, no drug is strong enough to be passed in functional doses through a bite. We're humans, not cobras." She peeled off a strip of tape one-handed, motioning for Will to hold the man down as she began binding his wound. "It couldn't have been the bite. He must have gotten the green stuff on him another way. Stepped in it or—"

Another scream cut her off. It was a woman's voice this time, high-pitched and in pain. Down on the ground, Lauryn couldn't even see where it had come from, but Will shot up off the floor like a gopher, his face pale and serious as he looked around. "Crap."

"What?" she demanded.

"Someone else just got bit," he said, dropping back down. "A nurse this time. Bastard just grabbed her arm and dug in."

Lauryn swore under her breath. As if things weren't bad enough. The staff was already pushed to their limits from having to deal with so many unstable patients. Add in biting and even the veterans were going to start panicking.

That realization must have been prophetic, because no sooner had the worry crossed Lauryn's mind than another scream rang across the ward. This one was followed by several other terrified shouts and the loud *bang* of a bed being knocked over. Cursing under her breath, Lauryn handed Will the tape to finish tying off the patient's wound and shot to her feet, sucking a breath to yell for everyone to just calm the hell down and remember they were professionals. But the angry words died on her tongue, because when she spun around to look at the far corner of the ward where the shout had come from, all she could see were beds.

Empty beds, with no one around them.

"Wait," she said, looking around in confusion. "Where did—"

Her words were cut short as one of the wheeled beds in the corner rattled and slid sideways. That was all the warning Lauryn got before a man exploded toward her, leaping off the floor between the beds like a tiger. It happened so fast, she didn't even have time to scream. She just dove sideways, knocking Will out of the way as the man flew past where they'd been to land in the cluster of terrified staff behind them.

What happened after was a maelstrom of bodies and blood and screams. All around the room, bloody-eyed patients were ripping themselves out of their beds and turning on the hospital staff like ravenous lions. The nurses tried to run, but the room was too crowded, and the panic slowed them down, making them easy prey for the gray-skinned monsters their patients had become. By the time Lauryn had pushed herself off Will, the screams were competing with the unmistakable sound of tearing flesh. The sound alone was enough to make even Lauryn want to vomit. That was what she was concentrating on when something grabbed her and yanked her off the floor.

The moment the hand closed around her arm, she began to fight, flailing wildly in an effort to keep whatever it was away.

"Stop," commanded a familiar voice. "It's me."

Lauryn blinked at the sound and looked up to see Talon standing over her, sword in hand.

It was a sign of just how messed up this whole situation was that the sight of a crazy man with a gleaming blade was almost enough to make her cry with relief. If things had been less dire, she would have, but Lauryn was too busy to break down right now.

"We have to get out of here!" she cried, grabbing his sleeve. "They're changing like Lenny!"

"They are," Talon agreed. "But we can't run."

"*Why do you always say that?*" she hissed as Talon reached down to grab Will next. "This isn't like under the bridge. Running is the *only* plan. We're facing a full-blown outbreak!"

She didn't realize how true those words were until she said them. All around the room, the bitten victims, including the tech she'd bandaged less than a minute earlier, were pulling themselves up from where they'd fallen. They rose like marionettes, their bodies cracking and bending at unnatural angles.

"You know, running is starting to sound like a great idea," Will said, glancing backwards at the heavy fire doors where all the medical staff lucky enough to be away from the beds when the situation had gone to hell were currently fighting each other to get out. "Let's—"

"We have to stay here," Talon said, his voice firm. "Look at them. They're hunters. If we run, they'll chase, and then there'll be nothing to stop them from infecting the whole hospital."

"Oh, come *on*!" Will yelled. "That's ridiculous. They're druggies, not zombies."

Lauryn wasn't so sure about that. By this point, most of the hospital staff who could run had done so, fleeing through the fire doors down the hall that led to the elevators. Behind them, the patients were in hot pursuit, their crooked bodies becoming more graceful—more *predatory*—with every step they took. It was like seeing the birth of a new kind of hunter in fast forward, and as she watched it go down, Lauryn realized that—in one way at least—Talon was absolutely right. Whatever happened, whatever was actually going on here, they could not let those things get up to the rest of the patients in the main hospital. She was still trying to figure out how to do that when a fresh chorus of screams rang out from the hall as the fleeing workers were taken down. This was followed by a few seconds of eerie silence, and then the creatures reappeared, stalking back inside the ward toward Lauryn, Will, and Talon.

The only prey left.

"That's it," Will said, raising his gun. "We need to run *now*. Stick close to me. We'll take the fire escape up to the street and—"

"No!" Lauryn said, grabbing his arm. "Talon's right. We can't run."

Will's face went blank in disbelief. Lauryn couldn't blame him. They were now the only unchanged people left in the giant ward filled with . . . she didn't even know what to call them. "Monsters" felt wrong, but they were definitely no longer human.

She scanned the room once more. At this point, every one of the original patients who'd been brought in had torn themselves off their gurneys. The rest of the medical staff—both the ones who'd run and those who'd been caught before they could—were down on the ground, but a few of the bodies were already twitching, their bloody eyes flying open in that horrified expression Lauryn had come to dread. The first ones were starting to rise, their gray, corpse-colored bodies slowly taking on the terrifying and oddly inhuman predator movement she'd seen before. Soon enough, they'd realize they didn't need to chase these three, and then the attack would come.

Under any other circumstances, that would have been cause for panic. Now, though, with seven floors of vulnerable patients waiting above them, it gave Lauryn an idea.

"We can't let them get upstairs," she whispered, gripping Will's arm as hard as she could. "We have to keep them down here somehow."

"Are you crazy?" Will hissed. "We can't stay here!"

"They haven't attacked us yet," she pointed out. An observation that made no sense now that she thought about it. "I wonder—"

"It's the sword," Talon said quietly, gripping the bright blade in his hands. "Demons are cowardly by nature. They only attack when they think they can win."

"Yeah, well, you might want to check the odds on that," Will muttered, clutching his gun. "'Cause they seem to be getting less afraid by the second."

He was right. The longer they stood without attacking, the bolder the changed patients became. Already, they were inching forward, surrounding the three of them in a ring of red eyes and long teeth. If they didn't move soon, they'd be cornered completely. The problem was if running upstairs wasn't an option, Lauryn didn't know where to go. Other than the fire doors, the burn ward didn't even have other rooms save for the bathrooms in the hall and the pharmaceutical closet at the room's far end. The one with a reinforced, key-locked door designed to protect hundreds of thousands of dollars' worth of prescription medication . . .

Right.

"Follow me!" she cried, pushing off the wall.

"Follow you where?" Will yelled as Talon ran after her. *"Lauryn!"*

But Lauryn didn't slow down. She couldn't. She could already feel the things' eyes on her as she broke into a run, sprinting around the toppled gurneys as she snatched the ID badge off her coat with her free hand. The moment she was in range, she slammed the plastic card against the black ID reader on the wall beside the door, frantically shoving the RFID chip against the pad until, after what felt like years, the light on the locked closet turned green, and the heavy deadbolt retracted with a click.

Lauryn shouldered the door, holding it open to let Talon and Will—who thankfully *did* follow her—run in before kicking the weighted door shut. It slammed closed seconds before the first of the pursuing transformed patients crashed into the wood. The second one hit the door hard enough to crack the reinforced security glass panel, but the door had been built to guard the hospital's investment from even the most determined pill addicts, and it held. When she was sure it would stay that way, Lauryn stepped back with a sigh of relief. "We should be safe in here."

"You mean trapped," Will said, looking around at the tiny space packed with plastic medicine dispensers. "There's only one way out, and if these guys are anything like the ones we dealt with yesterday, that door won't mean a damned thing in a few minutes. We had one rip open a patrol car, remember?"

"I don't think these are at that stage," Talon said quietly, peering through the tiny window at the top of the door. "At least, not yet."

"That's not really comforting," Lauryn said, looking around the safe room that was feeling more like a prison with every passing second. "What do we do now?"

Talon didn't answer. A lapse Will seemed to take personally. "Okay, that's it," he said, turning on Talon. "You and that other asshole, the one you called Black, seem to know a lot about this for a couple of random bystanders. Talk."

"I already told you," Talon said. "It's a sickness of the soul. They're being possessed." His expression turned grim. "Fully now."

"Whoa," Lauryn said, putting up her hands. "Are you for real? Like *The Exorcist* 'I'll swallow your soul' for real?"

Talon frowned, confused. "I'm not familiar with the reference, but I am speaking of demonic possession." He scowled through the tiny window at the things outside. "I don't know yet how the green substance Black used is involved, but all of the patients who were fighting it before have now been pushed fully into the arms of the enemy. If we are to have a hope of saving them, or ourselves, then we need to determine why."

Lauryn stared at him blankly for a moment before turning to Will, who was circling his finger next to his head in the universal symbol for "cuckoo." Unfortunately, that was a reference Talon *did* seem to understand, and he shot them both a quelling look.

"If you have a better explanation, I'll listen," he said, resting his sword on his shoulder. "But until then, you both might be better served if you opened your minds."

Considering they were cowering in a closet from something that looked a hell of a lot like a full-on demonic zombie outbreak, Lauryn was ready to give him that one. "Okay," she said with a deep breath. "I'll play. You called this 'a sickness of the soul.' I don't know jack about demons, but curing sickness is my job. How do we cure this one?"

"It would be easier to show you," Talon said, beckoning her over. "Come look."

Lauryn shuddered. "I'd rather not."

"Just come here," he said gently. "They can't hurt you."

She thought she heard the implied "yet" at the end of that sentence, but Talon was just standing there, looking as smooth and supremely confident as he always seemed to be. Biting her lip, Lauryn crept over to join him, standing on tiptoe to peek through the window as much as she dared.

"Look carefully," Talon said, pointing over the scrabbling claws of the ones trying to get in. "Do you see how they're all different?"

Lauryn didn't. To her eyes, the things waiting outside all just looked like crazed human patients who all happened to be exhibiting the same horrifying symptoms of bloody eyes, blue-gray skin, hallucinations, violent psychosis, and so forth. It was the same combination of symptoms she'd observed in Lenny last night, but while that was enough for the doctor in her to diagnose the problem, Talon was still waiting, so Lauryn dutifully forced herself to look beyond the obvious. To *really* look at the patients shambling beyond the door, and the more she looked, the more she realized Talon was right.

When Lenny had changed, he'd gotten huge. That definitely seemed to be happening to some of the victims outside—one in particular was so tall his head was pushing up the drop ceiling— but plenty of others were scrawny or bloated or simply deformed. They weren't all acting the same, either. Until now, Lauryn had been focused on the predatory ones that attacked, because they were the obvious threat. But while there were definitely several of these clustered around the door, just as many of the victims were hanging back in other parts of the room. Some looked to be searching the remains of their clothes for food or even prescription-pill bottles, which they devoured like they'd never get another. Still more were lying on the floor sobbing, their bodies shrunken and withered, like they were starving before Lauryn's eyes.

"I don't understand," she said at last, dropping away from the window. "They were all exposed to the same thing, and yet they all have different symptoms. How is that possible?"

"Because *they* are not all the same," Talon said, placing his hand on his chest. "In here."

Somehow, Lauryn didn't think he was talking about variations in biology. "You mean they have different souls," she whispered, her eyes going wide. "That's it, isn't it?"

"Exactly," Talon said, flashing her a proud look. "Evil enters through whatever doors we open for it. Rage, addiction, despair, selfishness—these are all weaknesses the enemy uses to break through our defenses."

Lauryn frowned. "You keep saying that—*what* enemy?"

"He means the devil," Will said, exasperated. "You know, big red dude? Horns, cloven hoofs, the whole nine yards."

"Go ahead and mock him," Talon said curtly. "But the devil is as real as any other force in the universe that drags man down. He preys on our faults and mistakes, exploiting whatever weakness we give him to pry his way into our hearts, and unless we cast him out again, he will never leave. Remember, 'The thief comes only to steal and kill and destroy.'"

Will rolled his eyes, muttering under his breath about crazy people and the idiots who listened to them, but Lauryn was no longer so sure of herself. She didn't believe in the devil any more than she believed in the tooth fairy, but it was just as stupidly dogmatic to dismiss reasonable explanations simply because they went against your preconceptions as it was to blindly believe. She wasn't willing to go so far as to accept that they were dealing with actual agents of hell, but she couldn't outright reject what Talon was saying, either.

Especially not when the evidence was clawing at the door.

"All right," she said slowly. "Let's assume for the moment that you're right and those people are possessed. How do we fix that?"

"For real, Lauryn?" Will cried, his voice furious. "You're

buying this? What are you going to do next? Call in a young priest and an old priest?"

"I just want to hear what he has to say," Lauryn snapped. "It's not like we've got another option."

"Hell yes we have another option," Will said as he pulled out his phone. "I'm calling in backup. Let's see how these things handle a SWAT team in riot gear."

Lauryn smacked his phone away. "Now who's crazy? We're dealing with an unknown contagion that passes by touch! You can't bring a bunch of nervous, gun-happy cops into that."

"That's still better than his plan," Will said, glaring at Talon before lifting his phone back to his ear. "Demons my ass."

Lauryn gave up after that, shaking her head as she turned back to Talon. "Please go on."

For some reason, her willingness to listen seemed to gratify Talon enormously. He actually cracked a smile, which seemed wildly optimistic as the monsters began to bang on the glass again. "It's a matter of scale," he explained, bracing his broad back against the door. "Most people can never be fully possessed by the devil even if they offer themselves to him. We are God's creation, and he has guards in place who protect us from such invasions."

"Protections," Lauryn repeated, remembering what he'd said on the street in front of her dad's house. "You mean . . . you?"

"I play a small part," Talon said with a calm that could have been humility or simply telling it straight. "And there are others, too, but we're not usually called upon to prevent possession. As I told the detective earlier, true possession is rare. Not because the enemy is not active—he is always looking for a way in—but because hell is very far away, locked beyond death at the bottom of the pit. Traditionally, only those who invite the enemy with open arms can offer their bodies to his lieutenants. In such cases, the lesser demons possess their hosts fully, using their human bodies to do horrible, terrible things. That said, I don't think that's what we're dealing with here. Traditional full possession takes years of focused effort and depravity, and lost as many of these addicts seem, I don't think it's possible for so many to have fallen so far all on their own all at once."

"I see," Lauryn said. "You think they were pushed." She thought about that for a moment, and then her eyes went wide. "Is that what the green stuff does? Do you think it could be some kind of demonic kick start?"

"I don't know," Talon said. "That's my best theory so far, but I fear this is bigger than what we've seen so far. Lincoln Black called the emerald liquid a catalyst, but these people were sick well before he arrived. Whatever he did merely sped up the process. A process, I'm certain, that was done *to* them." He glared over his shoulder out the safety-glass window where the patients' black claws were still scraping. "Whatever other sins they might be guilty of, these people didn't invite this evil. They were merely weak, and that weakness allowed someone to push them over the edge. But if they were pushed in against their will, that means we might be able to push them back out."

He *was* talking about an exorcism, Lauryn realized with a start. Even more surprising was how much the pieces were starting to click together in her head. As if what he was saying actually made a certain kind of sense.

"This possession," she said, following the logic. "We've already determined it's contagious through fluid contact—bites and so forth. If that's true, then this thing is acting like more like a disease than a drug."

Talon nodded. "A sickness of the soul."

"Right," she said, getting excited. "And diseases can be *cured*. We just need the right medicine."

"It's not the common cold," grumbled Will, who was apparently still listening.

"Good," Lauryn said. "The common cold still isn't cured, but I've already seen something work on this once." She turned to Talon. "Back in the alley, you saved Lenny and my hands by pouring something over us. What was that?"

"Blessed water."

Even when she was trying her hardest to roll with it, that was enough to make Lauryn wince. "Of course it was," she muttered, taking a deep breath. She couldn't quite believe she was actually going to say this, but in for a penny, in for a pound. "Got any more?"

Will finally looked up from his phone. "Holy water, Lauryn? *Really?* Are you going to try and tell me they're vampires next?"

"I'm not saying I believe in *all* this," Lauryn said quickly. "But I was there last night, and it worked. I don't know how, I don't know why, but I saw it happen, and I've got the burns to prove it. You know the saying: if it's stupid and it works, it's not stupid."

"This is," Will assured her.

Oddly, Talon looked just as doubtful. "It's not a bad plan," he said. "But there's a problem."

At Lauryn's questioning look, he reached into his coat and pulled out the plastic bottle he'd used on her fingers yesterday, turning it sideways under the fluorescent lights so she could see just how little water was left inside. "I haven't had time to refill it from yesterday," he said. "But even if it was filled to the brim, there wouldn't be enough for all of them."

"Gee, too bad this didn't happen near the reflecting pools out front, then," Will said sarcastically. "You could have baptized them all. Just dunked their sins away."

Talon looked deeply offended by that remark, but it gave Lauryn an idea. "For this," she said, tapping Talon's empty bottle. "What do you need besides water?"

"Just prayer and faith," Talon said, puzzled. "Why do you ask?"

Lauryn turned and reached into Will's jacket pocket. Sure enough, the lighter she remembered him always carrying around back when they were dating was still there, and she pulled it out with a grin.

"If I get you water," she said, flicking on the flame, "can you do the rest?"

She hadn't even explained her plan yet, but Talon's face broke into a triumphant smile. "Through God, all things are possible," he said proudly, straightening up to his full height. "What do we need to do?"

Lauryn pointed through the door's glass window at the automated sprayers for the hospital's fire system attached to the ceiling outside. "We use those."

"No," Will said automatically. "Absolutely not. I put up with this soul-flu-possession nonsense because you wanted to hear it, Lauryn, but this is where I draw the line. You are *not* going out there and risking your life for some holy water hocus-pocus!"

"Better than sitting in here waiting for those cops you just called to come in and shoot up my patients!"

"Exactly!" Will shouted. "They are your *patients* because you are a *doctor*, and doctors don't believe in this crap!"

"But they do believe in saving the people under their care," Lauryn said hotly, clenching her fist around his lighter. "I don't know if Talon's telling the truth or not, but I absolutely believe that whatever is happening to these people is not their fault. Even if it was, it wouldn't matter. The moment they entered this hospital, they became my patients. If there's a way to help them, *any* way, then I have to try. That's the whole reason I became a doctor!"

By the time she finished, Will looked like he was going to explode again, but Lauryn didn't give him a chance. "Let's go," she said, turning to Talon.

"Are you sure?" he asked quietly. "The detective is right—

this is going to be dangerous. I'll do my best to keep them off you, but even I can't be everywhere at once."

"Then I'll have to be fast," Lauryn said, trying to sound confident. "But we have to do something, and quick, because there's only two ways this ends when Will's SWAT team shows up: the patients bite the cops, or the cops shoot everyone. Either way, lots of people are going to die, and I'm not about to let that happen on my watch. Not if there's any possible way of avoiding it." She glanced down at the lighter gripped in her hands. "I say we give it a try. I mean, what have we got to lose?"

"Our lives," Will snapped, grabbing her hand. "You're not going, Lauryn."

"She is free to go wherever she wants to go," Talon said, dropping his own hand to his sword hilt. "God commands us to 'be strong and courageous, for the Lord your God is with you wherever you go.'"

Will sneered. "Yeah, well, God also had some very different things to say about the role of women."

"God's word has been misinterpreted from time to time," Talon said calmly, ignoring the barb. "She is free to go, Detective. You may not yet believe, but if you try to stop her from following what she knows to be right, believe that I will stop you."

There was no anger in Talon's voice when he said this. No malice at all. Only a conviction as stalwart and solid as the cement floor under their feet. Even Will must have heard it, because he looked away with a curse. Lauryn, on the other hand, had started to grin. She'd always had a love-hate relationship with Will's protective streak, but having a guy with a sword on your side definitely made it more bearable, even if he did talk like a walking Bible.

"That settles it, then," she said, her grin fading as the grim reality of what she was about to do set in. With a final bracing breath, she walked over to place her hand on the red fire alarm lever beside the door. "In or out, Will?"

Will swore again, and then he stomped to her side. "Fine!" he said, gripping his gun with both hands. "You're both crazy, which means I'm outnumbered, so let's just get it over with."

Lauryn flashed him a final, thankful look before turning back to the fire alarm. "On three," she said. "One, two—"

She flipped the lock and pulled it on two, an old doctor trick. She wasn't sure going early would work as well with this as it did with giving shots, but it was too late to change her mind. The alarm was already blaring, filling the tiny room with flashing strobes. Talon grabbed the door at the same time, yanking it open so fast the monsters outside tumbled in, landing at his feet in a scrabbling mass. Even thought it had been her idea, seeing them *right there*—inside the room that had been their sanctuary—was enough to make Lauryn freeze. She was still staring dumbly when Talon's deep voice thundered in her ear.

"Go!"

The order worked, and Lauryn charged forward, jumping over the piled monsters even as they pushed off the floor to grab hold of her coat. If she'd been alone, that would have been the end, but as he'd promised, Talon was at her side, swinging his sword like a bat to knock the transformed patients away from her. She had a vague thought that maybe she shouldn't be happy Talon might end up chopping off the body parts of her patients, but she had other things to worry about. At least she didn't hear Will using his gun. She couldn't check to look, though—she just kept running toward the nearest sprinkler.

Somehow she got there. Hands shaking, she clambered up on top of an empty gurney and held the lighter over her head, flicking on the flame and pushing right up against the mechanical heat detector in the sprinkler's nozzle. She wasn't actually sure how much heat was needed to set it off, but the answer was clearly less than she'd thought. Seconds after she pushed the lighter against it, the sprinklers went off. *All* of them, all at once, drenching the whole room in a spray of water so powerful, it felt like a rain of needles.

"Got it!" Lauryn shouted, ducking her head against the pounding water. "Do it!"

"Not alone!" Talon shouted back, grabbing her hand. "You have to pray with me."

Lauryn couldn't believe this. *This wasn't information he could have given me* before *we were surrounded by monsters?* "Are you serious?" she screamed. "I can't pray! I don't even believe in God!"

"You have to," Talon said, yanking her down off the gurney. "You wanted a miracle, remember?" He stabbed his sword in the floor in front of him and fell to his knees, dragging her down as well. "If you want something, you have to ask. Pray, and you shall receive."

Feeling like an idiot, Lauryn dropped to the ground.

"What the hell are you doing, Lauryn?" Will screamed.

I wish I had a clue.

She hadn't even gone through the *motions* of prayer since her father had stopped forcing her to in the eighth grade, and before then she'd never actually said a word to God on her own precisely because she'd never believed in him. Or, at least, she'd thought she hadn't. But down there on the ground next to Talon with an army of wet and extremely pissed-off maybe-demons bearing down on them, Lauryn discovered that the old adage about there being no atheists in foxholes was truer than she'd realized. So, with nothing else for it, she ducked her head, squeezing her eyes tight as she muttered the first real, sincere prayer of her life.

Please, she whispered. *Please, please, please.*

As prayers went, it was a pretty bad one. She wasn't even really sure what she was saying "please" for—healing her patients, their own survival, or all of the above—but she just kept saying it, begging whoever was listening to help them, *save* them.

To anyone else, it wouldn't have been much, but for Lauryn, it was everything. She'd lived her whole life proving she could do things by herself. Whether it was at school or with her father, she never asked for help. Never begged. Even when she was neck-deep in more work than anyone could possibly do, she'd kept her nose down and worked through. Not because she thought she would make it, but because admitting she needed someone else's work, someone else's *power* to achieve her goals was a far greater failure than actually failing.

That was how she'd lived her life, how she held her head up high. Everything she'd achieved—her grades, her place at the top of her class, her dream of being a doctor—she'd gotten on her own. But not this. This wasn't a test or an interview or a double shift. This was a disaster completely beyond her ability to handle, and if she didn't want her patients to die—if *she* didn't want to die—she needed more than she could give. She needed *help*, and as her father always said, the only way to get that was to ask.

She only hoped someone was listening.

Please, she begged again, squeezing her eyes even tighter. Please.

The words poured out of her, but when she held her breath to listen, there was no answer. She didn't feel any different, definitely didn't feel a miracle, but just as the despair began to wrap around her mind, Lauryn realized that the room had gone quiet.

And, more importantly, she was still *alive*.

That was enough of a miracle to make her eyes pop open, but it still took her several seconds to make sense of what they saw.

She was on her knees in an inch of water in the middle of the destroyed ward, and she was not alone. All around them, fallen over in the water like they'd simply gone to sleep, were the people who, a few seconds ago, had been trying to kill them. But the real shocker was that they looked like people again. There were no more bloody eyes, no more strange blue-gray flesh. Just hundreds of normal people lying still and calm on the floor under the still-spraying water, their wet faces slack with the deep relief of someone finally freed from pain.

It was so surreal, Lauryn had to look at Will to make sure she wasn't dreaming, but he looked as shocked as she was. The only person who didn't look surprised was Talon. He just looked proud, rising to his feet before holding out his hand to her.

Lauryn took it with shaking fingers. "What just happened?"

"A miracle," Talon said, pulling her to her feet.

Lauryn wasn't sure what to make of that. Honestly, she wasn't sure standing was such a good idea, either. Barely a second after Talon had lifted her up, she went right back down, her head swimming. In the back of her mind, the doctor part of her realized this was most likely a delayed reaction to shock, quite common given the fight or flight stress she'd just been under. But knowing what it was didn't make the effect any less severe. All she wanted to do was lie back down and go to sleep, and before she could force herself not to, Lauryn did just that, collapsing into a heap beside her patients just as the first officers of the backup Will had requested came barging into the room.

MY SOUL WAITS FOR THE LORD MORE THAN WATCHMEN FOR THE MORNING.
—*PSALM 130*

8
WATCHMEN

Will stood in the middle of the wrecked burn ward clutching his Styrofoam cup of terrible hospital coffee. Truth be told, he didn't even like coffee. He was just holding on to it because if he set the cup down, one of the crowd of nervous officers behind him would immediately try to get him another, and he had too much to deal with already.

It was now eleven in the morning, over three hours since he, Lauryn, and Talon had escaped the pharmaceutical closet and the whole of Mercy Hospital had become a crime scene for the weirdest case he'd ever investigated. If it wasn't for the fact that the whole thing had been caught on the hospital's security cameras, Will wasn't sure he'd have believed his own story.

But the strangest twist of all was that, despite being one of the largest violent incidents in Chicago history, which was saying something, there'd been no casualties. Every single one of the patients and the hospital staff they'd attacked had survived.

Normally, Will would have called that a miracle, but after Talon's supernatural mumbo jumbo, that word had been stricken from his vocabulary. So far as he was concerned, what had happened here this morning was nothing but an extremely unlikely combination of very good and very bad luck. Unfortunately, "luck" wasn't a story that went over well with the top brass, and as the witnessing officer, Will was in the hot seat to come up with a better explanation. He just wished he had one.

"Tannenbaum."

Speak of the devil—

Will turned around with a sigh to see Victor Korigan walking at top speed down the hospital hallway. The chief of police must not have gone to bed yet, because he was still wearing the same tux Will had seen him in last night. Yet somehow his dark eyes were alert and sharp as a hawk's as he strode toward Will across the puddles the fire sprinklers had left on the floor. "You'd better have a damn good explanation for this."

Will crossed his arms over his chest. "If you read my report—"

"If by report you mean the six sentences they gave me on my way over, I've read it," Korigan said. "What I want to know is why you were here to write a report in the first place. I ordered you to go to bed."

"I *went* to bed," Will said, which was technically the truth. "Then I got a call from a contact about a bunch of drug cases and came to investigate."

The chief's scowl deepened. "Alone? With no backup?"

"How was I supposed to know it would end like this?" Will said with a shrug. "I work Vice, not riot squad. And I *did* call for backup once the situation warranted it."

Korigan didn't miss a beat. "So why didn't you wait for it? We've got footage of you helping the doctor girl set off the sprinklers on three separate cameras. How do you explain that?"

"That was her idea," Will said quickly. "I only went along to keep her safe. You can't let a civilian run into danger like that."

"So it was just common heroics? And the fact that she's your former girlfriend has nothing to do with it?"

Will clamped his mouth shut, and the police chief sighed. "What about the man who was with you?" he asked, changing the subject. "The one wearing a sword. What's his story?"

"I wish I knew," Will said, and unlike everything else, that was the honest truth. Of all the things that had gone wrong this morning, Talon was the most frustrating. Will had fully intended to take him in for interrogation, but then Lauryn had fainted, and by the time he'd finished making sure she wasn't dead, Talon had vanished. None of the cameras had caught a thing, either. It was like the crazy man had just poofed into thin air.

Given how the police chief was looking at him, Will couldn't help but think his career was about to do the same, but Korigan surprised him. Just as Will was bracing for the old "hand over your badge," the police chief turned back to the crime scene with a resigned shake of his head.

"Done is done," he said bitterly. "The important thing now is that we get this situation under control, and that starts with a story people can understand."

Will frowned. "A story?" When Korigan nodded, he sneered. "We don't *need* stories. We have the truth. On camera, no less."

"Why the hell do you think I want a story?" the chief said. "I've had the mayor, the governor, and every major news outlet in the country crawling up my ass by turns all morning over this. Unfortunately, your name got out before I was able to get things on lockdown. Everyone knows by now that you were the man on the scene, which means I need you to make a new statement. Something that will make all of this make sense."

"But I already wrote my report," Will reminded him. "That's what happened. There's nothing else to say."

"Isn't there?" Korigan asked, flashing Will the same smooth smile he used for the cameras. "Traumatic events like this are famous for coloring how we remember them. I'm sure after you've rested a bit, you'll see things differently. Put this whole tragic event in a . . . new perspective, shall we say?"

"A new perspective," Will repeated, the cold coffee rippling as his hands began to shake with suppressed rage. "Funny, that sounds a lot like you're asking me to lie on my report. *Sir.*"

"Don't be ridiculous," the chief said. "That would be illegal, and I do not appreciate you making that accusation, Detective. I want the truth as much as you do, but the hallmark of a true story is that it makes sense. Now I'm sure you wrote that report to the best of your ability, but when memories—especially ones formed under traumatic circumstances—go up against facts, facts have to win out. Take this Dr. Lauryn Jefferson, for instance. She's been interviewed about this morning's events by several experts now, and every time, she claims her patients were under the effects of an unknown, extremely powerful hallucinogenic drug that is transferable through fluid contact, like rabies, and yet is also somehow dispersed by water. She's stuck to this story despite all of our narcotics experts telling her that the sort of drug she's describing is chemically impossible. Clearly, this otherwise excellent doctor is suffering under a great deal of stress, which has made her a highly unreliable witness. I've already talked to her superiors about it, and the hospital's agreed with me that she should be placed on medical leave for her own safety. I've had her statement tossed out as unreliable for the same reason. We can't be too careful with such a serious matter of public safety."

"Is *that* what you're calling it?" Will asked. "Because to me, it sounds like you had Lauryn's boss put her on psych leave so you'd have an excuse to throw out a witness story you didn't like."

"No—it's a witness story *you* shouldn't like," Korigan said calmly. "Perhaps it's slipped your notice that I'm saving your ex-girlfriend's career. I even convinced the hospital not to press charges against her for causing nearly a million dollars in water damage during her federally unlawful misuse of a fire-control system. That's a whole lotta nice I don't have to be. I'd think you'd be grateful."

"*Grateful?* For which part of this farce? Lauryn's *not* crazy. She's just reporting what she saw. What we *all* saw. It's on the damn cameras!"

"You've seen enough security footage to know cameras don't tell the whole story," the chief said, dropping his voice. "If you'd get off your high horse for one second, Tannenbaum, you'd see I'm doing you both a huge favor here. Your story makes just as little sense as hers, which is why I'm giving you a chance to re-think if that's *really* what you saw before this craziness becomes an embarrassing mark on your record."

Will opened his mouth to argue, but the chief didn't give him a chance. "People see a lot of crazy things when their lives are in danger. You're a good cop, Tannenbaum, but if you can't see that the report you wrote is some *X-Files* nonsense, then you need to go on medical leave even more than your doctor does. Now I'm going to make this as easy as possible for you. You can either rewrite your story of what happened here into something that actually makes sense, or you can stick to your guns and have your report thrown out as the ramblings of a deeply traumatized victim. Either way, your version of *this*—" he waved his hand at the soggy ward with its overturned beds "—is never getting out."

"You say that," Will growled. "But this isn't the kind of thing you can bury. There were *hundreds* of victims—"

"Whose testimonies are all questionable," Korigan finished. "Our experts are already calling this a mass delusion caused by the unusual potency of Chicago's new street drugs. How else can you explain so many people experiencing what was clearly not possible?"

"It's not a delusion!" Will yelled. "I'm absolutely clean, and I saw it, too. These things *did* happen."

"Of course they did," Korigan said, placing a sympathetic hand on Will's shoulder, which only pissed him off more.

"I'm not crazy!"

"Maybe," the chief replied. "Maybe not. But as of right now, you're on personal leave for medical reasons. If you know what's good for you, you'll go home, get some sleep, and put all this nastiness behind you. When you recover and realize how ridiculous you're being, you can come back to doing the excellent police work I expect from my officers. Do we have an understanding?"

Will understood perfectly. The police chief had a mess he couldn't explain, so he was burying it, and since Will refused to help shovel, he was getting benched. But this was one of those times when Korigan's slickness wouldn't save him. He might think he had everything tied up by discrediting all the witnesses and feeding the press a fairy tale, but Will wasn't a team player when it came to cover-ups. He didn't give a damn about his department's reputation. He'd become a cop because he wanted to protect and serve the people who actually needed it, which did not include his boss or the politicians who'd put him in power.

But while Will was more than happy to bust Korigan's cover-up wide open, he hadn't survived a decade of police work by being stupid. Bucking the system when things were this tense was a good way to get put down hard, so he decided to save the fight for later. He couldn't quite make himself pretend to be grateful that Korigan was "saving his career," but he managed to accept his medical leave with something like dignity as he made a show of packing up to go home.

He wasn't sure if it worked entirely. Korigan looked deeply

suspicious at Will's sudden change of heart, but the seeming surrender was still enough to get the chief off his back and out of his crime scene. The moment Korigan went back upstairs, Will dropped the act, leaving the other cops to finish up as he went off in search of Lauryn.

Tannenbaum was going to be a problem.

All the other officers had been more than happy to let the chief deal with the crazy mess that was the last few hours. It actually helped that no one could make heads or tails of what the cameras had caught inside the Mercy burn ward. Footage that made no sense was easy to write off, because cops, like mercenaries, were practical creatures. They didn't like things they couldn't explain. Mysteries meant extra work for everyone, possibly even federal involvement, so when Korigan had offered extra hazard pay in exchange for sweeping this morning's insanity under the rug, every officer had taken it no questions asked. Tannenbaum was the only outlier, an expected complication given his sterling reputation. But troublesome as that was, even he could be put down, especially since his ex was the other witness. All Korigan had to do was paint him as a desperate man going along with his former girlfriend's crazy story in an attempt to get back into her good graces, and no one but the conspiracy theorists would believe a word he said.

Unfortunately, setups like that took time, and time was exactly what Victor Korigan didn't have this morning. His hands were already beyond full dealing with the army of reporters that had besieged Mercy Hospital.

So far—thanks to a statement from Mercy Hospital's CEO, who'd gone along with whatever Korigan told him in return for the police keeping the press off their property—the mass-delusion story was holding. But while the press ate up the sordid and sensational story of crazed junkies driven psycho by bad drugs, it also put pressure on Korigan to crack down, which ran directly against his promise to St. Luke to keep the Z3X flowing. He was strategizing about how to reconcile the two and keep control of both situations as he jogged down the steps toward the underground deck his officers had claimed for their vehicles during the Chicago PD's occupation of the hospital's main building. But when he opened the door to the armored SUV that served as his official public vehicle during situations like this, he realized someone was already sitting in his seat.

"Jesus *Christ*."

Korigan jumped a foot in the air, pulling his gun automatically as Lincoln Black turned languidly to look at him from his cozy spot in Korigan's back seat, his sword beside him and his feet propped up between the front seats, where Korigan's driver and guard should have been waiting.

"Where are my people?" Korigan snapped.

"Taking a break," Black said, grinning. "Did you see my handiwork?"

Korigan lowered his gun with a sneer. "If you mean your *mess*, then yes. I saw it, and I'll be telling our mutual employer that you are actively jeopardizing his operation."

The threat only made Black's grin go wider. "How do you figure that? You think St. Luke doesn't know what his drug does?"

"*He* does," Korigan snapped. "But *I* don't. You didn't tell me Z3X turned druggies into *zombies*. Do you know how many fires I had to light under asses to keep this story from exploding all over us?"

"Nope," Black said, sitting up. "Don't know, and don't care. But you've got no cause to complain. Pulling off miracles like this cover-up is why you're getting paid the big bucks, isn't it? And speaking of."

He pulled a fat manila envelope out from under the white lab coat he was still wearing as he finished, wiggling it back and forth in front of Korigan like a bone in front of a dog before the mercenary snatched it out of his hands. "Is this what I think it is?"

"Your invitation to the ball," Black said, spreading his arms wide. "And I'm your fairy godfather."

Korigan ignored him. He ripped open the envelope to grab the thick stack of legal papers inside, reading through the papers as fast as his eyes could go. Sure enough, though, it was all there. Everything St. Luke had promised—control over his pharmaceutical empire and shell companies, all his wealth and property—it was all there in black and white, dated to be transferred to Korigan at the end of the week.

"What happens at the end of the week?"

The assassin wagged his fingers at him and hopped out of the huge SUV as nimbly as a cat. "Let's not ruin this by getting nosy. St. Luke is pleased with how you've handled things so far. Keep it up, and this'll all be over before you know it. Now." He tilted his head. "What's the word on Talon?"

The chief blinked, confused. "Who?"

"Big dude with the sword."

Korigan glanced pointedly at the archaic weapon clutched in Black's hands. "I thought that was you."

The assassin actually laughed at that. "I'm starting to like you."

"I could care less."

"Now you've gone and hurt my feelings."

Korigan didn't dignify that with a reply. He just reached for his phone, bringing up what little his boys had been able to scrape together about the third player in this morning's fiasco. The large black man with the sword who'd stuck to Dr. Jefferson like he was her own private guardian angel.

"There's not much to tell. We tried to do facial recognition on him using the pictures we scraped from the security cameras, but the quality's too low to get a match. And that's assuming he's even in our database. I've got an APB out on him as a person of interest. If he pokes his head outside anywhere in Chicago, my cops will pick him up."

"They can *try*," Black said with a snort. "If Talon could be cornered by pigs like yours, my life wouldn't be nearly as interesting." He frowned. "He was pretty hung up on that doctor chick. What's her story?"

"Everyone in the world seems to be hung up on Dr. Jefferson," Korigan said irritably, reaching into the car's glove box for the dossier his secretary had put together for him. "This is everything we've got. Knock yourself out."

Black snatched the folder out of his hand and flipped it open, poring over the pages with more attention than Korigan had seen the crazy bastard give anything else. "She's a regular Goody Two-Shoes, isn't she?" he said with a laugh. "Preacher's daughter, volunteer work with low-income patients, treating the homeless. No wonder the old man likes her." He flipped the page, and his face lit up. "And she has a *brother*."

Korigan didn't see how that changed anything, but Black was grinning like he'd just hit the jackpot. "I'm keeping this," he said, tucking Lauryn's folder under his arm. "Good work, Vic. I'm starting to be glad St. Luke ignored me when I told him to kill you."

Korigan fought the urge to come back at him. Black was clearly one of those people who loved screwing with others, but putting him in his place wasn't worth endangering his mission. Whatever airs he put on, at the end of the day, he was nothing but St. Luke's attack dog, the thug who kept the illegal side of his drug business in line. If he wanted to waste his time on the Jefferson girl's drama, Korigan was happy to let him. He'd already done his part to discredit her testimony, which meant Korigan's ass was covered. He had bigger problems right now, anyway, like the phone that was buzzing in his pocket. Probably the mayor again. That would have to be dealt with, but before Korigan stuck his head in any more bear traps, there was one thing he had to get straight.

"Don't mess with me again."

Black glanced up from Lauryn's file with an amused expression. "You're going to have to be more specific."

"You know what I'm talking about," Korigan said. "I know you think I'm just the cover guy, but St. Luke wouldn't be giving me this—" he held up the papers promising him St. Luke's fortune "—if your mission didn't depend on the work I do. So it doesn't help me when you keep info from me. You've already burned me once by not telling me how bad this Z3X crap would look before you blew it up in a public place, *or* that it was contagious."

That was what Korigan was most pissed about, actually. Drugs he could contain, didn't matter how crazy they made you. But drugs that spread like a plague? That got people panicked, and panic couldn't be reasoned with. Not with drastic measures at least, and good as Korigan was, even he had his limits.

"I don't care what St. Luke is doing to this city," he continued. "So long as I get paid, I don't care if the two of you plan to turn Chicago into your own druggie zoo. But if I'm going to do my job, you will not pull a stunt like this again."

By the time he finished, the grin had fallen off Black's face. "What makes you think you can tell me what to do? You're just the hired help."

"And you're just a psycho on a leash," Korigan said, standing his ground so Black would see he wasn't intimidated. "So I guess we're both St. Luke's bitch. But let's get one thing real straight: I know all of your boss's secrets. You guys screw me over again, and I will not hesitate to burn everything I have to screw him back. Get me?"

"Oh, I read you loud and clear," Black said as the smile slipped back onto his face. "That's why we picked you. You're a man who's used to having his back to the wall. But relax, Chief. You got nothing to worry about. Haven't you heard that the devil takes care of his own?"

Korigan didn't know what he was talking about, and didn't care. "You do whatever you want, I don't care, just don't get in my way. I'm going to get your boss his cover, but you pull a stunt like this again without giving me warning, and St. Luke's going to have to find himself a new dog."

"Are you talking about you or me now? Know what—it doesn't matter. Just keep telling yourself that you can do something to hurt St. Luke—or me—sunshine," Black said, turning away. "Now if you're done beating your chest, I've got an old friend to check in on. I'll swing by when I'm done to pick you up for the factory tour."

Korigan blinked. "What?"

The swordsman glanced over his shoulder. "You wanted in on St. Luke's narcotics operation. That's *my* turf. But I'll be happy to show you the ropes. Assuming your delicate stomach can handle it."

That was right. In his rush to keep this Mercy business on lockdown, Korigan had completely forgotten he'd demanded access to St. Luke's illegal businesses as well as the legit ones. Now that Black had reminded him, though, he was ready to go. It was obvious at this point that his ignorance about the realities of Z3X was a critical weakness, which meant it would have to go.

"I'll make time this afternoon," he said. "Be ready by three."

"I'll be ready when I'm ready," Black said, walking off into the dark deck. "Just make sure you are."

Korigan rolled his eyes. He'd had enough of the pissing

contest talking with Lincoln Black always turned into. But when he looked back to get the final word in, the parking deck was empty.

He turned in a circle, scanning the dark for the assassin he knew had to be there. Even creepy bastards like Black couldn't actually vanish into thin air. But no matter how hard he searched, he didn't find a thing. He was still looking when his driver and guard reappeared, laughing and joking with coffees in hand. They shut up the moment they saw their boss, but Korigan was too distracted to care. He just climbed in the car and told them to get him back to the office, pulling out his phone as he buckled in to resume cleaning up the epic mess Lincoln Black had left for him.

Lauryn sat hunched in a hard chair, watching the clock on the wall slowly crawl through yet another hour of what had to be the longest day of her life.

After setting off the sprinklers and passing out like an anemic, she'd woken up to find Talon gone, cops everywhere, and herself as the prime subject of interest for the entire city of Chicago. Just in the last three hours, she'd been visited by the hospital president, the chief of staff, the hospital's psychiatrist, the chief of police, three separate detectives, and a forensic investigator. Every single one of them had come into the visitation room the police had turned into a makeshift cell and asked her a dozen different versions of what were really the same three questions: How had she avoided being infected, why had she turned on the sprinklers, and where was the man who'd been with her?

Every time, Lauryn had given the facts as she knew them. No matter how skeptical the person interviewing her looked, she'd tried her best to tell the truth exactly as it had happened. This was partially because she'd been raised to be an honest person, but mostly because Lauryn didn't feel she had anything to lie about. Thanks to her and Talon's actions, everyone from the burn ward—patients and staff—had escaped relatively unharmed, and crazy as she knew it sounded when she told the story, Lauryn felt that was something to be proud of.

Or, at least, that's how she'd felt at the start. But as the morning dragged on and she was forced to tell the same story over and over, doubt began to creep into Lauryn's mind. It was all still there, the memories vivid and clear in the way only really traumatic events could be, but the further she got from the actual crisis, the more decisions that had made perfect sense at the time—trusting Talon, or running out into a room full of infection cases with zero protective gear to douse them in *holy water*—now just seemed plain old crazy. She stuck to them anyway, because, again, that was what had happened. But with every pitying look and skeptical frown from the parade of experts, Lauryn's doubt kindled and grew until she was no longer sure she wasn't as delusional as everyone else clearly thought she was.

By the time noon rolled around, she'd pretty much resigned herself to living in the tiny visitation room forever. Then, without warning, one of the hospital admins had come in to tell her the board had decided to place her on medical leave, and that she was free to go home. Lauryn had made him repeat that last part, because in her experience, suspected delusional patients didn't just get sent home. But the man was quite clear: citing lack of evidence, Police Chief Korigan had tabled the investigation into the events of the burn ward until further notice, and both the Chicago PD and the Mercy Hospital System CEO had agreed that everyone involved was to be given time off to recover, including her. Provided, of course, that she signed a gag order preventing her from talking to the press.

Even after he'd handed her the paperwork, she still hadn't believed it. She knew the Mercy Hospital disaster-recovery plan inside and out, and nowhere was there anything like this. *Especially* the gag order. But while the professional in her was incensed at the gross breach in protocol and the obvious attempt to hush things up, the rest of her was exhausted and more than happy to do whatever it took to go home.

She'd just finished signing the papers and was collecting her things from the police officer who'd been tasked with guarding her door when Will found her.

"Lauryn!"

She winced as he yelled her name, and then winced even more when he grabbed her arm and dragged her around the corner toward the exit.

"What are you doing?" she said, yanking her arm out of his hand at last.

"Getting you somewhere we can talk," he said, grabbing her again. "We don't have much time."

"We don't need time," she reminded him, pulling her arm free yet again. "And stop grabbing my arm like I'm your property. Anyway, there's nothing to talk about. I've already told every person in authority everything that's happened to me over the last twenty-four hours in triplicate. Trust me, there is *nothing* left to say."

Will glanced up and down the empty hall before fixing her with a glare. "Nothing?" he repeated. "So you think this whole 'letting you go home under a gag order and canceling the investigation' thing is totally normal, completely on the up and up?"

He had a point there, but what did he expect her to do about it? "It's done, Will," she said, shoulders slumping. "Sure, they're closing things up kind of quick, but what else can they do? Literally nothing about this situation makes sense. Even *I* don't believe my testimony anymore, and I lived it." She shook her head. "I know you're a detective and fundamentally incapable of letting things go, but everything ended up okay in the end. Maybe we should just leave it at that."

"*Leave it at that?*" he said, eyes going wide. "Chief Korigan just kicked me off the case—put me on *leave*—because I wouldn't change my report. He's burying this right in front of us, and you want me to just let that go?"

Lauryn opened her mouth to say . . . she wasn't sure, actually. In the end, though, it didn't matter, because Will had already cut her off. "There's something going on, Lauryn," he said, dropping his voice even lower. "Korigan's a brand-new police chief. Solving a case this big should be his ticket to fame, so why is he burying it instead of putting together a big task force to take out the drug dealers he's blaming it on? It doesn't make sense. Not unless he has skin in the game, too."

She rolled her eyes. "Will—"

"I'm not wearing a tinfoil hat, Lauryn. Trust me, I know how I sound, but I've been a cop for a long time. I've learned to listen to my gut, and right now every instinct I have is telling me that all of this is all connected. I've always known Korigan was a snake, but combine the appearance of this new drug with the unprecedented takeover of Chicago's narcotics market *and* the fact that we've got a police chief all but blocking the investigation, and even you have to admit there's got to be something bigger going on."

Lauryn bit her lip. She hadn't thought of it all together like that before. "I admit it's weird," she said at last. "But 'weird' happens all the time. Not everything has to be connected. Coincidences *do* happen, you know."

"Not like this," he said, moving closer. "Look, if there's anything I've learned as a detective, it's that nothing happens without a reason. When things don't add up, it's only because there's something you don't know, not because the world has suddenly become irrational. We just have to figure out how everything's connected."

Lauryn blinked in surprise. The logic Will was describing was exactly how she approached her own problem cases as a doctor. But while her own instinct was telling her to chase it, she was tired. So, so tired and sick of things she couldn't explain that it was hard to find any enthusiasm for Will's hunt.

"You're not wrong," she admitted. "But how are you going to do any of that? You just told me you were off the case. What are you going to do? Detective out of your apartment?"

"Technically, I'm only on medical leave," Will said. "But just because I'm down doesn't mean I'm out. It's still my job to protect this city." He glared at her. "You more than anyone should know about what it means to take an oath."

Lauryn winced. *Bull's-eye.* Will saw it, too, and he went in for the kill. "Someone knows what happened this morning, Lauryn," he said quietly. "I'm going to find them, and I need your help."

That was what she'd been afraid he'd say, and her shoulders slumped. "My help with what?" she asked, glancing pointedly at one of the hospital's ubiquitous TVs where the news was still running constant coverage of what they were calling "Havoc at the Hospital." "The whole city's seen the news by now. All the networks are reporting Chief Korigan's story about it being a bad batch of drugs, and why not? That certainly makes more sense than our stories. Face it, we're the weak links here. We can't do anything more than we've done already to prove our side of the story, even though it's the truth. Every contact you talk to is going to know you've got no leverage on this. Even if you do find someone who knows what's going on, they're not going to tell you anything."

"They won't," Will agreed grimly. "But it doesn't matter. I exhausted all of my normal contacts last night anyway, which is why I'm going straight to the horse's mouth. I want to question Talon."

Lauryn couldn't believe her ears? "Talon?" she repeated breathlessly. "But . . . you didn't believe anything he said. You called him crazy!"

"He *is* crazy. But that doesn't mean he doesn't know things," Will said. "I don't know what his story is or how he managed to vanish like that while the rest of us got caught, but I'd bet you a hundred bucks he'll be back, and he'll come to you."

There, at least, they agreed. But while Will sounded excited about cornering him, Lauryn would be perfectly happy if she went the rest of her life without having to see the mysterious Bible-quoting swordsman ever again. Given Talon's habit of popping up out of nowhere, she didn't think she'd be that lucky, but for now at least, things were slipping back toward relatively normal, and Lauryn was determined to keep them that way. At least until she'd gotten some sleep.

"You do what you want," she said tiredly. "I'm going home and going to bed. The papers are already filed to put me on medical leave due to a mental health crisis, and frankly I don't think that diagnosis is too far off. Maybe after some sleep, things will start to come together for me, but until then, I'm done."

"You can't just tap out on this," Will said as she turned to walk away. *"Lauryn!"*

"I'm done, Will," she said without looking back. "You should be, too. Go home."

She said that last part in her most serious voice, the one she normally reserved for telling patients their lifestyle choices were killing them, which, in a way, his were. Will had been hyper-focused on cases for as long as she'd known him. It was what had broken them up in the first place, but this time he was going too far, and she refused to help shove him any further down that self-destructive path. He really could lose his job over this, and while he might not care about that right now, Lauryn knew exactly how much being a detective meant to him. Just because she was tired of always coming in second to his work didn't mean she'd stopped caring about him, and right now, anyone could see he was in over his head. From the dark circles under his eyes, he needed rest even more than she did. But like most stubborn patients, telling him so would only make him balk, so Lauryn did the only thing she could do. She turned away, putting her back to him like a wall as she marched down the hall.

Cruel as it made her feel, it worked. Behind her, she heard Will start to follow, but then he stopped with a curse. When she glanced over her shoulder, he was rooted in place, glaring at her like he was trying to make her come back with sheer force of will.

Lauryn gave him a final scowl and kept walking. It was better this way, she told herself, picking up the pace. She might not want him to lose his job, but Will wasn't part of her life anymore. If he wanted to risk everything chasing after a mysterious event that the people in power clearly wanted to forget, that was his business. She wished him the best, she really did, but she had her own career, life, and sanity to think about, all of which she'd already nearly ruined with a morning's worth of sticking to her guns. Right now, her best hope was to go home, get some sleep, and hope that when she woke up tomorrow, everyone would still be in agreement that this whole mess was nothing but a blip of temporary mass hysteria too strange to go on her permanent record. It was a long shot, but it was the only hope she had at this point, and Lauryn clung to it like a lifeline, focusing on putting one foot in front of the other as she walked out of the hospital and through the gently falling snow toward the doctors' lot where her dad's car was waiting beneath a fresh layer of powder.

The moment she saw it, her whole body slumped. In the crazy

rush of this morning's disasters, she'd completely forgotten she'd run off with her father's prized Buick. Now she'd have to return it, which meant there was zero chance she'd be going home to her own apartment. The cops had only just given her back her phone, so she hadn't had a chance to check it yet, but even if Will was right and this was all being covered up, there was no *way* a medical disaster involving hundreds of people wasn't going to be all over the news. Her dad was probably having a fit at this very moment, which ironically made her feel a little better. Maxwell was the only person in Lauryn's life who would have seen her actions in the burn ward as something to be proud of rather than those of a crazy person. Too bad Lauryn could never tell him the truth. Not unless she wanted to be pestered about church and Bible study and going to seminary and all that other crap for the rest of her life.

That was a depressing thought, so Lauryn put it out of her head, vowing to never tell her father anything about what had happened as she opened the door and plopped into the Buick's freezing driver's seat. She'd actually started rehearsing what she planned say to her dad during the inevitable confrontation under her breath when she realized there was someone else in the car with her.

"Jesus Christ!" she cried, jumping so hard she whacked her head on the sedan's padded ceiling.

"Language," Talon said, cracking his eyes to glance up at her from where he was lying on the reclined passenger seat. "You shouldn't take the Lord's name in vain."

Lauryn chose to ignore that, clutching her pounding chest instead. "What are you doing in my car?"

"Waiting for you," he replied, like hiding in someone's car waiting for them to come outside was a totally natural thing to do.

"This is *not* okay," she said, angry she had to tell him that. "Get out."

Talon frowned and returned his seat back to the upright position. "I will if you wish," he said, moving his sword to rest between his legs. "But while I try to appreciate all the facets of God's glorious creation, I'd rather not ride my bike in the snow. Also, I thought you'd have questions."

Lauryn had a *lot* of those. She also had the beginnings of a very nasty fatigue-and-stress-induced headache that was threatening to explode all over her. But though she knew it was a terrible idea, in the end, her damned curiosity got the best of her. "Will your answers make sense this time?"

"I can only promise to tell the truth," Talon said. "Whether that lives up to your expectations, though, only you can decide."

That frustrating nonanswer didn't bode well for the rest, and Lauryn wasn't sure why she'd expected any better. She knew she should just kick him out, but even though she'd absolutely meant what she'd said to Will about putting all of this behind her, she found herself buckling her seatbelt instead.

This is absolutely crazy. Talon was the very last person she needed in her life. But tired and scared and over all of this as Lauryn was, she hadn't forgotten that Talon was the sole reason she and Will and probably everyone else was still alive. Putting it that way in her mind, kicking him out of her car seemed kind of ungrateful, especially since he was offering to explain himself. And anyway, it wasn't like this day could get any weirder.

"Okay," she said with a defeated sigh. "You can stay. But only because I want answers." And then, because she'd had politeness drilled into her since before she could talk, she added, "And thank you. You know, for saving my life again."

"Give thanks to the Lord," Talon replied. "For he is good."

She frowned. "Psalms?"

"One oh seven."

"Of course," she muttered, starting the car. "I bet you killed at Bible *Jeopardy*."

He gave her a confused look. "What is Bible *Jeopardy*?"

Lauryn sighed, slumping down in her seat. It was going to be a very long drive.

9

SIGNS AND WONDERS

Someone must have given an official statement that the crisis was over, because by the time Lauryn made it to the exit, the ring of news vans and emergency response vehicles that had besieged the hospital all morning was finally breaking up. No one even knocked on her window as she pulled out into the snowy street, pushing her way into the tangled mess of normal afternoon traffic. Even so, Lauryn bit her tongue, waiting until the towers of Mercy Hospital were safely out of sight before she finally worked up the courage to ask the question that had been burning a hole in her head all morning.

"So," she said casually, glancing at Talon. "Are you an angel?"

He arched an eyebrow at her. "Do you believe in angels?"

"No," she said quickly. "I'm a doctor. I don't believe in any of that stuff. It's just that, given what happened, I felt like I should get the obvious question out of the way."

"So you're asking if *I* believe I'm an angel?"

Lauryn shrugged, and he flashed her a smile. "What do you think?"

Her hands tightened on the steering wheel. "Honestly, I don't know. It would be so much easier to believe you're crazy, I was hallucinating, and none of that was real. But I was *there*. I felt it, saw everything with my own eyes, so . . ."

She trailed off with a shake of her head, but inside, she was holding her breath. She wasn't lying when she'd said she didn't believe in angels, but after this morning's events, Lauryn's ideas of what was and wasn't possible were no longer as set in stone as they'd once been. To be honest, part of her *wanted* to believe. For someone who found comfort in facts and rationality, the events of today had been a nightmare for Lauryn in more ways than one. At this point she'd have taken *any* explanation that would have put what she'd seen in some sort of understandable, explainable context—even angels.

"I'm not an angel."

"Oh," she said, feeling oddly disappointed, which was stupid. Finding out that the person riding in your car didn't think he was an angel should have been a *good* thing. Still, at least this meant Talon wasn't as delusional as she'd initially—

"I'm a soldier of God. Part of an ancient monastic order known as the Soldiers of El Elyon, God Most High."

Spoke too soon.

"An ancient monastic order?" she repeated skeptically, giving him the side eye. "Really?"

Talon side-eyed her right back. "After everything you saw today, *that's* the part you don't believe? Would you have been more satisfied if I had claimed to be an angel?"

Lauryn rubbed her eyes. "Look," she said tiredly. "I admit that today has been . . . different. But that doesn't change the fact that what you're saying is *really* hard to take seriously. I've never even heard of the Soldiers of El-whatever. Is that like the Templars or something?"

"The Knights Templar were a Crusader order created by the pope to push the Roman Catholic Church's conquest of the Holy Land," Talon said authoritatively. "My order is utterly different. The Soldiers of El Elyon—the SEE—answer to no earthly power. We are chosen by God himself to do his will on earth, and we go wherever he sends us. That's how I came to Chicago in the first place, and how I found you. Or did you think it was mere coincidence that I just happened to appear in that alley the moment you needed help?"

"Considering how much noise I was making, I don't think the situation needs a heavenly explanation," Lauryn said stubbornly. "Most people would run to help if they heard someone being attacked."

"That still doesn't explain what happened once I arrived," he said. "You helped me reach Lenny when he was lost, and then you saw me heal him when all of the others who'd been exposed to the green compound died. What could explain that save that God guided my hand and answered my prayers?"

Lauryn set her jaw stubbornly. "Just because I can't explain something doesn't mean God did it."

"What about the water?" Talon pressed. "You must have believed in the blessed water I poured over your hands, because you asked me to make more of it this morning. The sprinklers were *your* idea, and it worked. Those people were saved because you prayed for help and were answered with a miracle. You personally have received countless miracles over the last two days. How many more will it take before you believe?"

If the past few days had been blessed, Lauryn would be happy to do without miracles. "Just because I was willing to go along with you this morning doesn't mean I'm still on board now," she said. "I was trapped in a closet! Any solution sounds good when you're cornered. But there are a lot of perfectly valid reasons for why those sprinklers did the job that have nothing to do with miracles. Maybe the water washed off the drug residue that was causing the hallucinations. Or maybe the drug wore off on its own and it just looked like the water did it because of the timing. Just because something looked miraculous at the time doesn't mean everything that happened isn't explainable through normal, rational, scientific means."

When she put it that way, Lauryn almost believed her own argument. She could *almost* buy that what had happened this morning had a plausible explanation. But Talon was shaking his head.

"You're reaching too hard," he said. "One of the chief principles of rational science is Occam's razor, which states that among competing hypotheses, the one with the fewest assumptions should be selected. You're an intelligent, educated doctor. I'm sure you could come up with a thousand *complicated* explanations for why this morning wasn't a miracle if you tried hard enough. But wouldn't it make more scientific sense to accept the simplest explanation, which is that you asked, and God answered?"

"*No*," Lauryn said. "Because this isn't the Dark Ages, and God is never an appropriate answer to 'why did x happen?' in any kind of *reasonable* science."

Talon shrugged. "If you can't accept God as the answer, then I have nothing else to give you. I can only speak the truth, Lauryn. Whether you listen is up to you. You have been shown signs and wonders greater than any I have ever seen today. If you still won't believe in the face of so much evidence, I don't know what else I can tell you. Even so, I will not give up."

"Why not?" she asked angrily. "I just called you crazy to

your face. I'm never going to believe in this nonsense, so why keep pushing? Do you need to be right so badly?"

"I don't need to be right," Talon said, his voice deep and sure. "I *am* right."

As much as she wanted to call bullshit, the utter conviction in his voice made her tremble. He sounded more sure of those three words than Lauryn had ever felt of anything in her life, and she just didn't understand. "How do you know that?" she demanded. "Can you see God or something? Talk with angels?"

"No," Talon said. "But that's the nature of faith. We can't see gravity, either, but that doesn't mean we don't hit the ground when we fall. Faith is a real force that allows humanity to do great, some would say impossible, things. In Thailand, years ago, I saw a monk set himself on fire to protest the government's persecution of Buddhists. The whole time he burned, he never panicked. Never made a sound. The strength of his faith in the dharma was so great it allowed him to overcome the physical reality of his body's death. He was at peace in meditation from the moment the flames caught until the moment he fell to ash. What can we call that save a miracle?"

"Horrible."

"No more than how the very human government was treating his people."

"True." She bit her lower lip, afraid to say what was on her mind.

He saw her, though, and asked, "What?"

"Nothing," she said, looking back at the road. "I just find it really weird that you'd use a Buddhist monk as an example of faith. With all the Bible quoting, I took you for a holy roller."

"There is no contradiction," Talon said. "God is bigger than our labels. I am a Christian, but I do not presume to say that an infinite God is defined by my mortal—and therefore limited—

vision of him. He is our father. To some, she's our mother. To others, there are many faces that wrap into their vision of him. But however he appears to his children doesn't matter. He's there wherever and however we need him. That is the great mercy and understanding of the Almighty. He understands us in a way we can never understand him. That is why our faith never goes unrewarded, even if we can never fully explain why."

He bowed his head as he finished, and Lauryn sighed. "You sound just like my dad," she said irritably. "Not the multicultural thing. I don't even know if he's ever met a Buddhist. But he talks about faith the same way. He's the kind of guy who'd walk off a cliff without a second thought if he thought God wanted him to do it. But I'm not like that. You can talk about faith all you want, but so long as there's a chance of a logical scientific explanation, I'm *always* going to go with that, because the alternative is insane. I can't just believe that some all-powerful Creator is paying attention to our lives and manipulating us like puppets to his own ends."

"God does not manipulate," Talon said firmly. "He guides."

"Same difference."

He glared at her, a look she'd never associated with Talon in the admittedly brief time she'd known him—and Lauryn sighed. "I'm not trying to be insulting, but I've heard this sales pitch before, and I'm not buying. If God is real and cares as much about us as you claim, why doesn't he come down here and fix all the horrible things that are wrong with the world? All it would take is one giant sign in the sky, and the whole world would get its shit together. *That* would be a miracle, but according to you, he's mucking around blessing fire systems instead. What kind of sense does that make?" She shook her head. "None. I'm sorry, but I can't believe in something that makes so little sense just because you tell me to."

She tensed at that, fully expecting Talon to keep arguing,

but he just settled deeper into his seat. "Belief is hard," he said at last. "That's why God asks it of us. If it was easy to believe, everyone would do it, and faith would mean nothing. But those who believe without seeing are blessed in God's eyes."

"What about the rest of us?" Lauryn asked. "Are we SOL?"

"Never," Talon said. "We are never alone. God is everywhere, all times and places. He is with all of us always. All you have to do is reach out to him, and you will be welcomed into his arms as warmly and lovingly as those who've believed all their lives."

"And if we don't believe, what then?" she pressed. "Does he toss us to the devil?"

"No," he said firmly. "God never abandons us, but if the drowning man will not lift his hand to grab the rope, there's little God can do. You can't force salvation. It's a matter of free will. If everyone was forced to believe, then the decision to believe—to reject the devil and be faithful—would have no meaning. God gave us free will so that the choice to be righteous and good would be ours to make. Otherwise, what's the point? Without the ability to fail, success has no meaning."

By the time he finished, Lauryn was having bad flashbacks to her dad's Sunday sermons, but what more could you expect from a man who claimed with absolute seriousness to be a literal soldier of God? She really should just pull over and boot him, but something about what Talon had said just now and what he'd told her in the burn ward was bothering her—and since it would be cruel to kick him out on a busy road in the snow, Lauryn decided to go ahead and clear it up.

"Not to imply that I buy any of this—because I *don't*—but if you can't force someone to be saved, how does that fit with what you said back in the burn ward about those people being forced to fall?"

Talon's expression darkened. "That's different," he said, his voice grim. "Those people were suffering greatly, but not just from the pains and ills that cause people to turn to drugs in the first place. There was something else, an evil force weighing them down and leaving them open to a corruption far beyond the measure of their own sins."

"Exactly," Lauryn said. "So how does that jibe with all the other stuff you just said? Why is it God can't pull us *up* unless we ask, but the devil apparently can pull us screaming into hell whenever he pleases?"

"Because you're missing the part where those people had invited the devil into their lives," Talon said sadly. "Whenever we sink into temptation and evil, we open the door for our own destruction. It's not an absolute decision. A lost soul can always repent and choose salvation, but the devil isn't known for playing fair. That's why despair and fear are his greatest tools. If sinking souls never see they have a chance at redemption, or if they don't think they can be forgiven, it's the same as having no choice at all. By making us feel powerless and hopeless, he takes away God's greatest gift: our free will. Or, at least, that's how it's worked in the past. With this new weapon, though, the situation has changed. You saw their faces. Those people were trapped in their own minds. Even the most violent among them was terrified, babbling about demons and monsters, but all words of comfort couldn't reach them. They were imprisoned by fear."

In that, at least, Lauryn agreed. "The hallucinations do seem to be a key part of every version of the drug. What I don't get is why it's a drug in the first place. I mean, assuming for the moment that you're right and this is the literal devil's work, why does he need pushers?"

"For the same reason God works through miracles," Talon said patiently. "Choice. Just as you can't force a sinner to repent, you can't force a righteous man to fall. But drug users and gang members and people on the street are often suffering greatly. That makes them easy prey for the devil. It's a simple job to pull down a rock that's already sliding. The difference this time is that he trapped them first. A drug addict on the street can still be saved by a well-meaning passerby, but the victims we saw this morning were isolated, stuck inside their own hallucinations. At that point, the devil is able to control everything and all outside help is blocked."

Lauryn grimaced. Even without believing what he was saying, she had to admit that was a good setup. "So you think that's what the drug does? Isolates people so God can't reach them?"

"God can *always* find his flock," Talon said forcefully. "But he can't force them to take his hand. The decision to save yourself— *truly* save yourself and repent—is never an easy one. By contrast, the devil's road is simple. All he asks is that you fail, and with the drugs clouding minds that were already teetering on the edge, falling is always easier than climbing."

Given what she knew about the Bible, that actually made a lot of sense. Unfortunately, the metaphysical part of this wasn't what she was concerned with. "Going back to the part where this is a drug," she said. "I still don't understand how it's able to spread. Even if we assume you're right, and the drug is trapping targets in a prison of their own fears and despair to make them easier prey for the devil—which I still, for the record, do not believe in—how does that translate into normal, non-drug-using people being transformed into . . . whatever those things were because of a bite?"

"Sin has always been contagious," Talon said. "Those who keep bad company often fall into bad ways."

"But this was hardly a matter of falling in with the wrong crowd," Lauryn argued. "I knew several of the nurses who were bitten. They were good people, not druggies at the end of their rope. How did they turn so fast?"

"No one is without sin," Talon said, frowning. "But you make a good point."

Lauryn smirked, but it was hard to crow victory over a man who was clearly thinking over her words so carefully. "I think Lincoln Black accidentally told the truth when he called the drug a 'catalyst,'" he said at last. "Drug users are easy marks, but as I said, everyone sins. If the substance in question was designed to latch on to that, then it wouldn't matter if you took it as a drug or were exposed via a bite. So long as you were a sinner—and we all are—the end effect would be the same: you'd be trapped in the prison of your sin and tormented until, eventually, you fell. When that happens, the evil you admitted into your soul would have control of your body."

"And, in turn, the devil."

"Exactly."

That was a horrifying thought, and the only thing that kept Lauryn from panicking at the implications was a firm reminder that she didn't believe in any of this. After what had happened this morning, she could no longer deny that someone was drugging her city with a very dangerous substance, but it absolutely couldn't be the devil. Because that was *crazy*. Just like she was for going along with this as long as she had.

With that, Lauryn squared her shoulders. She owed Talon for saving her life, but she'd been more than fair about giving him the benefit of the doubt. Now, though, it was time to end this farce, and she slowed down, shifting into the slow lane as she turned to bid her guest farewell. "So where should I drop you?" she asked, keeping her voice light. "I know your bike's at the hospital, but do you have a hotel or . . ."

She trailed off hopefully, but Talon just shook his head. "I go where you go."

"That's too bad," she said. "'Cause I'm going home, and you're not invited."

"God sent me to Chicago to protect you," he said with a stubborn look.

She snorted. "Protect the nonbeliever?"

"You may not always be such," he reminded her. "But whether you believe or not, I can't leave your side now that Lincoln Black knows who you are."

That brought her up short. "The fake doctor?" When he nodded, Lauryn grimaced. "I'm probably going to regret this, but who is he? You guys seemed to know each other."

Talon's face fell into a scowl. "Just as there are those of us who follow and enact God's will, there are others who actively seek to pervert it. Black is one of these. He and I have clashed before."

"So I gathered," she said. "I take it that didn't end well?"

Talon shrugged. "It ended as it always ends. He tries to tempt me to murder and despair, I try to guide him back to the light. So far, neither of us has won."

"No offense, but I think you might be fighting a losing battle," Lauryn said. She'd grown up knowing guys like Black. Never anyone quite that bad, of course, but she knew a lost cause when she saw one. Talon, however, seemed resigned.

"The Good Shepherd never abandons the lamb. He may be a determinedly black sheep, but his is a soul like any other. So long as Black lives, I'll keep trying to reach him, and I will keep him from reaching you."

Lauryn shook her head. She was all for second chances, but letting a man like Black run around loose struck her as a capital-B Bad Idea. She was tempted to say as much before she remembered she was supposed to be getting this loony out of her car, not getting sucked deeper into his nut-job life. She'd been so busy arguing with him, she hadn't even realized she was nearly back to her dad's house in Englewood. If she didn't ditch him quick, she'd end up taking him home anyway.

"Okay," she said. "Seriously, I'm done. For real. Tell me where to drop you, or I'm just going to pick a curb."

"I'm not leaving you," Talon said again. "Not until you believe. You're too vulnerable like this, with your mind still in doubt."

"Trust me, I am *not* in doubt," she said. "You are hardly the first holy man to lecture me in this car, but I didn't buy this crap as a kid, and I'm sure as hell not buying it now. Not unless God's willing to toss me a miracle right now." She looked up through the windshield at the gray, clouded sky. "Hit me with your best shot!"

The words were mocking, but inside, a tiny piece of Lauryn was holding its breath. A tiny hope that, when nothing happened, as she'd *known* it wouldn't, turned into a surprisingly bitter sting of disappointment.

"See?" she said angrily as she pulled over to the curb. "Nothing. Now get out of my car."

As always, Talon didn't move. "God doesn't always speak through bolts from the sky," he said quietly. "Those who do his work and keep the faith often find their lives are full of small miracles."

"Oh, *please*," Lauryn said, rolling her eyes. "You mean like a child's laugh or the kindness of strangers?"

He smiled. "Kindness is always a miracle, but God's hand moves in more practical, straightforward ways as well. For example, your gas tank has been empty since we left the hospital, and yet your car is still running."

"Don't be stupid," Lauryn snapped. "My tank is not . . ."

The words trailed off as her eyes found the gas gauge. In her rush to get to the hospital this morning, she hadn't even looked at the Buick's tank. Now, sure enough, the red needle was well below the E. She was wondering how on earth the old gas-guzzler was still running when the car's engine suddenly shuttered and stalled.

"Damn," Lauryn hissed, pumping the gas, but it was no use. The car was dead. Thankfully, she'd already pulled over to kick Talon out, so at least they weren't broken down in the middle of the street. She couldn't stay here on a yellow line, though, so she switched on the emergency blinkers and coasted them into the parking lot of an old fast-food joint where a perfect downhill parking spot was miraculously available.

She regretted her word choice the moment that thought crossed her mind. Talon was looking too smug already as it was, sitting there with his things gathered in his lap like this stop had been planned from the beginning. But when Lauryn looked around to see where exactly they'd stalled out, her already sinking stomach took a nosedive.

Now that she was actually paying attention, this road looked familiar. *Very* familiar, and not just because it was the way to her dad's house. It was familiar because the parking lot where they'd stalled out was directly in front of her father's church.

"Missionary Baptist Outreach of Englewood," Talon read from the lit sign attached to the sanctuary's brick wall. As if she couldn't see it. "Pastor, Rev. Maxwell *Jefferson*."

"Don't start," Lauryn snapped, shoving open her car door. "Don't say a *word*. We were going to my dad's house, and he lives near his church. This is all just *coincidence*."

"If you insist," Talon replied, getting out as well. "But how many coincidences does it take before a smart woman like yourself reads the writing on the wall?"

She rolled her eyes, but Talon kept going. "You're the preacher's daughter," he said, looking at her over the roof of the car. "Surely you know the story?"

Of course Lauryn did. It was one of her favorites. When she was a kid, she'd loved the grisly, almost ghost-story-like tale of the Babylonian king Belshazzar who'd held a feast for all his nobles, demanding the Temple vessels be brought in from Jerusalem so that his nobles might drink from the sacred cups. But when he gave the order, a hand appeared and wrote mysterious, unreadable words on his wall. Terrified, King Belshazzar brought in his magicians and diviners, but no one could read what had been written.

In the end, his queen convinced them to call in Daniel, a Jewish prophet exiled in Babylon who was renowned for his wisdom. Belshazzar agreed, offering Daniel the third rank in his kingdom if he could read the words. Daniel declined the reward, but he *did* accept the task, reading the words, which were a warning to Belshazzar that God had authority over the kingdoms of mortal men. It was meant to be a reminder that even a king was merely a humble mortal before the Almighty.

Obviously—this was the Old Testament—proud Belshazzar ignored the warning and ended up being killed that very night by one of his own men.

As stories went, it was a good one. A ghoulish tale of hubris, classic Apocrypha stuff, but Lauryn didn't think Talon was referencing the story for its literary appeal. Given the context of their conversation so far, it was practically a threat. After all, King Belshazzar had *died* only hours after not taking God's signs seriously.

The thought had barely crossed her mind before she dismissed it. Lauryn was no king, and even if he could be a hardheaded bastard, Talon had yet to threaten anything. But though Lauryn was sure he hadn't brought it up to scare her, Talon knew his Biblical literature inside and out, and like all his references, this one was clearly meant to be a reminder. In the actual book of Daniel, the story of the writing on the wall was used specifically in comparison to the tale of another Babylonian king, Nebuchadnezzar, who unlike the foolish Belshazzar, *did* realize he was humble before God and changed his arrogant ways in time to save his life. Once she remembered that bit, Talon's point was painfully obvious.

Too bad Lauryn wasn't biting.

"I get it," she said sharply, glaring at him over the roof of the stalled car. "But joke's on you, because I'm not Belshazzar or Nebuchadnezzar or anyone else whose name would get you a billion points in Scrabble, and you're no prophet. You're a deluded man who thinks he's on a mission from God, and if there's any writing on the walls around here, it's just graffiti."

"So you say," Talon replied, unshaken. "But the point still stands. Just like Belshazzar, you have drunk from the vessels of God's Temple, but have not yet given him honor. Your words were written on the bodies of your patients, not the wall. That context should make them even clearer, and yet you still refuse to see. You have been given sign after sign, miracle after miracle, but you still don't believe, and while you waste time denying what's right in front of you, all of Chicago falls further into the enemy's hold." He shook his head sadly. "At this rate, by the time you do get around to considering that maybe all of these things are happening for a reason, it will be too late."

"Why?" she demanded, pressing her fingers into the door. "Why do I matter? You're the one who thinks he's a holy warrior. Save the city yourself."

Talon shook his head. "I can't."

"Well, if you can't do it, what hope do I have?"

"Every hope," he said without missing a beat. "That's why I was sent to find and protect you. Because *you* have been chosen."

Lauryn stared at him for several seconds, and then she pushed off the car with a frustrated sound. "I don't know why I bother," she said, marching across the street and up the church stairs. "Do whatever you want. I'm going in to find my dad and tell him I stalled his car."

She just hoped he was here. The house wasn't far, but it was still a longer, colder walk in the snow than she'd have been willing to brave. She should have known better, though. Car or no car, her dad's life revolved around his church, and as always, the moment she pushed open the door, there he was, sitting with a small group of older women at the long tables that ran down the center of the big area that served as their fellowship hall, making sandwiches. Why they were making sandwiches, Lauryn had no idea, but it was probably for something insufferably virtuous and, given the gruff look Maxwell shot her, way more important than anything she'd come here to talk about. But while her father's reaction left much to be desired, the women of the church gasped like she'd come back from the dead.

"*Lauryn!*"

A dozen delighted voices called her name in unison as she was nearly tackled by a rush of old ladies trying to hug her.

"Where have you been? I—"

"—heard you stole your daddy's car. You wicked girl! You should know better—"

"—so glad you're safe. My daughter told me there was an emergency at the hospital and—"

"Yes, I'm safe, thank you," Lauryn said, struggling to breathe through all the hugging and perfume. "We just had an accident, but it's under control. And I didn't steal Dad's car. I borrowed it. I'm actually here to bring it back."

"In one piece, I trust," Maxwell said, his deep voice disapproving as he finally looked up from the perfect sandwich he'd been folding into a square of waxed paper. "It's customary to *ask* before you borrow things, Lauryn. But since you're back, you can do penance by helping us finish up these bag lunches for our homeless brothers and sisters at the shelter."

Lauryn winced automatically at the order. She was debating whether it would be faster to argue that he didn't get to give

her penance anymore or just give up and make the stupid sandwiches when the women around her sucked in another collective
breath as Talon entered the room behind her. For a long heartbeat, everyone just stared, and then, like someone had given the
signal, they grabbed her and all started whispering at once.

"*Lauryn*, who is—"

"Is that your new man?"

"He's so handsome! Does he go to church?"

"—knows how to pick 'em. In my day—"

"No! No!" Lauryn said frantically, putting up her hands.
"It's not like that! Talon's just . . . um . . . someone I know from
the hospital."

The women's eyes went even wider, and Lauryn realized be-
latedly that this bit of quick thinking had not worked out in her
favor.

"So he's a *doctor*—"

"—why didn't you bring him over earlier?"

"—even *more* handsome—"

Mortified, Lauryn shot Talon a deeply apologetic look.
Crazy or not, no one deserved to have the well-meaning ladies
of Missionary Baptist sicced on them. But as with everything
else, Talon took the misguided complements in stride, politely
saying that he went to church often and that he was delighted
to be here, since where two or three gathered in Christ's name,
God was there with them.

The moment he quoted Matthew, it was all over. Just like that,
those twelve old hearts belonged to him hook, line, and sinker,
and Lauryn was completely forgotten. She barely had time to
get out of the way before the women grabbed Talon and ushered
him to the table, where they began trying to feed him from the
massive pile of food that always seemed to appear anytime more
than three people were together in the fellowship hall. The only
person there who didn't seem affected was Maxwell himself. He

simply welcomed Talon and then stood up, walking solemnly over to his daughter, who was seriously contemplating escape.

"Here," she said, shoving the keys at him along with two twenties from her wallet. "I'm sorry I took it without asking, but it was an emergency. I also ran it out of gas. This should cover it."

"Keep your money," he said, pushing her hand back. "I'm not mad you took the car, just that you didn't tell me you were going. A child should seek out her father in times of trouble."

"I'm not a child—"

"And speaking of trouble," he said, ignoring her—like always—to glance pointedly over his shoulder at Talon, who was now sitting at the table, making sandwiches like that was the entire reason he'd come here. "Who is that? And *don't* tell me he works at the hospital. 'Lying lips are an abomination to the Lord.'"

Lauryn gritted her teeth. If one more person quoted the Bible at her, she was going to go ballistic. "Not that it's any of your business, *Dad*," she said, "but his name's Talon, and he's the guy who saved me from getting ripped to bits last night. I was giving him a ride home from the hospital because, you know, gratitude, but then we ran out of gas and I was forced to coast in here. Again, I'm sorry about that, but the car's fine, so now that you've got the keys, we'll just be on our way."

The *both* of them. Because while Lauryn wasn't exactly keen to spend more time listening while Talon tried to convince her she was chosen by God, the idea of leaving him here to say that stuff in front of her father's congregation was miles worse. Unlike her, they would actually believe, and then she'd be in *real* trouble. But while she was obviously in a hurry to go, Maxwell was moving slower than ever.

"You're normally at work this time of day," he said, looking her up and down. "I heard on the radio that there was an emergency at the hospital. Something to do with drugs? They didn't say what exactly, but it gave me a bad feeling."

Lauryn fought the urge to roll her eyes. Her dad got "bad feelings" about everything that didn't directly involve living a Christian life. Of course, in this case, he was actually right, but Lauryn had learned if she didn't want to hear a lecture about the evils of the world and the fall of morality in the modern age, she should avoid agreeing with him whenever possible.

And after that car ride, she *really* didn't want another lecture.

"We did have a pretty crazy situation, but it's okay now," she assured him. "I've actually got the rest of the day off since they called me in early, so I'm going to go back to my place and crash. Naree's been really worried." As her overflowing voicemail box was proof of. "I should really get back home and calm her down. Thanks again for letting me stay with you last night, and, again, I'm sorry about taking your car."

"It's just a car," Maxwell said, surprising her. Her dad *loved* that car. "Before you go, though, I was hoping you could help me."

The question made her eyebrows shoot up. When her father wanted her to do something, he usually just dictated. The asking thing was new, so she decided to hear it out. "What?"

Maxwell's expression grew grimmer than ever. "Your brother didn't come home last night."

"Well, he went out after midnight," Lauryn reminded him. "Are you sure he's not just passed out at someone's house?"

"Not this time," Maxwell said, his brows furrowing in a way that made him look far older than he should. "I've had bad dreams all night, Lauryn. I've known for a while that Robert was in trouble, but it's gotten a lot deeper recently, and with all this news about some new drug, I fear the worst."

Lauryn's breath caught. She hadn't thought of that. Probably because she hadn't wanted to. Now, though, it was the only thing on her mind. "Have you talked to him?"

"Of course," Maxwell said. "But you know he won't listen."

Like father, like son . . . like daughter.

"We'll see about that," she growled, pulling out her phone. "I'll call Will. He works Vice. He'll know exactly what to say to scare him straight."

"You've been away from this neighborhood too long if you can even suggest that," her father said, exasperated. "Down here, young black men who get involved in things like this don't get scared straight. Especially not from some white cop their sister used to date. No—they go straight to life in jail. Robert's young and stupid and acting the fool, but he doesn't deserve to pay that price." He pulled out his battered old phone. "I've been calling him all night, but he won't listen to me. I was hoping you could give it a try."

Lauryn sighed. "You heard him last night. He's not going to listen to me, either."

"We won't know that until we try," her father said. "He's still your brother, and though he was bad at showing it, he always did look up to you. He's lost at the moment, but Jesus tells us 'there will be more joy in heaven over one sinner who repents than over ninety-nine righteous persons who need no repentance.' We must do everything we can to save him and bring him back to the light, before he's gone forever."

After what she and Talon had talked about in the car, that warning hit Lauryn a lot harder than it should have. It also made her angry, because Maxwell seemed to be more upset about losing a sheep from his flock than losing his *actual son* to the culture of drugs and violence that ran through South Chicago like a polluted river. Then again, maybe she was being too hard on her dad. Maybe God and the Church were just so much a part of his life, he didn't know how to talk about painful things like Robert without them.

Not that she was any better.

Lauryn winced. She always accused her dad of picking God over everything else, including his own children, but in her own way, she'd done the exact same thing. The moment she'd turned eighteen, she'd dropped her family like a hot potato and run off to chase her dream of being a doctor. She'd never even thought of what that would do to Robbie—it wasn't like the two of them had ever been close—but when she thought about how he'd yelled at her last night, accusing her of leaving them, she couldn't deny that he was right. She *had* left, and worse, she'd left him alone. Growing up, she'd had her mom and then Robbie to help her push back against her dad's ridiculousness. But Robbie was too young to remember their mother's death, and when Lauryn had gone, too, he'd been left with no one. Just a dad who cared more about his church and his ideals than his flesh-and-blood children.

Guilt hit her like a hammer, and she grabbed her phone, flicking through her contacts until she came to Robbie's number, which she couldn't actually remember ever calling before. She still wasn't sure if it would do any good now, but while Robbie's life wasn't her responsibility, he was still her brother. Her *baby* brother, and she'd left him alone in the same situation she'd worked her whole life to escape. Now he was out on the same streets the junkies she'd treated this morning had come from, and the idea chilled her to the bone. She wasn't stupid enough to think she could force him to change his thinking—only Robbie could save himself—but he still deserved better than she'd treated him. He deserved someone who cared, and for once, Lauryn was determined to be that person. He was her family, and if he was in trouble, it was her duty to help.

She just hoped he'd accept it.

As if he could tell just how uncomfortably close her thoughts were getting to what he'd told her in the car, Talon chose that ex-act moment to turn around and give Lauryn a questioning look. Unable to meet his eyes, she turned around as well, huddling in the lee of the church doors as she hit the call button and held the phone to her ear, waiting breathlessly as it rang to see if she was already too late.

> EACH PERSON IS TEMPTED WHEN HE IS LURED
> AND ENTICED BY HIS OWN DESIRE.
> THEN DESIRE WHEN IT HAS CONCEIVED GIVES BIRTH TO SIN, AND
> SIN WHEN IT IS FULLY GROWN BRINGS FORTH DEATH.
> —JAMES 1:14–15

10
BIRTH TO SIN

Will had never been good at following directions.

He was fine *most* of the time, but when orders came down that interfered with how he thought a case should be run, the words tended to go in one ear and out the other. Normally, he got away with this by achieving results. It was hard to punish a detective who regularly cracked hard cases. Today, though, Will was pushing it even by his standards. Not only was he back at the station (where he'd been specifically ordered by Chief Korigan not to be) *and* on his nineteenth hour of unreported overtime (in direct violation of Chicago PD officer safety regulations), he was at his desk calling contacts for a case he'd been ordered not to touch.

Any of those could mean serious trouble. All together, it was a trifecta that could cost him his badge. Another cop, one with more to lose, would have realized that and gone home. But Will was as bad at letting things go as he was at following directions he didn't agree with, and after the run-in with Korigan this morning, he was more determined than ever to bust this case wide open.

He just wished the case would cooperate.

After leaving the hospital, Will had gotten straight to work. Ten years as a vice detective had given him an impressive network among the street pushers and gangs all across Chicago, and he worked it like a spider checking its web, tapping each thread to see what he'd caught. But unlike yesterday when no one had known anything about a drug that made people go crazy, everyone was buzzing today about this new thing called Z3X. As one of his meth cooker contacts explained it, Z3X was an additive that was supposed to enhance the effects of other drugs. And apparently it worked—when he had access to it, he was able to sell triple the amount of rocks by cutting his product, and had people *begging* for seconds.

For a while, though, there wasn't much he could do, because there wasn't all that much to be had. Apparently Z3X had been around for months now in smaller doses, but since it was touted as nothing more than a cost cutter and it wasn't actually illegal by itself, no one had thought much of it. But starting yesterday, someone had been dumping the stuff on Chicago by the truck-load. Literally.

The last bit was so bizarre Will hadn't believed it at first, but every dealer, cooker, and pusher he talked to swore up and down that late last night, giant pallets of Z3X had just started show-ing up, arriving on huge flatbeds that were circling the South Chicago neighborhoods like ice cream trucks. But it wasn't just an increase in supply. These new loads of Z3X were supposed to be finer, stronger, and better all around than any of the stuff before, *and* it was being sold for dirt cheap. As one dealer put it, the drivers were acting like they were on a timed quota, practically dumping the stuff in the street if it wasn't selling fast enough.

These reports were further corroborated by Will's buddies on the force who drove patrol cars. Several of them reported pulling these same trucks over for suspicious behavior. Every time, though, they'd been forced to let them go again, because again, unlike the drugs it was meant to be mixed with, Z3X wasn't actually illegal, and the most they'd been able to do was give out a few traffic citations. One of the cops had actually picked up a packet of the stuff to take back to the lab, but it had come back clean. No controlled substances whatsoever.

The best lead Will had was that one of the key ingredients of Z3X seemed to be sulfur, but even this was still well within the legal limits for human consumption. Other than complaints that the stuff stank like rotten eggs, it truly seemed to be harmless by any measure Will could come up with, which put a real damper on police work. Those trucks might as well have been driving around selling nutmeg or baking soda for all that he could do about it.

But while the evidence all seemed to point to Z3X being a red herring, Will was getting report after report from his guys on the inside that this new stuff was legit. Some of the crazier pushers had even tried it straight, claiming that even without a real drug to mix with, it would tear you up. Plus, it was cheap. *Dirt* cheap, and getting more so by the hour. This morning, before the burn ward incident, one-pound bags of Z3X had been going for a mere five bucks. Now, at midafternoon, bags were going for a buck or less. Some dealers even claimed to have gotten theirs for *free*.

Under normal conditions, this kind of price free-fall would

have triggered people to hold off buying until they saw how low it got, but this situation was anything but normal. It was so strange, and the new Z3X *so* good, that the exact opposite was happening. Every dealer, wannabe dealer, and addict in the city was in a buying frenzy, scooping up as much Z3X as they could before the madness ended and prices went up again. Even normal people who didn't touch drugs were catching on. In some neighborhoods, it wasn't uncommon to see normal shop clerks and people waiting at bus stops break out running when they saw one of the trucks, chasing the driver down to get their own share of the Z3X craze.

The end result of this insanity was that Z3X had gone from a filler additive known only to people buried deep in the narcotics business to a household name in less than eighteen hours. Nothing should be able to move that fast. But while it was clear that whoever was behind this had pulled off the marketing coup of the century, Will still didn't understand *why*. Even if Z3X was made of the cheapest junk in the lot, someone was still paying to have it cranked out, packaged, and driven around all over Chicago. The scale of the operation was staggering, and in Will's experience, people with the kind of money needed to pull a stunt like this off didn't waste it. Someone had to be planning to make bank off this, but damned if Will could figure out how, or even who. The trucks and drivers were all rental operations who weren't obligated to tell Will anything without a warrant—a warrant he couldn't even request since he wasn't supposed to be working on this case in the first place. He was about to say screw it and just go follow one of the trucks home himself to see where all this stuff was coming from—because with this much in the city, they *had* to be making it in town—when he heard someone clear their throat behind his desk.

"You just couldn't let it go, could you?"

The tight, angry voice sent Will's fingers curling into fists.

"Afternoon, Chief," he said, closing the windows on his monitor before spinning around in his chair. "Didn't expect you back here so soon."

"I'm sure you didn't," Korigan said, arms crossed over the front of the rumpled chest of the tux he *still* hadn't changed out of. "And I'm pretty sure that's because I told you to go home."

"But this is where I like to check my Facebook," Will said with a smile. "There's no rule against being at work if you're not working."

Korigan's eyes flicked to the case files spread all over his desk. "And what's that? Light reading?"

Will shrugged. "Leftovers from this morning. I'm normally neater, but I figured cleanup could wait. It wasn't like anyone would come looking for them since you took everyone off the new drug case to handle your hospital hush-up."

The chief's eyes narrowed dangerously as he pulled out his phone. "Front desk, this is Chief Korigan," he said, glaring at Will. "Send a team up to Vice to escort Detective Tannenbaum out of the building."

"Whoa," Will said, putting up his hands. "There's no call for—"

"I gave you a direct order to go home and leave this be," Korigan said coldly. "You didn't. That's reason enough for me. And since you clearly have an issue when it comes to following simple orders, I'm also revoking your security clearance until further notice."

Now it was Will's turn to get pissed. "You can't do that!" he shouted, leaping up from his chair. "Dammit, Korigan, I'm just trying to do my job! There're drugs on the streets, and—"

"You're going to be on the street if you keep this up," the chief said, glancing at the door where two uniformed officers were coming in to remove Will from the building.

"You can't do this," Will said as the men came over to grab

his arms. "I'm a ten-year vet. You've been here six months. I've solved more cases than you've seen, and if you weren't in my way, I'd be solving this one! No one's going to let you—"

"No one has to *let* me," Korigan replied calmly. "I'm in charge here, Tannenbaum, and I'm not the one breaking the rules. You have a good record, but your lack of respect and compliance with the safety regulations of this department make you a danger to yourself and your fellow officers, and since you clearly don't care about that right now, I have to. Trust me, this is for your own good." He held out his hand. "Badge."

"You can't fire me over this," Will said through clenched teeth. "I'm doing my job."

"That's where you're wrong," Korigan said. "I could fire you five times over, but I'm not." He smiled at the uniformed officers. "We need good cops, which is why I'm putting you on leave until you remember that's what you are. I'm just taking your badge to make sure you stay there."

Will shot a pleading look at his fellow cops, but they just looked at their feet. "But—"

"*Badge*, Tannenbaum," Korigan said again, his dark eyes narrowing. "Don't make me do this the hard way."

That was not an empty threat. Will might have been in the right, but all the laws were on Korigan's side. If he fought now, the chief could do far worse than fire him. He could have him locked up for impeding a case, and then he'd never get to the bottom of this.

That was a risk Will couldn't take, and so, reluctantly, he pulled the lanyard holding his badge off his neck and handed it over. "You're making a big—"

"Gun, too," Korigan said coldly. "Now."

Gritting his teeth, Will pulled his weapon and laid it in the police chief's hands as slowly as possible. The moment he let go, Korigan turned to the officer beside him.

"Get him out of here."

"Come on, Will," the officer said gently as he grabbed Will's arm. "Let it go."

Will jerked his arm away, but it was an empty gesture. There was nothing he could do. Even if his fellow officers were on his side, Korigan was technically in the right on this, and thanks to that little "danger to your fellow officers" speech, everyone knew it. Looking out for your fellow cops was rule number one in the precinct. By invoking that, Korigan had just put Will on the outside of his own force even more than he had by taking his badge. If Will kept pushing now, Korigan could fire him on the spot and everyone would say he'd done the right thing. And from the crooked smile on the chief's face, they both knew it.

"Make sure Detective Tannenbaum makes it to his car," Korigan said, his voice warm with perfectly rehearsed worry. "I don't want to lose a good officer to his own hot head."

The other cops promised to look out for him as they led Will down the stairs. They watched him like hawks as he gathered his coat from the lockers, and then, as ordered, they followed him to his car, all but shoving him into the driver's seat and slamming the door in his face. "Go home, Will," the officer in charge said in that friendly but "seriously, don't try me" voice all cops get when they put on the uniform. "Don't make us send a car to tail you."

"I got it, I got it," Will muttered, slumping down in his seat in defeat.

The whole way out of the station, his brain had been scrambling for a way to beat Korigan's latest move. Now that he was actually out here in the cold, though, all he felt was tired. It was finally catching with up him that he'd been working almost nonstop for over thirty-six hours, and that, for all his effort and risks, he was no closer to solving the case than he'd been when he'd first interviewed Lauryn in the hospital. For all he knew, this Z3X business wasn't even related to what had happened in the burn ward or the green stuff the fake Dr. Black had tried to throw in Lauryn's face. It could be he was reading way too much into all of this. That maybe there wasn't a giant conspiracy, and Korigan was just burying this case for the mundane, petty reason of not wanting to look like an incompetent idiot.

Considering Korigan's high opinion of himself, that was more plausible than Will wanted to admit, and he reached up to rub his tired eyes with a sigh. Maybe it actually *was* time to go home. Or better yet, swing by and check on Lauryn.

Will knew that was a terrible idea the moment it occurred to him, but that didn't stop him from seriously considering it anyway. Scary as it had been, the time he'd spent with Lauryn had been a pointed reminder of just how good things between them had been before he'd thrown it all away by acting *exactly* like this. He always got obsessed over cases, chasing the truth until he'd worn himself down to the rivets and wrecked everything else that mattered in his life. Six months ago, it had been his relationship with the best woman he'd ever met. Today, it might have been his job. And while part of Will believed that it would always be worth it—that he did good work and kept people safe when no one else gave a damn—the rest of him was just tired. Tired of getting burned up, tired of pushing so hard all the time, tired of chasing shadows. It wasn't even like he made a difference. No matter how hard he worked, crime didn't stop. The city was never truly safe. Even now, people were out there running after the trucks that were handing out pallets of drugs like candy without a care in the world for the consequences. Why should he kill himself trying to save them when they couldn't even be bothered to save themselves?

That was a bitter line of thought, and Will decided with a sigh that it was time to get some sleep. *Actual* sleep, not the halfway kind where he lay on his couch clutching his phone. Because as big a liar as he might be about everything else, in one area at least, Korigan had the truth pegged: Will *was* exhausted, and that made him a danger to himself and others, especially when he started getting maudlin like he was now. So, with that, Will started his unmarked car and pulled out of the station, promising himself he'd revisit all of this tomorrow morning when he wasn't half-dead. But as he was turning out of the parking lot, a black limo turned in, cutting him off.

At the end of his patience already, Will leaned out his window to call the driver an asshole, but the angry words died in his throat. The limo was pulling up to the front of the station, and who should be getting in but Chief Korigan himself.

Will froze, brain racing. This could be perfectly innocent. Korigan had gotten his job by schmoozing with the sort of people who took limos everywhere. Maybe there was another party, and he was just . . .

His train of thought derailed as the limo door opened, and the light came on inside, outlining a profile Will recognized even through the tinted glass. It was the scary guy from the burn ward. The fake doctor who'd thrown the green stuff in Lauryn's face.

Lincoln Black.

And just like that, all of Will's plans for sleep went to hell. "Got you," he growled as he whipped his car around. "I've got you, you son of a bitch."

Adrenaline coursing through him, Will didn't waste a second. Leaning low over his steering wheel, he circled the lot and pulled out after the limo, following from a safe distance as the luxury car made its way through the pre-rush-hour traffic toward the river.

Robert's phone would not stop ringing.

After years of pretending he didn't exist, Lauryn had been blowing up his phone for the last half hour. The only reason he didn't just turn the thing off was because he was waiting on texts from his crew. He supposed he could have blocked her, but annoying as the constant buzzing in his pocket was, the satisfaction of knowing that perfect little Lauryn was throwing a tantrum over him was too good to miss. If he'd been less busy, he would have fucked with her good—picking up only to hang up, giving her to someone else, that kind of thing. But Robbie had *much* better things to do than harass his stuck-up sister tonight, so he shifted his phone to his outside jacket pocket where he wouldn't feel it going off every ten seconds and turned his attention back to what was really important here: his business.

"You done?" Angelo said, leaning on the railing of the stairs to the riverside warehouse where he'd asked Robbie to meet him. "I ain't got all afternoon."

"Sorry," Robbie said quickly, smiling apologetically at his supplier as he shoved his phone—which was already buzzing again—even deeper into his pocket. "I'm done. What did you want to show me?"

The dealer said nothing. He just shoved the door open and motioned for Robbie to follow. Robbie did so eagerly, chest thumping. Given how crazy this morning had been, he had no idea what to expect, but he was betting *big*. Like *Scarface* big. Cartel-lord-feeding-his-enemies-to-lions big. His imagination had been running wild ever since Angelo had called him in, but as he walked into the brick warehouse, the sight waiting for him made Robbie realize that he hadn't been dreaming nearly big enough.

"Holy . . . "

The scene inside the warehouse looked straight out of the movies. All along the cement floor, giant vats were set up like a grid of indoor swimming pools, each one filled to the brim with bubbling green liquid. At the bottom of each tank, a spigot poured the liquid into large drying racks where it quickly changed from liquid to the fine, black powder Robbie had come here to get. It smelled awful.

It smells like money, he thought greedily.

"That is a *lot* of Z3X," he muttered, trying and failing to count all the vats in front of him before turning back to his buddy Angelo. "And you're in charge of all this?"

"Damn straight," Angelo said, grinning wide. "I run this whole place from the top—" he pointed up at the metal grate ceiling of the warehouse's second floor, where armies of guys were loading huge buckets of the gray-black powder into baggies "—to the bottom." He nodded down toward the shipping bay, where the bundled baggies of Z3X were being loaded into trucks for delivery all over the city.

Robert nodded, trying his best to look pro. "How much are you shipping out?"

"All of it, man," Angelo said. "We been running at full capacity since orders came down to get this onto the streets last night. We've pushed half of it out already. This is just what's still left to go for tonight. That's where you come in." He looked Robert up and down. "How long you been working for me? Three months?"

Robert nodded, and Angelo smiled, slapping him on the back. "You done good, kid. Made a lot of money. I'm real proud. That's why I called you in today. I think it's time you moved up in the world."

That was exactly what Robert had been hoping. Angelo had been hinting that something big was coming for weeks now. Then, out of nowhere, he'd appeared in the club where Robert worked as a dealer and handed him a bucket—no joke, an actual orange hardware store bucket—of Z3X with the promise that if Robert sold it all, there'd be much more where that came from.

Including opportunity for Robbie's growth.

This was the break Robert had been waiting for. Angelo was

the dealer who supplied half the pushers on the South Side. He was a big deal, and when Angelo took personal interest in a person, their career took off—or they disappeared. Given how hard he'd been pushing this new Z3X crap, Robbie was confident he was about to get his invitation to the big leagues.

He deserved it, too. Most of Robert's clients didn't even know what Z3X was. Honestly, Robbie didn't, either, but that didn't matter. He'd sold it like it was candy, emptying the whole damn bucket into the party-mad crowd. He'd called his boss the moment he was out, and then Angelo sent over another batch. It had taken him all morning, but Robert had pushed that one, too. When he called in for a third, Angelo had given him the address for the warehouse and told him to come in person.

It was the chance he'd been waiting months for. When he'd first started selling, it was supposed to be temporary, just a way to make some quick cash until his music career took off. But his demo had been making the rounds for weeks now and he still hadn't gotten a single call. His drug business, on the other hand, had been exploding. He'd already made more cash in the last month than his dad made in a year, and that was just the money. There was also the part where bigwigs like Angelo got to sell to the really famous people, the big-time producers and rappers with the connections to get Robbie the break he needed. That was why he'd busted his balls selling whatever Angelo gave him, including this new Z3X stuff. It was funny, too, because Lauryn had always accused him of being a slacker. But Robbie didn't mind working like a dog when the reward was good enough, and from the way Angelo was smiling, tonight's was gonna be aces.

Speaking of, Angelo was still grinning down at his operation when he motioned for Robbie to follow him along the metal walkway. "It's a big day for us," he said, nodding to the giant thug with the gun who guarded the glass door to the factory's main office. "Big things coming. Whole city's gonna change. I need guys I can rely on more than ever, which is where you come in. You've been a minor player so far, but you've been a damn good one, and I think it's time for you to move up in the world."

By the time he finished, Robbie was grinning so wide it hurt. *Jackpot.* "I can do it," he said without missing a beat. "Just tell me what you need sold, and it's done."

"That's the attitude I like to see," Angelo said, sitting down on the leather couch that overlooked the production floor. "Then let's get you to work. You see all that?" He nodded through the window at the endless pallets of Z3X waiting by the loading bays. "Big Boss wants it on the street by midnight."

For all his big words, Robbie nearly choked. Being a low-level pusher, he didn't even know who the Big Boss was, but that order was enough for Robert to guess that he was crazy. *"All* of it? By midnight *tonight?"*

Angelo nodded, and Robbie bit his lip. He usually wrapped up his business when the clubs closed at dawn, but it had taken him longer than usual to finish selling Angelo's second batch of Z3X. Between that, lunch with his boys, and his drive over to the warehouse just now, it was almost three in the afternoon. That still left nine hours, including the evening, which was prime selling time, but . . . that was a *lot* of Z3X.

"Now you see my predicament," Angelo said with a "we're screwed" laugh. "But orders are orders. We got permission to do whatever we want on price. Hell, we can give it away for free if we have to. Whatever it takes to get every druggie, drunk, pothead, and pill popper in Chicago on Z3X before sunrise tomorrow."

"But . . ." Robert said, still confused. *"Why?"* 'Cause none of this made a damn bit of sense. "I thought it was supposed to be some kind of additive. It doesn't even do anything on its own, right?"

"It can if you take enough," Angelo said with a shrug. "But

that's not the point. We're pushers. Our job is to sell it, not brand it. I got my orders same as you, and word from the top is flood the streets. I don't even care how you do it. Hell, tell 'em it's a new kind of black cocaine. Druggies will take anything if it's cheap enough. I don't care if you give it away. Just get it out of here so I can make my quota, and it's all good."

He finished with a confident smile, but Robbie was more confused than ever. He'd only been in the serious pusher game for a few months, but even he knew the game was all about money, and there was no money for anyone when you were giving away your product.

"I can see what you're thinking," Angelo said. "I thought the same thing. When the order came down to put it on trucks and drive it around the South Side like we were the damn ice cream man, I thought the boss was crazy. I still do, but with money like this, crazy don't matter."

"What money?" Robbie asked, pointing over his shoulder at the massive Z3X production floor behind him. "All that's gotta cost bank to run, right? How do you make a profit on giving stuff away?"

Angelo spread his hands helplessly. "Not our place, man. That's the boss's call. But while I agree with everything you're saying, I've been working this operation all year, and I've learned to trust our employer. His orders don't always make sense at the time, but he always makes bank in the end. *Always.* And if you do your part, you will, too."

He reached over to the desk beside the couch as he finished and opened a drawer, pulling out a huge stack of hundred-dollar bills. The moment Robbie saw the cash, his mouth went dry.

"That for me?"

"All for you," Angelo said, wiggling the cash like he was taunting a dog. "Like I said, I don't know what the boss is planning with all this, but it's not our place to question. All you gotta know is that he's ordered all hands on deck, and he's put up the money to make that happen. So if you want the biggest payday of your life, here's what you do. You go out there and you sell like your life depends on it. You go to all your friends and get them to sell it. I don't even care if you give it away, but I want you to get everyone you know so high on this crap they can't see straight, and I want you to do it before the end of the night. Pull that off for me, Robbie, and this—" he wiggled the wad of cash in his hand "—is gonna look like paper-route money. So what do you say? You in?"

Robert was already nodding. "Hell yeah."

Angelo grinned and tossed him the cash. "Then get your ass out of here and get to it. Pull your car around to the loading bay and tell the guys on the floor I said to hook you up. I want your trunk so full—"

He cut off abruptly, his dark skin turning suddenly ashen, like he'd seen a ghost. Robbie was too busy stuffing the cash into his jacket to see why at first, but when he turned around at last, a man was standing behind him in the doorway. A tall, slender man with a—*Damn, is that a* sword?—strapped to his belt.

That was enough to send Robbie's stomach straight to his feet. He'd never seen this man before, but he'd heard the rumors, and it wasn't like there were that many scary giants with swords. This could only be Lincoln Black, the Big Boss's enforcer and the scariest man in Chicago.

He wasn't alone, either. There was a middle-aged man behind him who looked suspiciously like a cop. That was enough to make Robbie pause, but tough as the old cop looked, he wasn't saying shit, and he was staying well away from Black, which proved he had sense. Everyone—from bigwigs like Angelo to pushers like Robbie—avoided Black at all costs. There was no avoiding him now, though. He'd already shut the door in the maybe-cop's face, closing himself into the small office with

Robert and Angelo with a smile like a panther shutting himself in with the mice.

As the man with the most to lose, Angelo recovered first. "Black," he said, standing up. "I didn't expect you here so—"

"I didn't think I'd be coming," Black said, his voice sudden and smooth as a backstab. "All the reports say you're on target, which means we have nothing to discuss."

Angelo relaxed visibly at that, though not by much. "If you're not here about production, then why—"

"Personal business," the enforcer said casually, turning his dark eyes toward Robert. "A little bird told me you had a pusher coming up through the ranks by the name of Robert Jefferson." He looked Robbie up and down. "That you?"

Terrified, Robbie finally nodded, and Black's thin lips split into an even thinner smile before he turned back to Angelo.

"I'm borrowing him."

Robert's boss began to sweat. "But you can't. We've got a warehouse full of pallets to move. I need him for—"

"I'm borrowing him," Black said again, hand falling to his sword.

"All yours," Angelo said, sinking back to the couch.

Robbie shot him a betrayed look, and Angelo mouthed *Sorry*, but they both knew there was nothing to be done. In the underworld of Chicago, Lincoln Black was another name for God. Whatever he wanted, he got.

Robbie just hoped he wanted him alive.

Shaking so bad he could hardly stand, Robbie turned and followed the enforcer back into the warehouse. Since he'd said he wasn't here about production, Robbie assumed they'd go outside, but Black made no move toward any of the doors. He just told his silent companion—the one Robbie was starting to think couldn't actually be a cop no matter how much he looked like one—to wait as he turned and led Robbie up the stairs to the back half of the top floor.

Unlike the room full of packers Angelo had shown Robbie when they'd come in, this half of the warehouse's upper story was empty, just a big open space ringed in with plastic-wrapped pallets of Z3X waiting to be shipped. It was also apparently Black's private hangout, complete with a leather sectional couch in the corner, a wall of flat-screen TVs showing muted news feeds from across the country, a giant bar full of top-shelf booze, and a display of weaponry and old-school torture devices on the walls that would have put a museum to shame. The whole thing was arranged around a clear square of metal-grated floor from which Black could oversee the entire Z3X manufacturing operation below, though he didn't seem to be paying it any attention as he walked behind the bar, lovingly petting one of the shiny metal pokers hanging on the wall before turning to grab a bottle of whiskey that probably cost more than Robbie made in a month.

"Can I get you something?" Black asked politely. "Whiskey? Vodka? Or maybe something harder?"

He reached below the bar as he said this. When he came back up, he was holding a small baggie of heroin. Robbie licked his lips. He tried never to dip into his own stock—it was bad for business and the fastest way to fall out of being a pusher and into being a junkie yourself—but he had one hell of a soft spot for H. Even now when he was terrified, the little baggie called to him, and from the cruel look on his face, Lincoln knew it.

"Sounded like Angelo was making you one hell of a deal down there," Black said, opening the baggie and casually tapping a few grams of Z3X into the mix from a giant container of the stuff. "He plays a good drug lord, but at the end of the day, he's just another middleman trying to meet his quota. You and

I, though, we're different. We have ambitions." He glanced at Robbie. "You want to make it as a rapper, right?"

Robbie tore his eyes off the drugs at last. "How do you know that?"

"'Cause everyone wants to be a rapper these days," Black said flippantly. "You've also got your demo up all over the internet. Kind of a tip-off." *Oh yeah.* Feeling like an idiot, Robbie was about to ask why Black had been researching him when the taller man gave the baggie of H a seductive shake before pouring it out onto a silver tray.

"Tough business, music," Black said, stroking his long fingers through the white powder. "But not if you know the right people. Alone, you could try for years just to get an intern to notice you, but a well-connected man like myself could get you a recording deal just like that." He snapped his fingers. "That'd be worth something, wouldn't it?"

God, it would, but . . . "Why would you do that?" Robbie asked, incredulous. "I don't even know you."

"And I don't know you," Black said. "I don't give a damn about your music, either. But lucky for you, you've got something I want, and I'm *very* generous when it comes to getting what I want."

He held out his hand as he finished, offering Robbie the platter of pure white H cut through with the black lines of Z3X like he was passing around a tray of appetizers. "I'm a simple man," Black said as Robbie took the tray. "You play along, you'll get everything your heart desires. I've been doing this for a long time now, and everything guys like you kill for—drugs, girls, cash, record contracts—it's cheap for someone like me. I can get you anything you want, and all you have to do is do what I say. Easy, right? Of course, if you try to stab me in my back, I'll spread your guts all over town without breaking a sweat, but let's not get ahead of ourselves."

Robbie's hands began to shake on the tray. "What do you want me to do? Angelo's already paid me to push Z3X, so—"

"That's Angelo's problem," Black said dismissively. "The job I've got for you is much more important."

Given how crazy everyone was going over Z3X, and how much money Angelo had been willing to fork over just for a pair of extra hands, Robbie didn't see how that was possible, but he asked anyway. "What is it?"

Black's smile widened. "You've got a sister, right? Doctor at Mercy Hospital?"

Robbie blinked. Out of everything, that was the last thing he'd expect Black to care about. "You mean Lauryn? Yeah, she's my sister. What about it?"

"Nothing much," Black said casually. "She's just been keeping some . . . interesting company lately. And since we're throwing such a big party tonight, I thought we'd invite her and her new boyfriend. Just to spice things up."

Robert couldn't help himself. "Are we talking about the same Lauryn Jefferson?" Because other than that white boy she'd dated for half a second, his sister couldn't catch a boyfriend to save her life, and she was too straight edge to set foot in anything remotely resembling the kind of party Black would throw.

"I don't know," Black said. "You got another ER doctor in the family?"

Robert shook his head, and Black spread his hands like that was that. "I want you to call her and invite her over," he said, strolling back to his cabinet to pour himself a shot. "Her and her gentleman guest. Do that for me, Robbie, and I'll make your dreams come true."

That was a tempting offer, especially when Robbie knew the man in front of him actually had the connections to pull it off. Still. "You're not going to hurt her, are you?"

"Moi?" Black asked innocently. "What do you think?"

Robbie's eyes went straight to the sword on Black's hip, and the assassin began to laugh. "Yeah—that's what I think, too," he said, downing his shot in one smooth motion "But I didn't bring you up here to explain my motives. You're here—and *alive*—because I want to have a few words with the man who's become obsessed with your sister. Beyond that, though, I don't care about her. I'd go over to your father's house myself if I could, but in case you haven't noticed, we've got a lot going on right now, and preachers' houses are . . . let's say *difficult* for me to enter. You know how it is."

Robert didn't actually have any idea what he was talking about, but now didn't seem to be a good time to admit that. "So you won't hurt Lauryn," he said, making sure. "Just this guy who's with her?"

"More or less," Black said, nodding. "But trust me, he has it coming. I can handle everything once they get here, I just need you to make the call. Do that for me, and I'll take care of you." He smiled wide, a cruel, predatory flash of white teeth. "Trust me."

Robbie didn't see how he could trust anyone with a smile like that, but what choice did he have? Black wasn't someone you said no to—that, at least, was something he could trust. And it wasn't like he was actually interested in Lauryn. He just wanted the dude who was with her, which meant Robbie wouldn't be betraying his sister at all. He was just making a call . . .

"If you could justify this to yourself a little faster, that'd be great," Black said, snapping his fingers. "I'm on a schedule. In fact, here."

He walked over and grabbed the metal plate of H out of Robert's hands, taking a big pinch in his gloved fingers and shoving it under Robbie's nose. "This Lady H is the good stuff. Pure enough to snort, and she makes all the hard decisions easy. So go ahead, take a hit, and when you're done, this will all be easy."

He had a point there, and it wasn't like he'd be able to say no anyway, so Robbie leaned down and breathed deep, snorting the drug like he'd never get another hit.

The effect was immediate. Black wasn't lying about this being the good stuff, because the rush of intense pleasure hit him like a train. But just as Robbie was getting ready for the ride, the high shifted. For a long heartbeat, he felt like he was teetering on the first crest of a roller coaster. And then, without warning, he pitched over the edge, sliding in free-fall down, down, down into a pit like nothing he'd ever known where the darkness was alive and claws dragged him under.

"What—" he whispered, or thought he whispered. "What is this?"

"Top of the line," Black said, his voice coming from very far away. "Sin in a powder." Something cold and sleek slid into Robbie's limp hand. His cell phone, he realized dimly.

"You'll be tripping for a while, so I suggest you hold on tight and enjoy the ride," Black's voice drifted over him. "I have to go play tour guide for a dead man, boss's orders, but I'll be back in plenty of time to close the trap." He chuckled. "Your little bitch of a doctor's a slippery target, but she never could leave a patient in the lurch, and I'm betting that goes double for her brother. So you just sit there and focus on getting nice and pathetic. And in a few hours when the haze of your own private hell finally lets go just enough for you to cry for help, you know who to call." He tapped Robbie's fingers against the smartphone's cool screen. "Just mash it anywhere, and that phone will call your little doctor and her protector right into my loving arms. That's all I need from you, kiddo. Just be your weak, pathetic self, and when it's over, I'll take care of everything, just like I promised."

He patted Robbie on the head like a dog as he finished, but Robbie was too gone to care. All he could feel were the hands in the dark, the horrible hooked claws dragging him down toward a dark, hot place that reeked of brimstone and death. By the time he realized he was alone in the room, the stench was so thick he couldn't form words. All he could do was clutch the phone and wait, battling his way through the fear toward his sister. His last chance at escape.

11
INTENTIONS OF THE HEART

After trying, and failing, for twenty minutes to get in touch with her brother, Lauryn decided phones just weren't going to cut it. She wanted to go out and look for him herself, but Chicago was a big place, and from what she'd been able to dig out of her dad, the parts of it Robbie usually went weren't places she could search easily. She was also in no condition to search. Between the attack yesterday, a terrible night of sleep, and the crisis this morning, Lauryn was running on empty.

Maxwell must have seen it, because once it became clear she wasn't having any more luck with Robert than he was, he'd asked her to go back to the house instead, just in case her brother came home. When Lauryn had quipped that maybe *he* should go home and wait, Maxwell had gruffly informed her that he had a duty to his congregation. After that, she'd just given up, because God forbid her dad put anything—including his son—over his precious church.

The angry thought was reflex, but as soon as it was done, Lauryn knew she wasn't being fair. Given her own realization about her role—or lack thereof—in her brother's life, Lauryn could even admit there might be four fingers pointing back. Either way, someone had to help Robbie, and since her dad wasn't leaving his church anytime soon, the task fell to Lauryn. And Talon, since he still refused to leave her alone.

Since the car was stalled and there were apparently no more miracles on tap to get it going again, they'd had to walk. Thankfully, it wasn't far, and Lauryn knew the way by heart. Even with the snow, it was only ten minutes before they walked into her dad's living room.

Of course, Robbie wasn't home, so Lauryn plopped down on the blanket-covered couch in front of the door to wait for the little delinquent to show up. Talon dutifully took the spot across from her without a word, lowering his big body carefully into her father's rickety old chair with his sword across his lap. *That* would be a sight to greet Robbie when he came in, but for once, the thought of her brother freaking out couldn't bring a smile to Lauryn's face. She just wanted him to come home safe and sound.

And preferably not with a police escort. That was a depressingly likely scenario. But despite Lauryn's intention to wait by the door like an angry mama bear, she must have been more tired than she'd realized. One moment, she was sitting on her father's couch across from Talon, the next she was waking up in a dark room lit only by the last traces of the day's gray sunlight filtering in through the living room's lacy curtains.

She sat up with a curse, grabbing her phone off the table. *Six* PM. She'd been asleep all afternoon. There were no calls from Robert, either, which pissed her off even more. She was also hungry. Starving, actually, which made sense considering she hadn't eaten anything today. Fortunately, unlike everything else that had happened, hunger was a problem she could fix, and so Lauryn hauled herself off the couch and teetered into the kitchen to see what was for dinner.

Not much, seemed to be the answer. Her father must have still been at the church, because the usual offerings hadn't appeared in the fridge yet. Since no one in their family could cook, that meant Lauryn's choices were cans and boxes. She was waffling between beef stew and good old blue-box mac'n'cheese when she heard a strange, almost musical sound coming from the backyard.

Like most of the freestanding houses in this part of Chicago, her dad's home had a tiny postage-stamp square of grass for a backyard. A tall board fence gave it privacy from the identical yards of their neighbors, but the high walls also made the already small space feel even smaller. An illusion that was further emphasized by Talon, who seemed to be taking up all the space by standing right in the middle with his shirt off and his sword balanced like a feather in his outstretched hand.

"What are you doing?" Lauryn asked, glancing nervously at his cast-off clothes. "Aren't you cold?"

"The discomfort is part of the practice," Talon replied, swinging his sword in a beautiful arc through the air. The blade whistled as it flew, the musical sound Lauryn had heard before. "Comfort dulls the mind and makes you complacent. In the cold, everything is sharper."

"If you say so, sensei," Lauryn said, wrapping her arms around herself. "Can you at least put on a shirt? I'm getting cold just looking at you."

Instead of answering, Talon swung his sword again, but this time, he accompanied the move with a graceful kick that turned into a leap, sending his body moving like silk through the air. He followed this up with another series of rapid-fire moves, his body dancing weightlessly around the tiny square of grass.

By the time he came to a stop again, Lauryn's jaw was hanging open. She hadn't even known humans could move like that before this moment. She was still gawking shamelessly when Talon turned to her with a smile.

"Want to try?"

Lauryn blinked in shock. "What? Me?"

Talon moved toward her, flipping the sword in his hand to offer her the hilt, and Lauryn jumped back inside so fast she tripped over the doorstep. "No way," she said, putting her hands up. "I'll just stab myself."

"Being afraid of a weapon is often more dangerous than the weapon itself," Talon said. "Just hold it. Everyone should know how to handle weapons for their own safety, even if they never mean to use one."

Lauryn didn't know about that. That sword was *big*, not to mention heavy looking, and when was she ever going to need to hold a *sword* again anyway? But even as her mouth opened to tell him no, her fingers were drawn toward the wrapped handle. It really was lovely, she realized with a pang, the blade shining mirror bright in the evening's last sunlight.

Talon handed it to her slowly, easing the weight into her grip. But though the blade was definitely too heavy for her as she'd predicted, there was something about the weight in her hand that Lauryn liked *way* more than she'd expected. She'd never done anything physical as a kid, no sports or dance or martial arts. This was partially because her dad had never had the time or money to enroll her in anything and partially because Lauryn wasn't exactly what anyone would call coordinated. She wouldn't go so far as to say she was klutzy—her hand was steady enough in the ER—but her earlier comment about stabbing herself hadn't been an exaggeration. With the exception of scalpels, Lauryn and knives generally didn't mix. But this sword must have been special, because when she curled her fingers around the grip, she didn't feel unsure or uncoordinated at all. She felt powerful, like she was holding a dragon by the tail.

Talon must have seen it in her expression, because he gave her a knowing smile. "Go ahead," he said, stepping back. "Give it a swing."

Lauryn shook her head rapidly. Holding the beautiful weapon was one thing, but that edge was *sharp*. If she started flailing it around, she could take off someone's arm, probably hers. Before she could open her mouth to tell him as much, though, Talon cut her off.

"You won't hurt anyone," he assured her, stepping back until he was leaning against the back fence, well out of her way. "Just try."

She took a deep breath and looked down, flexing her grip on the blade's handle. It did feel lovely in her hand, perfectly balanced and heavy, but in a good way. A *strong* way, the sort where she swore she could already feel it moving. After a moment's hesitation, she moved with it, letting the sword's weight pull them both through the air in a wide sweep. It wasn't nearly as fast or impressive as anything Talon had done, but the move still made her feel like she was flying. A feeling that only got better with every additional stroke she made.

"It suits you," Talon said with a smile.

"Not really," Lauryn argued, blushing that he'd caught her having so much fun. "It's too big."

"We'll get you a smaller one," he assured her. "Someone who takes to a holy sword that quickly clearly needs one of her own."

That comment killed the moment like a shot to the head,

and Lauryn dropped her arm with a sigh. She was about to tell Talon that they were absolutely not rehashing the ridiculous conversation from earlier when her phone began to ring, buzzing and rattling loudly across the table she'd left it on in the living room.

With that, Talon was instantly forgotten. Lauryn raced through the house, almost tripping over the half step between the kitchen and the living room in her rush to get to her phone. Sure enough, when she snatched it up, it was Robbie's number, and she clutched the phone with both hands as she frantically hit the icon to accept the call.

"*Robbie!*"

The silence on the other end stretched on so long, Lauryn began to worry she'd gotten worked up over an accidental pocket dial. Eventually, though, her brother's tiny broken voice whispered, "Lauryn?"

"It's me," she said, whole body slumping in relief. "Where are you? Do you need help?"

"I don't . . . I . . ." He broke off with a shudder. "I need you, Lauryn. Been trying to call forever, but . . ." He gasped again. "Help me! They're everywhere, clawing. The *voices.*"

The terrified words made her blood run cold. Robert's babbling was nonsense, but it was nonsense she'd heard before. Just this morning, in fact, coming from the mouths of her patients in the burn ward. "Oh, Robert," she whispered. "What have you done?"

His only answer was a shaking, labored breath, and Lauryn closed her eyes.

"It doesn't matter," she said quietly. "Whatever's going wrong, whatever you're on, you're still my brother. We can fix this. I love you and I won't abandon you. Now tell me where you are."

There was another long pause, and then Robbie whispered

something that sounded like an address. Sure enough, when Lauryn tapped it into her phone, a map popped up for a warehouse by the river not too far away. Given how out of it Robbie sounded, she wasn't sure if that was actually right. The place looked all but deserted. It was all she had, though, so it would have to do.

"I'm on my way," she promised, hopping up to grab her bag and the emergency med kit inside. "Just hold on."

"Hurry," he whispered. "They're telling me they won't let me go until you come."

That sent chills down Lauryn's spine before she reminded herself that Robbie was likely high out of his mind. She'd suspected drugs from the start, of course, but until she'd heard the proof in his own voice, she hadn't let herself connect her brother with the strange outbreak gripping the city. Now, however, she had no choice but to face the truth. But terrified as she was, she refused to believe Robbie was lost.

"We saved the others," she said. "We'll save you, too. Hold on tight, kiddo. We're on our way."

Again, the silence stretched out forever, but this time, it didn't break. Robbie had hung up. On purpose or not, Lauryn didn't know, and she didn't care. She was already racing out the door . . . only to skid to a stop when she realized she no longer had a ride.

Cursing under her breath, she was about to march right back inside and call a cab when she heard the rumbling of a familiar engine. A few moments later, Talon pulled around the corner, perched on a bike exactly like the one she'd seen him riding the night he'd appeared under her window.

"Hop on," he said, tossing her a helmet.

Lauryn caught it without looking, her face bewildered. "Wait," she said at last. "Didn't you leave your bike at the hospital?"

"I did," Talon replied, lifting up the visor of his helmet. "But when I heard you on the phone with your brother, I knew we'd need a ride. When I went outside to look for one, I found this."

"Found," she repeated, looking at the bike more closely. "So that's not yours?"

He shook his head. "I believe it belongs to your neighbor three doors down."

"So you're just going to take it?" she cried. "What happened to 'thou shalt not steal'?"

"It's not stealing if you bring it back," Talon replied with infuriating calm. "And since it was waiting for me with the keys already in the ignition, I have faith that this was meant to be."

"*I* have faith that it's grand theft auto," Lauryn said, scowling. "Though I suppose you'd call it another miracle?"

Talon smiled. "'What we need, the Lord provides.'"

Lauryn doubted the actual owner would see it that way, but she was in too big a hurry to argue over Talon's suspicious ability to "find" things. She'd make Robbie pay the guy back for the bike later if it came to that. Right now, they were running out of time. "Let's just go," she said, shoving the helmet in her hands onto her head. When she was sure it wouldn't fall off, she vaulted up onto the bike behind him, wrapping her arms around Talon's broad back as he gunned the engine. He took off a second later, blasting down the quiet, snowy street with a speed that made her gasp. She held on with all her might, pressing her face into his coat to protect herself from the icy wind as she told him to go even faster, hoping against hope that they weren't already too late.

At the same time, not far away, Will was entering the third hour of his stakeout.

He'd followed Korigan's limo all over town, and the results had been *very* enlightening. Apparently, the police chief wasn't just covering things up to save face. If the places he and Lincoln

Black went to were anything to go by, Victor Korigan was neck-deep in the entire drug-making and distribution process for all of Chicago.

They'd ended their tour at a big warehouse by the river, which seemed to be acting as the distribution hub for all the Z3X trucks in central Chicago. Will hadn't been able to follow them inside, so he'd kept watch from a nearby alley, organizing all the pictures he'd taken during the drive into a massive and damning pile of evidence he meant to send to the DA (and the press) as soon as possible. He was especially proud of the shots he'd gotten of Korigan and Lincoln Black together, since Black's face—clearly recognizable from the hospital's security cameras—was the smoking gun of the whole case.

The only reason he hadn't sent it yet was because he wanted to make sure his case against Korigan was watertight. He'd underestimated the police chief twice now, and both times he'd regretted it. This time, Will wasn't budging until he'd built a trap so secure, even a slick eel like Korigan couldn't wiggle his way out. He was taking another set of pictures of the well-armed thugs standing around a van whose plates were registers to C-Company, the mercenary company Korigan had owned—and supposedly disbanded—before taking his current job as chief of police, when his ears caught the distant rumble of a motorcycle.

Looking back, Will couldn't say why that sound in particular had stood out. The city was full of bikes, not to mention he was sitting outside of a warehouse staffed entirely by guys in the drug business. Loud engines were the norm around here, and yet, for reasons he couldn't explain, this particular rumble made him look up from his camera just in time to see a bike with two riders pull around the corner of the side alley he'd chosen for his stakeout.

Two riders that looked an *awful* lot like Lauryn and Talon.

He dismissed the crazy idea immediately. Lauryn hadn't

been interested in his investigation this morning, but even if she'd changed her mind for some reason, there was no way, *no way* someone as smart as she was would be stupid enough to drive straight into a situation this dangerous. It had to be some other girl riding around with a big dude who carried a sword, just had to—

Lauryn took off her helmet, and Will swore a blue streak, jumping out of his car to grab her before the lookouts spotted them. He'd barely made it a foot before Talon turned around, smiling like he'd known Will was there the whole time.

"Hello, Detective."

Lauryn jumped at the greeting, which was the only part of this Will felt good about. At least he'd snuck up on someone. "What are you doing here?"

"What are *you* doing here?" Lauryn said, chest heaving. "You scared the daylights out of me!"

All the more reason for her *not* to be here. "I'm here for work," Will said sternly. "This is a stakeout."

For some reason, that announcement made her whole face crumple. "I knew it," she whispered, looking at the warehouse across the street. "I was hoping it was just a flophouse, but . . . This is where they make the drug, isn't it?"

"One of many," he said, puzzled. "But why are you here, then? You said you were done."

"I was," she said bitterly. "But then I got a call from my brother."

And just like that, Will understood. He'd met Lauryn's little brother only once before, when he'd picked the kid up for possession. At the time, he and Lauryn had just started dating, and he'd let him go with a warning so he wouldn't have to tell his brand-new girlfriend he'd busted her brother. At the time, he'd convinced himself he was doing both of them a favor, but he'd seen Robbie in the clubs plenty of times since. He'd always held off investigating out of respect for Lauryn and the hope that Robbie would turn himself around. Now, though, Will had a sinking feeling that all his leniency had done was cut the kid enough slack to hang himself. "He's in there, isn't he?"

Lauryn nodded, and Will swore under his breath. "And I suppose you think you're going in after him?"

"I have to," she said. "Will, I heard him on the phone. He sounded exactly like the burn ward patients did this morning before they went insane. What was I supposed to do? Leave him to his suffering?"

Call the cops. That was what he wanted to say, but considering he'd found this place himself by ignoring his suspension and following the chief of police, that wasn't advice Will felt comfortable giving anymore. Not that it changed the fact that a civilian like Lauryn shouldn't go anywhere near that warehouse.

"Forget it," he said. "It's way too dangerous."

She scowled. "I'm not going to just—"

"Then I'll go," he snapped, cutting her off. "I wanted to get a look inside anyway."

"You can't go," Lauryn cried. "You're not even medically trained. What are you going to do?"

"Bring him out to you," Will said, reaching into his glove box to grab his backup gun. "'Cause like hell I'm letting you go in there alone."

"She won't be alone," Talon said, cutting in for the first time. "I'll be with her."

"Like that makes it better," Will said, looking Talon up and down. "So far as I'm concerned, you're *both* nuts, and you're *not* going in."

Lauryn's glare turned dangerous. "I don't need your permission to save my brother. He's in there, possibly alone, suffering under the effects of the same unknown drug as this morning. He needs immediate medical attention, which means he needs *me*. I don't know how I'm going to swing that yet, but I am definitely not going to stand out here waiting while you go in alone. End of discussion."

Will didn't see how that was the end of anything, but before he could remind her that he was the one with the gun and the training, the big warehouse doors across the street rattled open, and a whole convoy of trucks began to pull out. Hidden in the tiny alley as they were, Will, Lauryn, and Talon didn't have to do more than step sideways to avoid being seen as the trucks drove by. A lucky stroke, to be sure, but considering how many trucks passed them, Will was having a hard time feeling good about it.

"Damn," he whispered, pulling out his phone to take a few more pictures. "How many of these are there?"

"What's in them?" Lauryn whispered back.

"Z3X," Will said. "It's an additive I've been tracking for a while now. The official story is that it's something they use to make the drugs stronger with no real effects of its own, kind of like how a little salt makes food taste better without actually being salty. Considering I've seen factories pumping out trucks of the stuff all afternoon, though, I'm not so sure that's the case anymore." At this rate, given how many of those trucks he'd seen roll out in the last few hours, there was probably more Z3X on the streets than the drugs it was supposed to enhance.

From the look on her face, Lauryn's thoughts were following the same track. "Do you think this Z3X could be related to the green stuff and all the other problems we've been having?"

"Do I think so? Of course. Do I have proof?" Will shook his head. "Before Korigan kicked me out of the office, we were running Z3X at the lab, and everything we found came back with nothing. So far as we can tell, it's just inert powder, a chemical cocktail of otherwise safe ingredients. We don't even know how it enhances drug effects. To be honest, before now, I kind of thought that was just some clever marketing to make junkies accept cut drugs."

Lauryn bit her lip, thinking. "That list," she said, her eyes sharp. "Did it include sulfur by any chance?"

Will nodded. "That was the first thing I checked. Sulfur was compound number two on the lab report, but there's not enough to be toxic."

"Even trace amounts are good enough for me," Lauryn said, rising up from her crouch. "For now, though, we should go. They just sent out a massive shipment, which means they'll be both chaotic and empty. We'll never have a better chance to get inside."

That was a damn good point, and Will was sick of arguing anyway. Lauryn was impossible to put off once she got something stuck in her head. The best he could do was go along and keep her from getting hurt.

"Fine," he said, grabbing a USB stick and connecter out of his pocket so he could pull the evidence photos from his phone. "You want to be crazy, let's be crazy. Just give me a sec to make a backup of what I've found so far for the DA and—"

He cursed under his breath. In the moment he'd looked away, Lauryn and Talon were already jogging across the street toward the gate the departing trucks had left open in the fence. Talon even had his sword out, guiding Lauryn through the dark like he was a paladin leading a siege on the enemy fortress. Swearing up a storm, Will backed up his photos as fast as he could and shoved the USB stick deep into his car's glove box. He'd have much rather gone ahead and sent them to the DA, interior warehouse photos or no. But without a careful note explaining what the pictures showed, the evidence wouldn't mean anything, and he had no time. He'd just have to do it later.

For now, he darted across the street, keeping his gun ready as he chased Lauryn and Talon into the shadow of the warehouse.

And high overhead, invisible in the dark, a tall man with a sword of his own stepped away from the factory window with a grin.

12

INTO THE LION'S DEN

The detective insisted on leading the way.

Talon was happy to let him. Bringing up the rear let him keep a closer eye on Lauryn, and after what had happened in the backyard, he needed to watch her more closely than ever.

His fingers tightened at the memory, gripping the hilt of his sword so hard it hurt. The weapon of a Soldier of El Elyon was a holy object, the physical proof of a warrior's strength, faith, and sacrifice. Receiving one was a sacred rite and a holy mystery unique to every SEE warrior. Talon's own had come to him via the hardest road imaginable. It was, in short, *not* something the average person could just pick up and play with . . . and yet that was exactly what Lauryn had done. But then, Talon had known from the beginning that she was no ordinary young doctor. The moment her voice had reached Lenny buried in the depths of demonic possession, he'd known she was the one he'd come to Chicago to find.

He only wished he knew why.

Talon had learned long ago that faith in the Lord was never misplaced. It was a lesson his old teacher had sacrificed everything to show him: that even when you didn't understand the path, God didn't make mistakes. If you followed and kept the faith, you would always arrive where you were meant to be. That was the road by which Talon lived his life, but even now, so many years later, it still hadn't gotten any easier. For all his faith and trust, it was hard to look at a girl who did not believe, who had no martial training and put no value on it, who refused to accept miracles even when they happened right under her nose, and not wonder, *why her?*

Why would God choose someone so unsuited? Surely, in all of Chicago, there was someone more qualified, more ready to take up this burden. *Surely*, it had to be so, and yet every sign so far had pointed squarely at Lauryn, and unlike her, Talon never ignored the work of God's hands. For reasons only God knew, Lauryn had been chosen, and that made it Talon's duty to protect, aid, and guide her. But while the physical protection part of that was easy enough, his attempts in the other areas were abject failures. At this point, Talon was positive that if Jesus himself came down on a cloud, Lauryn's reaction would be to stick her hand into the spear wound in his side to make sure it was real . . . and then send his sacred blood to the lab for testing.

But while the whole situation was frustrating beyond belief, Talon knew better than to expect an answer. The saying that "God works in mysterious ways" was there for a reason. Talon was hardly the first man to be baffled by the will of the Almighty. He couldn't make Lauryn believe any more than he could make her into the sort of pious, holy warrior he wished he'd been sent to find. All he could do was push ahead and remember that the Lord knew what he was doing, even when it didn't seem that way.

And speaking of . . .

"My god . . . " Will whispered as he pushed open the warehouse's metal door.

Lauryn had already crowded in behind him, her dark eyes gone wide. "How is there so much?"

Talon was wondering the same thing. From the outside, the warehouse had looked like any of the dirty redbrick turn-of-the-century meat processing houses that had dotted this part of the city since Chicago's boom days. Inside, however, was an entirely different story.

The cement floor, once used for packing, was now completely covered in huge metal tanks the size of swimming pools. The door Will had chosen for their entrance was a slightly elevated fire exit, a protected vantage point that both provided cover from the workers on the floor and gave them an excellent view of the emerald-green liquid being stirred inside each one and then pumped out onto a drying belt where it hardened and broke down into a blackish-gray powder. This, in turn, was scraped into huge bags by men wearing gas masks to protect their lungs from the noxious reek of sulfur that hung like a plague in the air.

There was also a suspended second-floor area where still more men worked like fiends, dividing the industrial sacks of powder into smaller personal-sized baggies, which were then loaded onto pallets and sent back downstairs via a lift to the loading bay. Since they'd just seen a shipment go out, Talon would have expected this to be empty, but the bay looked full to him, the pallets of powder stacked three-deep against the walls. A detail Will noticed as well.

"They must be making it faster than they can ship it," he said, pulling out his phone to start snapping pictures. "This is crazy. I've never seen drugs manufactured on this scale. And this is only one factory. They've got more." He gritted his teeth. "There must be more Z3X than people in Chicago by now."

Lauryn nodded slowly, but her eyes weren't on the pallets. She was staring at the vats on the floor where the emerald liquid was bubbling. "That's . . ."

"The same thing you found on Lenny," Talon agreed, nodding. "And the substance Lincoln Black tried to use on you."

"They're refining it," she whispered, looking furious. "That black powder is made from the green drug that was causing the OD cases!"

"It's worse than that," Will said bitterly, leaning over the railings to get a good shot of the vats. "*All* of that is Z3X. According to my sources, it's been added to every street drug sold in Chicago for months. What we're seeing here is just a ramp-up of production."

"But why?" Lauryn asked, confused. "This stuff *kills* people. Why would anyone want to fill the city with it?"

"Because that's the point," Talon said, his jaw tightening. Now, at last, it was all coming together. "Remember what I told you about the drug trapping sinners in despair? If what the detective says is true, then that's why all the patients in the burn ward this morning had the same symptoms despite all being addicted to different vices. Everything they took was laced with Z3X. That was the path. Once the drug pried open the cracks, all the demons had to do was come inside."

By the time he finished, Will was looking at him like Talon was the one high on drugs. Lauryn, on the other hand, seemed to be giving his words serious thought. That was more than Talon had expected, and he was starting to hope that Lauryn's faith was growing, when she suddenly turned back to Will.

"You have to call someone," she said urgently. "Supernatural hoodoo aside, whatever this stuff is, we know for a fact that it's extremely dangerous *and* contagious. I'm still not sure what the trigger is, but every addict in Chicago has to be full of this stuff by now. If they start to pop, they'll attack everyone around them, multiplying the problem exponentially." She began to shake. "If we don't do something quick, what happened in the burn ward this morning could happen to the entire city!"

"I know," Will snapped. "But who the hell am I going to call? I found this place by shadowing the *chief* of *police*. The same guy who's been hushing up what happened in the burn ward. I'd bet a million bucks he's been in on all of this from the start, which explains why it's been so hard to investigate. And besides, there's not a politician in this city Korigan isn't in bed with." And Will had seen personally just how tight his hold on the cops was.

"There has to be someone," Lauryn said.

"Who?" Will asked. "This place has been shipping Z3X like confetti all day. The fact that it's not being raided as we speak is proof of just how tight the crooked bastard's hold is. If I call for backup, he'll just order them to come arrest *me* instead."

"So go over his head," Lauryn said. "Call in the National Guard or something."

"I would," Will said. "But Z3X isn't actually illegal. And despite our theories, we still don't have actual material proof linking this stuff to the burn ward."

"What about all your pictures?"

"Those are for the DA," Will said. "I'm building an ironclad case to nail Korigan to the wall for this. And just in case Korigan's got the DA in his pocket, too, I'm sending the evidence to the state and national anti-corruption offices as well. Trust me, as soon as this blows up, he's going down."

"It's blowing up as we speak!" Lauryn cried. "Forget Korigan——we're talking about a possible citywide outbreak! *That's* what we need to stop."

"If you know how, I'm all ears," Will said. "But you're not

listening. The police chief of all of Chicago is in bed with this whole operation. If we call for help, all we'll be doing is letting him know that *we* know, which means we'll need to be silenced. That doesn't end well for us, Lauryn."

"None of this is going to end well if we don't do something," she said, fists clenching. "I'm not going to stand around waiting for people to die. First we find my brother, and then we're going to figure out how to shut down this factory."

"It won't matter," Will said tiredly. "Like I said, this is just their biggest facility. I saw a dozen more smaller ones, trailing Korigan earlier today, not to mention all the Z3X that's already out there."

She threw up her hands. "So we shouldn't even try?"

"I'm *trying* to keep you from getting killed!"

"I'm pretty sure my life would be a small price to pay for preventing an entire city from going through what happened at the hospital this morning," Lauryn said, lifting her chin stubbornly. "You do what you want. *I'm* going to save my brother, and then I'm going to do whatever I can to fix this. I'm a doctor—that's what I do. I fix things. It might not be enough, but at least I won't have to live with myself knowing I could have helped, and did nothing."

By the time she finished, Will looked ready to throttle her. Talon, however, was bursting with pride. He'd watched this back-and-forth with apprehension, but now he had nothing but confidence. She might not believe, but no one could argue that Lauryn's heart wasn't fierce, and in exactly the right place. "Come then," he said, cutting off Will, who was clearly not done arguing. "Let's find your brother."

Lauryn nodded and pulled out her phone, dialing Robert's number and going still, listening. Talon listened, too, but he didn't hear a sound. Either Robert's phone was silenced, or too far away to hear. But just as he was about to suggest a search, Lauryn's arm shot up to point at something over their heads. "There!"

Talon and Will both spun around to look, squinting up through the metal grate that served as the floor for the warehouse's second story. Sure enough, at the end of the wall, a light was shining down through the cracks. When they got closer, it became obvious it was from the bright LED glow of a smartphone screen lying facedown on the grate where it had dropped from the hand of the slumped figure collapsed beside it.

"Robbie," Lauryn gasped, the blood draining from her face before she turned and bolted for the metal stairs at a dead run.

Talon followed her instantly. A few seconds later, Will did, too, cursing under his breath about making as much noise as a herd of elephants—which Talon didn't actually disagree with. Thankfully, the giant machines churning the pools of Z3X made enough noise to cover, and they made it to the second floor without attracting attention.

Unlike the other half of the upper warehouse area, which served as a packing room, this part of the building's second story had been done up almost like a loft apartment. And in a corner where a leather sectional had been set up below some tasteful exposed lighting, a young man in a puffy jacket—whose face looked very much like his sister's—was slumped on the ground, looking like he'd fallen straight off the couches.

Lauryn ran to her brother's side without a word, but she hissed when she saw the baggie clutched in his outstretched hand. "What's that?"

"Heroin," Will replied instantly with the surety of someone who'd answered that question too many times to count.

"Idiot," Lauryn sighed, glaring down at her brother's unconscious face. "We need to get him to the hospital."

"No call for that," Will replied, reaching into his pocket. "He's just tripping, but I can fix that."

She glanced up, confused. "You can?"

"Vice cop, remember?" Will said, pulling out a plastic kit and holding it up for her to see. "We deal with this kind of thing all the time, which means I travel prepared."

Lauryn nodded like that made sense, but Talon was curious. "What is that?" he asked as Will unzipped what looked like a diabetic's insulin kit.

"Naloxone shot," the detective replied, pulling out a prefilled syringe and cracking the plastic head off the needle. "Instantly reverses the opium high. Even if he's OD'd, this should be enough to bring him back down to earth. Of course, it might not be a pleasant fall, but that's the price you pay for putting shit in your system."

"Just be careful," Lauryn said, biting her lip. "Just because Naloxone's common doesn't mean it's without risk. You could give him pulmonary edema."

"I don't even know what that is, but it hasn't happened yet," Will assured her. "Relax. Believe it or not, this is the most normal thing I've done all day."

He stabbed the needle into Robert's arm, and a second later, the kid shot up with a gasp, his eyes flying open to show the bloody sheen covering both whites.

Talon knew what that meant. "He's turning," he warned, grabbing the boy's shoulders and forcing him back to the ground.

"Not yet," Lauryn said back, grabbing her brother as well. "Robbie! Can you hear me?"

For a moment, Robert didn't seem to hear any of it, and then, just like Lenny, he blinked. "Lauryn?"

Relief broke over her face like a sunrise. "It's me," she assured him. "I'm here. We're going to make you better, okay?"

As she spoke, panic glazed over Robert's face. "You can't," he whispered, fighting Talon's hold. "There's no way out! The wings, the teeth—they're everywhere! They're almost here! They'll drag us all down to—"

He cut off with a choking sound, and Lauryn cursed under her breath as the bluish tinge began to seep up his arms where she'd grabbed them. "He's going!"

"So stop him!" Will said, putting his hands on Robbie's shoulders. "You did it before!"

Talon couldn't have put it better himself. For her part, Lauryn looked desperate. "I know," she muttered, eyes wide. "But I can't . . . I just can't pray over him and call it medicine! That's not how this works!"

"But it *is* how this works," Talon said, his voice firm as he stared her down. "It's time to believe, Lauryn. You've been shown the truth again and again. Now you have to embrace it and save your brother's life."

"Why me?" she whispered, her voice cracking with panic. "You're they guy with the holy water! I don't believe in this crazy—"

"You did in the hospital," Talon reminded her, his voice sharp. This was it, he realized. He'd been following all this time, blindly walking the path he'd been set with nothing but faith to assure him it would all work out. But now, as always, God had led him to exactly where he needed to be. Lauryn may not have believed in the beginning, but that didn't mean she couldn't see the light. That, Talon knew at last, was why he'd been sent to her. Not only to protect, but to guide. To lead her to where she needed to be, and now that they were finally here together on the brink, Talon was determined not to fail.

"There is no halfway in this, Lauryn," he said calmly. "Either you believe or you don't, but you know how to save your brother, because you did it before."

She shook her head. "I was desperate before."

"And you are desperate now," Talon said. "But God is there for us in our desperation. He is everywhere. He's offering you the rope, Lauryn. But *you* have to reach out. You have to be willing to take that first leap of faith, or you will never go anywhere at all."

He reached into his coat as he finished, removing the plastic bottle of blessed water that he'd refilled at her father's church. "You know what to do," he said as he held it out to her. "Now heal him as you've healed so many others, and believe."

Lauryn didn't reply. She just sat there, her whole body shaking like she was fighting something, and then Robbie's body lurched under their grip, his face contorting in pain. That must have been the last straw. Whatever else she believed or felt, Lauryn had always been a healer, and that was what she did now, grabbing the bottle of water from Talon's hand and dumping the whole thing over her brother like she was trying to drench him. And as the water fell, Talon knew. He knew it to his bones, knew it like he'd know a miracle happening right under his nose.

Lauryn finally believed.

Lauryn had no idea what she was doing.

Years of practice kept her calm on the outside—doctors *never* panicked—but inside she was a seething mess of fear and contradictions. Part of her actively hated Talon for making her do this, because she *knew* it wouldn't work. As her physiology professor used to joke, if faith healing worked, all operating rooms would be staffed with preachers. Every book she'd read, every day she'd gone to school, every hour she'd pulled in the Mercy ER was a pebble on the mountain of evidence that Talon was asking her to do the impossible, and yet . . .

She looked down at Robbie. Even dressed up in designer

wear, it was funny how much he still looked like the little kid she remembered, the brother she loved. She'd gotten so wrapped up in being a doctor, she hadn't even noticed she was losing him until he was gone. If she didn't save him now, she could lose him forever, but the only way to do that was to accept what Talon was saying. And while she knew he was right, that it *had* worked before, doubt still ate at her. She could almost hear her fellow doctors laughing at her for being such a sucker, buying into things she knew couldn't be true. She could imagine Naree with a look of incredulous scorn as she finally got back to her apartment and tried to explain all this to her roommate. The burn ward this morning had been one thing—there were atheists in foxholes—but this was *different*. Her life wasn't on the line. Robbie's was. If she did this, she'd be putting both of them in God's hands, the same God she'd spent her whole adult life rolling her eyes at. The fact that she was even considering it made her as crazy as Talon.

But she had to do *something*.

And so it went, logic against hope, belief against experience, back and forth and back and forth. She might have gone on like that forever, but then Robbie's body seized under her hands once again, his back arching up off the grate floor so suddenly, she almost lost her grip. And that was what did it, because she'd seen this before. She knew *exactly* what happened after the seizures started. Like everything else today, it made no medical sense, but as she fought her baby brother's violent thrashing, Lauryn realized she didn't care. Everything she'd been wrestling with was still true, but in the face of losing Robbie—of losing anyone else to this scourge—she realized it didn't matter.

She could be right all day long, and Robbie was still going to die. Despite all her years of medical training, all her knowledge, there was nothing she could do to save her brother, so Lauryn gave up trying to be right or logical. She stopped trying to explain what was happening, stopped trying to make sense of the nonsensical. Instead, she tossed the ego and bowed her head, mentally reaching out with everything she had to the God she'd spent her entire life ignoring.

Please, she prayed, the words falling out of her like tears. *You helped me before; do it again. Please save him. Please bring him back to me. Please, God, please, please—*

She was still begging when her brother gasped again, only this time it was an explosive sound of relief. Lauryn's eyes shot open; she grabbed Robbie's head with both her hands, and then without warning, she began to sob. Her brother's skin was going back to normal, the sickly bluish color draining away. He still looked like a junkie who'd just been forced out of a flying high, but compared to what could have been, the transformation was nothing short of miraculous.

In every sense of the word.

Even after her surrender, that realization was too much for Lauryn to take in, so she brushed it aside and grabbed her brother instead, squeezing him so hard it was more like a grapple than a hug.

"Lauryn," Robbie croaked. "Too tight."

"You damn *idiot!*" she sobbed, loosening her grip, but only a fraction. "Don't you ever do that to me again!"

"Do what?" he said, reaching up to grab his head. "I feel like crap. What did you do to me?"

"Kicked you out of your high," Will said.

The sound of his voice was much closer than Lauryn expected, and she looked up with a start to see him kneeling right beside her, glaring down at her brother like a wolf. "You've got a lot of explaining to do, kid."

Robbie blinked at him. "Who the hell are you?"

"Robbie!" Lauryn whispered, but Will just rolled with it.

"Detective Tannenbaum," he said. "Chicago Vice."

"Yeah—where's your badge?"

"He's a cop, Robbie," Lauryn said, rolling her eyes. "Trust me."

He must have, because her brother's eyes went wide. His fear was so transparent, Lauryn could practically see each step as he worked out what Will's presence here meant, right before he shoved her away.

"Aw, man," he said, putting up his hands. "The damn cops? You won't get nothin' from—"

"Save it," Will growled, pulling a pair of cuffs from his back pocket. But just as Lauryn was about to ask if that was really necessary, her brother jerked again, and she glanced up to see Robbie staring not at her or Will or even Talon, but at something behind them, his face going ashen.

"It's *him*."

He sounded so terrified, Lauryn's first thought was that he was still hallucinating, and then she heard it, too. Someone was coming up the stairs behind them. When she turned around, though, she saw that it wasn't one of the warehouse workers or even one of the bruisers acting as lookouts. It was someone infinitely more horrifying, because when she followed her brother's gaze to the stairs, the man from the burn ward was looking straight back at her, leaning on the railings with a sword propped on his shoulder. That was all she managed to see before Talon stepped in front of her with his own blade in his hands.

"Black," he growled.

"Call me Lincoln," the man said, his eyes glittering despite the lack of light. "Surely we're on a first-name basis after all the things we've been through together."

"Then you already know how this ends," Talon said coldly. "I've beaten you before."

"You sure you should be so cocky?" Black asked, his lips peeling back in a jackal's smile. "Pride's a sin, you know. I thought SEE warriors were supposed to set a good example."

Talon's eyes narrowed at that. Before he could reply, though, Will drew his gun and turned the barrel on Lincoln Black's chest. "That's enough posturing," he said slowly, giving them time to see the gun and realize he was deadly serious, despite his lack of a badge. "You guys can have your reunion later. Right now, I want hands where I can see them."

Lincoln shook his head with a long-suffering sigh. "Haven't we been through this before, Detective?"

"This is the last time," Will promised, motioning toward the door with his pistol. "Outside. N—*OW!*"

His order turned into a gasp of pain, and Lauryn whirled around just in time to see her little brother finish punching Will in the stomach. Or, at least, that's what it looked like. When Robbie's hand fell away, though, the detective's shirt was marred by a rapidly spreading stain of crimson. That was all she saw before he fell over.

"*Will!*"

She scrambled to the detective's side, rolling him over to examine the wound. It didn't look like anything too vital had been hit, but it was still bleeding too quickly for her own small hands to hold back, so she grabbed Will's hand instead, shoving his palm hard against the wound. She was looking around for something to use as a proper bandage when she noticed Robbie was no longer beside her.

In the confusion, he'd scrambled to his feet and run to Lincoln, his face beaming. "I got him!" he cried happily, showing him the pocketknife Lauryn hadn't even realized he'd had. "I got him for you, Lincoln! I called my sister, too, just like you asked. That makes us square, right? I can go now, rig—"

Fast as a striking cobra, Black's arm snaked out to wrap around Robbie's. He spun the younger man around in a smooth motion, positioning him so that Robbie's back was caught against Black's chest with his arm squeezing tight on his throat.

"No!" Lauryn cried. "Robbie, you idiot! What the hell do you think you're doing?"

"What any sensible animal would do," Black replied, squeezing until her brother's eyes bugged out. "Trying to save himself. But what your poor fool of a brother doesn't understand is that it's already too late."

"It's never too late," Talon said fiercely, drawing his sword. "Release him."

Lincoln grinned at the order. "Oh, it's miles too late this time, holy man," he said, his voice mocking. "Have you taken a look around at any point during your little intrusion? Which, by the way, you might want to work on. Even if I hadn't known you were up here the whole time, y'all bastards made enough noise that the whole building could have figured it out, and most of the bastards working here are high as hell." He shook his head. "But like I was saying, you assholes are months too late to stop this. All that crap with the emerald liquid and the ODs and the little party in the burn ward? That was warm-up—priming the pump, you might call it—but this ball was set rolling ages ago, and there's no stopping it now."

"It is never too late," Talon said again, making Black scoff.

"What, are you deaf, old man?" he asked, squeezing Robbie even harder. "There's no recovering from this. Game's over. You've already lost. You're dead, your girl's dead, the kid's dead, your detective buddy there's super dead. Damn, man, this whole city's dead! You could not have screwed this up more if you'd tried. At this point, the only thing left is for me to give the word and send you all on your merry way to hell. Unless . . ."

His eyes fell on Talon, and Lauryn's stomach tightened. "Unless what?"

"Unless you'd like to make a trade," Black finished, tapping his fingers against Robbie's throat. "I've got no use for another idiot cowardly pusher, but a SEE warrior? That's a different story."

Lauryn had already opened her mouth to say there was no way she was making a deal with such an obviously untrustworthy person, but Talon beat her to it.

"What do you want?"

Black's smile turned crueler than ever. "You and I have unfinished business to settle." He jerked his arm up, lifting Robbie clear off his feet. "You want to save the idiot? Here's my deal: you put down your sword and swear to your precious God to let me do whatever I want to you, *without* fighting back, until sunrise or death, whichever comes first. You do that, and I'll let all your little buddies here go free, no strings attached. The kid, the doctor girl, what's left of Mr. Detective there, they can all leave this place no worse for wear. Hell, if they hurry, they might even be able to get out of town before the fun starts. How's that for generosity?"

"Absolutely not!" Lauryn cried, whirling on Talon before he could say a word. "You are *not* sacrificing yourself for us! You don't even know if you can trust him."

"Oh, he definitely can't trust me," Black said. "But that's beside the point. See, if Talon there doesn't do what I want, baby Robbie's going to be short one head, and my boys down there" —he nodded down at the warehouse where, sure enough, several of the masked workers had stopped processing the orders and were now standing ready with their guns out— "get to take a fifteen-minute party break. I'm happy either way, so what's it gonna be, holy man? You or the kid? Choose quick, though. An offer this generous doesn't stick around for long."

By the time he finished, Lauryn was ready to punch that stupid smile right off his face. It just wasn't fair. There was no way, no *way* they'd gotten this far only to fail now. She refused to believe that this horrible man was right. There *had* to be another way, and she was racking her brain to think of it when Talon lowered his sword.

"I knew it!" Black cackled. "You never could resist being the martyr, could you?"

Talon's answer to that was a stony silence. Lauryn, on the other hand, had *plenty* to say.

"*No!*" she shouted, grabbing his arm. "You can't do this."

"If I don't, we could all die," he said stoically.

"If you go, you'll *definitely* die," she replied, digging her fingers into him. "Screw him and his deals. We'll find another way. You're the one who's always going on about miracles!"

"At least I know now that you were listening," Talon said with a warm smile. "But this is what I have to do, Lauryn. From the moment I met you, I knew I'd been sent here to help and protect you. 'The Good Shepherd lays down his life for the sheep.'"

The calm way he said that was enough to break even Lauryn's emergency-room-hardened facade. "You can't *die* for me!" she said, her voice panicked. "I just met you! I can't let you throw yourself away because my brother made a fatally stupid decision."

"But I'm not throwing myself away," he said, looking her in the eyes. "With one life, I buy three. That's a good deal by any reckoning, especially since one of those lives is a brave young woman who's finally learned to believe."

Lauryn had no idea how to answer that. She wasn't even sure if she could call the frantic surrender of common sense belief, but before she could think of another way to convince Talon not to do this, he turned his sword and pressed the hilt into her shaking hands. "Keep this," he ordered. "I don't want Black to touch it, and it might come in handy."

Lauryn didn't want to. If she took his sword, Talon would truly be defenseless. At the same time, though, the thought of that horrid man touching the beautiful sword made her stomach turn. But the longer she stood there, the more she realized he was right. Downstairs, the men with the guns had already moved to block the doors. All Black had to do was say the word, and they were all dead. It would take a miracle to get them out of this, and while Lauryn's opinion on miracles had definitely taken a turn in the last few minutes, she didn't think they'd be getting another one now.

But that didn't mean she was giving up.

"I'll take this," she said at last, clutching the sword with trembling fingers. "But only until I see you again. As soon as I get Will out, I'll be back to save you."

"Don't," Talon said softly. "It's what he's counting on." When Lauryn tried to argue, he raised his hand. "You fight me on everything, but not this. My life is my own, and I count it a gift to spend it in God's service. Promise me you won't undo what I've done here by coming back."

Lauryn shook her head frantically. "No—"

"Promise me!" Talon snapped, making her jump, and then he sighed. "Please," he said, more quietly this time. "I appreciate your loyalty, but you have your own work to do tonight, Lauryn. Don't throw yourself into the lion's den when I've sacrificed everything to get you out." He smiled. "Have faith. God does not lose."

Lauryn barely heard him. She'd already opened her mouth to keep arguing when Will gasped on the floor, sucking in a pained breath through clenched teeth. It was a terrible, deathly sound, and the moment she heard it, Lauryn knew she was almost out of time.

"I promise I won't come back," she said grudgingly, dropping down to help Will keep his hand against the wound. "But I'm not going to let this stand, Talon. We're going to find out what's going on here, and we're going to stomp it so hard, no one will ever breathe the name Z3X again. I swear, I won't let this be in vain."

"I'm counting on it," he said, giving her a final smile as he walked openhanded to stand unarmed in front of his enemy.

"Well, well," Black said with a delighted grin. "Looks like Christmas comes early this year." He let Robbie go without a second look, reaching out with his newly free hand to point to the ground at his feet. "Kneel."

After a second's hesitation, Talon obeyed, and Black threw his head back with a joyous laugh. "Just what I always wanted," he said, turning to Robbie, who was still doubled over, fighting to get his breath back now that he was no longer being choked. "Get the hell out of here. A deal's a deal."

For a moment, Robbie just stared at him like he didn't understand what Black was saying. Then, with a final guilty glance at his sister, he turned and fled.

"Robbie!" she yelled, but he was already gone, taking the stairs two at a time.

Lauryn watched him go with a bitter curse, but she'd deal with her brother later. Will needed her more right now, and she turned back to him with an angry breath, tearing off a piece of her shirt to make a bandage. When she'd bound his wound as best she could given the circumstances, she grabbed hold of his bloody hand.

"Can you stand?"

Still gasping, he nodded, and together, they got him to his feet. When he was steady, Lauryn slid Talon's sword under her arm so she'd have both hands free to help Will as they hobbled together past Black. True to his word, the assassin let them pass, even stepped aside so they could get down the stairs.

"Don't look so shocked," he said when Lauryn shot him a dirty look. "I can kill you at any time. But a chance like this"—he laid his hand on the still-kneeling-Talon's shoulder, making the warrior flinch —"comes once in a long, long lifetime. Now run away, little girl. While you still can."

Lauryn's jaw tightened. She'd never wanted to do violence to another person like she wanted to with Black at that moment. The only reason she didn't was the sound of Will's labored breathing in her ear and the warning look in Talon's eyes, reminding her of her promise.

"A deal's a deal," she whispered bitterly, sliding around Black to start down the stairs. The men in the warehouse kept their guns trained on her the whole time, but as Black had promised, no one made a move to stop them as she and Will hobbled down the steps, across the elevated fire escape, and back into the freezing night. The moment they were clear, one of the men stepped in and kicked the heavy door shut behind them, locking them out in the dark.

13

BOUGHT WITH A PRICE

By the time they made it down the stairs, Will was looking worse than ever. Even in the dark, Lauryn could see his color was fading fast, so she just stopped looking and focused on pushing ahead, using Talon's massive sword like a cane as she struggled to drag them both across the factory yard toward the alley where Will had parked his car. An effort Will seemed to be doing everything in his power to undermine.

"Stop it, Lauryn," he gasped, digging his feet into the snow. "You can't carry me all that way. I'm too heavy. Just drop me and run."

"Absolutely not," she panted, taking another step. "We're getting your car, and then I'm taking you to a hospital."

"There's no time," he said. "Black was right. I'd seen the fac-tories, but until Robbie, I couldn't fathom just how bad this was." He pointed at the snow-covered piles of Z3X on pallets that were stacked even out here. "It's all over the city. It's only a matter of time before they all end up like Robbie. You know what happens after that." He dug his heels in. "I'm just slowing you down. You need to *go*. Get out of town before—"

"I am not running!" she yelled at him, setting him down in the snow to search his coat for his car keys. "If I can't drag you to the car, I'll bring the car to you, but I *am* going to save your life, Will Tannenbaum. I'm not losing anyone else to this insanity!"

Will stared at her with pleading eyes, but he was too weak to do anything else now. The snow around him was already stained with a frighteningly large circle of red. Looking at him, Lauryn almost wished her idiot brother had thrown him into the Z3X instead. That, at least, she knew she could cleanse, even if she still hadn't taken the time to process how. A gut wound when you were stuck in the freezing cold snow with zero sterile tools, on the other hand, was a disaster she understood far too well. Enough to know just how bad Will's chances were if she didn't get him to a proper medical facility *fast*. But as her freezing fin-gers finally closed around the car keys in Will's jacket pocket, something cold and hard pressed into the hair at the back of her scalp.

Lauryn had never had a gun to her head before, but it didn't matter. The feeling of a pistol barrel pressed against your skull wasn't something you needed to see to understand. She froze at once, hands shooting up automatically while Will began cursing like a sailor on the ground beside her.

"That's enough of that," said an angry, commanding voice. "Turn around."

The gun pressed into Lauryn's head twitched to the left, and she obeyed, turning in place to see a group of four masked men in full combat outfits flanking a fifth man in an expensive suit, the obvious leader. But while Lauryn only vaguely recognized him as someone she'd seen once on television, Will was baring his teeth like a cornered animal.

"Korigan."

The name was enough to make Lauryn do a double take, and the chief of police flashed them a warm smile. "You're not looking so well, Tannenbaum," he said, frowning down at Will with his hands laced behind his back like he was observing a weak but still-rabid dog. "You should have taken my advice and gone home. I warned you this case was bad for your health."

"You bastard," Will growled, trying and failing to push up to his knees. "I knew you were crooked! But I've got you pegged now. I've got pictures tying you to every step of this. When the DA sees—"

One of Korigan's thugs planted his boot in Will's ribs, sending him toppling into the snow. Lauryn was already moving to help him when the man holding the gun to her head shoved the barrel down hard enough to bruise, forcing her to freeze yet again, helpless as Korigan nodded for the thug to grab Will off the ground.

"The DA isn't going to hear anything," Korigan said calmly as the man set Will on his knees in the bloody snow. "I knew you were on my tail. Don't worry, you were good enough that I never actually spotted you, but that didn't matter, because I knew *you*. The moment I saw you staring at my limo, I knew you'd never let it go. I could have offed you at any point after that, but Black had plans for your girlfriend there, so I let it slide. But while I've had fun watching you scramble after my dust, all good things must come to an end, which is why we'll be taking *this*."

He walked over and shoved his hand into Will's pocket, pulling out his phone.

"Like that'll work," Will spat. "You think I'm stupid enough to only make one copy? I've got evidence spread all over. You'll never get it all."

"Perhaps," Korigan said as he slipped Will's phone into his own pocket. "But tell me, Will, how will the DA get any of that evidence if you're not alive to send it? Even if you were smart enough to set up some kind of automatic forwarding, it won't matter. With all of Chicago caught in the grip of Z3X, no one's going to care about a corrupt police chief, and by the time they *do* care, I'll be untouchable. All your work will come to nothing, and in the end, you won't be anything but a footnote on a very long mortality report."

He finished with a smile that made Lauryn's skin crawl, but Will was staring at him in confusion. "Why?" he gasped at last. "I get why you're offing me, but why are you pumping this junk into Chicago? Why kill off the city you just bought your way into the top of?"

Korigan laughed out loud. "You think I care about this crime-riddled, freezing hellhole? This police chief gig was never anything but a stepping stone on my way to bigger things."

"That's why you unleashed this on us?" Lauryn cried, temporarily forgetting the gun against her skull as she whirled around. "Lenny, the burn ward, Robbie—all of that drama was so you could give yourself a *promotion*?"

"Not *a* promotion. *The* promotion," Korigan said as the goon forced Lauryn back down. "You know nothing. You were born in a land of peace and plenty. I was born to war. All my life, war has been with me. It's the water I drink, the air I breathe, and the food I eat. Even when I won, my reward was just a bigger battle with higher stakes. I never had peace, never had security. But with this move, all that finally ends. I've finally climbed high enough to reach the way out. Forever. Next to that, your suffering, their suffering"— he nodded at the dark city beyond —"it's nothing. Just the crying of spoiled children that I no longer have to hear."

"You're crazy if you think any reward is worth this," Will wheezed, glaring at the police chief with pure hate. "We're talking about a drug that turns people into monsters. *Contagious* monsters! How do you think this is going to end? There's nowhere in the world safe from that."

"Spoken like an ignorant man," Korigan said. "But trust me, I will be quite well taken care of. You, on the other hand . . ." He moved his hands from behind him and leveled his pistol at Will's face. "You're just a stain on the road."

The words washed over Lauryn like a splash of cold water, but it wasn't until she heard Korigan's gun cock that the truth of what was about to happen finally hit her. They were going to die. This man was going to shoot Will, and then probably shoot her, and there was nothing she could do. She wouldn't be able to keep her promise to Talon, wouldn't be able to help her city, wouldn't be able to do anything. Even now, she could feel the gun pressed into her own skull shift as the goon behind her moved his finger to the trigger. All he had to do after that was squeeze, and everything she'd fought for, everything she loved would be lost. But even as that realization struck her like a gong, Talon's words rang back as loud as cymbals through her skull.

God doesn't lose.

At any other point in Lauryn's life, that thought would have made her cringe. Now, it gave her strength, because it reminded her she wasn't alone. She'd been trying not to think too hard about what had happened when she'd healed Robbie in the warehouse, both because she'd been too busy and because if she did stop to think about it, she'd go nuts trying to make all the impossible things line up. Now, though, she was finally starting to realize that didn't matter. She didn't have to understand something for it to be true. It was there whether she understood or not, whether she *believed* or not.

But finally, Lauryn did believe.

After everything that had happened, she'd run out of excuses. All her pride was gone, leaving only the core, and that part of Lauryn—the little girl who'd always dreamed of helping people, of being the one who saved the day—*believed*.

With that single thought, freedom like Lauryn had never known swept over her. The near constant fear she'd been living under since she'd first spotted Lenny's collapsed body three days ago lifted from her like a blanket. She could still feel the pistol wedged against her skull, but she no longer feared it. Talon had said something along the lines of fear being just a way to let the enemy in, to deny that there *was* a plan and order in this chaotic mess of a world.

Though I walk through the valley of the shadow of death, I will fear no evil, you son of a bitch.

Holding on to her newborn faith, she suddenly leaned away, reaching down to grab Talon's sword out of the snow where she'd dropped it. Just like in the backyard this afternoon, the beautifully wrapped handle slid into her hands like it had been made to fit there, the bright blade almost leaping out of its sheath as she spun around, still crouched, to slice its gleaming edge into her stunned guard's leg.

Even as she did it, a part of Lauryn still didn't actually think it would work. She'd never even held a sword that wasn't made of plastic until a few hours ago, and she'd certainly never attacked anyone. But whether through a miracle or a mix of audacity and luck, she struck true. The blade slid clean and deep through the huge man's thigh, and he went down with a scream, his dropped gun clattering off into the dark.

For a heartbeat, Lauryn could only stare awestruck at what

she'd done, and then the reality of the situation came back like a thunderclap. A surge of adrenaline came with it, sending her scrambling through the bloody snow to take up a defensive position in front of Will.

She must have looked a terrible sight crouching there panting, the huge bloody sword up and ready, because the other guards all took a simultaneous step back. Even Korigan flinched before his face turned scarlet. "You idiots!" he screamed, whipping his own gun toward Lauryn. "It's just a sword! You've got *guns*. Shoot her!"

The men obeyed before he'd even finished, their shots cracking in the dark. Lauryn squeezed her eyes shut, waiting for the pain.

Pain that never came.

Despite the gunfire roaring around her, she didn't feel a single shot. After what felt like eternity, everything went quiet again, and Lauryn opened her eyes in wonder.

As ordered, all of Korigan's men had fired—she could see the smoke coming from the barrels of their guns—but not one of their shots had hit the mark. In what she could only call a miracle, every single bullet had gone crooked, striking the ground, the fire escape ramp behind her, even the pallets of Z3X stacked against the factory wall. Despite the men emptying their clips at her, not one bullet had touched Lauryn or the detective she was protecting. She was still staring in awe when the police chief finished reloading and swung his gun back up, emptying the new clip straight into her face.

Later, looking back, Lauryn was never able to say how she moved so fast. She knew it was impossible for the human body to outpace a bullet, and yet in between Korigan's finger hitting the trigger and the bullet traveling to her, she had whipped Talon's sword in front of her and blocked the first bullet. It struck the bright blade like a bell, ricocheting off with enough force to knock her backwards. The next several shots passed harmlessly over her head before Korigan adjusted his aim, shooting at her on the ground. But here, again, she blocked him. She didn't know how. Talon's sword seemed to be moving with a life of its own, dancing into the path of each bullet. This time, though, the shots didn't bounce off harmlessly into the dark.

This time, they bounced straight back, slamming into Korigan's chest.

The first shot knocked him back, but the second sent him spinning, sliding across the icy ground straight into the pallets of Z3X that had been stacked outside for pickup. Even then, logically, he should have landed safely. Being outside, all of the pallets were wrapped in heavy plastic, and each one had to weigh far more than Korigan did. But somehow, the moment he touched them, the stacked pallets came tumbling down, the bags bursting as they fell, burying Korigan and his cronies in an avalanche of pure, powdery, tar-black Z3X.

The factory yard went silent after that. Oddly enough, Will was the first to get his voice back, fighting for breath as he wheezed, "What was *that*?"

Lauryn looked down at the sword in her hands, the gleaming blade still mirror bright and unmarred from the bullets it had deflected. "I think it was a miracle."

For once in his life, Will didn't argue. He just closed his eyes with a pained breath. Which reminded her.

"Hold still," she said, dropping the sword as she turned around to place both hands on Will's wound. Even that small pressure was enough to make him gasp, and he fought to stay conscious.

"Ow."

"I know, I'm sorry," Lauryn muttered. "But I have to try something or you're going to die." Given the amount of blood in the snow around them, she was amazed he hadn't passed out already. Thanks to Korigan's delay, her chances of getting Will to a hospital in time were nil. If she was going to save his life, she had to stop the bleeding completely right here and now. Given how little she had to work with, that should have been impossible, but after everything that had happened, "impossible" didn't seem like such a high barrier anymore. After all, people were healed by miracles in the Bible all the time, and if prayer could cleanse people of Z3X, why couldn't it fix Will, too? It was worth a try if nothing else, and so Lauryn closed her eyes and prayed, sending up a wordless plea for help as Will's blood seeped through her fingers.

Now as before, she didn't feel any change. There was no flash of light, no sign that anything had happened, but when she opened her eyes again, Will's breathing was easier, almost like he was asleep. His color was still terrifyingly close to that of a cadaver, but she couldn't feel any fresh blood seeping through the scrap of fabric she'd used to stop the wound, and that was good enough.

With a prayer of thanks, she left Will and began to hunt for his keys. She'd dropped them when Korigan and his thugs had arrived, and with all the fighting, she didn't know if she'd be able to find them. But a minute later, her frantically searching hands grabbed them from where they were lodged in a snowdrift by the wall. She was about to go get his car and bring it over so she could load him into it when she heard the unmistakable sound of footsteps behind her.

The moment Black had let him go, Robbie had gotten out of there as quickly as possible. He'd raced down the stairs, heart pounding as fast as his feet. He didn't even know where he was running other than *away*, but somehow, he ended up right back where he'd started earlier that night: in Angelo's office. And Angelo wasn't happy about it.

"The *hell* you doing here?" he roared as Robbie slammed the door.

"Angelo, man, you gotta hide me," Robbie begged, holding up his hands. His *bloody* hands.

It didn't even faze his boss. You didn't get this high in the drug business without seeing more than your fair share of blood. But Angelo still looked pissed as hell, and now that his panic was beginning to calm down, Robbie was pretty sure he knew why.

"You asshole," Angelo sneered, walking around his desk to shove Robbie in the chest. "What the hell is wrong with you? I don't pretend like we're good people in this business, but man, that was messed up."

"I was just trying to save my skin!" Robbie argued. "You don't understand—"

"Oh, I understand," the drug lord snapped. "I saw it with these two eyes. You sold out your own sister, your damn *family*, to that bastard Lincoln Black. Just called her right in to his web, didn't you?"

"I didn't want to," he cried, desperate. "You gotta believe me, I didn't want to call her! But you don't know what Z3X is like when you take it like that." Even after whatever Lauryn had done, Robbie could still feel the clawed hands crawling over his skin, their oily voices sliding down his ears like tendrils. "You don't know what it's like!"

"You're right," Angelo said coldly. "I don't, cause I'm not stupid enough to take the product I push. I'm in this business to get rich, not turn into the junkies we sell to. Look at you, man. You took a shot of Naloxone and you're still strung out as hell. And then, like all that wasn't bad enough, you stabbed a cop. A *cop*! And not just any cop. You had to go and stab Will Tannenbaum. Do you have any idea how vindictive that bastard is?" He shook his head. "You better pray he dies, 'cause he will *never* let you get away with this. Even if he does kick over, stubborn bastard will haunt you."

"That's why I need your help," Robbie pleaded. "Come on, man, I know I messed up, but I'm in a real bad way and I need your help. You've got to get me out of here." That was no joke, either. He'd always thought of Z3X as just another drug to push, but that was before he'd had it straight. Now that he knew what it did, the full impact of what they were doing by spreading it all over the city was hitting him hard. He had to run, had to escape *now*, while there was still a chance. He was trying to think of a way to explain that so Angelo could understand, when the older man sat back down at his desk.

"I *got* to? Let's get one thing straight. I owe you nothing." Angelo snorted in disbelief. "I had you all wrong, Robbie. I thought you were smart, going places. I thought you had potential in this business, which was why I trusted you with my errands. I even let you run stuff uptown to the big house, which is a job I usually save for myself. I've been nothing but a saint to you, Robbie, but you know, I'm glad this happened. It let me see your true colors. We don't hold to a lot in this business, but what you did goes too far. Honestly, I ain't even mad at you for calling. You were high, and while I'm pissed you got high on the job, I don't fault junkies for their bad decisions. But after? When you stabbed the detective and ran for Black like a kid running to his mommy?" Angelo shook his head. "That's low, man."

Robbie began to sweat. "But—"

Angelo cut him off with a deadly look. "Anyone who sells out his family is slime who can't be trusted," he said, waving in one of the big enforcers from outside. "Thanks to your weakness, I gotta deal with Black's one-man torture party upstairs. That's two strikes, Jefferson, and I only give one. So if you know what's good for you, you'll get out of here before I finish the job, and if I ever see you in my territory again, you're dead. Got that?"

"Come on, Angelo," Robbie begged as the enforcer grabbed his shoulder. "Your territory's my home. I can't just—"

"Did I stutter?" Angelo asked calmly, stabbing his finger at the door. "Get out before I have Juan break your scrawny stick arms."

To make sure the point was clear, the enforcer began to squeeze, and Robbie decided he'd pushed far enough. The moment Juan let him go, he raced out of the office, fleeing past the vats to the warehouse's back door where he'd left his car. But when he reached it, he didn't turn it on. Instead, he slumped over the steering wheel, breathing deep as he tried to take stock of his life, or what was left of it.

There wasn't much. Sitting in his ice-cold car with the lights on, he could see his own haggard face reflected in the machine's shiny digital dash, and Angelo was right. He looked like a junkie. He'd never seen himself that way before. Drugs were always supposed to be a casual thing, something he did to make some cash and have a little fun while he worked on his music. But he hadn't been working on his music in a long time, and thanks to his cowardice, his alternate career was blown. Their boss, the Big Boss, had run off the other gangs and cartels years ago to make his operation the monopoly on drugs in Chicago, and Angelo was the man in charge of the entire South Side. Now that Angelo had blackballed him, Robbie could never work in this town again. But that wasn't the worst part.

The worst part of it all was that Angelo was *right*.

Robbie had acted lower than dirt, and he'd never felt it more than he did at that moment. Because even in the depths of Z3X, he'd known Lauryn would come. And that was knowing he hadn't thought—or cared—about her in years. All he'd cared about was himself, and now that all he had was himself, he didn't like what he saw. He hadn't set out to do this, but now that everything was down, Robbie realized for the first time that he really was the failure his dad always tried to make him feel like. He'd called his sister, his one and only sister, and when she'd come to help, he'd stabbed the cop, which he now vaguely recalled was her boyfriend, and run to Black for safety. He hadn't even thought about it. All he'd cared about was not going to jail and not getting Black pissed at him. He hadn't meant for things to go to hell, but looking back, he couldn't see how they would have gone any other way. Hell, he might have killed Lauryn, and he hadn't even had the balls to stick around and find out.

That thought was enough to make his whole body shake. Normally, he'd have said this was a perfect time for a hit, just a little something to calm him down, but after that last horrifying trip, Robbie didn't think he'd be able to touch drugs ever again. What he really wanted right now was a friend, but everyone he knew was in the business, which meant they'd be staying away from him now that Angelo had kicked him out—word traveled fast in the community.

He pulled out his phone anyway, scrolling through the texts that had come in while he'd been inside, in search of something—anything—to make him feel better. But all he got was a wall of missed calls and messages from his dad and Lauryn. That wasn't a surprise, since he'd been ignoring them all day, but seeing the overwhelming proof of their love and worry now just dragged Robbie lower still. He was about to throw his phone away when it vibrated one last time, and a new message popped up on the screen.

For a soaring moment, he hoped it was one of his buddies, but when he saw the name, his hopes fell. It was just his dad again. Old bastard never gave up. But as Robbie moved to erase the message, his thumb slipped, opening it instead, and the words glowed bright on the screen.

It's never too late.

His lips curled in a sneer. What did Maxwell know? It was way too late. Robbie had screwed everything up royally tonight. Assuming his sister was still alive, she'd never forgive him for this, and if precious Lauryn died, their dad wouldn't, either. Any way you looked at it, Robbie had left himself properly screwed. And yet he couldn't seem to tear his eyes off the words, reading them again and again until they burned into his brain.

He was still sitting there like an idiot reading the same line over and over when he heard the gunfire. He ducked automatically, dropping his phone in the rush to cover his head. Thankfully, the bullets didn't seem to be coming for him, but when he peeked back up over his dash to see who was getting shot, what he found hit him as hard as any bullet could.

Outside, less than a dozen feet away, Lauryn was on her knees in the snow, facing off against a man in a suit who was pointing a gun at her. Even in the dark, the man looked vaguely familiar, but before Robbie could place him, he unloaded his gun directly into Lauryn's face. The sight was enough to make Robbie scream for his sister. But while his voice was lost in the hail of gunfire, none of the shots landed. He didn't know how it was possible to miss at that kind of range, but the man couldn't seem to hit Lauryn if his life depended on it. And then, he saw her roll up with a freaking sword to block the last shots, bouncing the bullets right back at her attacker like she was the hero of a crazy movie. Even more amazing, this time the bullets flew *back*, sending the man stumbling into a stack of Z3X and bringing it down like an avalanche.

"Holy . . . " he breathed.

Robbie's eyes were locked on his sister. His perfectly fine, *living* sister as she crawled over to the detective—who was also alive—and began to bind his wounds. But even though Lauryn was being even more freakishly perfect than normal, the sight didn't sting like it usually did. Looking at her, all Robbie felt was relief. Relief and the strong urge to jump out of the car and go hug her until he was certain he hadn't messed everything up for good.

It's never too late.

The words came back like an echo, running through his head in their father's voice, and for the first time in a long time, Robbie listened. Maybe it *wasn't* too late? Yes, she'd be mad as hell at him, and rightfully so, but despite apparently becoming a sword-swinging badass since she'd gone to med school, Lauryn looked like she could seriously use some help. If he went over and offered, maybe it would repair some of the damage he'd caused being a dumbass?

Maybe she'd forgive him?

It was one hell of a long shot, but at this point—still coming down and blackballed by everyone he knew in a city that felt like it was going to explode at any second—any shot felt like a good one. At the very least, he wouldn't be alone.

That was more tempting than anything he'd thought of yet, so Robbie got out of his car and started toward her.

She must have been jumpy as hell, because even when he was trying to be quiet, she spun around at once, sword in hand. The moment their eyes met, Robbie froze, bracing for the dressing-down he knew he deserved, but it never came. Instead, Lauryn grabbed him in a huge bear hug, the giant sword clattering to the ground at their feet as she squeezed him so tight it hurt. Still unsure what was going on, Robbie could only hug her back, dissolving into sobs before he could even take a breath.

"I'm sorry," he bawled. "I screwed up so bad, Lauryn, and I'm so, so sorry."

He hadn't planned to say that. He certainly hadn't planned to cry, but it seemed to be the right thing to do, because his sister hugged him back harder than ever. "I know," she whispered. "But it's okay. I forgive you."

He didn't believe her. *"You do?"*

"Of course," she said, giving him a stern look. "You're my brother."

He knew he should shut up and take it, but he couldn't stop himself. "But why? I've done nothing to deserve—"

"You don't have to deserve forgiveness," she said, shaking her head. "It's given. You just have to ask and mean it, and I think you do." Her lips curled into a smile. "Besides—you never cry unless you mean it."

Robbie couldn't help it. He smiled back. "Thank you," he whispered, dropping his eyes.

"Always," she whispered back. "It's never too late to say you're sorry."

He froze, staring at her like a deer in headlights, his father's words echoing in his head once more, but Lauryn was already hurrying back to the detective. "Give me a hand!"

Not about to ruin this amazing turn of events, Robbie obeyed immediately, running over to help her lift the detective. "We can use my car," he said. "It's the fastest around, and closer."

"Thanks," Lauryn said, getting that look on her face she always got when things were bad. "He's stopped bleeding, but he still needs help."

Robbie nodded. "Hospital, then?"

She started to nod, and then shook her head instead. "This is going to sound crazy," she muttered. "But I don't think I was given this miracle just to save his life. I think there's something I have to do."

Miracle? "You're right. That does sound pretty crazy."

"It's been a crazy night," she said with a self-deprecating shrug. "But things are about to get bad, Robbie. You took Z3X—you know what it can do. Now that stuff is all over town, and I think I need to do something to stop it."

"How, though?" he asked as they carefully placed Will in

the back of Robbie's precious Charger. He winced a bit when the blood hit the upholstery, but the way he saw it, this was part of his penance . . . and he'd been meaning to change out the factory default cloth in the back seat anyway. "I've been pushing for the last twenty-four hours straight. Z3X is a done deal; there's no stopping it now."

Lauryn gave him a sharp look at the mention of pushing, but she didn't comment. "We can still stop more from going out, right? Kill the supply."

"Again, how?" Robbie said. "This factory's just one of twelve, and those are just the ones I know about."

She scowled, thinking, and then her eyes lit up. "What if we went for the head? The order to make all this Z3X didn't come out of nowhere. Someone has to be running all of this, and I bet they know how to shut it down, or at least mitigate the damage."

She finished with a hopeful look at Robbie, clearly counting on him to give her a name. It wasn't a bad guess—he had been working here—but unfortunately, he had none to give. Even Angelo didn't know who the Big Boss actually was. All the orders came through Lincoln Black, and he sure as hell wasn't talking. But just as Robbie was opening his mouth to tell her he couldn't help, he realized he did have *something*.

"I don't know who's running things," he said. "But I think I know where he lives. One time, my boss let me run a load of coke to a house uptown, no payment needed, and when I was delivering the stuff, I saw Lincoln Black at the party." *Buried under models, which was straight pimpin', but that isn't the sort of detail you tell your sister.* "I think that's the boss's house, or at least someone who knows him."

"That's good enough for me," Lauryn said, hopping into the passenger seat. "Let's go."

Robbie gawked at her. "Really?"

She shrugged. "Again, I know it sounds crazy, but I've learned to just take this stuff on faith. Now let's get moving." She leaned out the window. "I don't like the look of that sky."

Confused, Robbie looked up as well, but he didn't see anything unusual. Just a dark, overcast winter night sky in the city. The only thing notable was that there seemed to be a ton of birds, big black bastards that cawed when they saw him.

After his bad trip, that was creepy as hell, and Robbie didn't waste any more time. He ran around and jumped into the driver's seat, barely taking the time to buckle in before he hit the gas, peeling his tires in his rush to get on the road. They made it out just in time, too. The moment they were through the gates, a whole fleet of trucks started turning in to go pick up the next shipment . . . hiding the man who was just now crawling out from under an avalanche of spilled Z3X, his eyes shining like blood in the glare of the floodlights overhead.

BUT I SAY TO YOU WHO HEAR, LOVE YOUR ENEMIES,
DO GOOD TO THOSE WHO HATE YOU,
BLESS THOSE WHO CURSE YOU, PRAY FOR THOSE
WHO ABUSE YOU. TO ONE WHO STRIKES
YOU ON THE CHEEK, OFFER THE OTHER ALSO, AND
FROM ONE WHO TAKES AWAY YOUR CLOAK
DO NOT WITHHOLD YOUR TUNIC EITHER. GIVE
TO EVERYONE WHO BEGS FROM YOU, AND
FROM ONE WHO TAKES AWAY YOUR GOODS DO NOT DEMAND THEM BACK.
AND AS YOU WISH THAT OTHERS WOULD DO TO YOU, DO SO TO THEM.
—*LUKE 6:27–31*

14

OFFER THE OTHER CHEEK

For as long as there'd been an operation here, the southern half of the upper floor of the old meatpacking warehouse turned drug factory belonged to Lincoln Black. From up here, he could look down through the metal grating and observe the work below, but no one ever looked up. They knew better— he'd *taught* them better with his knife and fear, his two favorite weapons. Weapons he intended to put to good use tonight as he gazed down at his prey, still on his knees.

"Comfy?" he asked in a singsong voice, strolling over to grab a beer from the fridge in the corner. "I'd offer you a drink, but I wouldn't want to be accused of tempting you."

As ever, the SEE warrior said nothing. He simply knelt there with his back straight and his eyes level like he was trying to lose himself in holy meditation, which wouldn't do at all.

"How long have we been doing this, Talon?" Lincoln asked, walking back over to crouch in front of him so they were eye to eye. "Can you even remember anymore?" When he remained silent, Black's voice turned mocking. "Does that little honey of a doctor even realize how old you are, old man? 'Cause, damn, man, you're older than me, and I'm *old*." He brushed his fingers over his youthful face with a smile. "But you know what they say: do what you love and you'll never work a day in your life."

"And is *this* what you love?" Talon asked flatly, looking pointedly down through the grates at the sulfurous vats where St. Luke's drug was being processed for the masses.

"Honestly?" Black grinned. "This is the best damn day of my life. Like I said, this isn't something we cooked up on the fly. This city was doomed *months* before you even rode into town, and now, at last, we've reached the main event. All that down there—" he tapped the heel of his boot on the grate "—that's the dregs. The rest is already gone, pumped out into the city like cheap beer into a frat boy. Tonight, it'll all come to a head, and the whole damn world's going to get one hell of a wake-up call. We're talking legit Armageddon, and I've got a front-row seat right next to my favorite Jesus freak, who's bound by his own word not to fight back, no matter what I do." He sucked in a deep, satisfied breath. "Doesn't get better than that."

"It won't work," Talon said firmly, staring him in the face.

"It *is* working," Black countered.

"You will be stopped."

"By who?" Black demanded. "God? He's not here. He ain't doing shit. Or maybe you mean your tag team of Doctor Girl Wonder and Detective Boy Genius?"

He paused, waiting for the hope to flash in Talon's eyes. As ever, though, the warrior showed nothing, so Black decided to push. "They're done, you know. That's why I let them go. You see, kid detective forgot that his department-issued car was Lo-Jacked, and since he pretty much told Korigan to his face that he suspected him, Korigan's been keeping an eye on him. Of course, I didn't expect you to make yourself a present like this, but in case you still think your sacrifice means something, I just wanted you to know that Korigan and his C-Company goons are waiting outside for your little buddies as we speak." He sighed. "Such a shame. That girl was damn good at putting you in your place. I almost think I'll miss her."

"Lauryn's not dead," he said firmly. "God doesn't set tasks we cannot manage. He will preserve her."

"Would you care to bet money on that?" Black asked with a chuckle. "Oh, that's right, gambling is forbidden to you, just like all other forms of *fun*." He shook his head. "So let me guess, then. Your plan is to cross your fingers and wait for a miracle?"

Talon's jaw clenched for a moment before he visibly forced himself to relax. "Through God, all things are possible."

"So you claim," Black said, his voice smooth and cutting as he honed in on the weakness. "But that didn't do your last apprentice any good, did it? What was her name again?" He tapped his finger against his chin, making a show of thinking it over. "It was something deeply ironic. Faith? Chastity?"

He paused to let that hang, and Talon rewarded him with a shuddering breath.

"Hope!" Black cried, snapping his fingers. "That was it. Now, she was a fighter. Strong, fast, clever, hell on wheels with a sword.

Nearly gave me a run for my money . . . but not quite." He leaned down, hovering closer until his nose was practically touching Talon's. "You remember when I killed her, don't you?" he whispered. "How she *screamed* for God to save her? Kind soul that I am, I played along. I kept her alive for two days like that. Gave God plennnnnty of time to come do his thing. But he never did."

He tilted his head. "Why was that, you think? She was one of you. A faithful Soldier of El Elyon, one of God's supposed chosen. She called and called, but he didn't lift a finger to stop me or end her suffering. And if God didn't save *her*, what makes you think he'll do anything for your little Lauryn? She doesn't even believe."

By the time he finished, Talon's breathing was ragged. The sound made Black smile. *Closer and closer.*

"I still like to savor the memories," he said, straightening up again. "I especially liked it when she would scream for *you*. She gave up on God well before the end, but she never gave up on you. She just kept telling me over and over how her teacher was coming to save her, but you never did. I tried to keep her alive, but there's only so much a human body can take. By the time you finally decided to pop in, hers had given up the ghost. Hell, I had to pack her in salt to keep the smell from—"

Talon lurched forward with a roar, hands flying up to grab Lincoln's neck. For a moment, it looked like they were about to have a proper tussle, but then, less than an inch away, Talon stopped and collapsed back on his knees, his chest heaving.

"That's right," Black said with a satisfied smile. "You promised not to fight back, and you've always been a man of your word. A real paragon of virtue. Sometimes, I don't even think you're human."

He reached down to pat Talon's scruffy cheek as he finished, and the warrior rewarded him with a look of fury. "I could say the same for you," he growled, glaring up with the closest thing to hate Black had ever seen on his face. "What do you think you'll gain from this, Lincoln? What did I ever do to you to deserve this obsession?"

Black dropped his hand with a bitter smile. "You exist."

Talon didn't seem to know what to make of that, but then, he wouldn't. That was part of why Black hated him so much, because he didn't—*couldn't*—understand what life was like when you weren't blessed. But he decided, once more, to try to explain.

"It's the way you act," he elaborated, taking another swig from the beer dangling all but forgotten in his fingers. "You and the rest of your little God warriors run around telling people what to do like a bunch of holy hall monitors, but who gave you the right? You don't know any more about what's real or good than anyone else. You act like right and wrong are concrete objects you can see, labels on a sheep's ear saying if it gets to be a pet or go to the slaughterhouse, but you don't know a damned thing. Right, wrong, moral, immoral; it's all just arbitrary. Someone else's made-up fairy tale to tell other people how to live their lives."

"That's not true," Talon said. "There is a line—"

"Is there?" Black demanded. "Kill a poor man and no one cares. Kill a rich one and you get the chair. Kill one on the battlefield and you get a medal. Where's the line? They're all dead. It's all murder. The only difference is who's in charge." His lips curled in a sneer. "*That's* the line, holy man. That's what actually matters: who's on top making the rules. The only reason things get labeled as sins is because your God decided that's how it was, but even he can't make up his damn mind half the time. One day he's making commandments that Thou Shalt Not Kill, the next he's throwing a temper tantrum and flooding the whole world. And we're supposed to be made in this asshole's image!" He shook his head. "What does that say about him?"

"I think it says more about you," Talon said, tilting his head.

"We've done this for a long time, Black. Long enough for me to know some of your history. What happened to your mother—"

Black was back on him in a second, grabbing him around the throat. "You leave my mother out of this," he snarled.

"Why?" Talon choked out. "She's where all this started. Your mother was lynched for a crime she didn't commit, and rather than blame the men who did it, you blamed everything else."

"You don't know jack," Black said, shoving him backwards. "I blame everyone for her death 'cause everyone's to blame! You claim your God can do anything? Well, he didn't do squat when a woman whose only crime was being in the wrong place at the wrong time with the wrong skin color swung for a robbery she didn't even know about before the sheriff rode up to her house."

He could still remember it clear as day: the dust, the hot sun, the horse's sharp hooves falling on him as he tried to stop the men from taking his mother away. As always, the memory made him want to hurt things. That was fine. Talon was right here, and no one deserved it more.

"The only truth in this world is that we're *all* guilty," he said, tightening his grip on the bigger man's throat. "When a crime happened in a small town, the people demanded justice, so twelve godly men put their heads together and decided my mother was guilty. There was no evidence, but what did that matter? The moment those men spoke it, the lie became the truth. If there was any real justice in this world, God would have punished them right then, right there, but he didn't. And those men *swore on the Bible*! But no—no one punished them until I came, years later. Then, they regretted it."

Then they had *screamed*.

"They were just men," Talon said between labored breaths. "Men are fallible. They can be wrong. That doesn't mean God is."

"That's what I'm trying to get through your skull," Black

said, shaking his head. "Your God's no different. Like them, he says what's right and what's wrong and that's how it is. There's no argument, no logic, no mitigating circumstances on sin. He's a judgmental prick, not to mention a giant *hypocrite*. That's the worst part for me. I mean, the very first thing your Jesus says is to have mercy, and I could almost get behind that until I realized that every time I looked around God's world, all I saw were people suffering. We're all up to our necks in injustice and violence and war and disease and have been since the dawn of time, and here you come saying 'through God, all things are possible.' Like what? If that's true, then why doesn't God follow his own advice and come down here and be merciful? If he's so all-powerful, why does he tolerate all this? Why doesn't he fix it? Why does he let me do this?"

He released Talon and threw his arms down, gesturing with both hands at the vats of poison under their feet. "We're going to burn the world to ash," he said, chest heaving with excitement. "Tonight's nothing but the first domino in a long, long line. But my favorite part, my *favorite*, is that your God could stop all of this. He could strike me down with lightning, or turn all those vats into hundred-dollar-a-bottle wine. And yet . . ."

He froze, waiting. When nothing happened, he shook his head.

"See?" he said to Talon. "One big-ass disappointment. Here you've got a God who could do *anything*, and yet chooses to do *nothing*. It's enough to make a man want to see just how big a mess he can make, really tear things up to see just how much God will take before he finally gets off his lazy ass and fixes it."

"And is that what you're doing?" Talon said sadly. "Making things worse?"

Black snorted. "Better than walking around pretending to make things better. 'Cause I've seen the world, and, brother, you are doing a terrible job."

Talon shot him an angry look. "I can't speak for God, but anyone who's read a word of scripture knows that the Almighty suffers along with his creation. It wasn't always like this. He made us a paradise once, and we squandered it because we could not leave well enough alone."

"Oh, right," Black said, rolling his eyes. "Eat one apple because you don't want to be ignorant and *bam*, eternal suffering for you and your entire species. Really making your God look good there, bucko."

"They knew the choice," Talon replied. "God did not have to put the Tree of Knowledge in the garden. He could have left us no choice at all, no chance to fall. But he loved us too much for that, for without free choice, obedience means nothing. So he let us choose, and when we chose other than how he wanted, did he abandon us? No. He has cared for us always, leaving the gates of heaven open no matter how many times we betrayed him or turned our backs. The suffering on earth is caused by men like *you*, not God."

"So now it's all my fault?" Black said, shaking his head. "Funny how he's only all-powerful until it's time to take responsibility. But you are right about one thing: God loves him some obedience. Loves it so much that, according to you, he left a way to doom ourselves forever sitting in arm's reach just to see if we'd go for it. You know what that tells me? That your God loves obedience more than he loves any of us, and that's just messed up. Especially when you consider his demands."

"God asks nothing of us we cannot give," Talon said stiffly.

"You'd know, wouldn't you?" Black said, rolling his eyes. "You're one of the most obedient sheep in his flock. But what has that gotten you, old man? You live like a monk—no money, no sex, no *fun*. Just riding around on your bike from ghetto to ghetto doing God's work for decades on end. You don't get time off, you don't even get *paid*, since God has this whole 'easier for a camel to pass through the eye of a needle than for a rich man to get into heaven' nonsense. You know, if you guys had a union, that would be grounds to strike. But you won't, 'cause you already know God doesn't care about you. He just wants you to be good little obedient sheep and promises you mansions in heaven when it's over like some time-share con man, and you sit there and eat it up. Meanwhile, I'm over here doing whatever the hell I want, unpunished, rich as Midas, with women and drugs and anything else at the snap of my fingers. I've done everything you can call a sin into the dirt, and even though you've beaten me more times than I can count, you never do a thing to stop me." He grinned wide. "I think we can all see who's got the better deal here."

"Really?" Talon asked, sitting back on his heels. "If that's so, if your life is truly so much better than mine, why are you still so miserable?"

"What are you talking about?" Black asked, throwing out his arms. "I'm having the time of my life here!"

Talon shook his head. "I think you are very unhappy indeed, Lincoln Black, and you know it. You hate God because he didn't take away your hardships, but without suffering, we would never grow. That is why God permits suffering, because he wants us to be strong and stand on our own, not be coddled children. That is the lesson we learn in the SEE, and it has made us stronger than the strongest steel. But you will always be weak, because the only lesson you've learned from your suffering is that pain exists. For you, that is the end. You've never even tried to learn how to overcome it, or move beyond. You just wallow and blame God for not saving you when you won't even humble yourself to ask."

"That's where you're wrong," Black snapped, drawing his sword. "I've learned a *lot* about suffering over the years. In fact, since you seem to like it so much, I think I'll share some with you."

He finished by placing his sword against Talon's neck. The holy man didn't even flinch, but he would. Black had tortured many Soldiers of El Elyon in addition to Talon's old apprentice, and they all broke in the end. The trick was to remind them that, despite all their mystic trappings, they were only filthy, weak mortals same as everyone else. Sooner or later, they all joined him in screaming curses at the God they'd claimed to love. Talon would be no different—except for the part where Lincoln was going to enjoy it more than any before him.

How's that for happy, bastard?

With that delightful thought, he sliced the first cut down Talon's chest, taking care not to bleed him too much. Too much blood loss would make him pass out, and Black wanted this to last. So he took his time, alternating his strokes as he waited for the famous Talon of God to suffer his ultimate and inevitable break.

L auryn had never seen the city like this.

Despite the fact that it was barely nine, prime time for Chicago's clubs and restaurants, the icy streets were dark and empty. Though not silent. Even with the windows up, the wail of distant—and sometimes not so distant—sirens was constant. It sounded like every emergency vehicle in the city was out and on the job, but even with the disaster that implied, the blaring sirens were comfortingly familiar compared to the noises they covered up.

Every time the wailing sirens faded, the others sounds took over. Sometimes it was the birds. The flock she and Talon had spotted that morning must have just been the scouts. Now, they were everywhere, crows and vultures and carrion birds of every sort covering the telephone wires, window ledges, and rooftops of the city in a blanket of black-feathered bodies squawking constantly to each other like spectators waiting for the show to begin.

But creepy as the constant unfamiliar croaking of scavenger birds was, they had nothing on the screams that occasionally went off like gunshots in the dark. Each one triggered Lauryn's doctor's instinct to stop and see what the problem was, but she made herself ignore them. Stopping was *not* an option. Despite the seemingly empty road, there was movement in the dark. Sometimes it was just one: a hunched, inhuman figure shambling just off the road. Other times it was dozens, whole groups moving in packs from house to house and building to building like zombies in a horror movie. Alone or together, they always looked up when Robbie's car drove by, and there were always some following when she glanced at the rearview mirror, their bloody eyes gleaming in the orange streetlights.

Just the knowledge that they were back there was terrifying, so Lauryn stopped looking and focused on Will, holding him down to make sure the detective's miraculously closed wound stayed that way through the bumps and jostles as Robbie pushed his souped-up car down the icy street faster than she ever would have dared.

"We're not going to make it," he muttered, glancing wild-eyed in the mirrors at the figures shambling after them. "You know what? To hell with this. Let's grab Dad and get out of town while we still—"

"No," Lauryn said sharply. "Running won't help anything. You think all these people are just from the drugs?" Even if a third of Chicago had been on some kind of illegal substance, it wouldn't account for citywide chaos going on around them. "It's the contagion. This drug is spreading like a plague through the population, and it's going to *keep* spreading unless we find a way to stop it. We need to—*watch out!*"

She grabbed the handle as Robbie turned hard, narrowly

avoiding spinning out as he swerved to avoid the old woman with red eyes who'd jumped into the street to make a grab for Lauryn's door. By the time he got them back on track, Robbie looked like he was ready to have a heart attack. "Oh my God," he whispered. "Oh my—"

"Robbie!" she said sharply, making him jump. "Now is not the time to panic. Just drive. It'll be okay, I promise."

He shook his head. "Don't lie—"

"I'm not lying," Lauryn said, and she wasn't. There was no way she could have had the experiences she'd had tonight without reason, no *way* God would finally touch her just to let her fail. She wasn't sure how yet, but she knew they'd get through this if she just kept the faith and kept her head, so that was what she focused on, calling on everything she'd learned about how not to panic over her years in the ER. "Just get us there. I'll do the rest."

Robbie didn't look like he believed that, but he did keep driving, careening them through the city before finally smashing his car through an ornamental-fence gate and skidding to a stop in front of the largest mansion Lauryn had ever seen.

"This is it?" she asked, looking around in confusion. "But, this place belongs to Christopher St. Luke. He's one of Mercy's biggest donors, one of the leading philanthropists in the state."

"Hey, this was where I was told to go," Robbie replied with a shrug. "I warned you it might not be the right place."

He had, but the more Lauryn looked at the dark, shuttered mansion, the more sure she became that this was the right place. The birds that had been gathering over the city were thicker than ever here. It had been hard to tell when they'd pulled up, but as she stepped out of the car, Lauryn could see that every tree on the mansion's expansive riverfront grounds was jam packed with crows and buzzards and carrion feeders, all of whom seemed to be watching her, their black eyes glittering in the dark.

"Keep the engine running," she said quietly, leaning over to grab Talon's sword from the floorboards. "I'm going to go in and have a look around."

"You can't go!"

"I have to. I'll be okay—I promise."

Robbie's face turned ashen. "What am I supposed to do with him?" he asked, jerking his head toward Will.

Lauryn frowned. Honestly, she'd been counting on him to wake up during the drive, but he must have lost more blood than she'd thought, because he was still out. "Just make sure he doesn't try to get up," she said at last. "Whatever happens, do *not* let him follow me. He's lost way more blood than he should. If he moves too much, he'll pass out and hurt himself, and even with the wound closed, there's no telling what other internal damage might still be there. Tie him down if you have to, but *don't* let him go anywhere. I'll be back as fast as I can."

"Hurry," Robbie said, glancing over his shoulder at the busted gate. "It's quiet up here so far since these houses are so damn big and spread out, but I wouldn't count on it staying that way for long."

Neither did she. Lauryn already thought it was suspicious that no guards had come when they crashed through the gate. Considering this was supposedly a drug kingpin's mansion, she would have thought there'd be armed men all around them by now. But it was quiet. She tried to tell herself that this was just more proof of God's divine intervention, but this time, Lauryn wasn't so sure.

"I'll hurry," she promised. "But don't be afraid to run if you need to."

Robbie didn't look too happy about that, but he nodded, and then . . . "Lauryn?"

She looked down at him through the window.

"Be careful," he said, his voice stumbling. "I love you."

"I love you, too," she said, smiling to hide the growing dread in her stomach as she turned away from her brother to face the darkened house.

She wasn't exactly used to this prayer stuff, but a plea to God for safety definitely seemed in order as she climbed the once elegant, now frozen-over marble steps. She'd fully expected to have to break a window, but to her surprise, the doorknob turned when she tried it, the well-hinged door sliding silently open the moment she pushed.

Lauryn snatched her hand back. For all that this had been exactly what she'd asked for, finding an open door to your enemy's lair felt more like a trap than a blessing, especially once the smell hit her.

"Ugh," she muttered, putting her hands over her nose.

The moment she'd cracked the door, the smell of rotting flesh had hit her like a wave. She couldn't see what was rotting thanks to the dark, but it smelled like someone had left roadkill in a hot oven: a gut-churning combination of rancid meat and burning hair. But you didn't last long as an ER doctor if you had a weak stomach, and once the shock of the stench passed, Lauryn was able to push ahead.

Keeping Talon's sword ready in one hand, she lifted her phone with the other, using it as a flashlight as she stepped into an elegant foyer that still held the remains of what must have been one hell of a party. Everywhere her light fell, furniture had been toppled and, in some cases, crushed. Clothing—men's and women's—lay scattered around like confetti, and entire trays of canapés had been left to rot on the floor. There was also more than one puddle of vomit soaking the fine Persian rug, but not nearly enough to account for the stench. *That* seemed to be coming from farther in, because it only got stronger as Lauryn stepped away from the door. Breathing through her mouth, Lauryn was wondering what the hospital board would make of their favorite donor if they saw the state of his house when she heard a noise from the next room.

She whirled, sword clutched in her hand, but there was nothing to see. Just more dark. But then she heard the noise again. It was a sort of musical clunk, almost like someone had dropped a plate on a carpeted floor.

Step by step, she inched forward, creeping through the door at the end of the entry hall to peer around the corner into what appeared to be a ballroom. But as she was easing her head around the wooden doorframe, something black flew right at her face.

Lauryn jumped back with a scream, swinging Talon's huge sword before she could think better of it. In front of her, the black thing squawked and fluttered away, leaving her gasping. A crow. It had just been a startled crow. Now that she'd knocked the doors open with her wild swinging, she could see the ballroom was full of them. They were coming in through the veranda, where someone had left the glass doors open to the night. A great deal of snow had blown in as well, covering the stacks of pillows from what had clearly been an orgy room in an ironically virgin blanket of white. But while the rest of the room was still, the crows were having a grand old time pecking over the abandoned buffet table. Lauryn watched them squabble over the leftovers, using the normal behavior to try to coax her heart rate back down to sub-cardiac-arrest levels. She'd just about managed to return to something like calm when she heard yet another sound behind her.

Just another stupid bird, she told herself firmly. *Don't freak—*

That was as far as she got before a gloved hand closed over her face.

15

FEAR NO EVIL

This time, Lauryn couldn't even scream. She barely managed to breathe as she swung her sword wildly, not that it did any good. She was facing entirely the wrong direction, and whatever had grabbed her was stronger than any person had any right to be. Since fighting wasn't working, Lauryn dropped the sword and her phone so she'd have both hands to work on prying the gloved hand off her face. She was still trying when a man's angry voice growled in the dark.

"Didn't expect to see you here."

The words cut through her panic like a jagged knife. She knew that voice. She'd heard it less than an hour ago, but that was impossible. She'd already won that fight. But her miracle earlier must not have been as complete as she'd thought, because when the hand finally slid down to grab her shoulder, spinning her around before slamming her back into the doorframe, it was Victor Korigan's face that sneered down at her.

Or, rather, what was left of it.

Lauryn had seen a lot of Z3X cases by this point, but Korigan's bath in the pure Z3X powder must have been hundreds of times the normal dose, and the end effect was enough to turn even her iron stomach. His eyes were masks of blood, and his skin was entirely blue gray. It even seemed to be rotting in some places, which explained the stench she'd noticed when she'd first entered the house. But while the doctor in Lauryn was amazed at how someone could still be alive with so much obvious necrotic decay, the rest of her was fighting not to vomit. All of that was bad enough, but what really got Lauryn was how Korigan was still standing after taking multiple shots to the *chest*.

That mystery, at least, was quickly resolved as she spotted the bulletproof vest beneath his shot-up shirt. A safety measure she got a much better look at than she'd wanted when Korigan lurched forward, slamming her body into the wall with his own.

She dove for Talon's sword immediately, but whatever was going on with his body apparently didn't slow down Korigan's reflexes at all. He beat her by miles, snatching up the weapon with one hand while grabbing her neck with the other, his fingers digging into the tender flesh of her throat as he straightened up to glare at her.

"I should have known you'd find this place," he said, his voice rasping. "From the moment you first stumbled into this case, you've shown up everywhere you didn't need to be. But tempted as I am to kill you for doing *this*—" he turned to give her a better look at his gray, rotted face "—I've got a better idea. You're going to help me."

"You know," Lauryn said, choking the words out against the fist wrapped around her throat. "If you want me to cure you, you might want to try being a little nicer."

"Please," Korigan scoffed. "I don't actually believe in all this satanic crap. But St. Luke does. He's the one running this crazy train, and you're my ticket off it."

By this point, Lauryn was utterly lost. "How do you think that's going to work? I don't even know—"

She cut off with a gasp as his hand tightened. "Shut up," he snarled, sending little bits of rotted flesh pattering against her cheek. "Your opinion doesn't mean a damned thing. All that matters is that the SEE warrior St. Luke and his lackey Black are obsessed with thinks you're important enough to give you *this*." He tapped Talon's sword against the wall right beside her face. "That makes you leverage, Dr. Jefferson. Leverage I'm going to use to get out of this mess, and if you shut up and do as I say, you might even live through it."

That was a lie if Lauryn ever heard one, but she was screwed either way, so she played along. "Okay," she said, relaxing her body in a show of submission. "But even if you do trade me, what do you think St. Luke's going to give you in return? There's no medical treatment for Z3X exposure."

"Nothing you know about," Korigan said. "But St. Luke isn't stupid. Z3X is his creation, and you don't start a chain reaction this big without building yourself a way out."

Lauryn's heart skipped a beat. "You're saying there's a cure?"

The arm pinning her moved as Korigan shrugged. "Cure, antidote, treatment, I have no idea. But this is St. Luke. The man built his empire on drugs, legal and not, and now he's using one to take over this entire city. This whole thing was planned from the very beginning, and there's no way during all of that, St. Luke didn't build himself an escape."

For the first time since he'd grabbed her, Lauryn felt a surge of hope. Korigan was actually making sense. Of course St. Luke would leave a back door for himself, which meant there might really be a cure. Maybe finding it was why she'd been sent here! But elated as that thought made her, Korigan wasn't finished.

"There *has* to be a way to reverse this," he rasped. "But St. Luke's not going to give it away for free, and that's where you come in." He lifted his ruined lip in a terrifying grin. "I don't know what your connection to Talon is, but you'd better play your part and act like a good little font of mystical knowledge. 'Cause if you don't sell him on your value enough to get me access to that antidote, you're never going to see another dawn. Now—" he let go of her throat only to grab a handful of her hair, using it like a leash to yank her down the hall "—let's go. We've wasted enough time."

Lauryn didn't want to go anywhere with him, but with one of his hands holding Talon's stolen sword and the other clutched tight around her hair, she had no choice but to try to keep up. The pain in her scalp brought tears to her eyes as Korigan dragged her across the trashed, crow-covered ballroom to a door on the other side that led deeper into the house.

If someone had told her Chicago's most eccentric billionaire had a secret satanic lab hidden inside his house, Lauryn would have been understandably skeptical. Now, however, after Korigan had dragged her through the debauched ballroom, down a long hallway filled with blasphemous art and then through a false wall into a secret elevator, she was just wishing St. Luke had built his laboratory somewhere more convenient. As much as it hurt, though, she refused to show weakness, though she couldn't quite stop a sigh of relief when the crooked police chief finally let go of her hair to shove her inside the hidden elevator. But lovely as it was to finally be released from the horrible pain in her scalp,

Lauryn's relief quickly gave way to fear as the elevator descended deep below the house.

When the doors opened again, the view was very different. Spooky as it had been, at least the trashed mansion had been recognizably human. By contrast, the hallway in front of them now looked like some kind of alien prison with its harsh overhead lights, smooth concrete floor, and—worst of all—what appeared to be glass-fronted, steel-barred *cells* running down either side. With the lights off, Lauryn couldn't actually see what the cells contained. She was trying to decide if that was a blessing or a curse when Korigan moved to grab her hair again.

Desperate to avoid the pain, she put up her hands in surrender and walked forward on her own, staying as close to the lit center of the wide hallway as possible. On either side, she could hear the things inside the darkened cells, a terrifying mix of pained moans and horrible, inhuman buzzing. If she looked hard enough, she could even see them moving in the dark—hands pressing against the glass walls, masses writhing—so she didn't look. This, she realized, must be the zoo Korigan had mentioned. It was even more horrible than she'd imagined, so she tried to focus on other things, keeping her eyes straight ahead as Korigan walked her down the middle of the dark hall, her terrified mind clinging to the psalm her father had always made her recite whenever she'd admitted to being afraid. The one that had given her strength the last time she met Korigan.

Even though I walk through the valley of the shadow of death.

Korigan jerked her hair, making her gasp in pain. "I didn't permit you to speak."

Lauryn hadn't realized she *was* speaking, but the words wouldn't stop.

I will fear no evil, for you are with me.

"What did I just say?" he snarled, shoving her so hard she

stumbled. When he reached down to yank her back up, though, he froze, eyes wide with terror. Above his leather glove, the flesh of his wrist was rotting before their eyes, the gray skin flaking off in huge chunks to reveal the bone underneath. It was a horrifying sight, and for long heartbeat, they were both struck dumb before Korigan grabbed his sleeve and tugged it down, hiding the flesh from view.

"Go," he snarled, clutching his decaying arm to his side. "Hurry."

Lauryn didn't want to do anything he said, but she also wanted to escape this awful place, so she obeyed, picking up the pace as the two of them rushed through the rest of the dark, cell-lined passage to the doorway at the end. Here, the hall opened up into a much larger room. Normally, that would have made Lauryn happy. She wasn't exactly claustrophobic, but she'd never enjoyed small underground spaces, and anything should have felt like paradise after that horrible hallway. But even though this place was almost airy by comparison to the prison corridor, it was definitely not an improvement.

They had entered what was clearly a lab, but it was like no medical laboratory Lauryn had ever seen. Some of the machines were the same, but interspersed between them were horrible devices that looked like a cross between a mad scientist's creations and sacrificial altars. Recently used ones, given the astonishing amount of blood that coated their surfaces.

A day ago, any one of them would have been enough to make Lauryn freeze in terror. Now, though, given all the other hell she'd walked through to get here, she just turned away in disgust, scanning the bloody room for the reason Korigan had brought her here.

He was easy to find. In the whole giant room, there was only one person to be seen: a handsome older man in an unspeakably expensive tux standing in the middle of the lab with his back to them, his hands clasped at his sides as he stared into what could only be described as a pure black cube.

"Welcome back, Victor."

Lauryn jerked back. She knew the voice, of course. She wasn't even surprised to discover that Christopher St. Luke sounded exactly the same in person as he did on television. What she wasn't prepared for was what happened when he turned around, revealing a shirt front and white tie that were every bit as blood soaked as the rest of the room. There was blood on his face as well, painting a joker's smile across the smooth shaved line of his neatly trimmed beard as he flashed Lauryn a hungry grin.

"And you've brought a gift."

The sight of his bloody teeth was enough to make her gag. If Korigan hadn't still been holding her by her hair, she would have bolted right then and there. But even as she felt herself starting to crack, the memory of her father spoke clearer than ever.

Your rod and your staff, they comfort me.

"I told you to stop that," Korigan said threateningly, but St. Luke held up his hand.

"Let her recite her poetry," he said dismissively. "It has no power here. I'm far more interested in where you acquired *that.*"

"I thought you would be," Korigan said, holding Talon's sword up in front of him like a prize. "The girl got it from her God warrior boyfriend when your man Lincoln Black tricked the idiot into trading his life for hers. A bad move on his part, since I got her in the end." He chuckled. "So sad. All that sacrifice for nothing."

"So I see," St. Luke said, holding out his hand. "Give her here. And the sword. Quickly."

Korigan's gloved fingers tightened on Lauryn's shoulder. "No."

St. Luke arched a blood-splattered eyebrow. "No?"

"I did what you wanted," Korigan said. "I tied this city up and put it on the railroad tracks, exactly as ordered."

"And you have been paid handsomely for it," St. Luke said. "Everything you asked, I gave: money, power—"

"What good is all that when I look like this?" Korigan spat, pointing at his face.

"Whatever do you mean?" St. Luke asked innocently. "You've never looked better." He grinned at the decaying flesh that now covered half of the police chief's face. "Your true nature is showing through at last, Victor Korigan. Rotten on the outside as you are on the inside."

The police chief sneered. "Save your lies for your crazies," he said, yanking Lauryn back into his chest. "Our previous business is concluded. This is a new deal. You and Black have been obsessed with that drifter who calls himself Talon ever since you heard he was in town. This girl is his prize. I'll give her to you, and the sword, but in return, I want the antidote."

St. Luke looked surprised. "Antidote? To what?"

Korigan's rotting face turned savage. "Don't play stupid with me, old man. I know you built yourself a way out of this mess. Give it to me. Undo *this*—" he pointed at his rotted face "—and I'll give you the doctor girl that warrior of yours gave everything to save. We'll both get what we want, and then we can end this business cleanly like professionals."

"Ah, yes," St. Luke said wistfully. "Business. It's always *business* with you, Korigan. But what you don't understand is that, for me, this situation has never been anything but personal. Tonight is *my* victory. The payoff of many, many years' hard work." He paused there, flashing Korigan a smug grin. "Why would I ever build a way out of that?"

"Stop lying," Korigan said, though he no longer sounded so sure. "No one's crazy enough to infect an entire city without making an antidote!"

"Come now, Victor. You can't have it both ways," St. Luke said with a laugh. "You thought I was crazy enough to give you my fortune in return for less than forty-eight hours' worth of work. You can't then turn around and insist I'm sane enough to build a way out."

By the time he finished, Korigan didn't seem to know what to think. He just stood there staring at St. Luke with a look of bewildered horror. Then, with an unearthly howl of rage, he shoved Lauryn away. "You crazy bastard!" he screamed. "You knew this would happen!"

"I did," St. Luke confessed. "But you have no one to blame but yourself. A *smart* businessman should have known I'd never have been so free with my fortune if there was any chance of your surviving to claim it."

"Survive this, asshole!" the police chief bellowed, his voice transformed in rage as he threw Talon's sword to the ground. The beautiful blade was still crashing into the cement when Korigan pulled his cannon of a semiautomatic pistol out of his coat and aimed it with both hands, emptying the entire magazine straight into St. Luke's chest.

The rich man didn't move the whole time. Didn't even flinch as the bullets ripped into his already bloody chest.

And he *definitely* didn't go down.

"What the . . . " Korigan said, eyes wide as he pulled the trigger on his now empty gun again and again, getting only hollow clicks. "What the hell are you?"

"What you can become," St. Luke said, brushing his long, elegant fingers over the bloody holes Korigan had just made in his chest. His *unmoving* chest, Lauryn realized for the first time. "I told you, friend, it's too late. There is no antidote, no cure, no salvation for anyone in this city. Nothing can save you once the fall begins." He grinned wide, showing them a wall of bloody teeth. "You were all damned from the very beginning."

"NO!" Korigan roared, throwing his empty gun at St. Luke, who dodged easily. "I don't believe in any of this! I'm not—"

But he was. Even as he screamed that he wasn't, Korigan was changing, his body rotting before Lauryn's eyes. By the time his voice gave out, he looked like a walking corpse, not that it slowed him down. If anything, he actually seemed to be getting *bigger*, his putrid flesh pulsing and expanding as he stumbled toward St. Luke.

"You bastard!" he gurgled, the words mangled by his swelling throat as he grabbed the billionaire. *"I'll take you to hell with me!"*

"I'm afraid that's impossible," St. Luke said calmly, barely seeming to notice the huge, monstrous hands Korigan had wrapped around his torso. "You see, you've got it backwards. I've already been to hell, and I brought it back with *me.*"

His hand shot out as he finished, the elegant, bloody fingers punching right through the wall of Korigan's bulletproof vest and into the flesh beneath. It was a horrifying sight, but even when his entire hand was inside Korigan's chest, St. Luke didn't let go. He did the opposite, clenching his hand around the bones inside the bigger man's torso before he jerked down, using his own inhuman strength to force the thing Korigan had become to its knees on the floor in front of him.

"Accept your fate, Victor," St. Luke whispered, his blue eyes gleaming. "Embrace the monster you truly are, or die like so many others on this bloodiest, most beautiful of nights."

"Never," Korigan spat, his bloody eyes furious. "I will *never* be one of your monsters!"

St. Luke's face fell into a look of supreme disappointment. "Then die," he said, throwing the rotten man with a flick of his hand straight back into the black cube at the lab's heart that he'd been gazing into when they'd arrived.

With everything else that had been going on, Lauryn hadn't had a moment to spare for the strange dark cube at the lab's center. So far as she knew, it was just another unspeakable terror in the billionaire's collection. But the moment St. Luke threw Korigan into it, she realized she was wrong.

Though St. Luke had tossed the rotting pile of flesh that had once been Chicago's corrupt police chief with enough force to send him flying straight across the giant room, the moment he entered the shadows, all trace of what had once been Korigan— his body, his scream, even his stench—vanished. There was no ripple, no fading. He was simply *gone*, and the longer Lauryn stared into the darkness where he'd vanished, the more sure she became that it wasn't simple darkness at all. It was something else entirely, something no living soul should see.

"That takes care of that," St. Luke said, brushing his bloody hands together to remove the last remaining flecks of Korigan from his slender fingers. "Now." His eyes flicked to Lauryn. "Where were we?"

Up until this point, Lauryn had still been thinking of St. Luke as a man. When his cold eyes found her now, though, she finally understood the thing in the room with her was human in form only. But even as the primal terror that followed turned her legs to jelly and sent her to the ground, the words came again unbidden to her mind, louder than ever.

Even though I walk through the valley of the shadow of death, I will fear no evil, for you are with me. Your rod and your staff, they comfort me.

"More poetry," St. Luke said, his footsteps echoing on the bloody floor as he walked toward her. "It really is quite moving. But dazzling with language is an old con-artist trick: useful only on those too feebleminded to find their way through it. Tell me, little doctor, does that include you?"

He stopped when he reached her, bending over to look her in the eyes. He was so close, the blood from his bullet-riddled shirt—his, Korigan's, or someone else's entirely, Lauryn couldn't even tell at this point—dripped down to land on her clenched fists. Each drop was cold as snow and burned like acid, scoring her skin before she snatched her hands away.

"What are you?"

"You know," he said with a slow smile. "If you are what I think you are, you know. But the really interesting question here is who are *you*, Lauryn Jefferson?"

Lauryn set her jaw stubbornly. "A doctor."

"Really?" His eyes flicked to Talon's sword, still lying where Korigan had tossed it down on the bloody floor, several feet out of reach. "That's an awful big scalpel for a doctor."

"It's not mine," she said stubbornly. "It belongs to Talon, and he's going to be coming for it soon."

St. Luke grinned like that was a marvelous joke. "Considering he's with Lincoln right now, I *sincerely* doubt that. I know the Soldiers of El Elyon can seem infallible, what with their monk-like discipline and Biblical magic tricks, but take it from someone who's dealt with them for a *very* long time: planning is not one of their strong suits. So far as I can tell, their only strategy seems to be 'wait for sign from God, hope it turns out.'"

Lauryn set her jaw. "It seems to work for them."

"Does it?" St. Luke asked, turning around to wave his hand at the giant room packed full of lab equipment and nightmares. "Do you think all this was built in a day? Or a year?" He shook his head. "I've been working on this for *ages*. If the SEE had any real idea what they were doing, they'd have sent Talon to stop me last year, or the year before that. They most definitely wouldn't have sent him *alone*. But sadly for Chicago, God couldn't be bothered to send one of his cleanup crews around at a point when it actually would have done some good, which is why I have the free time to stand here discussing it with you. My victory is already assured. But just because the idiots who found you first are a bunch of disorganized, borderline psychotic Jesus freaks with terrible planning doesn't mean you're doomed to be one, too."

Lauryn blinked. "What?"

"You're obviously prime material," St. Luke explained. "I just met you a few minutes ago, but I already know that you're determined, driven, talented, and selfless to the point of absurdity. I know all of that because a SEE warrior—and not just any SEE, but their poster boy Talon himself!—latched on to you. He even went so far as to entrust you with his *sword*, which I don't have to tell you doesn't happen often. But just because he wants you for his team doesn't mean you have no choice in the matter. You still have your free will, which means there's still a chance for you to join the winning side."

"Which I suppose you think you're on?" Lauryn said, glaring.

"But of course," St. Luke replied. "That's not foolish pre-game bragging, either. As I've mentioned at least twice now, *I've already won*. My Z3X compound is spread all over Chicago. Even if your God decided to blow up every one of my factories right now, it wouldn't change a thing. The damage is done. There's nothing anyone can do to stop it now, not even me."

With every word St. Luke spoke, Lauryn's hope grew dimmer. She didn't want to believe him, but it was hard to keep the faith when she'd already seen the proof of what he was saying with her own eyes on the drive up here. But even as her belief that this could be fixed faltered, the ever-analytical doctor side of her still wasn't satisfied.

"Why?" she demanded.

St. Luke blinked. "Why what?"

She sat back on her knees, staring him straight in the face. "Why are you doing this? I've seen what Z3X does, and I still don't get it. What victory does driving everyone crazy achieve? All you've got is a city full of psychotic monsters."

"Not *monsters*," St. Luke said, his voice taking on the same irritated tone she'd heard in her own when she was trying to correct someone who wasn't listening. "Anchors. *Gateways.* Vessels for my soldiers."

"You mean demonic possession," Lauryn said, voice shaking.

"'Possession' is such a strong word. I prefer to think of it as an opportunity. You see, even I can't *make* people be evil. I can only tempt them until they become that way on their own, after which they're left open to me like a window left cracked for a burglar. Continuing this metaphor, Z3X would be the crowbar. It's a tool for widening what's already there. Every person suffering under the effects of Z3X was already on a bad path. All my drug did was speed up the process, opening millions of souls that would otherwise be very poor grips for us on this world into full-scale hooks."

Lauryn frowned. "Hooks?"

St. Luke nodded. "That part is very important. What you have to understand about hell, Dr. Jefferson, is that it's very far away. 'Cast into the deepest pit' isn't merely flowery Biblical prose. This world, the mortal world, is as far above us as heaven is above you, and it's protected by death."

This explanation left Lauryn more confused than ever. "How does death protect something?"

"It's the only way through," St. Luke explained. "Under normal circumstances, the only way a soul goes from here to hell is to die. The same goes for demons headed in the other direction. Unless we find a way to cheat the system, which I have found ways to do. But even then it's very hard, because, again, hell is very far away. That's where my plan tonight come into play, though."

"What do you mean?"

"What I mean is that hell doesn't have to stay so far away."

He lifted his bloody hand, curling the fingers into a shape like a hook. "Every soul Z3X opens up is a soul for us to get our hooks into. The more hooks we have, the better our grasp on this world, and the easier it is to pull things from hell *up*. Get a good enough hold—say, a major metropolitan area of around two million people—and you'd be amazed what we can pull into creation. Whole armies, maybe even a citadel of hell itself! And once you get one foot in the door, it becomes easier and easier to pry it open even wider, forcing the veil of death back until there's nothing in our way at all."

He finished with a deeply satisfied grin, leaning down until he was nose to nose with the doctor on the floor. "Now do you get it?" he whispered. "*Now* do you see what I mean when I say I've won? The moment that Z3X hit the streets months ago, my foot was wedged in that door. This whole time, I've been working on it, pushing it, wheedling it open wider and wider. At this point, I don't think I could close it if I tried." He pointed at the cube of darkness at the lab's heart. "Look and see for yourself, if you dare."

Lauryn didn't want to do anything he said. But curiosity had always been her great weakness, and in the end, she looked, lifting her eyes to the nothingness inside the black box no light could penetrate.

"Careful," St. Luke warned. "It stares back."

For once, Lauryn believed him. She could almost feel the darkness watching her, but horrifying as that was, she didn't think the blackness was the doorway to hell St. Luke was making it out to be. First off, there was no stench of brimstone, and second, St. Luke had said hell was far away. All the way on the other side of mortality. But if that was true, then that black cube in front of her was . . .

"Death," she whispered, chest heaving. "That's death."

"You *are* a clever girl," St. Luke said, reaching down to pat her on the head. "Good guess. Though I'm afraid what you see there is just the tip of the proverbial iceberg. The actual hole

I've dug is *much* bigger, and getting more so all the time. At this point, with so many hooks in so many hearts, I've practically pried open a highway, which means my work in this city is all but done. The only thing left to do now is give it one last, hard yank."

Lauryn's heart started pounding even harder. "And how do you do that?"

St. Luke wagged his finger at her. "Oh, no, darling. That's privileged information. Insiders only. But I'm in a very good mood, so I'll make you a deal."

"To what?" she scoffed. "Join you?"

"You say that like it's unthinkable."

"What else can it be?" she cried. "If I believe anything you've told me, then you're from hell. *Actual* hell, as in realm of unending torture. Even if you were destined to win, which I don't think you are, why would I *ever* choose to join a side where victory means literal hell on earth? In what possible world is *that* a tempting offer?"

"Well, it wouldn't be hell for *you*," St. Luke said. "You'd be with me, at the top. Take it from one who knows, my dear: ruling in hell is far better than serving in heaven. For one thing, *we* actually respect intelligence. Unlike those other guys who answer every reasonable question with mumbo jumbo about believing and trusting and other forms of blindness, we encourage skepticism. We also believe in proper compensation. You know SEE warriors take a vow of poverty and celibacy, right?" He shuddered. "What's the point of all that power if you never get to use it? But you're forgetting the strongest argument of all: *I've already won*. This whole thing's a done deal. There is no victory condition left for Talon and his ilk. And since a big part of my victory is to slaughter all who oppose me, you really might want to reconsider my offer."

"So that's my choice?" Lauryn said. "Join you or die?"

St. Luke flashed her a charming smile. "I like to keep things simple."

It was certainly that, but Lauryn wasn't changing her mind. "Your enemies aren't slaughtered yet," she reminded him. "Just because you're ahead doesn't mean you've won."

"Really?" St. Luke said, crossing his arms over his chest. "By all means, then, enlighten me. How shall I be defeated? Are you going to spout some more holy poetry at me? Move me to tears? Make an impassioned plea that will turn even my evil heart?"

"That wasn't what I had in mind," Lauryn said, lurching sideways to grab the hilt of Talon's sword from where Korigan had dropped it.

St. Luke's eyes followed the motion, and he sighed in disappointment. "So that's how it's going to be?" he said, shaking his head. "Foolish girl, you don't even know how to use that weapon."

He was right. Before today, Lauryn had never even held a sword. She didn't actually think she was holding it correctly now but it didn't matter. Just because she wasn't a fighter didn't mean she didn't know what to do. St. Luke's attempts to lure her over to his side had only made her more sure, because now more than ever, Lauryn knew Talon had been telling the truth. She *did* have a mission here tonight, and it wasn't to find an antidote. Everything that had happened over the last few crazy days had led her to this moment: here on her knees with the enemy right in front of her, looking *down* on her, underestimating her in every way. And the more Lauryn thought about that, the surer she became.

You prepare a table before me in the presence of my enemies.

St. Luke rolled his eyes as she stood up. "Fine," he said, exasperated. "You want to be foolish? Be my guest. Encouraging doomed acts of delusional hubris is one of my favorite hobbies, so let's go." He patted his chest. "Hit me with your best shot. Never mind that Korigan already tried that and failed. He was just an inhumanly strong monster of rage and greed. I'm sure you, the scrawny ER doctor who hasn't been to the gym a day in her life, will *definitely* do a better job."

Lauryn narrowed her eyes, pointedly ignoring him as she rose from the ground and walked past St. Luke toward the center of the bloody lab where the black cube waited.

"Okay, *now* I'm curious," St. Luke said, hurrying after her. "I know things look dire, but I hope you're not considering suicide. It's the only unforgivable sin, you know."

Lauryn ignored that, too, keeping her eyes on the watching dark as she moved closer.

You anoint my head with oil; my cup overflows.

"I wouldn't go much farther if I were you," St. Luke warned. "I've been a little overzealous tonight, and I'm afraid the boundaries aren't quite as clear as they used to be. Go much closer, and you won't come back."

That's what Lauryn was counting on. She walked right up to the edge, getting as close as she dared to the line of darkness no light could penetrate. Then, when she was right on the edge, she turned around and held Talon's sword up hilt first.

"You want it?"

St. Luke scoffed. "Please," he said, insulted. "You can't tempt the tempter."

"Can't I?" Lauryn said, wiggling the gleaming sword at him. "I still know very little about the SEE, but I know their swords are precious. Holy objects, even, and extremely hard to get. A perfect trophy for your victory, in other words." She smiled. "You want it, don't you?"

St. Luke didn't deny it, and he didn't take his eyes off the sword. For a moment they both faced off, Lauryn holding out the sword, the bloody man trying not to take it. Then, fast as a striking snake, St. Luke's hand shot out to wrap around the hilt.

Gotcha.

The moment his grip tightened, Lauryn wrapped her own hand tight around the sword's cross-guard . . .

And fell backwards into the wall of dark behind her.

As soon as she crossed the threshold, time slowed to a crawl. This was probably when her life was supposed to be flashing in front of her eyes, Lauryn realized, but she was too busy watching the panic cross St. Luke's face as he realized what was happening. Lauryn was taking the sword—*his* trophy—into the Great Beyond with her. Close as she was looking, she could actually see the moment he contemplated letting go, but if there was anything she knew about the devil, it was that he was greedy, and sure enough, St. Luke didn't go. Instead, he braced against the floor, stopping them both.

"Stupid girl," he snarled at her, his face warped by the hazy border of the doorway. "Do you think *I* fear death?" He nodded down at his bullet-riddled chest. "You're another story, though. You must be feeling it by now, the cold breath on your neck? The icy grip of mortality? It has you now, but it's still not too late." He leaned in closer, his face turning bone white in the dark. "Give me the sword, and I'll save you."

Surely goodness and mercy shall follow me all the days of my life.

Lauryn looked him dead in the eye. "You never save anyone," she growled. "And I will *never* let go."

And I shall dwell in the house of the Lord forever.

St. Luke's lips curled in a snarl of pure rage. "Fine," he spat, pulling back his leg to kick her the rest of the way in. "Then go ahead and—"

He never got to finish. The moment he lifted his leg to kick her, Lauryn lurched with all her weight. Unbalanced on a single foot, St. Luke's superior strength didn't matter. He had no leverage to fight her. After that, it was as simple as falling backwards, dragging St. Luke, who'd never let go of Talon's sword, into the abyss with her.

16

THAT ANY SHOULD PERISH

When Lauryn opened her eyes again, she was alone.

She blinked in confusion, looking around at the dark. The last thing she remembered was dragging St. Luke into the black cube, but the dark here wasn't anything like the cold, infinite dark of the abyss she remembered falling into. It was warm and familiar, the orange-lit half-dark of a city night. The rest was different as well: no more terrifying satanic lab or blood or even St. Luke himself. There was only her, standing alone on the snowy street . . .

In front of her father's house.

That couldn't be right. Lauryn turned in a slow circle, glaring at the peaceful, undisturbed snow around her for some sign of the trap this had to be, but there was nothing. Just her child-hood neighborhood as she'd loved it best, sleeping beneath a winter blanket on a quiet night, filling her with a deep, restful peace like nothing she'd ever known. Oddly enough, that was the clue that made the rest come together. Even in the deepest, snowiest night, nowhere in Chicago was *ever* this quiet. In a city of 2.7 million people, there was always someone yelling, some-thing breaking or moving about, and yet the night around her was silent. So silent, actually, that Lauryn couldn't even hear the puff of her own breath, which could only mean one thing.

She was dead.

This wasn't a surprise, exactly. She'd known where she was headed the moment she'd decided to take St. Luke with her. But knowing you were going to die and actually *being* dead were two entirely different animals. Still, it wasn't nearly as bad as she'd expected. As a doctor, Lauryn had always seen death as the enemy; the ultimate failure to be fought at all costs. Now she had to wonder if she and her fellow ER staff had been in the right all those times they'd wrestled someone back from the brink. If she'd known death would be this peaceful, maybe she wouldn't have fought it so hard.

Well, right or wrong, there was nothing she could do about it now. She didn't want to just keep standing here in the street, either. Apparently, snow was cold in the afterlife as well. Her booted feet were already starting to ache, so she stomped them on the pavement, looking around for some kind of sign: a light, pearly gates, anything to tell her what to do next. But other than the unnatural quiet, the street looked exactly as it always did. She was wondering if she was supposed to just start walking when she finally looked *up* . . . and nearly fell on her ass in the snow.

There was something enormous in the sky above her, and it was *not* peaceful or good. It floated in the night like a tower-ing thunderhead, but there was nothing fluffy or soft about the pitch-black battlements or the twisted towers that rose from the thing's peak like something out of M. C. Escher's nightmares. The main body was even worse—an ugly, pitted ball of dark volcanic-looking stone that didn't look structurally sound, much less capable of flight—but what really made Lauryn's blood run cold was the haze that surrounded it.

Her first thought was of billowing smoke, but as she watched the stuff move, she realized the cloud was actually made up of swarming *creatures*. Distance made them look no bigger than gnats, but Lauryn was certain the flying specks had to be at least as big as her, if not bigger, and there were thousands of them. No, *millions*. So many that their locust-like swarm darkened even the night sky. She was still staring at them in horror when she heard the crunch of footsteps in the snow behind her.

Before she could even think about it, Lauryn spun around, raising Talon's sword, which she'd only just now realized she was still clutching in her hand. But as she turned to face the new threat, she realized it wasn't one of the winged black things she'd seen overhead. It wasn't even someone she knew who'd died (which, considering where she was, Lauryn had been half expecting). It was someone entirely new, someone Lauryn—who wasn't sure of much at this point—was positive she had never met if only because there was no chance she would ever forget meeting a man like this.

He was ridiculously tall, easily the tallest person Lauryn had ever seen, and yet, despite this, he was perfectly proportioned, his strong body the athlete's ideal beneath his cloud-gray suit and white winter coat. His face was ageless and hard as stone, a sharp contrast to his deep brown eyes and dark skin, which were almost glowing with strength and vitality, though that might have been a reflection from the enormous golden wings that rose from his back, framing his shaved head in an aura of glory.

"Hello, Lauryn," he said, his inhumanly deep voice vibrating through her chest. "My name is Akarra. It is my pleasure to finally meet the Savior of Chicago face-to-face."

"Uh, same?" Lauryn replied awkwardly, unsure what else to say. She got nervous when moderately famous people came into her ER; an angel was completely outside her comfort zone, which was why she didn't process the rest of what he'd said until several seconds later. "Wait, savior of *what*?"

"The Savior of Chicago," Akarra repeated. "The person who shall rise to stop *that*." He pointed up, his glowing eyes locked on the nightmarish figure floating high above their heads.

Lauryn swallowed. "And what is that, exactly?"

"They call it Castle Delusion," the angel replied, returning his arm to his side. "A stronghold of the enemy. Normally, it is bound within their realm, but tonight the demon wearing the face of the man who was once Christopher St. Luke has used the corruption of thousands of souls to drag it all the way to the edge of the mortal realm. Now it hovers on the threshold of death itself, and even that final barrier is weakening. If nothing is done, the building pressure will sunder the veil that protects the world of the living from the worlds beyond, and the army of the enemy will spill forth."

By the time he finished, Lauryn felt like she'd swallowed a brick. At least now she understood why St. Luke had been so confident. Even the near-zombie-like outbreak Z3X had caused was nothing compared to bringing that . . . that *thing* into Chicago. "How do we stop it?"

"That is up to you," Akarra said.

"Me?" Lauryn said, wincing when she heard the panic in her voice. "Why me? I don't know what to do! I'm a doctor, not a soldier. What am I supposed to do against something like that— diagnose it?"

"That is up to you," Akarra repeated firmly. "It is not our

place to question the will of God. If you were chosen, it was for a reason. Trust in that."

With every calm word, Lauryn's frustration grew. "That's it?" she cried. "*That's* your angelic advice? I get that this is all part of God's plan, but I *really* don't see how I'm going to stop a giant flying hell fortress." She especially didn't see why, out of everyone in Chicago, God had apparently picked her to do . . . whatever it was she was supposed to do. Or why he'd waited until *now*. That thing was practically on top of them, and then there was the part where she was already *dead*.

"I know you have doubts," Akarra said gently. "All mortals do. That is how God created you. It is your nature to doubt and question, but it is your faith that shall see you through."

That answer was so like her dad and Talon and every freaking holy man she'd ever met, Lauryn couldn't help herself. "But that's so unfair!" she cried. "Why would God do this to us? If he loves us as much as you say, why does he leave us in doubt? Why did he leave us *alone*? If people knew God was real, they wouldn't get into half the trouble they do."

"I am a warrior," Akarra replied stiffly. "Not a sage or a prophet. Still, it seems to me that you have just answered your own question. The true measure of a person isn't how they conduct themselves when they are being watched, but how they act when they believe they are alone." He looked up at the sky. "God knows the heart of every living thing. He knows our evils before we do them, and yet he withholds his judgment until the act is done, because until that moment, there is always the chance to turn back."

Angry as she was, Lauryn had to admit that made sense. "No punishment before the crime, is that what you mean?"

The angel nodded. "God is just. But even after the sin has been committed, he does not turn his face away. His arms are always open to those who are truly sorry and truly repent. Fairness would dictate that those who commit crimes should be punished, and yet God is not fair. No matter how great the crime, he always chooses mercy, and for this we give him thanks."

"But why do *I* have to do it?" she asked again. "I didn't even believe in this stuff before tonight, and that was only after I got more proof of the divine than any actual faithful person should need. I'm a terrible Christian! I don't go to church, I—"

"Do you think God grades on attendance?" Akarra asked, his deep voice surprisingly angry. "Foolish child. God's favor is not bounded by your rules. He cares nothing for the strictures set down in holy books by old men. How you treat others less fortunate than yourself, the mercy and kindness in your soul, the courage of your deeds even when you do not think you will be rewarded—*these* are what God judges, and these are the things you have done that have made you worthy in his sight. He has read your heart, Lauryn Jefferson. He has seen your deeds, not your religion. It is what *you* have done that has made you worthy in his sight, and it is for that that he has chosen you to stand against the enemy's tide."

"So just me?" Lauryn said, her eyes going back to the sky. "Against *that*?"

"It is a terrifying task, and a difficult one," the angel agreed. "But he would not have given it to you if you could not do it."

Looking at that fortress, Lauryn wasn't so sure. "But how?" she asked again, trying to make the question sound pragmatic and not like she was freaking out. "I mean, leaving aside the obvious impossibilities of one me versus thousands of them, I'm still, you know, *dead*."

Akarra looked at her like she was stupid. "Has not God already proven time and time again that death is no barrier to him?"

"Okay, fair point," she admitted. "But if I'm supposed to do this, why are you here? Are you going to help me shoot that hell castle out of the sky or something?" Because that would be *awesome*.

The angel considered the question for a moment, and then he shook his head. "I don't believe I could. God is limitless, but I am not God. I am an angel, and as such I am bound by my nature just as mortals are bound by theirs. This place—" he gestured around at the silent winter night "—is your creation, the threshold of your death. It is a stillness where you can take time to decide, but the fact that Castle Delusion is visible even here is a sign of just how close the enemy is to breaking through."

Just saying those words made the angel shudder, and his face was more serious than ever when he looked at Lauryn again. "The veil *must not* be ripped. That barrier is all that divides your world from all the worlds beyond. Without it, there will be nothing to stop devils from walking as freely in your world as they do in their own."

"Wait," she said. "Just devils? Can you guys not come in and help us?"

"We *would* be able to walk among you," Akarra said cautiously. "But unlike the serpent's forces, we are bound by rules. A fight where one side plays fair and one doesn't is always doomed to be lopsided. But this is not to say we are powerless." Akarra pulled himself straight. "We are the soldiers of heaven, and we will fight as such when the time comes. But while we can kill demons and slow the forces of hell down, we cannot save humanity from itself. Only a human can do that, and you are the one chosen tonight. I am merely here to be your guide along whatever path you choose."

"Wait, I've got a choice?"

"There is *always* a choice," the angel said, giving her a quelling look. "Haven't you listened to anything you've been told?"

Talon had made a pretty big deal about choice. But even so. "If the choice is up to me, what are my options?"

"Whatever you are willing to work for," Akarra replied solemnly. "Your kindness in this life plus your sacrifice to stop St. Luke have already earned you a place of honor in your Father's house. If you wish, I can take you there now."

"You mean heaven?" Lauryn said, her eyes going huge. "Like, *heaven* heaven?"

The angel nodded. "But it is a choice you can only make once. If you go with me to that farthest shore, you will never be able to return to this one, and your place in these events will come to an end."

"But I thought my saving Chicago was part of God's plan?" she said. "If that's true, how can you offer to take me away?"

"God does not plan your choices," Akarra said as a smile ghosted over his lips. "He *is* all knowing, though, which pays to bear in mind. But obedience without choice is not obedience at all."

That was the same thing Talon had been trying to tell her this afternoon in the car, and Lauryn shook her head with a sigh. "Guess I should have listened," she said, looking up again at the terrifying fortress in the sky. "So what happens if I choose to stay?"

"If you decide to stay, you will be returned." His burning eyes flashed. "And you will fight."

Lauryn shuffled her feet in the snow. Honestly, quitting while she was ahead sounded pretty tempting. Despite Akarra's assurance that God wouldn't give her a task she couldn't handle, she still had no idea what good she was going to do against something like the fortress floating in the sky above her. But at the same time, running away, even to heaven, just felt wrong.

And I still have a sword to return to its rightful owner . . .

That was the realization that pushed her over the edge, and she turned back to the angel with a deep breath. "Okay," she said. "I'll do it. I'll go back. Don't know what I'll do when I get there, but I'll figure it out."

"You will," the angel said with absolute surety.

Lauryn nodded, trying to match his confidence, though she didn't quite think she managed. "So . . . how do I get back?"

"I can take you," Akarra said. "But first, you will need a weapon. That one belongs to another."

"Of course," Lauryn said, handing over Talon's sword. The angel took it with as much reverence as St. Luke had grabbed it in greed, making her wonder yet again just what was so special about the plain-looking blade. Given what Akarra had just said about getting her own weapon, Lauryn supposed she was about to find out.

"How do we do this?" she asked nervously. "Do I kneel or . . ."

Akarra shook his head. "Just take my hand."

Lauryn gave his extended—and empty—palm a skeptical look. But she was in too deep to back out now, and so, with a deep breath and a final look at the monstrosity above, she did as she was told, grabbing the angel's hand in her own like she was grabbing on to a lifeline.

The result was immediate. The moment she touched the angel's skin, golden fire raced up her arm. But though it consumed her in seconds, there was no pain. Only warmth and a feeling of absolute certainty that this was the right choice. It was like the moment when she'd first known she wanted to be a doctor, only infinitely more. Standing there with her burning hand wrapped around the angel's, Lauryn had never been more sure of anything in her life. For the first time ever, she had no questions, and she didn't even flinch when the peaceful bubble of death's threshold burst to leave her standing alone in what was left of St. Luke's horrible laboratory.

And in her hand, there was a sword.

It was beautiful. A mirror-bright, razor-sharp blade on a hilt as golden as the angel's fire. She was still staring at it in wonder when Akarra's voice boomed in her head.

Go, he said. *I must return a blade to another.*

"Already ahead of you," Lauryn said firmly, clutching her new sword as she bolted out of the bloody lab and back toward the elevator leading to the surface at a dead run.

H ad enough?"

Talon kept his head down, ignoring Lincoln Black's mocking voice to focus on the breaths that just might be his last. He had no idea how long this night had gone on, but his body was definitely nearing its limit. There was no piece of his skin that was not bruised or cut, no movement he could make, no breath he could breathe without setting off a shot of crippling agony. Even holding perfectly still was painful. A fact his jailer clearly relished.

"Hurts, doesn't it?" Black whispered in his ear. "Welcome to my world, old man. But you should thank me. Pain means you're alive. *Really* alive, not that ascetic monk crap. But as much as I'd love to let you sit and wallow, I can't let you miss this. Open your eyes." When Talon didn't obey fast enough, Black struck him on the cheek. "Open them!"

Talon was tempted to keep them closed just to spite his enemy, but the pain was already too great, and he was still only human. Slowly, tiredly, he cracked his eyes open to see the agent of his enemy standing over him like a mountain, a crooked smile on his taunting face. "Here," he said. "I've got something for you to see."

He grabbed what was left of Talon's jacket and started to drag him, bumping his body across the rough metal-grated floor. Every jolt kicked off a new pain, leaving Talon on the verge of passing out by the time Black lifted him up, propping his body against the warehouse's brick wall so he could see out the window.

"Take a look," he said, delighted. "I heard tell that Chicago was your old stomping ground before you threw it all away for Jesus, but I bet you've never seen it like *this*."

Talon had never wished something was a lie so hard in his life, but for once, Black was telling the truth. Through the window of the warehouse's second story, he could see the city lit up in the night, but not in the usual way. He'd seen that same orange light reaching to the clouds once before, long ago. Then, they'd called it the Great Chicago Fire. Through the pain, he wondered if there'd be anyone left alive to name this one.

"Isn't it beautiful?" Black cackled, pressing Talon's face into the cold glass. "The whole city's burning like a campfire, and the firemen can't even get in to fight it because they're all busy getting in touch with their true natures thanks to St. Luke's little drug." He leaned down to press his ear against the window, and his face lit up. "You can even hear the screams!" He laughed delightedly. "And look down in the streets! There are packs of the infected bastards roaming down there like wild dogs. It's absolute and utter anarchy. And here I thought I'd lost all faith in humankind!"

He finished with a joyful shout that made Talon feel physically ill. "You're sick, Black," he whispered, glaring up at the younger man. "You need help."

"No, *you* need help," Black snapped, jerking him away from the window. "Too bad there's no one to give it to you. I'll be honest, I've been waiting to see what nonsense you'll pull out of your holy ass this time around, but it's nearly dawn and so far?" He shrugged. "Nothing. What's wrong, SEE warrior? No miracles left in the tap for you?"

Talon turned away, but Black grabbed his chin, forcing him to look through the window again. "You're missing the best part," he whispered, forcing Talon's chin up until he was staring at the sky. "Look at the smoke and you'll see it."

Talon didn't want to see, but he couldn't look away, because Black was right. High overhead, the smoke from the fires was swirling with the dark clouds and the flocks of carrion birds to make a shape in the sky. Looking at it was like trying to spot the shadow of a fish under the water, but Talon had spent his whole life looking for such signs, and he saw this one clearly. Something was coming. Something *big*.

"What is that?" he whispered.

"The future," Black whispered back. "*My* future, and you don't have a part." He shook his head. "Poor Talon. You made a good run of it, but we've won. While you holy rollers were off thumping your Bibles and condemning the people who needed you most, we were here ripping the world apart to remake in our image. Gotta be an improvement, right? I mean, can't possibly be worse than this hypocritical hellhole your God made. He slapped the whole thing together in seven days, *with* vacation. That's some shoddy construction. Clearly, it's time for an upgrade."

"That is not an upgrade," Talon said savagely, turning on Black. "I don't know what they promised you, but you've let the wolves in by the front gate, and they're not going to spare you when they start to rampage."

For a moment, he almost thought that threat got through, but Lincoln just bared his teeth. "Good," he snarled. "This meek little flock needs a shake-up, and unlike you, I ain't no sheep."

He turned away after that, leaving Talon leaning on the wall staring at the burning city. It was the longest he'd left him unobserved, and Talon knew he should be using that, but he couldn't seem to move. He was just so tired, and the enemy was so far ahead. He wanted to believe that Lauryn was out there, but he didn't even know if she was still alive, or how she could fight this if she was. He'd never questioned God's choice, because the Almighty did not make mistakes, but as he watched the smoke curl up to add definition to the thing in the sky, Talon couldn't help but wonder if maybe, just this once, he'd been wrong to blindly trust his instincts. He didn't regret saving Lauryn's and Will's lives, but he was bitter about having to make the choice in the first place. How many people could he have saved if he'd been down there on the streets with her? How many innocents had fallen tonight because he'd been stuck here satisfying Lincoln Black's sadism?

How many had he failed?

Talon closed his eyes. Always. *Always*, that question returned to haunt him. No matter how hard he fought or how much he improved, it was never enough. When the chips were down, he always failed someone who deserved better. Decades ago, it had been Hope, his first apprentice. Now, it was Lauryn, left out there alone, and who knew? The night wasn't over. Maybe by the time the sun rose, he'd realize he'd failed all of Chicago. Even if Black set him free right now, he was too hurt to fight. He didn't even have his sword. All he could do was sit here and pray for God to forgive his weakness and comfort the city he'd failed so utterly, and he was closing his eyes to do just that when he felt a warm hand land on his shoulder.

He jerked instinctively, already looking for Black. But for once, it wasn't the assassin. It was no one. The space behind him was empty, and yet Talon could feel the hand gripping his shoulder harder than ever, the fingers warm as sunlight, filling his body with strength and his mind with a memory of another time, long ago, in another life.

Finally.

Talon gasped, his pain forgotten as the memory flooded

through him—the wings of fire, the promise of a greater purpose.

You are not forgotten, the angel's voice said. *Loyal Soldier of El Elyon, God Most High, you have endured through great hardship, and you have held fast. You have turned the other cheek, sacrificed pride, and striven to return a lost sheep to the flock. Such work has favor in the eyes of the Lord. Your prayers have been heard, and your pupil is anxious to have you back at her side.* The fiery touch moved to Talon's right hand. *Will you fight once more?*

"I will," Talon gasped, the joyful words jumping from his lips. "Always."

Then rise, the angel commanded. *And take back what the enemy would steal.*

As the words faded, the fire went with them, but not before leaving a familiar weight in Talon's hand. When he looked down, he was clutching his sword, but not as it usually looked. His sword had always been a simple cross blade, brightly polished through care and wear, but still mundane metal. *This* weapon glowed with the reflection of angel fire, and everywhere the shadowless light fell, his wounds vanished, leaving him whole.

"The *hell*?"

Talon lifted his head to see Lincoln Black staring at him in disbelief, and then the assassin bared his teeth. "Oh, *hell* no!" he shouted, drawing his own crooked black sword with a scrape of metal on bone. "You ain't going nowhere. You're *mine!*"

"I can never be yours," Talon said, standing up. "I am already claimed body and soul by he who made me best, as are you."

"I hate when you talk that Godspeak!" Black spat, lifting his blade. "This won't be like last time, old man. That's our castle in the sky, not yours. Power's in our court now."

Talon shook his head sadly. "If that's what you call power, I pity you."

"Save your pity for yourself, asshole!" Black roared, swinging at him, but the blow stopped cold, the black sword striking Talon's bright white blade like a hammer against an anvil. For a moment, Black just stood and stared, and then he jumped back with a string of curses so foul, Talon had to shake his head. It was already clear any words he spoke would fall on deaf ears. After burying himself so deep, violence was the only language Black still respected. If Talon wanted to reach him, he would have to answer in kind. He just wished he felt worse about that as he turned and joyfully raised his own sword to meet Black's attack.

Father forgive me . . .

> PUT ON THE WHOLE ARMOR OF GOD, THAT YOU MAY BE ABLE TO
> STAND AGAINST THE SCHEMES OF THE DEVIL. FOR WE DO NOT
> WRESTLE AGAINST FLESH AND BLOOD, BUT AGAINST THE RULERS,
> AGAINST THE AUTHORITIES, AGAINST THE COSMIC POWERS
> OVER THIS PRESENT DARKNESS, AGAINST THE SPIRITUAL
> FORCES OF EVIL IN THE HEAVENLY PLACES.
> —*EPHESIANS 6:11–12*

17

THIS PRESENT DARKNESS

In his long years of wandering, Talon had learned many ways of using his body as a weapon. He considered it a soldier's duty to master as many forms of fighting as possible, even if he hoped never to use them. But while all the skills he'd learned were useful in their own ways, his favorite style was the Japanese art of Aikido, and not just because it was beautiful. He loved it because of all the martial arts, Aikido was the only style he'd encountered that stressed the safety of both the attacker as well as the defender. At the heart of its philosophy was a longing for harmony and a deep respect for all living things—using your opponent's own momentum, aggression, and strength against them to nullify violence with stillness. Learning it had been a humbling, enlightening, joyful experience, and it was that hopefulness Talon held dear now, using his favorite style to flip Lincoln Black's attacks back on him.

"Screw you and your fancy Judo moves!" Black bellowed, narrowly escaping Talon's grab to try and put him into a submission hold. "This is a sword fight, asshole."

"I'll fight back when you give me something to swing against," Talon said, smiling. "So far, all you've done is flail around like a mad dog."

"I'll show you mad," Black yelled, swinging wildly, his black sword flying so fast it vanished into the dim light. "I'll show you *death!*"

Normally so cool and collected, Black's anger was consuming him, and his sword crashed into Talon's, hitting so fast, all Talon could see were the sparks as it struck. Black lashed out again and again, wailing with all his might, but to no avail. No matter how hard he struck, how fast he went, Talon's stance did not falter. He simply stood and took it, standing steady and implacable as a mountain until, at last, Black stepped back.

"You stubborn bastard," he panted, chest heaving as he tossed his black sword away. "Fine—I'll play your game." He walked over to the bar and grabbed a bottle of whiskey, taking a long swig. "You want to play defense?" he said when he was done, wiping his mouth on the back of his gloved hand. "Dodge this."

The words were barely out of his mouth before his other hand, the one he'd slipped behind the bar while his free hand grabbed the whiskey bottle, came up holding something long and pipe-shaped with a string sticking off one end. It wasn't until Talon saw the tiny flicker of fire on the string's end, though, that he realized the thing wasn't just pipe-*shaped*. It was a pipe *bomb*, and it had just landed at his feet.

Talon dodged only through the grace of God. He lurched to the left, gripping his blazing sword tight as he rolled behind one of the warehouse's metal support beams. It was poor protection, but in the split second before the bomb went off, it was all he had. He'd barely covered his head before the bomb exploded with a deafening *boom*, sending the metal shrapnel that had been packed inside shooting like bullets in all directions. Several pieces whizzed right by his head and shoulders, passing so close he could feel the heat of them on his skin, but between the iron and the angel's protection, he managed to avoid actually being struck. Even so, he was still in a protective crouch when the explosion finally ended, the ringing boom giving way to Lincoln Black's echoing laughter.

"And that's how we do it downtown," he said, his voice mocking. "Plenty more where that came from, old man, so why don't you come out? We'll play *catch*."

The final word was accompanied by the sound of something being thrown, but Talon knew what he was up against now, and he did not hesitate. Black's voice was still ringing when he rolled to his feet, sliding around the pole he'd been using for cover to slice the second pipe bomb—which Black had indeed just tossed at him—out of the air.

The moment his flaming sword hit, he worried he'd made a mistake. It was clear from the hand-filing marks on the pipe's surface that these were homemade explosives, not purchased ones. He had no idea how they'd react to being cut, which was a problem given that he'd sliced this one directly in front of his face. From his grin, Black clearly expected it to explode, but Talon's sword passed through like a fish through water, carving the flying bomb neatly into two halves that flew harmlessly past, clattering to the ground behind him.

"You and your miracle *bullshit*," Black snarled, tossing the third bomb, which he'd been ready to throw at Talon, back into the box full of explosives hidden behind the bar. "That should have been your head, you goddamn cheater!"

After a whole night of talking to Lincoln Black, Talon didn't feel the need to dignify that with a reply. He simply raised his sword again, stepping to the side to avoid the gaping hole the first bomb had left in the wooden floor.

"That's how you want to play, huh?" Black said, vaulting over the bar. "Okay, fucker, let's *play*."

He turned to the weapons displayed so carefully on the brick wall behind him and grabbed the largest item—a huge weighted chain with a wicked-looking hook on the end. He'd barely gotten the thing off its hanger before he swung it, aiming to sink the barbed hook deep into Talon's leg.

As ever, Black was astonishingly fast. But he was also the enemy Talon had trained all these years to face, and he dodged the hook with time to spare.

The chain, however, was another matter.

He was still spinning out of the way when it wrapped around his legs, binding them together and sending him to the floor. He was trying to kick back up when Black appeared above him.

"What's the matter, holy man?" he taunted, yanking the chain tight. "All tied up and nowhere to—"

His words were cut off, leaving him gasping, as Talon struck upward, slamming him with the flat of his shining blade. The impact sent him flying into the wall behind the bar, breaking the bottles in an explosion of glass. He fell to the floor next, gasping and sputtering as thousands of dollars' worth of top-shelf liquor landed on his head. He'd just made it to his knees when Talon's sword appeared at his throat.

"It's over."

"The hell it is," Black gasped, glaring up at him. "You don't have the balls. You've never had the balls to kill me, and that's where you fail, Talon, because I ain't ever going to rest until I take you to hell with me."

"But you're already there," Talon said sadly, looking around at the lonely room full of vice and pain. "You blame me and God and everyone else, but the truth is you've built your own hell here, Black. You could leave at any time, let go of your bitterness and live a better life. But you would rather stay miserable in a world where your problems are someone else's fault than accept that the real enemy here isn't me or God. It's you."

"Then end it," Black said, chest heaving. "You've already written me off. Finish the job." He lifted his head to press his neck against the blade of Talon's sword. "Do it."

For a moment, it seemed like Talon would. He edged closer, pressing his sword along his enemy's neck, and then he relaxed.

"No."

Lincoln Black's eyes flashed with fury. "What?"

"No," Talon said again, lowering his weapon. "I'm not going to kill you."

For a moment, Black just stared at him in disbelief, and then he lurched forward. *"What is wrong with you?"* he screamed. "How many times is it going to take before you learn I don't stop? Do you really think that if you keep letting me go, I'm going to come around? See the light and go to Jesus? Is that what you think is going to happen?"

"It's what I hope," Talon said. "There is always hope."

"If you believe that, then you're stupider than I thought," Black spat. "'Cause I ain't ever gonna stop. If you don't kill me, I'll—"

His words cut off as Talon's sword returned to his neck. "I've heard it all before," Talon said calmly. "But no matter how hard you try, you can't pin your sins on me. Everything you do, you choose, and that's on you, not me. But I will not kill you, Lincoln."

"Why not?" Black demanded.

"Because I'm not like you," Talon said softly. "God doesn't give up on people, and neither do I. There is always a way out. You can still—"

"What?" Black sneered. "Repent? Fucker, *please*. You really think your God would take me? After all this?"

"Yes," Talon said. When Lincoln rolled his eyes, he crouched down in the broken glass to look him in the face. "This is why God's mercy is infinite. Because when there are no limits, there can be no sin so great that it can't be forgiven. Salvation is *always* possible. Always, for anyone. Even you. You just have to want it."

"Then we're at an impasse," Black said. "'Cause I'm never going to want what you're selling, and I'm *never* going to stop coming after you."

"And I'll never stop offering you an out," Talon said, grabbing the weighted chain Black had dropped when he'd hit the ground. "But the ball's in your court now. You're a smart man, Lincoln. When you're tired of being on the losing side, let me know. I'll always be waiting to lift you up."

"*I don't want your pity!*" Lincoln roared, struggling as Talon wrapped the chain around him, pinning his arms and legs to his body until he was trussed up like a roast. "Let me go, you damn—"

But Talon was already walking away, leaving the defeated assassin screaming impotently at the top of his lungs. It was a temporary solution. Black was nothing if not resourceful. Even a chain wouldn't hold him for long. He would be a problem again soon enough—he always was. Tonight, though, he was out, and Talon had bigger problems, starting with the Z3X factory beneath him.

The workers must have fled during his fight with Black, because by the time Talon reached the floor of the warehouse where the vats were churning, all the control stations had been abandoned, the machines left pumping and churning on their own.

With no one in his way, it took only a few minutes for Talon to shut down the whole operation. When he'd rendered all the machine control consoles into metal slag with his sword, Talon turned his attention to the foreman's office, and poked through the scattered papers and spilled beers until he spotted what he was looking for: a brand-new cell phone sitting in its charger, its screen bright and unlocked, ready to be used.

"God provides," Talon said, wiping his bloody hand on the scattered papers before picking up the phone to tap in Lauryn's number.

By the time Lauryn finally made it out of St. Luke's hellhole of a house, she'd never been happier to breathe fresh air. That was, until she saw what was floating in it.

"Damn," she whispered, almost dropping her new sword as she craned her head back to stare at the massive shadow hanging low in the smoky sky.

It wasn't complete, not yet, but what Lauryn could see left no doubt in her mind that this was the same castle she'd seen on death's threshold. It got clearer as she watched, the lines of the horrible towers emerging from the black smoke like a ghosts through the fog.

"Damn," she whispered again, darting down the mansion steps. "Damn, damn, *damn*."

In the rush since she'd woken from death with a sword in her hand, Lauryn hadn't had a chance to stop and sort things out. She still wasn't precisely sure what was happening, but one look at the sky was enough for her to know they were running out of time. But even though the rest of the world seemed to be sliding into chaos, there was one good thing waiting for Lauryn when she stumbled out the mansion doors, and he was standing next to her brother.

"Will!"

Will was leaning on the door of Robbie's car clutching his wound, his face taut and angry. Beside him, Robbie was pacing nervously, biting his nails as he'd done when he was a kid. They both looked enormously relieved to see her, which was only fair since Lauryn had never been happier to see two people in her life.

"I'm sorry, L," Robbie said as she ran toward them. "I tried to keep him in the car, but—"

"It's okay," she said, running to hug them both. "I'm just glad you're alive." She pulled back to have a look at Will's wound. "How are you feeling?"

"Not bad considering I got shanked," Will said, glaring at Robbie, who winced. "But, Lauryn, what the hell were you thinking going in there alone? You could have been—"

"I know," Lauryn said, cutting him off before she had to lie about the fact that she had been through every bad thing Will was clearly about to say, including death. Because none of that mattered anymore. They had bigger problems to deal with.

"Come on," she said, tossing her sword into the car. "We need to go."

"Nice sword, sis."

"Thanks," she said with a tight grin.

"Go where?" Will demanded. "Lauryn, what happened to you in there?"

She sighed. "You wouldn't believe me if I told you."

"Try me," Will said, glancing up at the shadow of the castle in the sky. "My suspension of disbelief is pretty high right now. I mean, last thing I knew, I was dead from a gut wound, and then I wake up feeling pretty decent only to find Robbie shooting what looked like zombies off the car with my gun."

"You should just be happy I got them before they got you," Robbie said, his eyes wild and shaken. "This apocalypse crap is nothing like the video games."

"I'm afraid it's about to get worse," Lauryn said grimly. "That thing in the sky? It isn't going to stay a shadow much longer. We have to stop it before that happens."

"How the hell do we do that?" Robbie cried.

Lauryn's shoulders slumped. She had no idea. She hadn't known what to do when she'd asked to come back, and she *still* had no clue. All she knew was that if she was, in fact, chosen for this task, then there had to be a specific reason God had picked her out of everyone else. Whatever the answer was, it had to be something only she could do, a solution only she could find. Maybe she was meant to find a cure or—

"Damn," Will said, glancing over his shoulder. "They've spotted us."

Before Lauryn could ask what he was talking about, she saw it. Outside the mansion's walls, figures were moving down the street, their bloody eyes glistening in the light of the street lamps as they peered through the gate Robbie had plowed down when he'd driven them in.

"You just had to break the gate," Will said, checking his gun. "*And* you used up all my ammo."

"Hey, I was just trying to survive," Robbie said, jumping into his car as fast as he could. "Let's go!"

Will got in more slowly, wincing as he bent over to squeeze himself back into the car's rear seat. "Too bad we don't have a fire hose full of that holy water stuff you used on Robbie," he grumbled. "Couple thousand gallons of that and we could just wash all this away."

Lauryn froze, her eyes going wide, and then she lurched down to grab Will. "What did you say?"

"That you could wash it all away," he repeated, giving her a funny look. A deserved one, because from the way her cheeks ached, Lauryn knew she had to be grinning like a maniac.

"That's it!" she cried.

Will looked more confused than ever. "What's it?"

Lauryn couldn't answer; she was too busy working things through. It was all snapping together in her head—what she'd learned from Talon, St. Luke's explanation, what she'd seen on the other side—and as the pieces connected, a plan began to form in her head.

"I got it," she whispered, clenching her fists in triumph before she leaped into the car.

"Got what?" Will demanded as Robbie hit the gas.

Before Lauryn could answer, her phone buzzed in her pocket. The number wasn't one she recognized, but at this point she was happy to talk to anyone who was still sane, and she wasted no time raising the phone to her ear. "Hello?"

"It's me."

The deep, familiar voice made her eyes close in happiness. "Talon!"

"Holy crap, for real?" Robbie cried. "Talon's still kicking after Lincoln Black?"

"Of course," Lauryn said proudly. "Who do you think you're talking about?"

By the time she finished, her brother's eyes were wide as billiard balls, and she grinned into the phone. "I think you've impressed the jaded youth."

Talon chuckled at that, and then his voice turned serious. "Are you all right? How's Will?"

"Actually, we're all doing great," she said, looking over her shoulder at Will, who seemed to be nearing the end of his patience. "How are you? I mean, you're clearly alive, but are you—"

"I'm fine," he said, and to Lauryn's surprise, she believed

him. Life as a doctor had made her very good at picking up hidden pain in people's voices, specifically over the phone, but despite everything she'd feared, Talon really did sound just fine, and very determined. "And Lincoln is dealt with, thanks to you." She heard the grin on his voice. "I got your present just in time."

Lauryn glanced up at the shadow in the sky. "Well, if there was ever a time we needed miracles, it's now. You've seen the sky, right?"

"I have," he said grimly. "What's your plan?"

Lauryn blinked in surprise. "How did you know I had a plan?" She'd only just thought of it herself a few second ago.

"Because you always have a plan."

His instant, confident answer was the best compliment anyone had ever given her. "I think I've got something that might work," she said. "Do you remember where my dad's church is?"

"I do," he said. "I'll be there as fast as I can."

"We'll meet you there, then," Lauryn said firmly, glancing at Robbie, who nodded. "Drive safe, the streets are crazy."

"Same to you," Talon replied. "Have faith, Lauryn. We'll get through this."

"I know," she said firmly. "I do. And, Talon?"

"Yes?"

"I'm *really* glad you're okay."

"As am I," he said. "See you soon."

Lauryn smiled and cut off the call, turning to Will, who was waiting impatiently.

"Why are we going to your dad's and not getting out of town?"

"Because we have to finish this," she said firmly. "If we run, all of Chicago's going to fall to this. But I think I've got a plan for how to save these people."

"I don't know if there's any saving this," Robbie said, his voice cracking as he finished turning the car around, finally facing them toward the gate he'd busted down on the way in . . . as well as the crowd of monsters waiting beyond. "This situation's only gotten worse since you went in. I wouldn't be surprised if the whole city was infected by now." He shook his head. "I'm not even sure we can get back to the South Side."

"We have to," she said. "Look, if there are any sane people left, they'll be at Dad's."

"How do you figure that?" Will asked.

"Because Z3X can't make people be monsters," she explained. "It can only augment the sins that are already there. But my dad's congregation is full of the most legitimately godly people I know. If anyone can resist this outbreak, it's them."

"Wait, so we're betting on the prayer circle?" Robbie said, shaking his head. "We're dead."

"Just drive," Lauryn said, placing her sword in her lap. "I'll explain the rest once we get there. Right now, you need to drive, and I need to think."

"Then get in the back," Will grumbled, moving over. "I'll take front."

"And do what?" Lauryn asked, climbing out of her seat into the back.

"Improvise," Will said, grabbing Robbie's tire iron off the floorboard. "The rest I'll leave to you."

Lauryn blinked. "Really?" Because blind trust wasn't an attribute she normally assigned to Will Tannenbaum. But when she gaped at him, he just shrugged.

"This kind of thing will change a man's perspective," he said as he climbed into the front. "We'll get you to church. You just make sure you know what to do when we get there."

That was the last thing she'd ever expected him to say, and it made Lauryn smile. Her brother, on the other hand, looked like he was going to hurl. "Just hold on tight," he muttered, revving the engine. "It's about to get bumpy."

The words were barely out of his mouth before he floored it, shooting his sports car right up the wrecked gate and *over* the transformed monsters lurking on the other side. For a moment, they were airborne . . . and then the car crashed back to earth, bottoming out in a shower of sparks and swerving wildly before Robbie got control again, flooring the pedal as they raced back down the street and back toward the smoke-stained skyline of Chicago.

And overhead, the vultures screeched in delight as the phantom castle began to emerge from the clouds.

18

BOLD AS A LION

Getting home was even more terrifying than driving to St. Luke's mansion had been.

Before, the shuffling figures had just been glimpses, shadows in the dark, eerie emptiness. Now, the illusion of stillness was completely gone, and in its place, monsters openly roamed the streets.

Even knowing they were just transformed people and not *actual* monsters, there was no other word that fit. Everywhere Lauryn looked, creatures with ashen skin and bloody eyes, wearing the tattered winter clothes of normal Chicago residents, roamed the city in huge hunting packs. There were no more cars, no more screams; even the sirens had gone silent. In the time between when they'd arrived at St. Luke's and when she'd come stumbling out, the entire city had been dragged under by the spreading virus of Z3X, and as the last uncorrupted people on the streets, Lauryn, Will, and Robbie had the attention of every single one.

"I can't shake them!" Robbie screamed, spinning the wheel as he changed their course again and again. "They're everywhere!"

"They're hunting us," Will said, keeping his tire iron close. "Like animals."

"We'll be fine," Lauryn said, clutching her sword as she watched the black shapes chasing their car in the mirror. "Just get us to Dad's."

"What do you think I'm trying to do?" Robbie yelled. "I—"

"Robbie!"

"*What?*"

"Don't panic," Lauryn said, quietly now. "I swear to you we can get through this. We're still in a car, which means we're faster, and if any of them get close, Will and I will—"

A jolt cut her off as something huge crashed into the car, almost running them off the road. By the time Lauryn recovered, she realized it was a man, or what was left of one. A huge boulder of a human, his skin grown over in giant plates, had bowled into the side of the car like a charging bull. He was still there, too, holding the car back with his massive hands as Robbie frantically gunned the engine, squealing the tires to no avail. Will was leaning out the window, bashing at the thing with his tire iron, but the demon man didn't even seem to feel it as he broke the windows one by one. He was about to rip the passenger door off when Lauryn leaned out through the broken rear window and swung her golden sword at him.

The attack was reflexive. Lauryn still had no idea what she was doing. She just flailed her weapon. But even though she hadn't put any thought or skill into the attack, someone upstairs must still have been looking out for her, because the blow struck clean, slicing through the demon's clawlike hands where they gripped the door. The moment his hold vanished, the squealing tires grabbed the pavement, and the car lurched, shooting them down the road to safety.

"That," Lauryn gasped, pulling her sword back inside. "I'll do that."

"Right," Will panted, looking impressed despite himself. "Good job."

"I swear," Robbie muttered, gripping the wheel with both hands as he looked around at the black, nightmarish shapes in the rearview mirror, "if I live through this, I'll go to church every day. I'll never touch drugs again. I'll—"

"Robbie," she said, her voice calm. "Just drive."

He closed his mouth and nodded, hunching over the wheel as he wove them down Chicago's grid of streets toward home. When she was sure her brother wasn't going to panic again and crash them, Lauryn turned back around, readying her sword to guard the broken windows from the next attack. Will did the same, holding his bloody tire iron like a bat as he watched the figures moving through the night, but whether by good luck or blessing, that attack was the last. Once they'd cleared downtown, they didn't encounter another large group all the way back to Englewood. Lauryn was starting to think they'd cleared the worst of it when her brother slammed on the breaks.

Lauryn, who had been turned around, found herself smashed against the back of the front seats. Will recovered first, scrambling back up with his tire iron ready. "What the hell was that?"

Rather than answer, Robbie raised a trembling hand and pointed out the front.

Clearly, Lauryn wasn't the only one who'd had the idea to get to holy ground. The street running up to her dad's church was a parking lot, but while normally Lauryn would have been delighted to see evidence that so many people were apparently still untransformed and able to get to safety, cars weren't the only thing in their way.

"Crap," Will whispered. "That's going to be a problem."

Understatement of the century, Lauryn thought grimly.

Down the road, on the other side of the wall of cars, her father's church was surrounded by a sea of transformed demons. Just like the ones they'd seen on the way over, these came in all shapes and sizes. Lauryn didn't see any as big as Korigan had gotten, but several came damn close. Others were small and twisted, climbing over the abandoned cars like goblins. Big or small, they were all focused on the brightly lit church and the terrified crowd Lauryn could now clearly see inside. But despite watching the people like wolves watched sheep, not a single demon appeared to have set foot past the church steps.

It wasn't for lack of trying, though. A giant mass had actually piled up on the threshold, shoving and clawing at each other in a frenzy to get at their prey. But no matter how hard they pushed, they couldn't seem to move forward. It was like the church itself was protected by an invisible barrier. Lauryn was still trying to figure out how that worked when she heard a familiar rumbling coming down the empty road behind them.

By the time she whirled around, Talon was already climbing off his motorcycle, sword in hand as he turned to nod at Lauryn, who could only grin in relief. "You have no idea how happy I am to see you,"

"Same to you," Talon replied, looking pointedly at the sword in her hand. "It suits you, as I knew it would."

Before Lauryn could ask what he meant by that, Will cut in. "Wait," he said, looking from Lauryn to Talon and back again. "You *both* have swords now?"

Lauryn glanced down at her blade, which was lighter, golden, and obviously different from Talon's. "You didn't notice the difference before?"

"I was kind of busy," Will said, exasperated. "You know what, I don't even care. Swords for everyone! All I want to know is can you use them on *that*."

He pointed at the wall of demons surrounding the church like a moat, and Lauryn bit her lip. "I don't really want to," she confessed. "Despite how they look right now, those are people. They're just possessed."

"Wait, possessed?" Robbie said frantically. "I thought they were zombies?"

"They are human," Talon said firmly. "Or they were once."

"And can be again," Lauryn reminded him. "That's what we're here for. We just have to figure out how to get through to the people inside."

"Well, they don't seem to be able to go past the stairs," Will observed. "Good thing, too. Those doors are basically cardboard."

"It's not the doors that matter," Talon said, moving to the front. "It's the place. Even when they're commanding a possessed human, no demon may set foot in the Lord's house."

"Great," Robbie said. "Any place where those things can't go sounds like where I want to be. You guys with swords just need to cut us a path and we're home free."

"I'm not attacking them!" Lauryn cried, scowling at her brother. "Weren't you listening? Those are innocent people." He opened his mouth to protest, but she cut him off. "*Mostly* innocent—but they still don't deserve to be cut down when they don't know what they're doing."

"But they're attacking us," her brother argued.

"They're victims," Lauryn argued back. "You were like that, too, Robbie. Should we have cut you down?"

That shut him up right quick, and Will sighed. "We have to do something," he said quietly. "This peace won't last forever while we make up our minds."

He was right. Already, a few of the demons from the rear of the pack were turning toward them. The sight of their bloody eyes was enough to make Lauryn cringe, but just as she was scrambling to think of what to do, Talon stepped in front of her, drawing his sword, which shone like fire in the night.

"What are you doing?" she hissed. "I thought we agreed no killing!"

"Death is not the only tool for a holy sword," he said, giving her a wise look. "Have a little more faith in me, Lauryn. No harm shall befall the innocent."

Lauryn wanted to believe that, but she still didn't see how him swinging a giant sword wasn't going to end in a bloodbath. Before she could ask for a better explanation, though, Talon charged forward, raising his sword like a torch above his head as he crashed into the back line of the demons.

The moment he connected, a blinding light filled the dark street. Will and Robbie turned away with pained shouts, but Lauryn felt nothing but awe. Despite the blinding light, she could see everything clearly: the motion of Talon's body, the way his sword swept away the corruption, leaving each demon almost human looking before it hit, but not to cut. Instead, Talon's razor-sharp blade struck each member of the crowd softly as a blade of grass and firmly as a mountain, pushing them aside to clear a path.

"*Go!*"

The command thundered, and everyone—even Robbie— obeyed. They ran as a group, following the guiding light of Talon as he moved in front of them, parting the demons like Moses parting the Red Sea all the way down the street until, at last, they reached the clear safety of the church steps.

"Oh, thank God," Robbie said, scrambling to the doors. "Thank you, thank you, thank you."

Lauryn felt the same, but she didn't have time to run up. She was busy dealing with Talon, who'd doubled over as soon as they made it, his light fading as he began to pant. "Are you okay?"

"Better," he said, chest heaving, though his face was a joyous smile. "I haven't been gifted with power like that in a long, long time."

"It was amazing," Lauryn agreed, looking back at the demons, who were now clawing at the barrier harder than ever. "I saw it. You came close to healing them! Could you—"

"No," Talon said, shaking his head. "The corruption is still there. It was just pushed back when I came near because the devil runs from the light. But I would have to cut the contagion out of each one individually to cleanse them, and there are just too many." He shook his head, still panting. "I hope whatever you've got in mind is enough for a city."

"That's what I'm aiming for," Lauryn said, reaching down to help him up. "Come on."

By this point, Robbie had already made it to the doors and was frantically beating on them, yelling for someone to let them in. A few seconds later, the door flew open, and Miss Yolanda stormed out with a fury, pointing a shotgun and a cross straight in Robbie's face. "Get out of here you—*oh!*"

She lowered the gun at once, grabbing Robbie in a bear hug in the same motion. "Thank Jesus you're all right!" She turned around to the crowd behind her. "It's okay! It's Maxwell's children!"

Through the open door, Lauryn saw a crowd of men, women, and children on their knees. Some she recognized as regulars from her father's congregation. Others were strangers, but they all had objects of faith—crosses, rosaries, stars of David, copies of the Quran, whatever they could carry—clutched in their hands, and they all looked terrified.

"What's going on?" she asked as Miss Yolanda shuffled them inside.

"Ain't it obvious?" the old woman asked, resting her shotgun on her shoulder. "It's the end of the world. Judgment Day." She nodded at the crowd. "When it started, we all came here, and good thing. The Lord's House kept us safe, but things outside keep getting worse." Her eyes went to the shadow of the floating fortress in the sky outside, and she crossed herself. "We're all praying for our souls. So glad you're here, Lauryn. You should join us."

"I can't yet," Lauryn said, pushing away. "I need to talk to my dad. Where is he?"

"Lying down a moment," she said with a frown. "He's been leading the prayers and keeping things together ever since this started. Poor man was practically dead on his feet before we could convince him to take a rest. He's in his office."

Then Lauryn knew right where to go. "Thank you!" she called over her shoulder as she ran down the hall.

"Best make it quick!" Miss Yolanda yelled after her. "Emergency broadcast just went out saying all of Chicago's in some kind of containment zone. The National Guard will be rolling in soon as they can, but that won't keep the devil out." Her voice started to waver. "It's the end of everything!"

"No, it's not," Lauryn said firmly, stomping down the hall with Talon, Will, and Robbie right on her heels.

I hope.

Like most of the community rooms in the small brick church, Maxwell's office was in the basement, squeezed in beside the choir rooms. It was a tiny closet of a space made even smaller by her father's insistence on keeping and displaying every gift anyone had ever given him. After decades of ministry, this meant there was no longer room for anything but a tiny table, a chair, and a threadbare couch. Her father was stretched out on the latter, lying with his eyes closed and his worn Bible in his hands. He jerked awake when Lauryn entered, blinking in the lamp like he wasn't sure what he was seeing, and then his dark eyes began to shimmer.

"Lauryn," he whispered, heart in his throat. "Robert."

"Hi, Dad," Lauryn whispered back. "We—"

Maxwell lurched up before she could finish, dropping his Bible on the floor in his rush to grab his children. "I thought you were dead!" he cried, clutching them both to him. "Thank you, God! Thank you for sparing my children!"

For a moment, the three of them just stood there wrapped in the tangled knot of each other's arms. It was the closest they'd been to being an actual family Lauryn could remember, and she would have happily stayed there forever. But they didn't have forever. They might not even have until morning unless she moved quickly.

"Dad," she said, breaking away at last. "I need to talk to you."

"What?" He shook his head. "No, baby, you need to go upstairs with the others and pray. The end is—"

"No. It's. Not," Lauryn said firmly. "I know things look really bad, but this isn't the Apocalypse. It's just an attack, and if we don't want to go down, we need to fight back."

Maxwell gave her a severe scowl. "Lauryn," he said firmly. "I know you don't believe, but surely you've seen what's happening? The signs in the sky—"

"No, that's actually not it at all," she said quickly. "I have seen them, and I *do* believe."

"*You* believe?"

The question came out blatantly skeptical, not that Lauryn blamed him. "I do," she said with a sheepish smile. "You know how you always used to say God would give me a sign? Well, tonight he smacked me upside the head with one, and I'm telling you, God *is* not ending the world. He wants us to make sure that *doesn't* happen. I know this is going to sound really crazy, but everything that's happened tonight isn't due to God's wrath.

It's the result of an attack by hell on Chicago. That said, the creatures out there aren't demons. They're transformed people. Those are our neighbors, and they need us to save them."

"She speaks the truth," Talon said, stepping into the tiny office as well. "Your daughter has received and worked miracles this night, Reverend. She is right. If we're going to have a hope of saving our city, we need to fight."

"Fight?" Maxwell said. "Are you insane? We're not warriors. We're just—"

"You're faithful," Lauryn said. "That's all that matters. Despite the plague sweeping through Chicago, everyone here has managed to avoid being infected. That's a sign of great faith and character, which means you all have everything you need to fight this. I can show you how, but you have to trust me . . . and you have to be brave enough to go out there and do it."

Maxwell's eyes went wide. "Go out?"

"I know," Lauryn said. "It sounds crazy even to me, but I swear this is how it has to be. Every one of those transformed people out there is acting like a hook. That thing you saw in the sky? It's a fortress full of demons, and the demons possessing all those people are helping to pull it into our world. If they succeed, and it bursts through, it really will be Armageddon. But we can stop it before that happens. We just have to heal those people. I already know how. I did it this morning in the hospital. I did it to Robbie."

Maxwell gasped. "Robert? You . . . ?"

"So they tell me," he said guiltily.

"It's true," Will said, leaning in the doorway. "I saw it with my own eyes."

"And he's not even a believer," Lauryn finished, smiling at her father.

"I'm *really* not."

But Maxwell wasn't listening. He was still shaking, looking

at his daughter like he'd never seen her before. Finally, he asked, "How do you know all this?"

Lauryn took a deep breath. Here went nothing. "An angel told me."

If she'd said that to anyone else, that would have been the end of the conversation, but her father was different. Unlike her, he'd always believed. That was why she'd stayed away for so long, because she'd thought *he* was the crazy one. Now, she could only hope that Maxwell would see past the hurtful things she'd said before and take her at her word. She should have known better, though, because Maxwell didn't look angry or doubtful or even smug that she'd finally seen the light. He just looked happy.

"I knew he'd reach you," he whispered, patting his daughter's shoulders. "I knew you were made for the Lord's work, Lauryn." He turned around and bent over, scooping his Bible up off the floor. When he had it firm in his hands, he turned back to her with a determined look. "What do we need to do?"

Lauryn grabbed him and hugged him tight. "Thank you," she whispered. "Thank you for believing me."

"I always believed in you," he whispered back, kissing her cheek before he pulled away. "Now I assume you'll need to talk to everyone?" When Lauryn nodded, Maxwell pushed his way out of the office. "Then let's go."

Still grinning, Lauryn followed happily, hurrying after her father as he strode up the stairs with astonishing speed. By the time they made it back to the fellowship hall, everyone seemed to be waiting for them, but Maxwell just held up his hand. "My daughter has something to say," he said, motioning for Lauryn to get up on the little stage at the room's far end. "She's seen the light and knows how we can all be saved. Listen to her. She speaks the truth."

That was enough to set the room fluttering, including, unfortunately, Lauryn's own stomach. She'd been so determined to fix this, she'd completely forgotten how much she hated talking in front of crowds. But it was way too late to back out now, and so she forced herself to climb up, taking a deep, terrified breath before turning to address the room.

"I'm Dr. Lauryn Jefferson," she said, speaking as loudly as she could. "I know many of you think this is Judgment Day, and I know it looks that way, but I'm here to tell you it's not. This destruction is not God's doing! It's a plan by a very evil man to sacrifice our city and bring hell into Chicago."

She paused there, waiting for the inevitable heckling that was bound to follow a statement that insane, but the crowd stayed silent. Apparently, being trapped in a church by a demon mob changed what you were willing to accept as fact, and when it was clear the people were still on board, Lauryn continued.

"We can't let this happen," she said, voice trembling. "But to stop it, I need your help. The creatures outside our doors aren't monsters. They're your neighbors and friends who are being used like puppets, and we're the only ones left who can save them. Now is not the time to cower behind closed doors. Now is the time to come together and take our city back! Again, I know that sounds insane, but God wouldn't call us if it wasn't possible. I know we can do this if we work together, but I won't force anyone who isn't willing. If you want to stay, stay. But if you're willing to fight, come with me to the Ohio Street Beach."

For the first time, someone spoke up. "What's at Ohio Street Beach?"

"Safe access to Lake Michigan," Lauryn said with a grin. "I know how to beat this, because I've cured it before. Water and prayer can remove the corruption. It's just like scrubbing a wound clean. With all of you helping, we've got all the prayer we need, and if we get to the beach, they'll have to go through the water to get to us, which will also slow them down. At that point, all we have to do is grab hold and wash them clean again."

"It's a baptism," Maxwell said, his face breaking into a smile. "Of course! It all makes sense. But there have to be thousands, *hundreds* of thousands of possessed people out there. We're barely a hundred. How are we going to cleanse them all?"

"That's just it," Lauryn said. "We don't have to cure everyone, at least not all at once. Remember: each one of those people is a hook the enemy is using to drag hell into our world." She looked back at the crowd. "You've all seen the fortress in the sky, right? That's what they're trying to bring through. That's why they needed the whole city—because it takes that much power to force something that big into our world. But if we can banish the demons out of enough people to knock out even a fraction, they won't have the critical mass necessary to actually break through, and that will buy us the time we need to cure the rest."

By the time she finished, her heart was pounding. That was the first time Lauryn had actually spoken her entire plan, and it had actually come out sounding even better than it had in her head. She just hoped everyone else thought so. It was one thing to say they should fight back, but quite another to ask a group of normal, mostly elderly people to go out into the demon-riddled city of Chicago and baptize monsters who were trying to kill them in Lake Michigan in the middle of the night in *November*.

But as with everything else that had happened tonight, she should have had more faith. She'd barely finished explaining before Miss Yolanda stood up, shotgun in hand. "I told you those people just needed Jesus," she said proudly. "I've been to Ohio Beach plenty of times. We can take the church vans."

Her words were like the stone that kicks off an avalanche. The moment she hopped on board, the rest of the room began talking loudly, making plans for how they were going to get across town and what they'd do when they got there. Several had already grabbed their stuff and pronounced themselves ready to go right now. It was such an extreme turnaround from the terrified huddled mass they'd found when they'd first arrived, Lauryn almost couldn't believe it. Her father, however, seemed to be having no problem.

"It's hope," he said, giving her a wink. "You gotta remember, we thought we were going to die. Now you're here telling us we're not, and more, that we can save the people we'd already thought we'd lost." He shook his head. "It's amazing how much more lively a person gets when they've got something to fight for."

"I guess you're right," she said, staring in wonder as the crowd began to self-organize.

"Of course I'm right," he replied, pulling the church van keys out of his pocket. "I'm your father."

As ever, that made Lauryn roll her eyes, but Maxwell was already off, calling for volunteers to drive those who wouldn't fit in the vans. She was about to hop down off the stage and join him when Will appeared beside her.

"Are you sure about this?" he asked, reaching up to help her down.

"I think so," she replied. "I mean, I don't *feel* sure, but it makes sense with everything I've learned."

And if I'm wrong, then we're all dead, and it's all moot anyway. So there's that.

From the look on his face, Will was thinking the same thing, but he kept it to himself, turning to the crowd that was already streaming toward the back of the church where the vans were parked. "I can drive," he said. "I'm a cop. I've had combat-driving training."

This sparked a huge argument about how no stranger could know how to drive their vans better than they could. Honestly, Lauryn wasn't sure who was right, but she could have hugged

Will a thousand times for the show of support. Unfortunately, she had no time. Will was already off, and she had work to do. So, sword in hand, she turned around herself, making a beeline through the remaining crowd to start planning exactly how they were actually going to pull this off.

19

BRIGHT AS CRYSTAL

To Lauryn's surprise, getting the people to the beach was actually the easiest part. Because of its focus on missionary work, Missionary Baptist had four very sturdy, very large passenger vans. These were enough to fit most of the crowd, and those who didn't fit had the cars they'd driven to get here. Getting them back into those cars was a bit hairier than getting to the vans since the cars were on the street where the mob of possessed people was still waiting, but just like before, Talon was a machine, clearing the way with great sweeps of his sword to let the people run back to their cars. They did it, too, which was what surprised Lauryn the most, though after what her father had said, it shouldn't have. These were the kind of people Z3X hadn't been able to touch. That meant they were exactly the sort to rush into danger to help others, and that's what they did now, piling into the cars and vans to form the convoy that would take them all safely to the water.

As one of the few armed people, Lauryn had taken point, riding shotgun in one of the vans. Leaning out the window and using her sword like a beacon, she led the charge through the dark city in what had to be the most surreal experience of her life. As Talon had shown her earlier, the demons fled before the holy light. She couldn't get hers to shine anywhere near as bright as Talon's, but it was still enough to clear a path through the wide roads leading to the lake. She still had to smack off the few that were fast enough to jump at them, but while that should have been terrifying, Lauryn wasn't afraid. Even as her heart pounded, she felt nothing but the excitement and satisfaction of knowing she was finally back on track. After being at the mercy of monsters for so long, she was *finally* fighting back, and it felt amazing.

The medical professional in her was tempted to chalk this up to some kind of grandiose delusion brought on by extreme fear. But the rest of Lauryn—the one who'd jumped to her death and then come right back again—felt only a bone-deep satisfaction as the whole convoy rolled to a stop at the cement barrier separating the highway from the dark lakefront.

"This is it!" she cried, hopping out. "Everyone, get in the water!"

This command was met with hesitation, not that Lauryn blamed them. It hadn't yet gotten cold enough this winter for the lake to actually freeze, but it couldn't have been more than a few degrees above ice. To make things even worse, it was choppy, the black water driven up in large, terrifying waves. Under any normal circumstances, going into that kind of environment without a proper wetsuit would kill you, but these were hardly normal circumstances, so Lauryn led the way, charging into the freezing water up to her thighs.

Sweet merciful Lord . . .

And he was. It was definitely cold, but not nearly as cold as it should have been. In fact, once the initial shock had worn off, the water actually felt warmer than the air, which was a miracle if Lauryn had ever seen one. Even so, she gave it a full minute while everyone unloaded, going into the water up to her chest. Only then, when she was certain she wasn't sending these people to their hypothermically induced death, did she raise her arms and wave the others in.

"Come on!" she yelled. "Before they get here!"

"What makes you think they're coming?" Robbie yelled back, looking at the water like it might bite him. "It's not like we can send them an invitation."

This was enough to make the crowd look doubtful, but before Lauryn could respond, Talon hopped out of the last of the cars, his sword still glowing like fire. "They'll come," he said, his deep voice ringing over the wind. "Wolves will always hunt the sheep. Look."

He pointed at the streets behind them, and several people in the crowd gasped. Down in the water, Lauryn couldn't see why at first, but she could smell it. There was a foul odor of sulfur on the wind. It drifted down to the lake from the dark city like a warning, stirring up the vultures roosting in the trees that lined the shore.

That was enough to overcome the crowd's reluctance. They charged down the beach into the lake, wading into the dark water with only a moment's hesitation, and just in time. By the time the last of their group was in up to their knees, the first demons had appeared on the highway above, looking down at the people in the water with their glistening eyes like a pack of coyotes eyeing a coop of chickens. But just as Lauryn was about to start taunting them down, the situation changed.

It happened like a shift in the wind. There was no buildup,

no warning. One moment, everything was as it had been all night. The next, a great sound rang out across the city, a horrifying, skin-crawling mix of hunting horn and the ripping of something that should never be torn. It echoed in the night, vibrating through the air like knives. Then, with a final sickening lurch, the castle in the sky tore its way into the world, and the winged demons Lauryn had seen on death's threshold poured through like a waterfall.

Even as it was happening, Lauryn couldn't describe what she was seeing. Watching the . . . the *things* pouring from that hole was like trying to focus on an optical illusion, probably because no human eye was ever meant to see a creature of hell in the flesh. All she could tell was that they were horrible and enormous, easily dwarfing the cars they'd left abandoned on the road. Already, the night sky was blacker than black with the shadow of their wings, and they were still coming, tearing and clawing and ripping the hole wider as they wiggled through the gaps between the castle and the hole it had ripped in the sky.

"What do we do now?" she whispered at last, turning to Talon, who was standing in the freezing water next to her. "This whole plan was to stop the castle from ripping through—how can we do that if it's already happened!?" There was no way. She'd failed. "I was too slow," she whispered. "We have to scrap this, turn back."

Talon shook his head. "There's no turning back from this."

"But it's not what we're here for!" she cried. "I brought these people out to cleanse possessions, not fight actual demons." She flung her hand up at the nightmare in the sky. "We can't fight *that*."

"We can't," he agreed quietly. "We are still only human."

"Then what hope do we have?"

"The same we always had," he said, clutching his sword as he lifted his eyes heavenward. "Faith."

She knew he was right. It was the same lesson she'd been learning all night, but it was still hard to believe when an unspeakable, unknowable death was sweeping down on you from the sky, its claws already uncurling to pluck the people—*her* people, the ones who'd answered her call—out of the water like eagles snatching fish. She could already see death coming as the demons swung down, and she shot back to her feet, raising her hands to be first since this was her idea and therefore her responsibility. But just as the first of the fiends swept in low to pluck her out of the water, a second, vastly different call rang out.

This time, it did not bring fear. This call was bright as a trumpet and sweeter than the first morning light. As it broke across the city, a new rupture blossomed in the sky, unfolding like a flower, and when it opened at last, light poured out, and everything changed.

Again, they were winged creatures, and again, they were impossible to look at directly, though not for the same reasons. This time, it was blinding light that forced Lauryn to lower her eyes as flights of angels with wings like fire and swords that matched hers and Talon's spilled forth into the world and crashed straight into the enemy.

"Soldiers of El Elyon!"

The deep command made her jump, and Lauryn looked up just in time to see Akarra swoop down to join them in the water, his feet resting on the waves like they were dry land. Just like on the threshold of death, the stern dark-skinned angel was huge and beautiful and terrifying to behold, but Lauryn felt no fear. It was simply impossible to be anything but awestruck in the face of so much glory, and all she could do was fall to her knees, lowering her face to the icy water.

"Rise," Akarra commanded. "Your fight is not over."

Lauryn scrambled to her feet, stumbling in the sand before Talon caught her and dragged her the rest of the way up. When she was standing again, Akarra turned and pointed to the fortress in the sky. "They have breached the sacred barrier," he said, his voice rumbling with fury. "They tread where no creature of their sort should dare, and they will suffer for it." He bared his teeth savagely before turning back to the humans. "In the meanwhile—" he smiled at Lauryn "—you've done well, little doctor. You used your head and solved the riddle, as we knew you would. Keep up your good work, and together we will push back the tide."

"But how?" Lauryn asked, looking up at the horrible shape of the hell fortress. "My entire plan was to stop that thing. How can I do that if it's already here?"

Akarra smiled. "Just because they have made it through doesn't mean they can stay." He glared up at the highway where the transformed demons were still watching. "Remove the hooks they have placed in the people, and that fortress shall fall right back down into the pit. All will be well, young warrior, if you but keep the faith. We shall watch over you and guard your heads, and I swear now that no harm shall come to you from the sky. But you need to focus and do God's work on the earth."

By the time he finished, Lauryn could only nod. The angel nodded back and took off, shooting into the sky with a single flap of his burning wings. It was only then, when he was gone and the shock of his light had faded, that Lauryn realized everyone on the beach, including Talon, was staring at her.

"That was an angel," her father whispered, his voice trembling. "An *angel* spoke to you!"

"Yeah," Lauryn said awkwardly, unsure how else to answer. "I told you I talked to one earlier . . ."

She faded off with a wince. The moment she'd admitted the truth, her father had fallen to his knees in the water. "My child is blessed!" he cried, grabbing her hand.

"*Dad!*" she yelled, face burning, especially when the others started doing it, too. "No, stop!" she cried, putting up her hands. "I'm not, that is—we don't have time for this!"

That was a truth Lauryn wished she didn't have to point out, but it least it got their attention. Up on the ledge, the demon-possessed people were massing on the road like predators waiting for their chance to strike. When the people in the water started kneeling, several of them must have seen their chance. By the time Lauryn yelled out, they were already down on the beach, loping across the sand toward the people in the water. It should have been a terrifying sight, but it was what Lauryn had come here to do, and after the creatures, the possessed humans didn't look so bad anymore. Either way, she was ready. She just hoped the others were, too.

"Do what I do," she said, moving to grab the first monster as it hit the deeper water and slowed down. "Now!"

She grabbed the transformed person—a midsized demon with long grasping fingers and a drooling mouth that made her want to retch—around the neck, using its own momentum to take them both down. The moment it was in the water, she dunked its head, tipping the creature backwards like she'd seen the priests do for river baptisms.

"You are cleaned," she said, voice shaking as she fought to hold it down. "Come back to us!"

That was definitely not the canonical prayer for an exorcism, but it didn't seem to matter. The faith behind them was what did, because the moment she spoke the words, the monster stopped thrashing. Between the dark and the muddy water, it was impossible to see what was happening, but Lauryn could feel the body shrinking and changing in her hands. When it was over, a woman broke the surface with a gasp, her bloodshot eyes wide and horrified and her mouth open in a silent scream. For a moment, she stood there frozen, and then she collapsed, falling into Lauryn with a relieved sob.

"Oh, *thank you*," she cried. "It's over. Thank you!"

"You can thank me by doing to others what I did to you," Lauryn said, setting the woman gently on her feet in the lake.

For a moment, the woman stared at her in absolute confusion. An expression that only got worse when she looked around and saw others doing what Lauryn had done, catching the possessed demons as they charged and dunking them in the water. There was definitely some divine help going on, because even the oldest, frailest men and women were having no trouble forcing the biggest of demons into the water, washing them clean with a prayer. And when they rose again, they were human. And terrified, especially when they looked up and saw the battle raging in the sky between the fire-winged angels and the black-winged hellspawn.

"Do not be afraid!" Talon yelled, holding a particularly large demon under the water until he turned back into a man. "Help or move out of the way, but do not panic. Fear is the devil's rope, and he will tie you down if you let him."

Lauryn wasn't sure if that was the right thing to say in this situation, but it seemed to do the job. Once they got over their initial shock, several of the transformed people moved to start helping others. Good thing, too, because Talon had also been right about the possessed being drawn to them like predators to sheep. In the few minutes since they'd started, the crowd of possessed people had turned into a tide, and the longer they stayed in the water, the bigger it grew. Hundreds, thousands, Lauryn couldn't even begin to count, but as minutes turned into hours, their numbers grew and grew until the lake was full of people helping others.

The demons on the other side began to turn away.

"They're running," Lauryn said, panting with exertion.

"Because the enemy is a coward," Talon replied, wiping the lake water off his face. "He always runs the moment he loses the advantage. Look up and see for yourself."

Lauryn gasped. She'd been so busy trying to keep pace with the tide of demon-possessed humans charging after them into the lake, she hadn't had a moment to check on the battle with actual demons raging above their heads. When she did, though, her heart leaped.

In the time they'd been washing the corruption St. Luke had placed into the citizens of Chicago, dawn had broken, and the demon's charge had broken with it. The horrifying castle was still visible, but it was fading as Lauryn watched, its twisted towers and toothlike battlements melting like frost in the morning light. As it diminished, the few winged demons that hadn't yet been cut out of the sky began fleeing back to its shadow, their horrifying bodies winking out as they fled back to the hell they'd come from. By the time the actual sun broke over the lake's edge, the castle was gone completely, leaving the sky blue and clear and cold in the winter light.

"It is done."

The booming words made Lauryn jump, and she looked up to see Akarra standing on the water in front of her, his stern face split by a grin of triumph. "You have done well in the task you were set, Lauryn Jefferson," he said proudly, putting out his hand. "I'll take your sword now."

"What?" Lauryn said, clutching her sword. "But . . . but I thought it was mine."

"It is," the angel said. "That is a holy sword forged of your own clear soul. But such weapons are not for laypeople. If you wish to go back to your old life as you said, you must return it to our keeping."

That *had* been what Lauryn had said. But now . . .

"What if I don't want to go back?"

The angel looked at her in surprise. Lauryn was pretty shocked, too. This whole time, all she'd wanted was to get away from the crazy and get back to her normal life working the job she'd studied so hard to get. Now, though, after everything that had happened, life at the hospital felt like a distant memory. She never wanted to stop being a doctor, but there was also no way she could just forget leading the charge and being a warrior.

No way she could forget *this*.

"What if . . ." She swallowed, clenching her fists as she gazed up at the angel. "What if I wanted to stay?"

"Then you must pay with your life," the angel said solemnly. "As that one has." His burning eyes slid toward Talon. "The path of righteousness is straight and narrow, but the path of a Soldier of El Elyon is a razor's edge. It can be yours if you wish to walk it, but it will cost everything you have, and once you begin, the only escape is death."

That was a pretty tall order. Even Talon looked a bit uncomfortable. "It's not an easy calling," he said quietly.

"Neither was med school, and I got through that just fine," Lauryn pointed out, gripping her golden sword tight. "Look, the whole reason I became a doctor in the first place was to help people. Tonight, I helped save all Chicago! I might be pretty new to this faith stuff, but I'd have to be delusional to miss a sign like that." And the more Lauryn thought about that, the more certain she became. The rightness she'd felt earlier was still there, burning in her stomach like nothing had since the moment she'd first known she wanted to be a doctor. Now, as then, she knew, knew beyond a shadow of a doubt, that this was what she was meant to do, what she *wanted* to do, and Lauryn had never had a problem going after what she wanted.

"I can do this," she said firmly. "I'm supposed to do this. I *want* to do this." She glared at Talon. "Teach me."

The SEE warrior sighed and looked at the angel, who laughed. "The willing serve best," Akarra said, smiling at Lauryn. "Do as you feel is right, and keep your sword. You've earned it . . . and I don't think I'd be able to wrestle it from you before I have to go."

Lauryn's eyes went wide. "Wait, you're leaving?"

"We must," Akarra said. "This is the mortal world, the realm of human choice. We have no more place here than the demons we chased out. Now that they are gone, we must go as well, but I have a feeling that we will meet again, Lauryn Jefferson. Our enemy is far from defeated. If you choose to walk this path, you will be needed again."

"Good," Lauryn said, clutching her sword to her chest. "It's nice to be needed." Otherwise, what was the point?

She left that last part unspoken, but she had the distinct feeling the angel heard it anyway as he vanished into the morning sunlight. "Then fight well, little doctor," he said, his voice little more than an echo. "Until we meet again."

And with that, he was gone, leaving Lauryn alone next to Talon in the freezing water. "So," she said, smiling up at him. "How do we do this?"

Talon frowned, his face troubled, but before he could give whatever dire answer he was obviously considering, Lauryn was tackled off her feet into the water as her brother, father, Will, and at least a dozen others rushed in to hug her.

On the other side of the barrier, on the threshold of death that connects this world to the world beyond, inside the grand observation hall at the heart of the now retreating Castle Delusion, the creature who'd worn Christopher St. Luke's face for the last decade roared with rage, kicking the table of ornate delicacies that was supposed to have been his victory banquet across the rough stone floor. When the skeletal slaves scurried in to clean up the spilled plates of human hearts and sacrificial offal, he kicked them as well, sending them screaming back into the dark corners of the fortress.

"No!" he snarled at the spilled blood on the floor. "This was not how it was supposed to end! *You told me I would win!*"

I did, the blood replied, the words vibrating through the connection it created from this half world of death to the deeper hells below. *But I only said as much because I believed your reports of your own cleverness. How was I to know you were such a bald-faced liar?*

"It matters not," St. Luke spat back, rubbing his mortal shell's bullet-riddled chest. "Chicago was only one city. My reach spans the globe. I'll do it again." And this time, he'd do it better. This time, he'd leave nothing to chance. "Besides, it wasn't a total loss. It was only for a few minutes, but I still breached the barrier and brought our fortress into the mortal realm. That's better than any demon's done in a thousand years!"

It is, the voice in the blood agreed. *And that is why you have not been dragged back to hell to answer for this failure.*

"Then send me back so I can build on it," St. Luke snapped.

The voice in the blood sighed. *About that. I'm afraid you've been a little rough on the meat puppet we gave you to use. Now that you've dragged it with you into death, it'll take a great deal of effort to send you back.*

"I didn't drag it into death! That little SEE groupie pushed me!"

Same difference, the blood said idly. *I'll still have to send you back. That's hard enough when your meat sack's alive. Yours is dead. Do you know how much blood that takes? How much sacrifice? How do I'll know I'll get my investment back?*

"Because I'm the one with the power," St. Luke reminded him. "You might be a king in hell, but in the mortal world, you're just another demon. I, on the other hand, am one of the richest men in the world with connections all over the globe." His face split in a grin. "You can't afford to let me die."

That was the truth, and they both knew it.

Very well, the blood rumbled. *But this is your final chance. Fail us again, and the next time you die, Zariel, we'll leave you in that mortal shell to rot.*

"There won't be a next time," the demon Zariel promised, pulling St. Luke's corpse tight around him like a suit. "Now send me back." *I've got unfinished business to take care of.*

The blood on the floor rippled with a long-suffering sigh, and then pain grabbed Zariel like a vise, squeezing him into a stabbing point as the dark magic forced him—and what was left of St. Luke—through the barrier of death and back once more into the world of the living.

ACKNOWLEDGMENTS

The authors would like to thank everyone that assisted in making *Talon of God* a reality. Special thanks go out to John Bellamy, Murphy Batiste, Peter McGuigan and Kirsten Neuhaus of Foundry Media, David Pomerico and Rachel Aaron. Your unwavering faith and dedication to this project helped turn an idea into a reality. To our Gurus, Grand Masters, Pastors, Preachers and Spiritual Guides who took time to polish these "rough stones" into diamonds. Additional thanks goes out to the team at HarperCollins—Priyanka Krishnan, Angela Craft, Shawn Nicholls, Anwesha Basu, Pamela Jaffee, and Jeanne Reina—who helped to make this novel the very best it could be. And lastly, we want to thank our Parents, Elders and Ancestors for the "spark" and everyone who reads and enjoys this work. Your support makes everything possible.

Dr. Wesley Snipes
Ray Norman

With over seventy films to his acting credit and eighteen as a producer, DR. WESLEY SNIPES has a unique diversity that has made him one of the most beloved and sought out talents for the past thirty years. In addition to his presence in Hollywood, he is also an entrepreneur, including the innovative "Project Action Star," a social media and television project which is forthcoming. A skilled practitioner of numerous martial arts disciplines, he has taken the physical expertise he honed choreographing fights scenes in movies like *Blade* and his vivid imagination to write the action-packed *Talon of God*, his first novel.

Hailing from Chicago, RAY NORMAN received an Engineering Degree from the University of Illinois and a Law Degree from Southern Illinois University. He's worked as an attorney recruiter and corporate headhunter, as well as ghostwritten books on health, nutrition, and spiritual self-help. In addition, he's a script writer, and including an original stage play, *And You Thought Your Family Was Crazy*. In his spare time, Norman enjoys reading, working out, watching movies, and dining at fine restaurants. In the near future he plans on getting his private pilot's license. *Talon of God* is his first novel.